THE SILENT MOTHER

BOOKS BY LIZ LAWLER

The Next Wife

I'll Find You
Don't Wake Up

LIZ LAWLER

THE SILENT MOTHER

bookouture

Published by Bookouture in 2021

An imprint of Storyfire Ltd.
Carmelite House
50 Victoria Embankment
London EC4Y 0DZ

www.bookouture.com

ISBN: 978-1-80019-736-7
eBook ISBN: 978-1-80019-735-0

CHAPTER ONE

21 AUGUST

Ruth wheeled her overnight suitcase to the door. Apart from the bed showing evidence of a restless sleeper with its tangle of sheets, the room was as tidy as when she'd checked in. She stepped out into the corridor and let the door close behind her, breathing deeply to calm her racing heart. It had been beating uncomfortably since receiving his voicemail yesterday. Something in his voice said she needed to be worried. She stared at the black screen of her mobile, willing it to light up and display a new message. She didn't want to call. He'd asked her not to, leaving her blind to what was going on, though it hadn't stopped her sending him a text when she arrived at the hotel. She hoped to surprise him by letting him know she was already in Bournemouth and not travelling this morning. She hoped they would meet up, but he hadn't replied. She had to respect his wishes. They were similar creatures, needing time alone to filter out anxiety so they could focus on staying calm. She listened to the message again.

'Mum, sorry to do this to you without warning, but I'm in a bit of bind to be honest and could do with your moral support. Don't be shocked, but I had to go before a magistrates' court. Try not to worry. I haven't murdered anyone. But I'm now up before a judge tomorrow at Bournemouth Crown Court. Don't call. Please. We'll talk tomorrow. And wear your no-nonsense suit. You look a warrior in it. My barrister is named Jacob Cadell. He seems good. So, fingers crossed. Okay, hope to see you there… and love you.'

Her stomach dipped at hearing the false bravado again. Thomas was not easily unnerved. She couldn't remember him ever being afraid. Despite telling her not to worry, she was worried. Very worried.

She studied her appearance in the mirror on the wall in the elevator. The black tailored jacket and trousers suited her long lean body perfectly. The pretty pink brooch on the lapel saved the plain white shirt and black-laced brogues from looking too masculine. It was her Christmas gift from him last year, worn for good luck. The hairs on her arms and on the back of her neck stood up as she shivered. Would he need good luck? A stray blonde hair fell across her face and she tucked it behind her ear irritably. Flyaway hair was not the image she wanted to present today. Her son needed a warrior at his side.

As ready as she could be to face this barrister before proceedings began, she stepped out of the lift. There was no need for her to check out of the hotel as she had already paid, and no need for her to move her car from the car park, as Bournemouth Crown Court was right next door. She'd got her bearings last night while she sat outside the hotel having a coffee and saw it was only a short walk along a pavement. She'd found herself thinking about the location of the hotel, as the family next to her shared they were visiting a very sick relative in Bournemouth Hospital, directly across the road. While a young couple, further away at another table, shared with anyone with reasonable hearing, they were flying to Zante in the morning. She wondered at the number of people who came through its doors for the purpose of being near the hospital, the courthouse, the airport. Afraid, anxious or happy. The building had no doubt given respite to a lot of troubled souls; hers being one of them.

She hoped that Jacob Cadell, the barrister, was good. She had googled him. His picture showed a man in his sixties with grey hair, and she was shocked that the majority of cases he defended were for serious violence, serious sexual offences, weapons and fraud and armed robbery, and hoped Thomas just plucked his name off the internet and hadn't chosen him for any of these reasons. She straightened her shoulders as she began the short walk. If Thomas's crime could not be dealt with at a magistrates' court it had to be more serious than a motoring offence or minor assault. What had he done to require a barrister? She breathed in sharply. She would soon find out.

The entrance to the court was daunting with a semi rotunda front, set in a wall of green glass. Though only just opening, people were already milling outside and Ruth picked up on the anxiety showing in some faces, in their raised voices and rapid pacing. A young woman was clinging to a young lad, crying. Another lad stood out from the group he was with as the only one wearing a jacket and tie. He was laughing too loudly and smoking his cigarette too fast.

Moving past them she entered the building and without being asked took off her jacket and placed it with her phone, car keys and handbag in a plastic tray before stepping through the body scanner. She asked the security officer where she might find Jacob Cadell and was directed to a reception desk where she told the woman behind the glass screen she was Thomas De Luca's mother.

Ruth's heart sank as a woman approached her wearing a court robe and tatty unpolished shoes. Her hair had the tell-tale residue of dry shampoo and could have done with a good brush. She hoped this woman wasn't standing in for Jacob Cadell; if she paid so little attention to her appearance, what attention did she give clients?

'Christine Pelham,' she said, introducing herself without offering her hand. 'I'm Thomas's solicitor. I represented him at Poole Magistrates' Court. Mr Cadell and I are just reading through the pre-sentence report, but Thomas will have had his appointment with probation and so will be aware at least in general terms of the recommendation.' The solicitor gave a brief polite smile. 'We're just waiting for your son to arrive.'

Ruth wondered if she'd turned white. *Pre-sentence report.* Thomas was to be sentenced. What happened to the trial?

The woman looked at her watch. 'I'll show you where you can sit while we wait.'

Dazed, but with legs still working, Ruth followed her up a flight of stairs to the first floor where she was shown to rows of seats in a long corridor. Closed doors led to the courtrooms. Before she could ask anything further the woman hurried away leaving Ruth shell-shocked. With a trembling hand she got her phone out and rang her son. 'Where are you, Thomas?' she whispered urgently when he failed to pick up.

She recognised the man walking towards her. Jacob Cadell was shorter than she'd imagined him to be from his photograph. His shoulders looked too broad for a man of his height and would have suited a rugby player. He was dressed in wig and gown and brought with him a sense of solemnity, which was softened by his kind smile.

'Mrs De Luca?'

She shook her head. 'No. Thomas has his father's surname. I'm Ruth Bennett, Thomas's mother.'

He nodded congenially and sat down beside her. 'Well, he's only a little late so not time to worry yet. His case is being held in Court Three and I'm hoping he'll be either first or second on the list. Have you heard from him?'

'No,' she answered a little breathlessly. 'We haven't spoken at all. Thomas only let me know yesterday about being in court. I'm afraid I don't even know what the charge is.'

The barrister frowned. 'Oh dear, then this has come as a shock to you.' He settled a bundle of manila folders onto his lap. 'Thomas was arrested for assault, then further charges were brought against him later. He appeared before a magistrate in Poole back in May, where the case was then passed to the crown court for sentencing, which was when he engaged my services.'

Her stomach somersaulted. Thomas had been dealing with this since May? It was August. For over three months he hadn't breathed a word. 'So when was his trial?'

He slowly shook his head. 'There wasn't one. He pleaded guilty.'

She recoiled from him in shock, pushing hard back into her seat. 'For what?' she cried in a raised voice, drawing the eyes of those around her.

The barrister kept his own voice low. 'Common assault and… theft of hospital medicines. Given that Thomas has no previous criminal record I'm hoping to get him a community sentence.'

Ruth knew for sure she had gone white. Her blood pressure had fallen to her boots, the oxygen sucked from her lungs. She put her head in her hands, leaned forward and breathed in deeply. When she felt able to sit up again, she raised her head slowly. 'You said *hoping*.'

His slight nod didn't give her confidence, nor his words. 'The prosecution will suggest that the variety of drugs and the quantities may indicate sale rather than consumption. But there is little evidence to support that. His early guilty plea will be taken into account. Unfortunately, midazolam was found in his system, which he has not given an explanation for. I believe the taking of this drug impaired his good judgement. Having gained his full registration as a doctor at the age of twenty-five, and completing his first year of practise, he is clearly a man who briefly steered down the wrong pathway after being on the right path all his life. This is a man who deserves leniency.'

Ruth wondered if he was practising his summation. If so, it wasn't working on her. This was her son he was talking about. She knew how hard Thomas had worked all these years. Her mind was racing. Palms sweating. He made it sound like Thomas was a drug addict. 'This sounds like a trial.'

'It isn't,' he replied. 'It's a hearing. The prosecution's role is to summarise the case against the defendant to the judge, to assist with sentencing guidelines, but there is no jury in the sentencing process. The judge makes the final decision.'

'Midazolam,' she said in a leaden voice.

He nodded. 'Yes, it's—'

'I know what it is,' she interrupted. 'I'm a doctor too. What I don't know or understand is why it was in my son's system. This isn't a case of a mother not knowing her son. It's the very opposite. Thomas has never taken drugs in his life and nor would he. Why would he plead guilty and lose the benefit of a trial? That's what I'm finding hard to fathom. I guarantee, one hundred per cent, he is innocent of these charges.'

He looked at her frankly. 'I'm afraid you'll have to ask Thomas that question. I wasn't there from the beginning to counsel on his plea.'

'What quantity are we talking about?' she asked.

'Hundreds,' he quietly replied.

In a daze she whispered, 'Hundreds of tablets.'

'Yes. Painkillers, antibiotics, sedatives. Tablets you can't buy over the counter.'

Leaving Ruth with her heart clamouring, the barrister said he'd drop back shortly. She felt sick, her stomach churning, an emptiness in her gullet waiting to be filled. She saw people coming up the wide stairs and walked over to stand at the top so she could watch them coming through the body scanner, gathering up their bags and loose items to put back on shoulders or in pockets. She didn't see the dark hair of her son. What was he playing at, being late for court? Didn't he know he could be arrested? Nerves were pressing her bladder, but she didn't want to leave her spot in case she missed his arrival. She needed to ask him why he didn't want a trial. Christ, she hadn't expected something like this to happen today. She'd ended her speculation at imagining him trimming hedges or cleaning walls wearing a high visibility tabard as community service. She hadn't imagined him going to prison.

A few minutes later, she spotted the barrister walking along the corridor, his expression, thank God, calm. He led her away from the top of the stairs, back to the row of seats, probably so as not to cause congestion by standing in the way of people coming up them. He sat down beside her again.

'Any word?' he asked.

'No, not yet,' she answered with a bright hopefulness in her eyes, but worrying the man might declare Thomas a no-show. 'When he does arrive, do we just wait here to be called?'

He pointed to a door. 'No. You'll go through that door to the courtroom. Thomas enters by another door to a semi-partitioned area known as the dock. The view is a little restricted, I'm afraid, but you'll be right beside him and able to see him in profile.'

Ruth quivered. This was all real. Happening right now. Her son might be going to prison today.

As if on cue, Christine Pelham appeared. Ruth scrutinised her. Was she the reason her son pleaded guilty? Was she too busy that day to do her job? Ruth wanted to tear into the woman and ask her what the hell happened, but stopped herself at the worry she saw on Christine Pelham's face.

'Jacob, I need an urgent moment of your time,' she said in a hushed voice.

The barrister immediately stood up and walked a few feet away so the woman could converse with him in private. She was speaking rapidly, but quietly, so Ruth wouldn't hear. Ruth also stood, waiting for them to finish and tell her what was going on. Her son had pleaded guilty to a serious crime and this woman hadn't even come to court dressed respectably. Ruth was having a hard time holding onto her temper. She was having visions of Thomas being arrested for not showing up at court and being given the sternest sentence as a result. Time was ticking on, she realised. It was now time to worry.

She tried phoning Thomas again. She needed to get to the bottom of the situation fast and undo some of the damage. What possessed him to plead guilty? Had his solicitor advised him to do this? He had to have had a reason. Or did he see no hope? Why hadn't he spoken to her at the beginning? She knew people and would have hired him the very best solicitor in the land. Why had he not come to her for her immediate support? They were close and didn't keep problems or secrets from one another. She was his confidante and was good at finding solutions. She would have wanted to help, she was his mother, and when needed, *his warrior.*

From the corner of her eye she saw Jacob Cadell turn towards her. She knew from the moment he slid his wig from his head. From the moment Christine Pelham backed away, the slow movement so telling. She knew why Thomas wasn't answering his phone.

A feeling, felt only once before in another lifetime, pressed hard against her ribcage. She needed to avoid hearing this man's words and block out what he was about to say. She felt the touch of his hand against hers and wanted to snatch it away. How had he got this close without her realising? She had to restrain herself from clamping her hand over his mouth. She was only seconds away from hearing something that would change her life forever. The long stretch of corridor behind and before her seemed to have disappeared. She could see nowhere to run.

'Please shut up,' she said. Even though he had yet to say a word. 'Please don't speak.'

His eyes locked on hers and she saw his deep regret at what he was about to do. 'I'm so terribly sorry to have to tell you, but we've had word as to why Thomas hasn't arrived. Local police have entered his flat and found him. I'm so very sorry, but it appears your son has taken his own life.'

Ruth stood perfectly still. She had once had a patient say to her they could feel their body shutting down as they got ready to die. She wanted it to happen, rather than embrace what was to come. She was not brave enough to feel that type of pain. It wasn't supposed to happen. She'd taken his being alive as a given, never thinking that his life could end. It couldn't have happened, that Thomas was no longer breathing, that his breath had stopped. That he was no longer her beautiful breathing boy.

The pain caught her by surprise. Around the throat. It stopped her from escaping anywhere in her mind. It ripped deep into her belly, then sharply across her chest. The pain found a way in to let her know it was real. Her beloved boy no longer breathed. He was dead.

CHAPTER TWO

31 DECEMBER

New Year's Eve and Bournemouth town was busy with shoppers. Ruth avoided some well-wishers calling out Happy New Year by crossing to the other side of the road and keeping her head down. She was not up to facing such happiness with her heart this heavy, and was liable to cry if she said it back.

She'd been walking the streets of the seaside town since early morning and it seemed different from her memories of twenty years ago when she holidayed there with Thomas. It had been vibrant then, with baking sunshine. Now it was cold, the shop she was passing empty, collecting dust on its windows while the doorway collected the homeless. She couldn't help noticing them. Compelled by the eyes staring at her she went into a supermarket a few shops along and returned a short time later with two carrier bags of food, which emptied fast. She hadn't seen the town in August as she only visited the courthouse, and then, of course, the mortuary.

Feeling guilty, knowing she would be staying warm tonight while people huddled in the cold, she wished she could do more than just give them a little food, but it would take a miracle to break the cycle of homelessness.

She headed away from the shop doorway towards the stone steps that would take her down to Lower Gardens, a public park of leafy green space that was lit up like a fairyland, the trees covered in white and pink Christmas lights. She'd had a picnic on the grass there once, sitting under one of the trees while Thomas ran back and forth for crusts off their sandwiches to feed to the ducks.

She crossed the gardens and exited at Pier Approach. The beachfront promenade welcomed early revellers, the bars and cafés busy, a live band and a funfair keeping everyone entertained. The excited squeals of children's voices could be heard from the Big Wheel. Standing more than a hundred feet tall, the structure was lit up like a perfect white spider web hanging in the sky. Ruth walked away from the noise, heading for the pier. Post sunset, the sea was a shade of purple and the golden sand had changed to a reddish brown. The beach stretched for as far as the eye could see and she could understand why Thomas wanted to live here. He'd loved surfing and living by the sea. Just as his father had. She said that in his eulogy. And more.

The funeral was a small private gathering. Her sister Pauline and brother-in-law Nigel, along with Thomas's grandparents, Nonna and Nonno De Luca, and his uncle Marco, were the only ones there. She hadn't wanted to invite anyone else for fear of them harbouring unkind thoughts if they were aware of what Thomas was accused of. Mercifully, there'd been little reported on the event of his death. As there was no trial, most people were unaware of what he was facing the day he died. In Bath, none of her colleagues were aware. They knew her son took his own life, but not the circumstances surrounding his death. But then Thomas had been living away from Bath for seven years. He'd formed new friendships over the years and had lived far enough away for him to be off the radar. She doubted the same could be said of Bournemouth. Everyone he worked with would know what he was arrested for. Gossip was rife in a hospital. His friends would know. His colleagues, too. Perhaps even his patients.

Heaviness pressed her throat. Proving Thomas innocent was going to be a colossal undertaking, when she had only her own belief to go on, and an anonymous letter posted to her more than a month ago that sat at the bottom of her bag. Was it madness to have come here? The anonymous letter gave her so little direction. Barely even a letter, but a small sheet of paper with a scraggly edge at the top where it had been torn from a spiral notebook. The person had written just a few words.

To the mother of Thomas De Luca. Please come to Bournemouth and uncover the truth. Please come and undo the damage that has been done.

Someone wanted her to do what she had already planned to do – clear her son's name. She needed no urging, especially from someone anonymous.

She had closed up her home and given up a GP partnership in order to carry out this duty for her son. She had taken a new job as a locum GP, was starting it in two days' time in a place where she knew no one. She would be a stand-in for a doctor taking maternity leave. She'd been a partner for ten years and knew all of her patients by their first names and had given it up for a job that wasn't even permanent. She did not need urging. She had to do this for her son's memory, the last thing she would do for him.

She prised out of Jacob Cadell the name of the person who called the police. Maybe the person was irrelevant – it could have been anybody on the ward who was concerned about Thomas's behaviour, so the name was only important in so much as it was a starting point. The woman might not know anything, but until Ruth spoke to her she was an important witness.

Ruth had used this information to start her mission. She had used her position as a doctor to get her to the right place. It had taken a fair few calls to find out which GP practice had this woman as a patient.

Where Ruth was going to work might be the worst place on earth, but to her it was a gift that a temporary vacancy had become available. Not that she was attributing it as a miracle or seeing it as mystical, as on UK Indeed, and a half dozen more job sites, locum doctors were in high demand. She was taking this drastic step, taking actions she never would have considered she would have to do in her old life, even to the point of compromising her professional ethics. She needed no damn urging. No reminding of her duty as a mother.

She could think of nowhere else to be that was more important than where Thomas had lived. This place had been his home and it was stamped forever with some of his history. He had died here. She was there to find out why.

She didn't believe for a second that he was guilty, despite evidence to suggest otherwise. At his inquest she'd heard some of it, but not the details. It was not a trial. It was to find out the circumstances of his death, his state of mind. She knew only the bare bones that she persuaded Jacob Cadell to tell her over the phone the day after her son's death: Police were called to a hospital ward. Thomas was causing serious disruption. He'd assaulted a security guard. While at the police station, hospital personnel searched his locker and found stolen medicines. The inspector authorised a search of Thomas's flat in the reasonable belief that the premises may contain evidence. A large quantity of drugs was found under his bed. It raised the question of him selling prescription drugs.

Outside the coroner's office speculation was added to her limited knowledge by a reporter trying to waylay her departure. *Is it true Dr De Luca tampered with medication, refilled broken ampoules with water?* Thankfully, he'd been unaware who she was, as revealed in his parting shot: *Did you work with him*? Ruth refused to believe any of it. The Thomas she knew was admirable. It was not just a mother's conviction that her son would do no wrong. Thomas wouldn't break the law. His ethics and morals had been far too strong for him to do something like that. It was not in him to go off the rails and throw away all the goodness of who he had been. A young man who had been decent and kind and only ever wanting to be a doctor to help others.

The post-mortem found alcohol and diazepam in his system. The urine toxicology reported infrequent use of diazepam. A frequent user has an identifiable diazepam pattern and will show the presence of certain metabolites. Chemical analysis showed a negative result for other substances. For someone purportedly taking drugs, no one seemed to find that fact in the least interesting – his body showed no evidence of a habitual user. He had taken his life with only enough sedation and alcohol to make it easier to do what he did. He could have taken so much more and ended his life that way. Thomas was not a drug taker, despite them being in his system when he was arrested.

Was she mad to be doing this? She was leaving herself wide open to be hurt even more, if that was at all possible. Grief was delivering physical pain to her body every day. In her wrists and her feet. Along the blades of her shoulders. Excruciating aches had appeared overnight in places she had never felt pain before. At forty-four she'd been blessed until that day in August with feeling no different to when she was in her twenties. Now it hurt to swing her legs out of bed in the mornings or hold a kettle while it filled with water.

Her one comfort was in knowing she was finally here. She hadn't dropped everything immediately after his death because her ingrained sense of responsibility wouldn't allow her to do that. Perhaps the nature of her job or bringing up a child alone hadn't afforded her the right to just walk away. She'd always been aware of her duties. She could take comfort in that being the reason for why she had not come sooner.

She shook her head. She couldn't fool herself. She knew her reasons for not coming sooner went far deeper than an obligation. She had been scared to come. While she stayed away the reality of what happened could be shelved until she came to terms with his death. His death was only one part of this story. Why it happened was the part she was terrified to face. She didn't want to find out she couldn't prove him innocent. That he was guilty. That she had a son she had never really known.

Her appointment at the police station earlier chilled her to the bone. While waiting to collect Thomas's possessions she had gazed around reception. She'd been surprised to see doors to interview rooms made mainly of glass. Each room was small, then made smaller by a glass wall partition – one side for customers, the other side for police. It made her uncomfortable when she noticed one of them was occupied, like she was watching something that should be private. Then her eyes clocked the grey door in the very far corner – Custody Suite – she sat then for the rest of the time imagining Thomas being brought in there.

She tried focusing on a poster. Tips to help with an anxiety attack. Look around for five things to see. Four things to feel. Three things to hear. Two things to smell. One thing to taste.

It hadn't helped. The only thing she could focus on was the grey door. There were no glass panels to peek through like with the interview rooms. She could only imagine the cells behind it, seeing Thomas inside one and him seeing the other side of this locked grey door. Not knowing when it might open again and set him free. But perhaps hopeful, at that point, of nothing worse to happen, unaware his freedom had already gone.

CHAPTER THREE

The flat was on the first floor of a large Victorian house with two flats above and another below on the ground floor. Thomas had lived there for over a year but she never got around to seeing it, as every couple of months he had visited her instead.

On autopilot when the landlord contacted her to close the lease on the flat, she paid for the next month's rent, and when that month passed she paid up front for a whole year, asking him to throw away perishables but to leave everything else as it was. She also asked him not to reveal her identity or her relationship to Thomas to the other tenants. She hadn't even met the man. He'd posted her the keys with an almost indecent haste; possibly relieved he was able to carry on renting it so soon after what had happened. If he thought it odd that she would choose to live there he wasn't saying anything, and, in any case, she didn't care. She was not afraid to be in the place where her son had died. It was the last place he'd breathed. And she wanted to feel close to him.

Ruth let herself in the main front door and climbed the carpeted staircase. She used a second key to open the door to the flat and saw her suitcases where she'd left them that morning on the tiny hall floor. She hadn't gone further inside as she would have found it difficult to leave again after seeing her son's things for the first time since his death. She entered the sitting room and switched on the main light, preparing herself.

The first thing she noticed was the shape of the room, long and narrow with an opening at one end for a galley kitchen that at one time would have been a cupboard. The electric hob was largely redundant by the look of things, as a microwave and kettle sat on top of it. A tiny sink tucked into one corner butted against a square countertop, beneath which, thankfully, was a fridge. In the sitting room a well-stuffed armchair faced the only window with a small table and a lamp next to it, books piled on the floor beneath it. He loved reading as much as her, and like her he never seemed to find time to read all the books he wanted. A large bookcase took up most of one wall and was crammed on every shelf with medical textbooks and a dozen or so box files, most likely containing his work from his medical student days. A narrow desk was squeezed into the remaining space. Her eyes fell on the object placed on top of it. A soft blue woollen scarf, neatly folded.

She pulled out Thomas's belongings from her shoulder bag, still in police evidence bags: his laptop, iPad, mobile and diary, and placed them down on the desk. The police officer she dealt with had eyed her curiously, perhaps thinking she had taken her time in coming to get them.

She stepped back into the small hall, an open door revealing his bedroom, big enough to accommodate a double bed and wardrobe. The other door was closed. She placed her hand against it, waiting a few seconds before opening it. The shower curtain was pulled across, hiding the bath. Unhurried, she pulled it back and stared at the space where her son had died. It shone spotless and the curtain looked new. The sink and the shelf above it were empty of the usual toiletries. Not even a bar of soap or toilet roll was left. She assumed the room had got messy and everything had been thrown away. Whoever had cleaned and cleared out the room had done a good job, as Thomas had done an equally good job in covering the walls with his blood. He'd taken no half measures. She'd seen the room in a photograph. He'd cut deeply, ensuring his arteries spurted. The surgical blade had been found on the floor, fourth tile from the left side of the wall.

She knelt beside the tile and ran her hand over the dry enamel. Her boy had died in this bath and she could only pray he drifted away quickly, that there was no time for fear or pain. She wondered at what point he made the decision. He left her a voicemail asking her to come and support him, but he didn't wait for her. He must have contemplated what lay ahead for him the next day at court. A possible prison sentence and a shattered dream.

As far back as she could remember, even at primary school, he had dreamed of being a doctor. He hadn't wished to explore other careers, and he didn't choose the path just to follow his mother. His theory was that he was born to be a doctor, as why else was that all he dreamed of? He'd wanted to go far in medicine, not simply to climb a ladder but to learn things that could bring real change to people's lives. Thomas had been after the ultimate goal – to find cures for illnesses presently uncurable, to preserve life for those whose lives would otherwise be cut short. Her son had dreamed big for a while, and she would always be proud of him for that.

Achingly tired, she got off her knees and went back to the sitting room. The single bulb hanging from the ceiling gave a gloomy light and made it hard to see if the walls were painted cream or white, or whether the carpet was grey or beige or even blue. She switched on the lamp by his armchair and then sat down in its softness and felt the agony of that day all over again. She could smell the soap he used. She pushed her face into the velvet fabric to be sure. The scent of it had rubbed off on the material, along with another scent of wood and earthiness that brought tears to her eyes. He was there with her in that chair like a comfort blanket wrapping her.

Why did you do it, Thomas? You didn't need to die, you sweet, foolish boy.

*

She was roused some hours later by the sound of fireworks. The New Year had come. She unfolded herself from the chair and went into the hall to search her case for the bottle of whisky she'd packed. A leaving present from Sue, the receptionist. A Glenmorangie single malt. She found a glass in the kitchen and poured a generous measure, then felt a lovely heat in her throat that soon curled in her belly as she swallowed it down. She poured a second measure, which she would take to the desk to sip while she looked at her son's things.

She pulled open the long single drawer and saw an assortment of stationery. Biros, notepads, Sellotape, stapler. Two items drew her attention more: a rubber ball of elastic bands that looked to be the same one he made while studying for A levels, and an origami fortune teller. She'd shown him how to make them when he was a child as a way of getting him to learn numbers and colours. She picked it up and positioned her index fingers and thumbs into the four hollow pyramids and gently pushed the four corners together. Blue, red, green and yellow. She chose a colour and flapped the fortune teller one way, then the other, spelling out the colour blue. On the inside flaps she saw a choice of four numbers and this time flapped the fortune teller to the count of two. She then carefully peeled back the flap to read her fortune.

Here's a cheery theory: Everyone thinks you're guilty.

Ruth inhaled sharply. It was not what she'd been expecting to see. Normally, there was something nice to read in this game. Like, you'll be rich one day or everyone likes you. She placed the fortune teller on the desk, and then unfolded it carefully. The messages were soul-destroying.

You will have a crap day, with lots of people pointing the finger at you. You may be innocent but your accusers won't believe you.

One day soon you will become very famous, with your
mugshot splashed everywhere.
Save your breath and tell them lies, then they'll believe you.

Ruth raised a trembling hand to her mouth. He had been tormenting himself playing this silly game. Why hadn't he just come to her? Their relationship had been strong. He must have known she would never think him guilty.

She folded the sheet of paper and put it back in the drawer. Then her eyes wandered to his diary. She wanted to read it. In all the years he'd been writing diaries, she'd only ever peeked inside one of them once – the day after his fourteenth birthday when he refused to come out of his bedroom after getting home from school. Concern had made her look and had then made her smile and vow never to invade his privacy again. She'd memorised word for word what he'd written.

I hate Mum. She has embarrassed me for life. She actually tried to squeeze a spot on my chin before I could get into the car, and Denise saw her. Now she'll never go out with me and it's all Mum's fault.

The diary on the table in front of her was a grown-up version of the ones he wrote in as child. Plain, dark blue and not covered in football stickers. She hesitated to open it, wondering if he'd mind, wondering where she should start. At the beginning, at the end or just somewhere in the middle. Then it dawned on her what day it was. *How strange.* Exactly one year ago he had started this book, so she would start at the beginning.

1 January

Brilliant New Year but paying the price today. Can't be arsed to get out of bed but I'm starving. Can't believe I snogged her.

Stupid move as I have to work with her. I hope she doesn't remember and was as drunk as me. Don't want or need a girlfriend in my life. Maybe at forty. Or at a compromise, thirty-five. Until then I'll settle for the odd quickie.

Is there anything in this room I can eat to save me leaving it? Glory hallelujah… spotted a lonesome Snickers bar in my thought-to-be empty Christmas stocking.

Nah, no good. Still hungry and now need to take a piss. (Sorry about language in case I suddenly die and someone reads this, but I'm talking to me on these pages not you!)

Ruth found herself smiling. Reading his diary brought him to life and was giving her an insight into his private thoughts and character. So far she'd learned nothing startling, only that her son had been a healthy male with normal habits.

She flicked through a few pages but stopped when she saw the word *Fuck.*

23 January

Fuck. What have I done? I should have gone home. I wonder if I should text her and play it down. Say I was drunk and can't recall much after falling asleep on her couch. Will she be the type to accept that and just go away? Hopefully, think no more on it. Memo to self: stick to beer in future! And don't be a fucking moron!

Ruth was intrigued, not about her son's sex life or lack of finesse, but about this woman and how well she might have known Thomas, how she might have viewed him. He was arrested on 18 April, so what she was reading took place three months before then. Was this woman in his life in April? She flicked through the days and stopped at a page that had more writing on than the others.

3 March

I cannot believe that I have met her. I am not meant to meet her until at least thirty-five but she is here right now in my world. I know it's the real thing as I have never felt more myself with anyone. She looks at me like no one ever has before. A secret look she passes me every time I look in her eyes. The maddest thing of all is neither of us wanted this. She is like me and wants to concentrate on her career. Yet we cannot draw apart. She talks about the amount of time we spend together and we agreed to limit it as we both have goals. Yet we cannot now sleep without the other by our side.

The only blight is I might have to move. My stupid mistake in January won't go away. I'm worried she'll turn up at the door. Her text messages make out like she can't stop thinking about that night. Making me uncomfortable to be around her at work. Tomorrow I'm telling her I've met someone. Then she'll hopefully let it drop. Fingers crossed.

Ruth rose from the chair alarmed, as if what was happening was right now, and not in the past. He'd said *fingers crossed* in his voicemail when he'd been hopeful of Jacob Cadell being good. And now the same expression had been used about someone else. From what he'd written he'd had problems with the woman he slept with. The fact he thought he might have to move made it sound like more than just an annoyance. What had he been afraid would happen?

She walked over to the window to stare out. Reading that passage had left her hollow. *He had fallen in love.* At the same age his father fell in love. She despaired over how life could deliver the same fate to both father and son at the same age. Except Thomas died unhappy. Alone. *Knowing* his life was about to end.

He must have pleaded guilty because he saw no way to prove himself innocent and saw no benefit to a trial. She would find out the truth. She would do it as the last role as his mother. She would prove her son was innocent.

CHAPTER FOUR

Rosie Carlyle entered her ground-floor bedsit and felt the hair rising on the back of her neck. *What the hell? Her clothes.* T-shirts and pants and blue jeans neatly hung over the radiators. The washing machine was on when she went out. She hadn't emptied it. She was positive. If she had she'd have hung the clothes over the airer so as not to block the heat. Her gaze took in the neatly made bed and folded pyjamas, while her senses strained to pick out sounds that would tell her she was not alone. Her eyes slid towards shadows, where someone might hide, wishing the low-energy bulb in the ceiling would hurry and brighten or that the bedside lamp was on. The bed was a divan, so not possible to hide under. The wardrobe so packed, a mouse would have a job finding room.

In a panic she turned swiftly and shut the front door, then hurried and checked the back door. It was locked, but fear drove her to tilt back a chair and jam it under the handle. It didn't make her feel any more secure. Someone got in, even with it locked. She just prayed it was Anabel, playing a horrible trick.

Her best friend, who hadn't even wished her Happy New Year, who now didn't want anything to do with her, who wouldn't answer her texts or calls and was doing this to punish her. Like every bad thing that ever happened was her fault. Rosie only suggested they keep quiet and say nothing to protect Anabel. Rosie had tried reasoning with her but to no avail. Anabel wanted to blame her for what happened when they were children, and blame her now as well for what happened last summer. All these years Rosie had been protecting her and now Anabel was threatening to tell their secret. She was holding onto her silence to frighten Rosie, and was doing a good job of it. Anabel was likely to be believed if her version of events differed to Rosie's. Couldn't she see what she was doing would do neither of them any good and only hurt both of them in the end?

They had been friends forever, surely that stood for something? It's not like Rosie was going to tell anyone what Anabel did. She had nothing to fear. Rosie was the one having to worry, the one panicking each time her friend threw a wobbly, who was having to take little blue-and-yellow tablets with an extra pill here and there to take the edge off nerves ready to snap. She was living with the constant fear that Anabel would crack. Since last summer she'd become snappy with Rosie. Seizing any excuse to find fault with her, before then using the silent treatment. Why couldn't Anabel see none of it was Rosie's fault, and accept her own mistakes? Resentment of Rosie being able to shrug things off was probably the reason Anabel was behaving like this. Rosie didn't have a choice but to put aside her concerns. Any mistakes Anabel made Rosie always had to sort out. She'd had to sort out what to do when they were children, otherwise Anabel would have got taken away. Rosie was the planner, the doer, always the one out front, the one who had to decide on everything. Where they should go. How they should dress.

What do you think I should do, Rosie? What do you think I should say?

Anabel hadn't objected to the suggestion in the beginning, only when it was too late. Now she was all twisted inside about it. Driving Rosie crazy. Rosie couldn't turn back time. Nothing could be undone now.

She picked up the nearly empty bottle of vodka on the table. There was enough for one small swig. She had come home from a party across the road feeling tipsy, but felt sober now. She didn't even know the people across the road, that's how bad things had got. Accepting a party invitation to a house full of strangers, just so she had somewhere to go. This time last year they were still together at a party. Though, that's when things started to go wrong. Rosie couldn't deny Anabel's behaviour upset her. But she got over it. She forgave her and supported her instead. She had gone through a shitty experience and had needed Rosie.

'Well fuck you, Anabel,' she said bitterly.

In a cupboard under the sink, she found a bottle of Metaxa. She'd bought it in Rhodes Old Town for them to share in the room, but it stayed unopened and came home with them instead. She unscrewed the cap and poured some in a glass, then sat on the edge of her bed and gazed at the hole in the carpet. She had lived there six years and had four walls and two doors, not counting the bathroom door. Her bedroom, kitchen and living room all in one place. It was perfect if you didn't mind not walking around and were inventive with how you placed furniture, but it would be no good for someone with claustrophobia.

Holiday photographs covered the walls, some of them curling from being up a long time. Rhodes, Ibiza, Crete, Majorca, Turkey, Benidorm. It would be difficult to tell where any of them were taken, as all showed similar scenes. Anabel or Rosie on a beach, by a poolside or in a bar. Rhodes was the best. They both found boyfriends, so neither felt like a third wheel. Rosie had been a true friend, making sure Anabel looked her best, that her clothes flattered her, her spray tan hadn't run, her nose and eyelids weren't getting red.

Rosie arranged all those holidays. She would have arranged one last year, except Anabel wouldn't stop moping and agree. Rosie wanted to cheer her up. Do something nice for her and go somewhere special. The Maldives or the Seychelles. What had Anabel ever done for her? Nothing. Zilch. All the years of Rosie putting in the effort of making sure Anabel was happy and looked nice, where was *her* input? Her effort to ensure Rosie had a good time? Her effort – to stand there like a gormless baby with her thumb stuck in her mouth – embarrassing her half the time. *Grow up, Anabel,* she muttered in her head. *Or at least stop sucking your thumb.* It hadn't looked so gross when they were eighteen and Anabel looked fourteen, but now at twenty-seven she looked pathetic.

Anabel chose to forget those things, like she chose to forget about her friend on New Year's Eve.

She stood up and breathed deeply, and calmed her anger. She knew deep down Anabel loved her. Anabel was just going through a hard time right now, and probably didn't care if it was affecting Rosie.

Rosie needed a second drink, or else a pill. She had enough prescription meds to last her the week if she cut them in half, but by then she'd be climbing the wall. She had a smear test booked for Friday, so she could ask for more then. Although she had better come up with a less alarming reason than the one she gave before. She'd had to lie through her teeth before the doctor would issue another prescription, by getting her to believe the imaginary dog that ate her tablets had been checked out at the vet's and his blood tests and stools were clear. This time she'd make it simple. Her mum had cleaned her place and thrown away what she thought was rubbish.

Rosie checked again that the front door was definitely locked before pouring her drink and putting her mind back to the excuse she would give, testing it for holes. She didn't want to walk out of the surgery empty-handed. The only hole, which didn't matter as nobody would know, was her mother wouldn't clean her place. She had never even seen where Rosie lived. Poor woman had enough trouble cleaning her own home. Anabel had a lot to be thankful for with her nice close-knit family. Her mum always on hand. She was probably still scoffing down food, eating herself silly at her family's party. In the last few months her body had ballooned while Rosie's had gone thin. They were opposites when it came to dealing with stress. Anabel took comfort in food, Rosie in vodka and pills.

She'd go and see her tomorrow. She wouldn't put it off any longer. With it being New Year's Day, Anabel might see it as a new start. There was a shop around the corner near where she lived, so Rosie would nip in, then over a box of chocolates and a bottle of vodka they could bury the hatchet. She'd behave in a jokey manner and thank her first for coming into her home to make her bed and hang out her washing, then watch for the guilt to come into her eyes. If reassured it was her, she would attempt to sort out this rift between them, as it really couldn't carry on into this new year. Rosie's nerves couldn't take it.

Rosie was done with cowering. Anabel had left her to dangle long enough. Rosie was going to cut that rope and walk. But not before she let Anabel know she was on her own. If she talked, Rosie would talk, too. She needed to know what Anabel was planning. Then no one else needed to get hurt.

CHAPTER FIVE

For the first time since August she woke refreshed. Ruth had slept deeply in Thomas's bed, though not in the same linen. It smelled fresh, the fragrance of washing powder wafting from the pillowcases when she climbed into the bed. She wondered if she'd misjudged the landlord, that he had thought to do this as a kindness. She was phoning him today and would ask. She needed to know a few things, like where to do her washing. There was no space for a washing machine or oven in the tiny kitchen.

She explored a little more. The one wall cupboard in the galley kitchen held a measly collection of mugs, bowls and plates and one glass tumbler, used to hold a handful of cutlery. The other was on the desk from her whisky last night. On one of the shelves she found a toastie maker and an array of dried goods. Porridge, coffee, rice, pasta, and dried milk. She would go shopping and stock the small fridge, which she was relieved to find had freezer space for at least two microwave meals.

She put the kettle on to make a black coffee, and took the box of porridge and a bowl from the cupboard. She should eat. She'd lost essential weight and needed to put it back on. As a doctor she was aware of the perils of malnourishment. She required fuel to give her the energy to do her work, both the job she was starting tomorrow and getting paid for, and for the one she would do in her own time. When in town she'd look for a pharmacy and pick up some vitamin D, fish oil capsules and turmeric. She could do with a boost. Grief had taken its toll on both her body and mind, but she owed it to Thomas to stay well. It was not going to be a walk in the park. The police found only damning evidence so she faced a hard task to find something to challenge it. All while dealing with grief.

Simply opening his wardrobe was enough to shatter her. Only willpower stopped her climbing in to bury herself in his clothes. She shut it quickly, fearful of his scent escaping if left open too long. To avoid that, she hung the contents of one of her suitcases from the picture rail in his room. She'd packed her suits and blouses on their hangers, which was fortunate. She would live out of the other suitcase for underwear and casualwear. Her trainers, warm ankle boots and work shoes were neatly under the bed. Thomas's size eight slippers were keeping her feet warm now – only one size bigger than her own. He'd taken after his father with his small feet, but after his mother for his height, standing two inches taller than her five ten. He'd taken after his father for his smile too. That smile had given her Thomas.

It should have been a normal holiday in Pompeii, not the undoing of her life plan. He'd been working on an archaeological site that she accidentally trespassed upon. He'd exploded at her in a heat of anger. In Italian, of course, and the reason she stayed to listen to him, not knowing whether she was in trouble. She'd kept silent and was escorted from the site with her head held high. Later that day while sat at a café drinking a glass of red wine he'd spotted her from his truck, and discovered she was English and hadn't understood a word he'd said. Then he smiled.

It had been an impossible affair from the beginning. Their plans were tumbled upside down. When the holiday was over she stayed another week, and when uni started again she found a job in a bar. September and October found them revising their plans. They would make it work. She could study in Italy. Go to medical school in Italy. Live in Italy. Flora De Luca welcomed her with open arms. Those same arms held her when on Christmas Eve the *polizie* came to tell them there'd been a fatality. She thought it happened while he was at work, in a place where accidents could happen. But it had been on a street, witnessed by others, including the jewellery shop owner. He'd walked out of the shop carrying a small blue box, which he opened to look at again. He'd not seen the bus coming. He'd been looking at the ring.

She had cried over Pietro De Luca, and Flora De Luca had cried with relief when Ruth found out she was carrying his child as her son's memory would live on. Her original life plan was revised again and most of it panned out the way she'd imagined it first time, except it took a little longer to achieve. She was twenty-nine and Thomas was ten by the time she qualified as a doctor.

After drinking her coffee and eating some porridge she disciplined herself to get dressed and ready to go out and not touch his things. She would allow herself time after she'd organised her new life. She was going to be living in this town for several months and rushing to find everything out in an instant was only going to tire her. She needed to recover her energy first, and remain invisible. She was able to go about her business with quiet anonymity, as her name was not De Luca. That was her best advantage to finding out the truth. As Ruth Bennett she could get close to those who had known Thomas without them being aware of who she was.

Investigate them quietly. Unobtrusively. Until she had all the pieces of the puzzle perfectly in place.

Then she would know who did this to her son.

CHAPTER SIX

The key to the front door didn't work when she returned from shopping.

A woman standing in the front garden smoking a cigarette suggested she give the key a wiggle. 'You have to do that sometimes,' she said. 'We keep telling Henry it needs a new lock.'

Ruth took her advice and was rewarded with the door opening. Henry, she surmised, must be the landlord's first name. She'd only addressed him as Mr Thorpe and he hadn't suggested she should do otherwise when they spoke earlier on the phone while she was queuing to pay for her shopping. The conversation lasted less than a minute, long enough for him to tell her there was a washing machine on the ground floor in a utility room, where she'd also find her son's bike, which he was happy for her to keep there if she wanted. She'd check out the bike later.

She turned to her helper. 'Thanks. I'll know next time.'

Dressed in a slightly shabby pink puffer jacket the woman looked to be in her thirties. Ruth guessed smoking was her reason for being outside, unless she normally went out in slippers and pyjama bottoms. Ruth saw she had a ring on each of her fingers and wondered if it made her hands feel heavy.

'Kim,' the woman said, smiling. 'I'm in the flat below you. Saw you move in yesterday. Hope the noise last night didn't disturb you. Had a bit of a party.'

Her pale blue eyes were curious. Too curious, Ruth thought, and still caked in last night's make-up. Her badly dyed blonde hair looked unbrushed as if only just lifted from a pillow.

Ruth smiled back. 'Nice to meet you, Kim. I'm Ruth. And I didn't hear a thing to be honest. Just fireworks at midnight.'

'Cool. And everything's all right up there? No problem getting anything to work?' she asked. 'Any problems with Wi-Fi, the tenant on the top floor sorts it all out. You should have the shared password. If not I'll write it down and pop it under your door.'

'Thanks, that would be great. But no, everything's fine otherwise.'

'Well, that's good then. It's been empty a while. Last person to live there was in August. Thought Henry had decided never to rent it again.'

'Why?' Ruth asked, as if curious.

'You squeamish?' Then, before Ruth could answer, Kim bizarrely slapped her own head. 'Forget I said that. I've got a thick gob sometimes.'

Ruth bit her lip as if amused. 'I'm not squeamish. I've seen a dead body before. I take it you're referring to something like that happening?'

A reluctant nod was given. 'Yeah. Poor bloke topped himself. Young as well.'

Ruth feigned shock to cover up for the pain she was feeling. It was hard to hear a stranger talking about her son like this. 'That's sad. Why?'

A conspiratorial look entered Kim's pale eyes. 'Heard he was a drug dealer. A doctor, no less. Nicking drugs off the NHS.'

'Really?' Ruth replied, hiding her reaction at hearing her son's reputation shredded.

Kim nodded. 'Police were here. Not that they carted much away. A sports bag is all. I got a look in through the door. Didn't see a single cannabis plant.'

Ruth suspected this was a disappointment. 'What was he like?'

She smiled in a coy way. 'Cute.' She shook her head as if bemused. 'You wouldn't have thought it, mind. He looked too much of a health freak to be a dealer. Rode his bike like one of them formula racers in all the proper gear. It's miles to the hospital from here and he biked it every day for fun.'

She probably meant a Grand Tour cyclist, but Ruth didn't correct her. What she'd said was interesting. Her observation of Thomas was quite correct. He'd given up red meat and dairy products years ago and would only consider not walking or cycling if both his legs were broken. 'Well, it sounds a sad story. He must have felt very alone to have taken his own life. Did he not have friends or a girlfriend to stop him?'

Kim shrugged. 'He had the odd bloke or woman visit. Not often. Saw one woman he obviously didn't want visiting because he pretended to be out when she called. He was there. I saw him going up the stairs before she arrived, but I did him a favour and told her he'd gone out. She didn't look happy when I told her it again next time as well.'

Ruth wanted to ask more, but to do so might arouse suspicion. She picked up her shopping bags instead. 'Well, I better put this lot away before it perishes. Nice talking to you, Kim.'

'Likewise.' She pulled a crumpled packet of cigarettes from her pocket. 'Might as well have another fag after saying all that. Save me coming out for a bit. You need anything, give me a shout,' she called as she stepped back outside the house again.

As the door closed behind her Ruth wondered how much more Kim might know about Thomas. Maybe she should invite Kim and her other new neighbours round for a drink. Some of them might have known him well. She would bide her time, though. What was most important was to infiltrate their lives slowly to achieve her goal.

*

It was early evening when she realised Thomas had lived without a TV or radio. She wanted to listen to the six o'clock news. It was a small thing to discover but added to her picture of how he'd lived. He may have spent his spare time reading. Kim had slipped a piece of paper under her door with the Wi-Fi password, so she could watch it on her own laptop, but she didn't want to fetch it out of her case just for that. On her next outing she'd buy a TV for some company in the evenings. She liked having it on in the background sometimes when at home. For now, though, she settled for listening to some music on her phone while she sat at his desk. She opened the diary to where she left off the night before.

4 March

I should have saved my breath. I told her and since then she's not stopped texting all day. Even while sat at the fucking desk a few feet away she sent texts. Professing sleepless nights, for fuck sake. It was a stupid mistake. Because of too much booze!!! I don't know what the fuck to do. Everyone likes her. Jed fancies her. I wish the fuck she'd ask him out and get her mind off me. To top it off, Mr Mason thinks I'm the one who lost the patient's notes. Jed didn't help, standing there saying nothing. He saw me put them on the bloody desk. Thank God we now put everything on the computer. Bloody things are meant to have done away with hard copy. But not for Mr Mason. Tomorrow I'll find the fucking thing and slap it in his hand. Probably him who lost them in the first place with him always having to swap his reading glasses and distance glasses. The man is permanently searching for them. Glad it's not my gallbladder he's taking out tomorrow…

5 March

Well, well, well. Notes found under desk. Me thinks not. They're as thick as a brick. If they'd fallen on the floor there would have been an explosion of paper everywhere. I'm pretty sure who put them there and wish there was CCTV above the desk to show it. On the plus side, she left me alone today. So hopefully she's happier for her little revenge.

Hope of that went out the window. She just texted. Shall she come over so we can talk? I gave a short reply. In capitals. With lots of exclamation marks. NO!!!! Mum would exclaim over the overuse of exclamation marks, but I'm worried to fuck how she knows where I live. Thank God I'm away this weekend. Maybe over a glass of wine I'll ask Mum her advice. I want to tell her about C.

Ruth was unsettled again. If he'd asked her advice she would have told him she was hearing warning bells and that he should act quickly and appropriately and apologise to the woman. He'd slept with her and should have taken care how he handled matters afterwards. The woman may have thought he cared for her deeply. While growing up she'd tried to instil good morals in him, to treat everyone with respect. Especially the old and infirm. How to treat women had been a whole other subject and Nonna De Luca had had plenty to say on that. Thomas had adored her and she had adored him. She would have ripped him in two if he'd shown any untoward behaviour to a woman.

Ruth remembered his visit in March quite clearly. He hadn't mentioned anyone whose name began with C. They'd talked about his work, ordered takeaway and watched *The Untouchables.* He never even hinted there was something wrong. She wished he had named the woman as she couldn't work out if C was the one he'd slept with or the one he was in love with. The situation with the patient's notes smacked of something a little sinister, as if they were hidden deliberately. It put a patient's wellbeing at stake. Had this woman done that? Or had Thomas become paranoid because she wouldn't go away?

Ruth picked up her mobile and opened the Notes app. She added to the one name already jotted down: Mr Mason, Jed, and C.

Before calling it a night, she wanted to take a look at the days following his arrest. From 18 April to 21 April, nothing was written. Were the pages blank because he'd been too shocked to write or had he been in a cell in a police station and unable to?

22 April

Just writing this is making it real! How has this happened? I can make no sense of any of it. I don't have answers to explain the drugs. What's worse is the police don't believe me. Nor does my solicitor. She asked if I had reason to self-medicate for an injury. What the fuck does she think? That I broke a leg or something and just decided to take something for the pain? Oh, sure, that really makes sense. I don't even know what I'm meant to have taken. The doctor in A&E asked me what I'd taken and looked at me sceptically when I answered nothing. Maybe for back pain or an old injury? the solicitor then suggested. I don't know if she has something wrong with her hearing but she can't seem to hear me when I say I don't know how it got in me. Nor how those drugs got in my locker or under my bed. Clearly someone put them there, but it wasn't me! I'd like to offer a possible suggestion, but it might lead to more trouble. The police already think I'm lying about texts on my phone from so-called buyers without them reading one that was open to interpretation. But which was also true. I'm a moron for writing it. I should have held back. Kept it a private thought. The best thing I can do is keep my mouth shut. And pray something comes to my rescue. I am up to my neck in shit. Friends I thought I could count on have distanced from me as if I've suddenly contracted a contagious disease. Thank God I have her in my life otherwise I don't know what I would do.

An ache in the bridge of her nose intensified as Ruth held back the tears. She was too angry to cry. Had the police read his diary? Had they thought every word a lie? Diaries were for writing one's innermost thoughts. That was the whole point of them. Surely they didn't think he made this up just for their eyes? His diary confirmed his innocence, surely? His confusion had screamed his despair. He couldn't explain any of it, not even how a powerful drug was in his system.

If they could read this page and still charge him it was no wonder he'd pleaded guilty. He'd had no one on his side, including his goddamn solicitor. How on earth had they thought him guilty of stealing for gain, a lowlife who preyed on the needs of others? It was laughable. Twenty-five years of age and the worst he ever did was get a detention at school for refusing to do some homework. Her anger boiled. They must have thought they'd been handed him on a plate. A nice young man of good character and manners pleading guilty. Yet the only evidence against him was in a locker, in a sports bag, in his system, *on his phone.* Jacob Cadell never mentioned that. Had the police tracked down the people who sought to buy drugs from him? Maybe if there had been a trial Jacob Cadell would have pointed this out and would have picked at the evidence until there was nothing left. But he'd come to the rescue too late. Thomas had already pleaded guilty.

Well, they would soon come to learn she was not going away. Not until she had what she came for.

CHAPTER SEVEN

The building looked like it might have been intended as a church, with its tented roof and steeply pitched slopes pointing sharply to the sky. Yet it was modern, built in the last decade. Perhaps it was decided it would benefit the community more as a GP surgery.

She dismounted the bike and undid the strap of Thomas's helmet. She would text Henry Thorpe shortly and ask him to support her in a white lie should anyone ask why she was riding his previous tenant's property. She wanted him to say it was unclaimed so he was letting her use it. Kim had gaped at her this morning when Ruth wheeled the bike out the front door. She'd been outside smoking again. Ruth smiled and thanked her for the password for the Wi-Fi and moved swiftly on.

She heaved for breath, glad she had never succumbed to smoking. She could barely breathe now, her windpipe was so tight. Most of the route was uphill and she couldn't work out the gears properly – it had almost killed her. What possessed her to ride the bike? She didn't know. Stupidity, she guessed. Thankfully, she had fresh clothes to change into and antiperspirant in her bag.

Conscious of her clammy skin and glazed face she dived into the patients' toilet as soon as she set foot inside the building and gave herself a quick strip-wash before donning her smart clothes. Navy tailored slacks, white collared shirt and black leather loafers. She tidied her hair, retouched her make-up, then, satisfied, she unlocked the door. She sensed she was being observed and looked across the foyer to the reception desk. Three women in matching blouses and nearly matching hairstyles were watching her. Ruth smiled politely and walked towards them. Before she could speak the one with bobbed grey hair got in first.

'You know those toilets are not for general public use. They're for patients only.' She then folded her arms in a disapproving manner.

Ruth turned and stared back at the toilet door, taking her time to examine it. Then she gave another polite smile. 'I'll make sure to remember next time. Perhaps it should have a notice on it.'

The woman jutted out her chin. 'Shouldn't need one. People should already know that.' She turned to the women at her side to rally support. 'Isn't that right?' she asked.

They were either more polite than their colleague or had picked up on Ruth being someone who'd not just wandered in to use the loo. Bobbed-hair number two stepped forward. Her rich brown hair was quite pretty and she had warm brown eyes. 'Would you by any chance be Dr Bennett?'

Ruth nodded. 'Yes, I am.'

The grey-haired woman, who at a guess was in her sixties, didn't back down at learning this as she tutted and said, 'Well, why didn't you say? We thought you just wandered in. We get a lot of that with having a row of shops next to us. They treat it like it's a public convenience.'

Ruth had heard enough of toilets and changed the subject. 'So, you must be the receptionists?'

The third woman nodded. 'Yes. Though Joan is senior to me and Mary. I'm Sally.'

It didn't take much to work out who Joan was. She already looked more in charge and apparently impervious to rudeness from the way she now pointed a finger at Ruth. 'If you go to the door behind you, I'll let you in and tell Dr Campbell you're here,' she said bluntly.

Five minutes later Ruth sat in an empty consultation room, waiting for Dr Campbell. She'd been silly to start off like that, aggravating the senior receptionist. A good receptionist could make life so much easier, ensuring surgeries ran smoothly and doctors and nurse practitioners were looked after and not run ragged. But if you got a Rottweiler, one who put patients through an interrogation before they could book in, or who thought grilling a doctor was part of their job, they could make life difficult. She hoped Joan was just having an off day.

The office door opened and Ruth stood as Dr Carol Campbell entered the room. She was a petite woman with short dark hair, and around Ruth's age. She was one of the partners at the practice and had interviewed Ruth for the job. Dr Campbell closed the door and leaned back against it before letting go a theatrical sigh. 'Am I glad you didn't change your mind. The whole world and his wife want a doctor today. We should ban Christmas to save on the carnage. Overindulgence will be the problem for most of them.' She sighed again, then grinned. 'Welcome to the mad house.'

*

Despite the warning there were lots of patients to see, Ruth wasn't seeing her first patient until two. She was given the morning to familiarise herself with the surgery's computer system. Apart from the practice having customised the layout and added specific templates it was much the same as the system she'd used in Bath. She got to grips with the basic functions pretty much straight away and was confident with how to check appointments, bring up blood results, create reports, print prescriptions, fit notes or patient information leaflets. The practice had gone paperless a year ago.

Ruth was impressed so far, especially when Dr Campbell brought her a lunchtime coffee latte. She didn't stay long to chat; she was just making sure Ruth was happy with how everything worked before afternoon surgery began. Ruth assured her she was. In truth, she felt guilty. What she had done was unethical. She had searched the patients registered at the practice and now had contact details for the woman who reported Thomas. She felt as bad as if she'd stolen petty cash and was relieved she would not have to do something like it again. She was law-abiding and had felt uncomfortable the moment she started searching. Dr Campbell's kind act had increased her feelings of guilt. Ruth had to remind herself she did it for a good reason. Her purpose for being there was to find information to help clear Thomas's name. She was not going to hurt the woman. She just wanted to talk to her. That's all. So she could stop fretting, and concentrate on her new job.

The afternoon flashed by. Five patients. Five ailments all caused by an overindulgence of some sort. Dr Campbell had been correct. A patient with a flare-up of gout. A patient with dyspepsia from too much port. A patient having a feeling of bloating and *yuckiness.* A patient with heartburn, and a patient with persistent diarrhoea from nonstop eating of nuts since Christmas Day. When satisfied they were otherwise well she gave them simple advice to stop their symptoms. Abstain from rich food, alcohol and smoking.

She was now waiting for her last patient, and heard a tap at the door. The man who entered hobbled as he made his way to the chair. He smiled grimly as he sat down. 'Pain's worse when I rest it,' he said.

Ruth was already developing a diagnosis. 'In which foot?' she asked.

'Right one. Had it all over Christmas. In the heel and arch. Worse in the mornings. Not so bad when I get walking, but stabbing when I stop and rest.'

'Can you remove your socks and shoes for me so I can have a look?'

'Sure,' he replied, quickly slipping off his trainers and socks, and then his jacket and jumper. 'I'm sweltering after just walking in here. Normally walk miles in a day without breaking a sweat.'

She studied him. He was tall and fit-looking, probably lifted weights. His muscular shoulders and arms filled his T-shirt. She lowered her gaze to his feet as his amused gaze met hers.

'Can you raise your toes off the floor for me, please?'

He managed to lift the toes of his left foot with no problem, but his right toes barely moved and caused him immense pain in his arch when he tried. She then asked him to lift his feet up one at a time so that she could see his soles. The heel of the right foot was marginally swollen. 'I'm thinking you have plantar fasciitis. The symptoms you describe go along with that. The ligament connecting your heel to the front of your foot gets damaged if too much pressure is on it. Exercising on a hard surface or wearing shoes with poor cushioning will do it, so soft insoles in your shoes will help. Rest it on a stool and apply an ice pack every two to three hours, and do some gentle stretching exercises. Take paracetamol if you're not already, and unless it gets worse perhaps come back in two weeks so we can see how things are.'

While he put his shoes back on Ruth washed her hands at the sink in the corner of the room.

'I hope it eases. I'm on my feet for a lot of the day,' he said.

She returned to her desk and had her back slightly towards him as she documented the examination. 'What do you do?' she asked. 'Do you require a fit note for work?'

She could hear him breathing, and heard him give a little sigh. 'I'm a policeman. A beat cop, so no surprise I've got bad feet. But no, I don't need a fit note. I'm on annual leave this week.'

She briefly turned to give him a sympathetic look and caught him studying her.

'We've met before,' he said. He sounded very sure, and was still staring.

Ruth felt the back of her neck prickle. 'I don't think so.'

He nodded. 'Yes, we have. I was your driver that day.'

Her heart rate accelerated as he continued to examine her features. *Her driver. That day.* She remembered being put into the back of a police car after coming out of the courthouse and sitting there forever before the vehicle moved. She had to wait in that car so as not to arrive at the morgue before Thomas. She felt disturbed that she should now be reminded of this by her patient. It felt wrong, unprofessional even, to have mentioned it. The same as it would be wrong if she saw a patient outside of surgery and reminded them of seeing her at an awkward or painful time.

She carried on with the task of typing her findings in his medical notes and was startled when his hand touched her shoulder. She turned in her seat quickly to dislodge it. He was smiling at her kindly, and it made her uncomfortable that he knew intimate things about her private life. He was good-looking in a self-assured way, she realised, and she was suddenly conscious of his near proximity and the closed door.

He stood back and regarded her as if knowing her well. 'I remember how dignified you were. Most people can't contain their emotions. I thought about you a great deal afterwards, to the point I was going to phone you and see if you were okay.'

Ruth shook her head at him and spoke coolly. 'I wouldn't have wanted that. I was quite all right, thank you.'

A small smile appeared on his face, irritating her madly because it seemed as if he thought she had to say that. She was beginning to think he was smarmy and wanted shot of him.

Relieved as he walked to the door, he unnerved her further.

'Say, how about having a drink one evening?'

Ruth managed a polite smile as she shook her head. 'Thank you, but that wouldn't be appropriate.'

He raised an eyebrow at her answer. 'Why not? Unless you've married since the summer or got a boyfriend?'

Her cheeks flushed with colour and her mouth slightly opened. How did he know she'd been unmarried before then? Or that she'd been without a boyfriend? Had he checked up on her after driving her that day? She felt a little sick at the thought of it, but more so at the thought of him being by her side that day as she gazed through the viewing window at her son's body. She remembered there had been a policeman with her and now realised it was him.

Standing up to make herself feel less intimidated, she didn't hide her annoyance. 'I think perhaps next time, Mr Wiley, it would be more appropriate for you to see one of the other doctors here at the practice.'

He puffed out his cheeks and shook his head. Then brazenly shrugged as if it were no big deal that he'd just hit on his doctor after informing her he'd driven her to see her dead son.

Finally, he opened the door and left the room.

Ruth sat down with relief. She noticed her hands trembling. The unexpected meeting with the policeman had left her shaken. He had met her briefly on what was to be the worst day of her life. What he witnessed that day should have remained deeply private. He had intruded on her last moment with her son, by watching her. She hadn't wanted anyone in Bournemouth to know she was Thomas's mother, but now this overbearing and overconfident man had just let her know he knew exactly who she was.

CHAPTER EIGHT

Half an hour later, still shaken, she changed into her cycling clothes. The building had gone quiet and she guessed most staff left at five thirty. It had been a strange day and her last patient had unsettled her. In her old job, even with consultation-room doors shut, she would know who was working in them and always felt safe. She hadn't met any of the other doctors or nurses yet, and it had felt quite isolating all day in that room alone.

She was fitting her helmet on when Joan came out of the building to hand her a wad of blue paper towels. 'It was raining an hour ago so thought you might need these to dry your bike. Tomorrow, bring it in through the back door. There's a storeroom to the left where you can leave it.'

Ruth smiled at her gratefully, glad there'd been someone in the building aware she was there. She thanked her, and put the paper towels to good use by wiping the saddle and handlebars. She mounted the bike and rode away, relieved that her intended destination was downhill, and not far from Thomas's flat. In a short while she would meet the woman who had reported Thomas.

With a gloomy expression, Ruth followed the traffic along the busy road, concerned she was in for a disappointment and maybe even disapproval. The woman might have an unfavourable opinion of Thomas. Ruth might hear details that wouldn't help at all. And how did she introduce herself? As a new doctor at the surgery or as Thomas's mother? If she said she was a new GP where this woman was a patient it wouldn't go down well, and rightly so, as the woman would know she had been tracked down. Ruth was so desperate to uncover the truth, she hadn't given thought to any of this. She had no option but to stay positive. Refuse to allow hurdles to get in the way. It was either going to go well or badly wrong. She was not going to unearth everything at once. Keeping that in mind would help to keep her going and would stop her from being too hopeful of an instant result.

*

Ruth wheeled the bike onto the pavement and leaned it against a green metal BT box. If invited in, she would wheel it to the front door. She was glad she was not in her car, otherwise she'd be driving around still, looking for somewhere to park.

The row of tall houses on each side of the street gave her a feeling of claustrophobia. The small red brickwork was a dominating feature making the road look too narrow between the facing houses. Ruth liked to look out of a window and see the colours of nature – a green field in the summer, stark black trees in the snow. She didn't want to look out of a window and see into someone else's home.

She was fortunate she could choose where to live. While some people had no choice. As a doctor she had been in a lot of homes, and saw how people had to live. On top of each other, sharing communal stairs and lifts that sometimes didn't work. Homes where children were without a garden, so they went to the park instead, which might work for some families but not all. Getting children ready to go out was an uphill battle for some parents, when it meant getting ready all the necessary equipment that goes with them. Baby bottles and nappy bags and changes of clothing loaded onto a pushchair, that then tipped backwards the minute the toddler was free to get out of it. Having a garden didn't make that any less a struggle, but it would lessen the amount of times having to go through it.

She was remembering these things from being a mother herself, and she only had to concentrate on one child. Trying to get Thomas ready for nursery had been like a mini-workout some days. His arms and legs pushing out of clothes she was trying to put on. Then when finally ready to walk out the door, late for work and nursery, Thomas would need a wee or a poo or his shoes put back on, which had to be found first. Those first years she was always behind, always catching up, chasing her tail running around in circles.

Putting her memories away, Ruth focused on the house she was visiting, wondering whether to keep the helmet on. It would make her less memorable with her hair covered. The woman might not recognise Ruth then at the surgery. Ruth could use Thomas's surname and say she was Mrs De Luca, or just say, Thomas's mum. She didn't need to mention she was a doctor. She was in Bournemouth and decided to take the opportunity to meet someone who might be able to tell her a little about how Thomas was that day. There was no need to make it more complicated.

She needed to stop procrastinating and just knock on the door. She was chilled from standing there dithering. She took a deep breath, then with shoulders back, went up to the door and rang the round black bell next to the flat number. She stepped back and waited. She gave it a minute, then pressed the bell again. Then a third time for luck. She let another minute go by before giving up. Luck wasn't on her side this evening. She would try again tomorrow.

She was about to get back on the bike when she froze, hearing the purr of an engine. Maybe it was the woman returning home. Ruth scanned the cars close by, then stepped out into the road so she could see further along. Ruth couldn't see any lights on in any vehicle. She peered at the windscreens trying to make out if there was a driver in any of them. It was easy to see into the cars that were next to her, but not so easy when parked further along in the dark.

The noise then stopped. The engine switched off. She waited awhile, expecting to see a person getting out of a car, but no one appeared. She went back on the pavement, wondering if she'd missed them getting out, but no one was there. It might be perfectly innocent behaviour, but as she was standing out on the road clearly scanning the cars, it would make sense if the driver got out and reassured her.

A moment later, she was ready to cycle away, when she heard the car again. The same soft purr. She felt a shiver down her spine. Something didn't feel right. She didn't like the thought of someone being able to see her, while she couldn't see them. To show she wasn't bothered at being made to feel nervous, she raised a hand and waved.

She was halfway along the road when she heard the power of the engine. It wasn't a purr like before, but a roar. Someone was revving the hell out of it, pressing their foot on and off the gas pedal. Ruth cycled faster to get to the end of the road, then turned to look for a car behind her, but the road was clear. It was still hiding among the other vehicles, with its lights off.

She hoped the stupid person got stuck there, and couldn't get their car out. Disturbing people in their homes, probably frightening dogs and waking babies, and getting kicks out of scaring people in the street. She hoped the pillock was stuck there all night. It would serve them right.

She was on her road when a thought occurred. The person might have been trying to get their car out. They may have been making that racket to get people out on the street to move cars that were blocking the driver's car in. Ruth didn't know whether she should laugh. Either a poor sod or a pillock was sat in it. She couldn't decide. What she could be sure of, she was not cycling down that road again. She would take her car and find somewhere to park, or she would get a taxi.

CHAPTER NINE

Rosie turned into Anabel's road stiff with cold. Her toes felt like they might break off, her fingers burned. She had not worn warm enough clothes and had forgotten hat and gloves. She would raid Anabel's wardrobe for the return journey, otherwise she'd perish or end up with pneumonia. Earlier, it was drizzling but mild, now it was bitter.

She stared across at Anabel's windows and almost cried, as she saw the same thing as yesterday. Black glass, lights off, not home. 'Shit,' she muttered. *Where the fuck was she?*

Like Rosie, Anabel had the ground floor, but with no back garden to sit in, so no access to the rear of the building to see if a light was on in the bathroom. Although, she would have had to be in there a long time not to have a light on in the living room. It was dark at four, it was now ten past six.

Rosie noticed a pink car outside Anabel's flat. It was parked with the headlamps off and the interior in darkness, but someone was sitting in it. The driver's door opened and a woman got out. Without even thinking, Rosie darted back around the corner into the little shop. Anabel's mum was the last person Rosie wanted to see.

The shopkeeper recognised Rosie from the night before and gave a welcoming smile, probably hoping to see her spend more money on chocolates and vodka. The bottle had only been 70cl size, yet cost nearly what she paid for a litre bottle in a supermarket. She would buy another bottle as she was in the shop, but only because it would save her going out tomorrow. Through the shop window, she saw Meg Whiting peering through Anabel's letterbox. She dug out her purse and quickly paid, declining the offer of cheap bars of chocolate on the counter, ready to dash as soon as she had her change. There was no point in stopping to ask Meg where her daughter was if she was looking for her through a letterbox. She would be better off getting home and getting warm again, and maybe emailing Anabel instead of texting or phoning. Anabel might be surprised by Rosie doing that and might reply. Yes, she would email her as soon as she got home.

Preparing for the cold again, she swung out of the shop too fast and barrelled straight into the woman.

Anabel's mum looked shocked. In fact, she looked as white as a ghost. She grabbed a hold of Rosie's shoulders, partly to steady herself but mostly to hang on to Rosie, as if fearing she'd disappear.

'I saw you turn back. You saw me and shot off like a bullet. Is it because you don't want to tell me where Anabel is?'

Rosie shook her head, wishing she'd taken time to wash her hair or at least tie it back. Anabel's mother was a hygiene freak, always obsessing about cleanliness both in her home and in the people around her. Anabel's jeans used to wear out from so much washing rather than the actual wearing of them.

Rosie decided she'd be honest with the woman. 'I didn't know she wasn't home until I got here and saw no lights on.'

Meg Whiting took a shuddering breath. Her voice was filled with alarm. 'Where is she then? Where can she be?'

Rosie shook her head again, wondering if she should be concerned. The woman had a tendency to get neurotic over minor problems. 'I don't know. I haven't spoken to her for a while.'

Her eyes turned frantic. 'What's a while? A day? Two days? A week or what? When did you last speak to my daughter?'

Rosie managed to step away as the woman lifted her hands and dragged them through her hair. Since none of her texts or voicemails had received a reply, the last time she'd spoken to

Anabel was Christmas Eve, and then only briefly considering they'd not spoken in over two months before that. She was saved from answering as the woman interrupted her thoughts.

'I haven't been able to get hold of her since the day before New Year's Eve. She didn't turn up at the house for the party, and didn't phone or text either. No one has seen her. We've reported it to the police, but they don't seem worried as we have nothing to give them to cause concern, other than that this isn't like her.' She stared at Rosie, suddenly suspicious. 'Are you sure you don't know where she is or why she's not communicating with any of us? Is she pregnant, Rosie, and has gone off somewhere? You can tell me. I won't be shocked.'

Rosie inwardly sighed. Anabel was twenty-seven. If she was pregnant it was hardly something she would need to hide. Rosie was worried, though, now she'd heard the circumstances. Anabel missing her parents' New Year's Eve party was a surprise. She went to their parties every year, which was a pain as by the time they got in a nightclub every decent-looking bloke was taken. It was a family 'thing', a Whiting tradition she never wanted to miss. But as she hadn't been there, where had she been? Was it possible she'd been in Rosie's home for all of that evening, while Rosie was across the road at the neighbour's party? Perhaps she didn't make Rosie's bed and hang out the washing to frighten her, but because she was bored and looking for something to do?

Why didn't she let her mum and dad know? Was it a spur-of-the-moment thing? She wanted time alone? Christmas Eve, when Rosie bumped into her in town, she was poker-faced and would have stayed mute if Rosie hadn't fallen backwards over a dog. When Rosie's ankle got entangled in the lead and the dog played tug of war and tugged her down the street it had been like a comedy sketch. Anabel had burst out laughing, something Rosie hadn't heard in a long time. Rosie didn't care that her elbow was bleeding and tailbone almost broken, she was happy to hear Anabel laugh.

But the laughter ended abruptly when Rosie asked how she was. Anabel stared at her with wounded eyes and said her life was ruined. Had Anabel taken off to decide what to do? She could be somewhere on the other side of the country in a police station confessing everything or changing the story to make Rosie sound guilty. Rosie kept her expression calm, while her stomach filled with worms.

'I doubt she's pregnant. She may have found a boyfriend, though. Perhaps she's with him, still nursing a hangover from New Year's Day. Have you been into her flat?'

The woman jammed her hand in her pocket and fetched out some keys. 'I was about to when I saw you. Will you come with me so we can look together?'

Rosie nodded, then took the keys from the woman's trembling hand and crossed the road. She let her enter the flat first then followed. A couple of envelopes lay on the mat, which Meg walked past. The one-bedroom flat was chilly, the radiator stone cold. The heating had been off for more than a day, Rosie reckoned. She'd stayed there enough times to gauge the coldness of the place. It felt strange without Anabel there. Strange and different. She noticed things as if seeing Anabel's home for the first time. The colour of the rug and the cushions on the sofa complimented the wallpaper in the living room. The throw in a pale shade of orange draped over a small chair in the corner. Photographs on the wall in attractive frames. Plants in stylish pots. And everywhere clean.

She had a sudden urge to leave. She realised, all at once, an emptiness. Contentment, fulfilment, culmination of a meaningful life. This was all accessible to Anabel. She lived while Rosie existed. Rosie closed her eyes. She didn't need her head messed up with nonsense. Fancy cushions hadn't made Anabel happy. She'd run away from her home and Mum and best friend, which should be Rosie's only concern right now. Not whether one of them was having the better life.

While Meg toured the kitchen, Rosie headed for the bedroom. She did the sensible thing and checked under the bed. Her small suitcase had gone and there was no other place Anabel could have stowed it. She opened the wardrobe and saw gaps in the clothes, which confirmed that Anabel had deliberately gone away. At least they knew she hadn't been abducted. She'd break the good news to her mother.

Making her way out of the room, a smell drew her attention to the wastepaper basket. A black banana skin lay on top of other rubbish. She fetched it out in case it was suggested they start cleaning the place. She was about to walk away when she saw thick blue writing on a piece of paper. She picked it up, then gave a small gasp, which thankfully went unheard. If Meg Whiting read this message she'd go back to the police.

> *You ought to have been caught. When will you pay? Chip chop chip chop – the last man dead.*

Rosie could hardly breathe. Her heart pounded in her chest. *Anabel must have talked.* She had told someone and now someone else knew. There could be no other reason for her getting this letter. Someone wanted paying. She couldn't keep her trap shut and had now run like a coward without even letting Rosie know.

Fear churned inside her. She didn't care that Anabel was gone, she cared only about who she'd told. What she'd said. Did she say it was her fault alone? Did she mention it was Rosie as well? Rosie was scared and was thinking fast. About Anabel, about New Year's Eve, about her clothes on the radiators.

If she'd run away before New Year's Eve it was not Anabel who had come into her home. Someone else had. Someone unknown. Someone who now knew their secret.

CHAPTER TEN

Ruth abandoned the microwaved supper of tinned potatoes and precooked salmon as she read something painful in Thomas's diary. Any notion to carry on enjoying the food given up on as her taste buds turned her mouth sour. She grabbed a glass of water to wash the taste away, and shakily read the passage again.

16 August

It hurt my heart to leave her today. I wanted to stay in her arms and stare out the window and make shapes out of the clouds, but she stubbornly refused to play. The only horse she professed to see was the one in the name of the bar across the road. I am so damn scared that I'm not going to get many more days of lying with her and looking out of that rooftop window. How do I stop this? Someone really has it in for me and posted my photograph from the newspaper on FB. 300 likes! I want to hide! If not for Jed Nolan everyone would have seen it and read it. Thank God he managed to get the person to take it down. My heart keeps hammering and the only place where I feel safe is with her. But I can't do that to her. I can't involve her in this mess. I'd rather cut all ties now than spoil what we had. If I could have one wish it would be that she had not met me to save her this hurt.

Ruth gulped back tears. He'd written this six days before he died. The raw pain she was feeling would settle more quickly if she could control it. If she let it slice her open it would take longer to recover and take what precious energy she had left. She needed to focus less on the emotional journey her son endured and more on finding out who put him on it in the first place. At least she now had Jed's surname and a place she could look for. A bar with 'horse' in the name, not far from where his girlfriend lived. In a house or flat with a rooftop window. She wanted to meet this woman, to see what she was like, and see what she knew.

Closing the diary, she put it away in the drawer. Without passwords she couldn't open his Facebook page, or his iPad and laptop. If she took his mobile to a shop they'd probably unlock it for her, but clear out his entire phone in the process. She was now regretting not tackling this problem beforehand as it would take time to sort out. In the meantime, the bundle of post waiting to be opened would have bills to pay for accounts that she could not use. Nothing was simple.

Her plan to come to Bournemouth with just one name to go on hadn't led anywhere today. Apart from down a street to listen to a scary car. Once she was home she had tried phoning her and heard the message: 'The user's mailbox is full. You cannot leave a message at this time.' So no luck at all. Ruth would keep trying, of course, it was only her first attempt, but it was frustrating not to have met her, after the ordeal of getting her address.

She had learned something new about Jed, though. He'd shown kindness to Thomas. Ruth picked up her phone before she could change her mind and googled 'Thomas De Luca Bournemouth'. She held her breath as his photograph appeared. He looked strained and was staring straight at the camera. The headline made her screw her eyes shut.

DOCTOR PLEADS GUILTY TO STEALING HOSPITAL MEDICINES.

It was an unbearable read and painted him in a deplorable light. Ruth could only imagine his anguish at seeing himself written about in such an awful way, having to bear the indignity of being labelled a thief. A life destroyer, rather than lifesaver. The coroner reached the right conclusion as to cause of death, but not the right conclusion as to *why* Thomas did it. It wasn't because he couldn't face what he'd done. It was more likely he couldn't bear to be thought guilty. Ruth believed this with every fibre of her being and only her resurrected son coming back to tell her differently would change her mind.

As she picked up the half-eaten meal to take to the kitchen, she heard a knock at the door. She quickly placed the plate down, then hid Thomas's things in the desk drawer. She opened the door hoping she didn't appear flustered.

For some reason the man standing there reminded her of a teacher. In a shirt and tie and dark green corduroy jacket over navy chinos she could imagine him in front of a blackboard. The black-framed glasses and short dark hair made him look studious and intelligent. He greeted her by holding out to her a shiny silver key. 'Your new key for the front door. The lock has been changed.'

She recognised his voice. Henry Thorpe, her landlord.

'Thank you,' she said.

He eyed her curiously. 'You are Miss Bennett, aren't you?'

'Yes, of course I am,' she replied, sounding slightly affronted at being asked this way, as if he suspected her of being an imposter. 'Would you care to come in and check I'm the only person here?'

He entered the flat in a carefree manner as if her invite was genuine, leaving her to stand at the door while he casually carried on through to the sitting room. He turned and inspected her again. 'I was expecting an older woman. You don't look old enough to have been Tom's mother.'

He said Tom like he knew her son and in a way that sounded nice, and she instantly forgave him his behaviour. 'I had Thomas when I was nineteen.'

He stared around the room. 'I've had the flat kept locked so none of the other tenants know that it's still full of Tom's things, but if they see inside they'll wonder why it's still here.'

Ruth gaped at him, with her mouth open, thinking about her stupidity. Hiding a laptop, phone and iPad when all his belongings were all over the room. It could have been Kim at the door and then her cover would have been blown. 'God, I'm an idiot,' she exclaimed. 'Why didn't I think of that?'

'I expect you've had a lot on your mind.' He patted the pockets of his jacket, then searched his trouser pockets before the frown from his face disappeared when he reached into the breast pocket of his shirt and found what he was looking for. He pulled out a long key and handed it to her. 'There's a cupboard on the landing outside your door. If you like, you can store Tom's things there. The furniture was already here so it's just his books really, and clothes, I imagine.'

She clasped the key firmly in the palm of her hand. 'Thank you. And thank you also for preparing the bed with clean linen. It was thoughtful.'

He gave an awkward nod, then walked over to the bookcase. 'I have a couple of Tom's books that I'll return next time I'm here.'

He seemed stand-offish. She wondered if that was because of Thomas. As landlord, Henry Thorpe would know what Thomas had done. Ruth now felt awkward. Perhaps she wasn't welcome to stay here after all.

He stood with his back towards her and studied the shelves. 'He read all of these.'

He said it quietly and seemed locked away in thought. She hesitated to say something, then he turned and stared straight at her. 'I can hardly bear to be here with him gone.'

Ruth felt her heart go still as her eyes fixed on him, trying to see through the glasses on his face. He sounded so sad.

'You liked my son,' she said.

He nodded. Then seeing something register on her face he quickly shook his head. 'No, not that way. You misinterpret my liking for Tom. I liked him as a very fine person. I liked the direction he was heading. We had similar interests and outlook on life. I would class Tom as a good friend.'

Ruth stared away from him. What he said didn't make sense. Not according to the diary she'd read. Friends had stepped away from Thomas when he most needed them. Disappointment may have kept Henry Thorpe away. The very fine person he liked may have been sullied in his eyes. She gazed at him now, scornfully, and her voice dripped with sarcasm. 'Really? A good friend? So where were you when he was going through hell? Where were you the night he took his life?'

He didn't react to her anger. His expression of sadness remained unchanged. 'I wasn't here when it happened. When he was arrested and during the months that followed I was on the other side of the world. The first I knew about it was when my sister, Marlene, telephoned and told me of Tom's death. I flew back immediately, of course, but too late to do anything. I would have helped him if I'd known. Typical of Tom to keep the most monumental trouble of his life quiet from anyone who cared about him. He was quite capable of hiding things, never wanting to burden anyone with worry. But I shan't forgive him if he kept quiet for fear of me thinking him guilty. No, I shan't let that go if you can hear me, Tom.'

Ruth sank into the armchair with legs suddenly gone weak. 'You think he was innocent,' she half whispered.

He stared at her like she was a puzzle. 'Well, don't you?' he asked harshly.

She laughed a sound not fully formed that came out more as a bark, which was followed by her teary smile. 'I was beginning to think I was the only one who believed him innocent.'

He breathed deeply and dropped his shoulders as if a weight had been lifted. 'Anyone who knew Tom would know he was not capable of committing such deeds.'

'Yet the police charged him.'

He shook his head as if trying to flick that fact away. 'The police could only work with the evidence available to them. I spoke with a sergeant when I got back. Everything was stacked against him and then Tom rolled over and pleaded guilty.'

Ruth felt let down by his choice of words. He'd made it sound like Thomas was weak. She would have preferred him use the word *flattened.*

His gaze went round the room as if searching for something before it settled on the bottle of whisky. 'Do you mind?' he asked, picking it up.

She shook her head and a moment later was handed the glass she'd been drinking water from with a whisky in it instead. He found the twin glass and emptied it of cutlery. 'Tom rolled over, but he would have had a reason. I've wracked my brain and the only one I can think of was to protect someone. Find that person and you'll find the guilty party.'

Ruth made no comment. She liked his amendment, but she was not prepared to reveal why she was there. He might understand her reason for wanting to keep her relationship to Thomas private, but she doubted he would approve of her using anonymity to question other tenants. As it would be done so in a dishonest way.

'So what are you going to do with yourself in Bournemouth?'

She gave a small shrug. 'Get to know it, I suppose. Go surfing, like Thomas did. This was his home. It will be… nice to see it.'

His expression showed his surprise. He looked perturbed when he walked into the little kitchen and washed and dried his glass, putting cutlery back in the tumbler, before returning it to the cupboard. Then he came back into the sitting room and said something she was not expecting. 'Please don't take offence, but you rather took me by surprise. I was hoping you were here to put right a travesty of the truth. I mentioned the only reason I could think of, hoping you might want to find that person. Tom wasn't guilty of those crimes. But somebody was, and they're still free.'

He left soon after, leaving Ruth's mind stuffed with questions. Had Thomas protected someone? *Had* he known there were stolen drugs in his locker? Or had he been oblivious as he stated? *I can make no sense of any of it. I don't have answers to explain these drugs.*

Unless of course he did have answers and the words in his diary were for others to read? Had he tried to outsmart the police to protect someone? If so, was she someone he loved? Perhaps C? Ruth decided it had to be C after thinking about the way Thomas wrote his sentence: *I want to tell her about C.* If referring to the woman causing problems, he wouldn't say it like that. He wanted to tell his mum about someone special.

Perhaps C had stolen the medicines and Thomas hid them. Would he do something like that? Break the law? Act so flagrantly? Ruth always thought not, but she herself broke the law today because of someone she loved, abused her position as a doctor to access confidential information. But why then did Thomas end up with drugs in his system, resulting in behaviour that got him arrested? He denied taking anything, which left the possibility someone gave him something. Perhaps the person he protected? Why couldn't the anonymous letter writer have told her more? They must know something if they believed Thomas was innocent. Did they know who was really guilty? Was their reason for staying anonymous deeper than that? Was the letter writer in fact the guilty party? Someone who needed to salve their conscience? Who better to ask for help than the mother?

Trying to fit the pieces together was as impossible as trying to fit wrong pieces of a jigsaw puzzle together. The picture would not hold. It would buckle if pieces were forced to fit. Ruth should take heed of that. She could hold onto the idea of her son being innocent only so long as she didn't try and pin the blame on another innocent person. Otherwise it would come full circle, with a person standing wrongly accused.

She got up from the armchair and felt her legs aching across her thighs and in the back of her calves, and debated whether to cycle again tomorrow. If she wanted to get fitter she should. She'd been good on a bike once. She should not let the thought of the person in the car stop her from cycling.

In the kitchen she threw away her dinner and washed the plate, knife and fork and her glass. Henry Thorpe had seemed to know his way around. He'd emptied the tumbler of cutlery, instead of asking if there was a spare, as if he had done it before when a glass was needed. He spoke of Thomas like he knew him well. He had told her something she had not been aware of until last year, which was that Thomas was quite capable of hiding things. He had then carefully worded what was tantamount to a lecture. If he'd said any more she would have blurted out her real reason for being there. She wondered if he thought her callous coming only now.

She wondered what Henry Thorpe did for a living, whether his income came solely from renting property. He was around her age, she guessed, and had classed her son as a good friend. While she didn't find that odd, she was a little surprised as he seemed like a serious man who would prefer to spend his time in serious company. She would love to ask him what he and Thomas talked about, if only to give her another insight into Thomas as a young man still emerging. To hear someone speak of him who knew him as a fully grown adult made her feel she had missed out on this part of him. Next time she would ask him more, and she would also call him Henry as it would seem strange now to call him Mr Thorpe after what they had spoken about and after drinking whisky together.

When she climbed into bed she felt guilty that she wasn't feeling as heavy hearted as she had in all the days and nights before. She felt guilty for feeling like a tiny part of her heart hurt less, a tiny part that should still be hurting for Thomas.

Turning onto her side she placed her head on his pillow, and as if they had been waiting for their cue, slow tears slid over the bridge of her nose to join those sliding off her cheek. She was used to them by now. They had been coming every night for a while. She didn't have to be thinking anything for them to fall. They just came when she put her head down. To remind her it was still real.

CHAPTER ELEVEN

Ruth's first week in her new job passed quickly. She'd been given the same consultation room each day and it now had her name on the door. The light blue walls and darker blue flooring already felt familiar. She was still only on nodding terms with the doctors and nurses, which she didn't mind as she was not there to make friends, but on good terms with the receptionists. Joan had turned out to be a sweetheart, providing her with little comforts for the room. A kettle and a mug and some flavoured teas, so she could make herself a hot drink if she didn't have time to come out of the office. Joan seemed to have decided to take her under her wing as Ruth now knew where she could shower, and had a locker where she could hang clothes to save bringing them in every day. She'd persevered with riding Thomas's bike and now changed gears like a pro, which helped her arrive at work sounding less like she was having an asthma attack. She zipped along the long red-brick road, as she now called it, without worrying if a car should follow. At the speed she was doing, in traffic, a car would have a job to keep up. She was getting fit, but not having much luck at the red-brick house. There were still no lights on.

Her evenings also passed quickly as she was kept busy with sorting out Thomas's things. His flat was now empty of most of his possessions. She managed the task without bumping into any of the other residents, but suspected they were, like her, at work all day and then relaxing in their homes at night. It had taken two evenings of careful trips to move it all into the cupboard on the landing. Cupboard didn't really describe it, though, as it was bigger than the galley kitchen in the flat. She had wanted to go through everything before putting it out of sight, but it would have taken her longer… maybe a year. She would look at everything once this was all over. She would take it back to Bath with her so that she could take her time and not miss a thing, because no one wanted to see these things more than her. She'd left his clothes in the wardrobe, as no one would see them there. Now, if Kim or the other tenants knocked on her door, they would see the flat as hers.

She had one more patient to see before the weekend began. She read the medical history while she had time, paying attention to the historical use of drugs prescribed, the gradual increase in dosage for fluoxetine, and that zopiclone was on a repeat prescription. She wondered if the zopiclone went on a repeat prescription due to an error, as it was usually only prescribed for short periods. The patient's history described sleep disturbance as being part of the cause of depression. A stress-related event or a trigger was not recorded.

Ruth slipped her shoes back on as she heard the knock at the door. The woman who entered was thin, with lank pale hair. She slouched into the room and sat quickly with her hands clenched together in her lap. She was booked in for a smear test. According to her medical notes, Rosie Carlyle was twenty-seven and being treated for depression, anxiety and insomnia. Ruth thought anorexia might have to be added as well, as her BMI was unquestionably low. Her wrists stuck out of her sleeves like twigs.

Ruth gave her a pleasant smile. 'Hi, I'm new, so we haven't met before. How are you?'

The woman shrugged, then proceeded to bite at fingernails that were already chewed to death and looked sore with inflamed cuticles. Ruth prompted an answer by asking the question again. This time she got a reaction. Her hand flew from her mouth and waved agitatedly, as if wiping something fast. 'I need a new prescription,' she said rapidly. 'My mum threw away my pills thinking they were rubbish.' Her expression was angry as if this were Ruth's fault somehow.

Ruth hid her own reaction. She was not surprised by the request. Twice before this patient had asked for a further prescription as tablets had got lost or *eaten*. She wondered if this appointment was kept solely for the purpose of getting a further prescription.

Ruth proceeded carefully. 'Would you like me to call you Rosie or Miss Carlyle?' Ruth worked to the same rule with every patient, making sure to always ask for consent to examine them or to learn how they preferred to be addressed.

'Rosie will do,' she answered sullenly.

'Well, Rosie, this will be the third time this has happened. I don't wish to sound harsh, but it will be the last time we do this.' Ruth was not going to mention her concern over the zopiclone as she would discuss it first with Dr Campbell.

Rosie visibly relaxed. 'Thanks. It won't happen again.'

Ruth doubted that, but again didn't say. Instead, she asked if Rosie was agreeable to having the smear test done. Rosie nodded.

The rustle of paper towel indicated she had climbed on the couch and was ready. Ruth saw shoulder blades stand out like wings on her back. She had undressed fully for some reason, apart from her bra, and was sitting with her knees drawn up to her chest, her head lowered to rest on them. She was stick-thin all over. Ruth asked her to lie back and relax.

Afterwards, Rosie dressed while Ruth typed up some notes and prepared the prescription. Ruth gave her seven days' worth of medication as Rosie's repeat meds would be available after then. She then stood, ready to leave, but didn't walk to the door. She was staring at the wall with troubled eyes.

'Was there something else you wanted to discuss?' Ruth asked in a kind voice.

Her eyes slid away from the wall and she shook her head. 'Nothing you can help with.'

Ruth studied her for a moment. 'You won't know unless you try me.'

Rosie eyed her cautiously and then asked about patient confidentiality. Ruth reassured her the only time a doctor cannot honour a patient's privacy is when a patient is going to hurt themselves or hurt someone else.

Rosie sat back down. Her eyes found Ruth's. 'Do you ever feel like life is just a waiting game, that no matter what you offer, it isn't enough for some people? That it would be better sometimes to not have expectations? ' Her tone of voice was brittle, like she was about to cry. 'My best friend has gone away, and I can't trust her anymore. It's like she's gained an advantage and doesn't want to be friends any longer. She's left me to cope alone with all this.'

'What are you coping with, Rosie?'

She stiffened and her expression hardened. 'Try this for size,' she answered. 'I live alone and I come home to find someone was in my home. They took my washing out of the washing machine and hung my clothes over the radiators in my room.'

This concerned Ruth. It sounded like a very strange occurrence. She wasn't sure she believed what Rosie was telling her. 'Have you reported it to the police?'

'No. No point. Nothing was taken.' She laughed bitterly. 'I have nothing worth taking.' She blinked as if surprised as she touched her wet cheeks. She looked at her wet fingertips, then shook her head firmly from side to side.

'Do you like yourself, Rosie?' Ruth asked gently.

She grabbed a tissue from a box on Ruth's desk and scrubbed her eyes unnecessarily hard, then looked at Ruth coolly. 'If you think who you are matters to people, then that question is about impressing them, not about liking yourself. Once you start thinking of reining in parts of yourself, you stop being significant.'

Five minutes later, Rosie was gone from the room, leaving the damp tissue on the desk and her doctor feeling disturbed. Something in her character unsettled Ruth. Rosie had good reasons for feeling depressed. She was living alone, had no friends, her best friend had gone away, and strange things were happening in her home. If she thought these things were real she should report it to the police, like most other people would.

Ruth was glad she had agreed to come and see her again on Monday. In the meantime, she would refer her for a mental health assessment and hope an appointment could be made soon. After completing her notes and referral letters she rose from her chair. It had been a strange end to the day. Rosie Carlyle had got to her. She was a spikey little thing. With an intelligent mind. Only a little older than Thomas, and it seemed like she had no one to turn to. Ruth was very conscious of what Thomas had done to end his life – his mind must have been deeply traumatised. Rosie's mental health – unable to cope, feeling unsafe, without a sense of connection with people, her friend – was a worry.

She glanced around the office, thinking how quickly she had settled in. She was looking forward to the glass of wine she'd promised herself. Her first evening out in Bournemouth. It would be good for her own mental health to do something new.

CHAPTER TWELVE

Ruth dismounted the bike and stared at the bar she researched yesterday evening. She'd found a few pubs with horse in the name. One had been knocked down, another had changed names, while others were closer to Poole or didn't have neighbouring properties close by. So she was fairly sure The Horsemen might be the one. In the images she brought up on her laptop the frontage had been painted a few times, garishly at one point in excessively bright colours. It was currently painted a muted dark green and was more fitting to the age and style of the building. She had studied the area and street on Google Earth. Some of the houses opposite the pub had rooftop windows and she was hopeful that one of those windows belonged to C. The pub had an evening menu, so she would eat out for a change. She could relax a little with nothing to rush back for. She looked presentable enough having come straight from work. Her trainers were clean and Thomas's cycling trousers did the job of looking smart without being too snug a fit.

It was still early and only a couple of tables had been taken. Before going in she stood outside the bar working out which windows would give her the best view of the buildings opposite, and was pleased to have the one of her choice. The table for two was a bonus as she would probably be left alone while eating. She chose chunky chips and scampi off the menu so she could eat with fingers and concentrate on what was going on outside. The street was busy with cars and pedestrians. Some of the shops on the other side of the road were still open. It would be easy to miss someone going in or out of the private doors between them if she looked away.

Sipping her second glass of wine, and pleasantly full, Ruth watched the street from the window, trying to imagine what C might look like. It might not happen, of course. This might not be the right pub. She might not live in any of the flats above the shops. She might have moved away. Ruth could knock on a few doors and ask if a woman lived there who knew her son, but she wouldn't in case no one had ever heard of C or Thomas. She'd rather have the hope of meeting her than no hope at all.

She took another sip of her wine and cast a glance at the lamppost where the bike was locked. It was safe. The helmet was clipped to her bag so she didn't lose it.

Her gaze went back to the doors over the road. In the last hour and a half she hadn't seen anyone using any of them, though lights were on in some windows. By matching up curtains and blinds, she could work out which windows belonged to a single flat. It occurred to her suddenly that there might be a back way in as well. She hoped not.

Another ten minutes went by and she was starting to feel too relaxed. Her eyes were beginning to glaze over. The street was less busy with fewer people and cars passing by. The bar was busier, and much warmer.

She was almost in a trance when she was jolted to awareness at the sudden squealing of brakes from outside. She watched two men and a woman change direction and rush out into the road. They were gathering at the front of a stationary car. Ruth instinctively stood, grabbing her rucksack and jacket. She passed the bartender and shouted, 'Haven't forgotten to pay. I'm outside. Think someone's hurt.'

Moving fast she went out the door and headed towards the car and gathering crowd. A woman lay on the ground, still but softly moaning. She was alive. Ruth immediately stopped a shaken-looking man from what he was about to do.

'Don't move her,' she said loudly and clearly for all to hear. 'Let me at her, please, I'm a doctor.'

The shaky man started apologising. 'Sorry, I was just going to raise her head a little,' he said, showing her a jumper he was about to use as a pillow.

Ruth was aware of that, which is why she stopped him. She smiled kindly. 'Best not before we know what her injuries are. Did anyone witness the accident?' she asked.

A woman behind her spoke. 'I don't think she was hit. It looked like she fainted and fell in the road.'

A man said, 'I didn't feel the car hit her. Though I thought I wasn't going to be able to brake.'

Ruth heard him wheeze as he heaved in air. She turned to the man with the jumper. 'Help the driver and get him to sit down and take slow deep breaths. Did anyone call an ambulance?' To which more than one voice yelled, 'Yes.'

Ruth concentrated on the woman. She had been assessing her the whole time, looking for signs of injury or bleeding. She was lying on her side already, which would help keep her airway clear. She got closer to look at her face.

'Hello,' she called. 'Can you hear me? Can you open your eyes for me?'

The eyelids fluttered, then lifted. They stayed open as the woman focused.

Ruth smiled. 'Hi, I'm Ruth. Do you want to tell me your name?'

'Catherine,' she said, 'with a C.'

'Can you remember what happened, Catherine?'

'I think I fainted again,' she replied in a weary voice.

'Are you hurting anywhere? Can you feel pain in any part of your body?'

'No, I'm quite comfortable.' She gave a small, tired laugh. 'Probably because I'm on my side.' She was lying on her left side and wore a loose beige raincoat.

The woman behind Ruth spoke again. 'She's pregnant.'

Ruth turned to speak to her and recognised her as the woman who served her food. 'Do you know her?'

She nodded. 'A little. She comes in now and again. She lives up the road. Purple door.'

Ruth felt her chest fill with air as she steadily breathed in. So not in the houses across the road, but not far. Hers was a purple door. Her gaze went back to Catherine. *Surely this couldn't be her. She was pregnant. It wasn't her. Did she have a rooftop window?*

An ambulance could be heard in the distance. It would soon be with them.

Catherine gazed at Ruth anxiously. 'Have I hurt my baby with the fall?'

Ruth reached out and gently held her hand. 'Babies are very robust. Try not to worry. They'll soon check you over. Do you know what you're having?'

'A boy,' she answered softly.

Ruth wanted to ask her if she was Thomas's C, to put an end to the ridiculous hopefulness squeezing her heart. *It wasn't her.* She must stop this foolish notion. This pregnant woman just needed help, not some desperate mother hoping that some of her son had survived. The poor woman would be horrified if she knew what was in Ruth's mind.

'Ambulance is here,' someone shouted.

Ruth slowly got to her feet to make room for the paramedics. She told them her findings and let them take over. She waited till the ambulance had gone and then made her way back to the pub to pay her bill.

The woman who worked there accompanied her. She handed Ruth her bank card and a receipt. 'Poor love. Bet it gave her a scare. She nearly lost it once already.'

Ruth pulled on her jacket and unclipped the helmet from her rucksack, making ready to leave. The woman had turned to a gallery of photographs. She pulled one off the wall and showed it to Ruth. 'After losing him it would have been a travesty.'

Ruth stood like a statue as she gazed at the faces of the young man and woman. Then, in slow motion, she gently drew her finger down his face.

The woman tutted. 'Life's so unfair sometimes. Always takes the good ones.'

She then put Catherine and Thomas back on the wall.

When the woman turned back, Ruth was gone.

*

Keeping the lights off, Ruth went over to the window. She gazed at the orange glow of streetlights, along the road, thinking about Catherine with a C. She couldn't help smiling, thinking of Thomas's diary. Perhaps Catherine presented herself to Thomas the way she had to Ruth this evening. Thomas would have homed in on it. He might then have teased and called her Catherine with a C, and in his diary, he abbreviated. To simply call her C.

Ruth couldn't decide what emotion was hurting her most. Sadness or joy. They were so intertwined it was impossible to feel one without the other. The same to be said for loss and hope. Catherine, she imagined, if she loved Thomas, must feel that way too.

Ruth had not expected to be coming home this evening knowing her son's baby was on the way. In the instant of knowing, she wanted to stop what she was doing, for fear of Catherine being involved.

Her eyes were drawn to the front garden. She gazed curiously at Kim. Wondering what she was doing, going behind a bush. Had she lost her key, been taken short and in desperate need of a wee? She was standing, not crouching. Standing and not smoking.

Ruth pondered. Hoping she was wrong. That there was a perfectly innocent reason for her standing there. A moment later, though, a very broad-shouldered man came through the garden gate. He stayed still, then his head turned. He had either spotted Kim or she had called to him.

Ruth couldn't see his face. A beanie hat was pulled down low over his large head. He moved towards Kim. Face to face, his size diminished her average build and height. He reached out his hand the same time Kim reached for his. Then they drew apart and his arm went behind his back, his hand into the back pocket of his dark trousers. Before Ruth could blink he was gone out the garden gate, a rolling movement of powerful shoulders and large head, ambling along the street. He reminded Ruth of a large bear.

In the garden below her window, Ruth watched Kim light a cigarette and lean against the garden wall. With nothing more to see, she was about to turn away when a second figure appeared by the garden gate. She gave a small groan, and stopped watching. If Kim was in trouble, she didn't want to witness her being taken away by the police. She didn't approve, if Kim was doing what she thought, but nor was she immune to the situation. The woman would be feeling fearful, and perhaps embarrassed. She didn't need people watching this. She needed a bit of dignity.

Thomas had a hospital ward watching him. Some would have turned away, while others watched. Not wanting to miss a thing. Ruth could never be a watcher. The hardest part of her job was watching someone suffer – physically, mentally, despairingly, angrily – she didn't watch for fun.

She watched because she had to.

CHAPTER THIRTEEN

Rosie stood the long lengths of batten against the wall before studying the back door. The chair she'd put against it had not moved. It was still exactly how she'd left it, tilted back and jammed under the handle, but it wasn't secure. The stupid door didn't lock properly. She'd tested it repeatedly, even going so far as to lock it from the inside and removing the key and then walking down the side alley to get to the back door. If she lifted the door up by the doorknob then turned it, the door unlocked making it easy to get in.

She placed the Wilko carrier bag on the table and fetched out the new hammer and nails. She intended to nail the door closed so it couldn't be opened again. She'd reported the faulty lock to the letting agency as soon as she discovered it three days ago, and was still waiting for them to fix it. So she would do the job for them, and if they dared complain about damage she would ask if they thought it was okay to risk her safety when anyone could walk in.

She took off her coat, cleared a space for the wood, then realised she needed a saw, which she had not bought. Her intention was to have lengths of batten nailed to the doorframe and across the door all the way down like a ladder. Stumped by the problem, and annoyed for not thinking of a saw, she glared at the wood. She could try breaking it with her knee. In frustration she went to her bag to find her emergency cigarettes, probably stale by now, then hunted for a lighter. In a kitchen drawer she found matches and a solution to the problem of not having a saw. A breadknife.

Several hours passed before she finished. Her arms were hanging from her shoulders like heavy rubber and her right palm had blisters. She was on the verge of crying, as in the last half hour it dawned on her she was building herself a cage or a prison. She slumped her head down on the tiny kitchen table, and didn't care she was breathing in sawdust.

Anabel still hadn't been in contact. Not even with Meg. Rosie knew this because every day Meg let her know. She wished she could have given her a false number, but Meg insisted she have it before Rosie left Anabel's flat.

Rosie wished she could run away, that there was someone she could run to. That person had always been Anabel.

Born a decade after two sons, her brothers had grown and gone by the time Rosie was ten and it felt like she'd never known them. Ron and Max were just names of brothers she had, their photos on her mum's mantel the only reminder they were related. Rosie had been like an only child. When new neighbours moved in next door, with a daughter the same age as Rosie, it felt like her life began. She'd found a sister and friend rolled into one.

She supposed in some ways it was her dad's death that made her family a bit dysfunctional. They became less close with one another. Her mum spoke to her brothers, but Rosie never did, nor ever saw them. Rosie supposed her dad's death hit her brothers harder. They'd had him longer as a parent and maybe seeing the family home reminded them of him too much. Rosie coped better. She had her friend.

Two peas in a pod, people called them. They went to school together, studied A levels together, chose careers together. They did everything together and now Anabel had betrayed her. She needed to know where Anabel was and who it was she told. Between them they could pay the person to go away.

Her phone pinged and she glanced at it apprehensively. Anabel's mum again. She opened the message and felt her heart slam.

Rosie, police might call. Be great if you can help them with any names of people Anabel knows. Thank God they're now taking it more seriously. Anabel was a no-show at work so colleagues are now concerned x

The added kiss was such a false note. The woman was frantic, no doubt, and would add a hundred kisses if it got her daughter back. Rosie let out a soft moan, then her sore fingernails went back between her teeth so she could gnaw on them while she worried.

Anabel spoiled every chance Rosie had of being happy. She wouldn't be content until Rosie was miserable. She had done the same when they were kids, pushing her way in to Rosie's father's affections. *A little poppet,* he called her.

She started humming as she gnawed dry sore skin, occasionally singing a few words from the nursery rhyme. *When will you pay me? When will that be?* Until she was humming and moaning and saying words and chewing strips of bleeding skin.

CHAPTER FOURTEEN

Ruth could have phoned from the ward, using the internal number to get through to the Maternity Unit, but preferred to be somewhere more private. She also wanted to get some fresh air. She'd forgotten how warm hospital wards could be, and tugged off the plastic apron she was wearing over the scrubs. She dug her phone from her pocket and called the maternity ward, standing outside in the cold winter sunshine.

A few minutes later, she thanked the doctor and disconnected the call. She was unsurprised to hear that Catherine Dell was discharged following a vasovagal attack – a faint, in other words. Miss Dell would have a follow-up with her midwife today. When Ruth asked how far along in the pregnancy was Miss Dell, the doctor said she was twenty-six weeks and, having fainted before, was advised to take it easy.

Ruth felt a bittersweet tug at her heart, knowing history was to be repeated. Thomas never met his father, his son would not meet his. Had Thomas known Catherine was pregnant? Ruth hoped not. She would find it difficult to bear if Thomas knew he was leaving behind an unborn child. Putting her phone in her pocket, she headed back to the ward.

As a locum GP, new to the area, she'd asked to see the services available to the community. Her guide, a modern matron called Terry, had organised the visit and given her a tour of all the departments, before leaving her on the Surgical Admissions Unit, where Ruth wanted to spend some time. Ruth didn't tell Terry, of course, that her reason for being there was so she could talk to the staff who had worked with Thomas. She was giving up hope of talking to the woman in the red-brick house. There was no point keeping going there if she was never home. The woman might even have moved away. At the hospital she got to meet more than one witness, although, her visit so far had not been particularly helpful. Striking up a conversation with people who were busy wasn't easy. No one stood still long enough for her to say more than two words to them. The nurses, the cleaner, a doctor, an occupational therapist – all of them had been run off their feet since the moment Ruth got there. It might have been better to have just asked Terry if he could arrange for her to see someone about what happened. It wouldn't have been an unnatural request.

She dismissed the notion as quickly as it came. At some point she did want to hear the hospital account, but not before she finished finding out what she could on her own. What Ruth was after was hidden. Which is why she was there incognito, presenting herself only as a new GP, and not as Thomas's mother.

She used the hand sanitiser on the wall as she came back on the ward. A staff nurse who she hadn't met came out of an office. Ruth said, 'Hi.' Maybe she would have better luck talking to this one. She looked less rushed.

The nurse glanced at her lanyard and Ruth explained she was there for a visit, and asked if she could tag along. The nurse vaguely nodded. Ruth followed her into the treatment room and watched her set out four injection trays on the worktop, then take four giving sets from a wall-mounted plastic box and four 10ml syringes from a smaller box. She was a quiet young woman of neat appearance, with brown hair in a sleek bun, and shoes very polished.

'Can I do anything to help?' Ruth asked.

The nurse shook her head, gave the briefest smile, and carried on with her task. From a box on the counter she grabbed ampoules of sodium chloride and dropped two a piece on each tray.

'There,' she said. 'I'll just fetch their prescriptions.'

'Would you like me to start drawing up the saline?' Ruth offered. 'I take it it's to flush their cannulas?'

The nurse seemed undecided. After all, Ruth was a stranger, and even though wearing a loaned set of blue scrubs, the lanyard around her neck said VISITOR. 'No, that's okay. I prefer to do it one at a time, and at the patient's bedside.'

Ruth was not offended. It made sense and was a safer practice. 'Well, if there's anything I can do, please ask. I won't mind. I haven't even introduced myself properly. I'm Ruth Bennett, a new GP to the area. I just wanted to get a feel for the hospital.'

The nurse looked politely interested and said, 'I'm Chloe, and if I seem grumpy it's because Saturdays are my least favourite day. I've been waiting on a junior doctor all morning to write up a few antibiotics so we can send some patients home.'

Ruth expressed sympathy. 'It was the same when I worked in hospitals. Not sure it will ever change. But it seems nice here. Some of the patients I spoke to can't praise it enough.'

'It is a good hospital,' Chloe professed proudly. 'The best, and I've worked at a few. I'd certainly be happy for my mum or dad to be treated here.'

Ruth nodded. 'Well, I think it's splendid from what I've seen. Staff are super friendly, which says a lot about the morale here. It must have been at rock bottom after what happened with that doctor. That can't have been easy.'

Her expression showed she was not comfortable with this comment. 'I'm not sure we should talk about that. Like you say, it wasn't easy.'

'I'm sure it wasn't. It must have felt like such a let-down.'

She folded her arms across her chest. Her initial tone was disapproving. 'He was actually quite pleasant, Dr De Luca. In fact, very caring. And then gradually you couldn't help noticing things. Theatre would ring and ask if his phone or his bleep was on the desk. He always seemed to be looking for something he'd lost. Then when he did have his bleep, he'd turn up at a ward when no one had bleeped him to come. I wondered if it was caused by sleep deprivation from working insane hours or stress from doing the job. You see it a lot with junior doctors, the worry of missing something being seriously wrong with a patient.'

Ruth breathed in as quietly as she could, trying to hide her despair. Hearing Thomas portrayed like this, like he was falling apart, wasn't easy for her.

'I suppose you could think that when someone behaves out of character. It was out of character, I take it?'

Chloe shrugged. 'It's hard to say, to be honest. How well does anyone know someone really? The day he was arrested was awful. That was a Saturday, but Mr Mason was here thankfully. There'd been an emergency operation in the morning, new admissions coming in, so the ward was busy. Then out of the blue Dr De Luca appears. He starts stumbling about the ward, knocking over patients' things. A water jug, then a drip stand. Then he just stood there, laughing like a fool, clearly under the influence of something. When porters and a security guard came, he evaded them by running up and down the ward. Then the guard caught him and Dr De Luca threw him to the floor… The man banged the back of his head. When the police came he laughed his head off at them. When Mr Mason tried to reason with him, he told the consultant to fuck off. It was horrible, really horrible, because after that he began to cry. Which made some of the patients cry. What was truly awful, though, was that we couldn't get to them. Someone said he had a weapon, a surgical knife, and to stay clear of the area.'

Ruth saw in her eyes she was reliving it. 'He then got aggressive with the police, so two more officers came, until eventually they had him pinned to the floor in handcuffs, and his legs strapped so he couldn't kick out at them. They carried him out of the ward like that. Four of them. And all the while we could hear him crying.'

She shook her head slowly, staring absently at the far wall. 'None of us were really surprised he took his own life. He seemed so incredibly unstable, that it wasn't really a shock.'

Chloe's description allowed Ruth to imagine every detail. She could hear and see him. He would have hated it, to have been so out of control. It just didn't make sense to her. *Thomas wouldn't have taken drugs.* He was on duty when it happened. She cemented that thought in her mind and murmured as if agreeing with the nurse. 'It sounds like it was a nightmare to deal with, not a nice experience for anyone to witness.'

'It wasn't,' she retorted. 'It affected us all, especially after what he did to himself.'

'Did you receive counselling?' Ruth asked.

'It was offered, but I don't think anyone went for it.'

Ruth decided she would ask an impertinent question. 'Did anyone think he was innocent?'

Chloe's expression turned cool. She unfolded her arms and pressed her hands together. 'Do you mind if we don't talk about this anymore, it's really upsetting?'

'Of course not,' Ruth replied, immediately contrite at forgetting the effect the conversation might have, but wishing Chloe had given an answer. 'I'm sorry for bringing it up.'

'It's just I'd rather forget about that day. Forget about him.'

Ruth somehow managed to produce a sympathetic smile. 'I'm sure you do. Well, I'll let you get on if there's nothing I can do to help?'

Chloe's reply was glib, then a little sanctimonious. 'No, nothing. To be honest, you'd be better off observing. It's very busy here.'

Ruth let it go. Chloe had told her things she didn't know. Painful things she needed to know. Her boy had been strapped down while he was crying. She had needed to know these things.

But, oh, how she wished she didn't.

CHAPTER FIFTEEN

Ruth stayed out of sight while Dr Nolan wrote up prescriptions for the patients going home. He was the junior doctor Chloe had been waiting for all morning. Ruth noticed the fair curls over his forehead. He looked too young to be a doctor, like he was playing dress-up in clean-looking scrubs and a stethoscope around his neck. As he stood to leave, Ruth fetched her bag and said a quick farewell to Chloe and another nurse. Then she dashed.

She kept behind him along the corridor to the hospital restaurant, and while he was at the hot counter display she went into the ladies to change, bundling the scrubs in her bag. When she came out he was sitting at a table with his food in front of him. She bought a coffee and made her way to his table. He looked surprised as she pulled out a chair opposite him, perhaps wondering why she didn't choose the empty table right beside him. But, perhaps thinking her not unattractive, he smiled.

'Hi,' she said. 'We just came from the same ward. I'm a GP, new to the area. I was hoping to meet you.'

He set his knife and fork down, letting the food wait. He was interested, all right. His eyes travelled the length of her slim-fitting jeans, admiring her long legs. She decided it was time to enlighten him, not let him get his hopes up. She hadn't let her hair down for that reason, but to remove the knobbly pins digging in her scalp. 'You knew my son, Dr Nolan. Thomas De Luca.'

He was instantly startled and half rose from his chair, before settling back down. '*I'm sorry?* I thought you said we just came from the same ward. That you're a GP, new to the area?'

'I did. I am. The staff showed me around wonderfully, but when I saw you I thought I'd use the opportunity to meet you. I didn't get a chance to meet Thomas's friends when he was alive.'

His face turned awkward and he fumbled for the bottle of water on the table. 'I'm sorry for your loss.'

Ruth smiled and sat down. 'Hey, I'm not here for that, but to say hello. Thomas regarded you as a friend. I just want to hear about that.'

He cleared his throat a couple of times, looking uncomfortable, his gaze shifting absently to the empty tables and then to the floor. He was avoiding looking at her, and it crossed her mind he didn't want to talk about Thomas. She sat silently until his gaze came back to hers, until he saw her knowing look. 'So, not a friend then?' she remarked, keeping her tone light and just curious. 'I got that wrong. I thought you were, because you got that article taken down off Facebook.'

Blotches of red appeared on his cheeks. Then his forehead turned ruddy. Ruth stared at him curiously, a suspicion growing, confirmed as his face got redder. 'Oh dear. I got that wrong as well,' she said, in a dry tone. 'I'm glad Thomas wasn't aware. He thought you saved the day.'

'Look,' he blustered. 'That was an idiotic thing to do which I regretted the moment I did it.'

'Of course you did,' she replied softly. 'Three hundred likes later.' She stared at him frankly. 'If it's not too difficult a question to answer, why *did* you do it?'

He sighed heavily and briefly closed his eyes. 'I don't know.'

She stayed silent. She noticed the way he spoke, his enunciation of syllables. Was he trying to impress on her that he was a well-spoken young man and only did things like this on the spur of an idiotic moment?

He quietly muttered under his breath, 'I don't fucking need this.' Then seeing her face express something similar, he huffed, 'Sorry. It just pissed me off, hearing how saintly he was after what he'd done. Some people still didn't believe it, even though the police found drugs in his home.' He sounded more natural now. At least sincere.

'So you wanted to put them right? Ensure there was no doubt about his guilt?'

'That's right, I did.'

Ruth picked up her hot drink and took a sip. 'This is good coffee,' she said. Then she carefully placed the large cup back in the saucer. 'Was there never any doubt in your mind he was guilty?' He quickly stared away, but not before she saw something shift in his eyes. 'Was *that* doubt I saw?'

'You saw nothing.' He shook his head. 'Nothing in the scheme of things. He was guilty. And that's a fact.'

'But,' she pressed, 'something you're not saying says otherwise.'

He folded his arms, agitated. 'Look, I don't have to talk to you. I could report you. What do you think the staff on the ward would say if they knew you were Thomas's mother?'

'You could report me,' she answered calmly. 'But is that what you want to do, Jed?'

His eyes rebuked her for using his first name. Ruth used it deliberately. She wanted this conversation to sound personal. To mean something to this man. 'Come on, Jed,' she said, in a cajoling, encouraging voice. 'Talk to me.'

He sighed heavily, then dragged his hands down his face. 'There was an error in one of the dates when Thomas was recorded as working.'

Ruth gazed at him keenly. She'd not expected him to say anything like that. 'What sort of error?'

'A record had been kept of the dates when drugs went missing.'

'By whom?' she asked, surprised.

'I don't know. I presumed it was done by pharmacy. That it was them who noticed drugs going missing, and they put it in place to catch the person. None of us knew drugs had gone missing until Thomas was arrested. Then it all came out that it had been happening over a period of weeks, drugs missing from different wards, A&E, theatres. All the places where Thomas worked. Except this one date was wrong. He wasn't on duty that day. I was.'

Her eyes widened, her voice dropped. *'You?'*

'Yes. Thomas swapped shifts with me as it was my birthday the next day and I wanted it off. I worked his shift that day. He had the day off.'

'What drugs went missing?'

'A whole box of diamorphine.'

Ruth let this information sink in. 'So you were there, so you know he didn't take them.'

'We didn't know drugs were missing at that point,' he said firmly.

Her face was astonished, her mouth open. 'Are you kidding?' Her voice was disbelieving. 'A box of diamorphine goes missing and nobody notices?' She laughed harshly. 'So when were you enlightened? Where was this record of when drugs went missing? How did you get to see it?'

He shrugged. 'The day after he was arrested there was a copy of it on a desk in one of the theatre department offices, so I had a look. The dates started back in February. Entries of drugs missing. It was mostly small quantities. Morphine, fentanyl, pethidine, ketamine, antibiotics, even.'

Ruth was flabbergasted. It seemed incredible that someone just left this document lying about, given that it was evidence and Thomas had been arrested. 'This copy. What happened to it?'

'It was shredded. The receptionist ripped it from my hands.'

'So the official document? Did someone from the pharmacy department question you?'

'No. I was questioned, but not by them. By human resources and the investigating team. No one from the Surgical Admissions Unit was involved in the investigation. I was never shown the official record. No one mentioned it during my interview. My memory of it is vague. It was like a spreadsheet, with handwriting in some columns, making it a bit scruffy.'

'You said it all came out that it had been happening over a period of weeks. How did you hear about it? Who told you?'

He stared morosely. 'I meant gossip. It came out in gossip. People discussing it on the ward. He'd got away with it by taking small unnoticeable amounts at a time from different places.'

Ruth didn't care to remind him a whole box of diamorphine was hardly an unnoticeable amount. 'So a copy of a document and idle gossip is all you had to go on?'

'Look,' he said, with a bite in his voice. 'I was mainly asked about my own actions. Whether I noticed anything out of the ordinary. I was asked what I'd noticed about Dr De Luca's behaviour, whether there was anything of concern. Which I had. His manner changed. He was tense, guarded and then on a couple of occasions his behaviour was erratic. Thomas lost a patient's medical notes, then tried to blame a nurse. She would have taken the blame, too, to save Thomas getting it. Then he accused her of hiding his phone! Shouted at the poor girl. If she was on duty I'd introduce her. You couldn't wish for a nicer person. You'd see how far off the mark he was blaming someone like her.'

Talking about the nurse who was wrongfully accused by Thomas had set Jed's eyes ablaze. He was firmly in her corner. Was it because he had feelings for the nurse or simply cared how a colleague was treated? Ruth couldn't help wondering if he was jealous. He had just revealed, in telling her about a patient's lost medical notes, that the woman Thomas had slept with was this nurse. For some reason Ruth had imagined her as clerical, perhaps because Thomas described her as sitting at a desk.

'Would it be possible for you to contact her? I'd like to meet her.'

He shook his head. 'No, she's not on duty. She's off sick at the moment. Since your son died, it affected her quite badly. She phoned for the police to come to the ward that day, which for someone like her would have been a hard thing to do on a colleague.'

Ruth was quietly stunned. Jed Nolan had no idea what he had just revealed. That *this nurse* was who Ruth had been trying to track down. She was the whole reason for working where she was because *this nurse* was a patient there. On top of that, this was the woman Thomas slept with. The mistake that wouldn't go away, who was now proving elusive. Ruth wanted to sit still and think about what this all might actually mean. She couldn't back down her immediate thought as she was already thinking it. *Was this a scorned woman?*

'I put his picture on Facebook because he behaved like a dick.'

Ruth was startled out of her shock by the blunt admission, and felt saddened that this man felt his behaviour was justified. He was a doctor, for God's sake. He should have been more aware of Thomas's state of mind. 'Maybe so. But I think being arrested, facing prison time, and his career over, were enough punishment. Or have I missed something here? Do you think his suffering wasn't enough? It must have been pretty bad for him to want to take his own life.'

He squeezed his eyes shut and quietly said, 'I never would have expected Thomas to do that.'

'But stealing drugs is something you would have expected him to do?' she asked, keeping a check on the tone she used. She wanted his honest opinion, not some trite remark because he wanted shot of her.

He sat quietly and seemed like he wasn't going to answer, so she wasn't expecting to see him shake his head. 'No, I wouldn't. All Thomas wanted was to be a doctor.' He laughed harshly. 'He never let up.'

'Did you tell them this when you were interviewed?'

He shook his head.

'Did you tell them about the discrepancy you saw on this scruffy piece of paper?'

Again, he shook his head.

'So how do you account for that, Jed? Do you think the person who kept this record made an error in dates? Do you think that's what happened?'

'I don't know.'

She glanced at his plate of food. The mash and beans looked cold. His expression woeful, Ruth took pity on him. 'Last question, Jed, then I'll go. What did you think exactly when you heard what Thomas had done?'

He mumbled something under his breath. Either another expletive or something he didn't want her to hear. 'What was that?' she asked.

His jaw clenched as if biting back the reply. He inhaled noisily through his nose, then the moment passed and he spoke. 'I said, I thought no way did he do that.'

Ruth stood up and as she passed him she patted his shoulder lightly. 'That's right, Jed. No way. Remember that when I prove you right.'

*

Ruth took sanctuary in her car where she berated herself for her own stupidity. It didn't add up how Thomas had access not just once, but over a period of time, to steal these drugs. From memory, standard procedure for controlled drugs was that they arrived in wards in sealed bags, accompanied by the controlled drugs order book. The medication then had to be signed for by a registered nurse with the date and time received. The new stock was then entered into the controlled drugs register. Checking the stock of all controlled drugs entered in the register happened at least once a day, depending on the department and their requirements. Any processes involving controlled drugs had to be witnessed by an appropriate member of staff alongside a registered nurse. Any discrepancies had to be reported straight away. The drugs were kept in a locked cupboard and its key was kept by the designated registered nurse. In a document of some fifty pages or more, standard operating procedure detailed the requirements for safe, secure handling of medicines. Yet, she was meant to believe no one noticed a box of diamorphine missing. She was meant to believe that the controlled drugs accountable officer, often the hospital's chief pharmacist, left a copy of a record kept of dates when Thomas stole drugs lying around for anyone to see? It seemed more than just carelessness. It seemed impossible.

The CDs accountable officer may well have decided to identify the cause for any discrepancies, especially if they were suspicious of misuse. In that case the hospital should have alerted the police, which may then have led to them installing a covert camera. According to Jed Nolan, Thomas was helping himself to drugs regularly, so surely after the first few occasions someone would have challenged this? They wouldn't let it go on from February to April. Who was spying on him to know this? Because whoever it was would have had a hard job keeping tabs and would have to have been constantly at his side. And checking it was no one else taking them, of course. As while it was true the keys were kept by a designated person, doctors, ODPs, registered nurses had to have access to the drugs cupboard. In some departments they were constantly accessing the drugs cupboard: the emergency department, theatres, ICU. Regardless of how busy they were, though, two people had to check out controlled drugs. The law required it.

Someone kept a record. Someone put Thomas's name in a column. Who did that? Did the police or hospital have the original? She banged the steering wheel in frustration. She wanted to know how this all happened. She *now* wanted a meeting with the hospital.

In anger, she took out her phone and googled Christine Pelham's law firm. She needed to contact her. When she got through to an answering service she had to bite her tongue before leaving her message. She wanted the solicitor to call back. Though being a Saturday, that was unlikely to happen till Monday. The woman should have done right by Thomas the first time. Ruth had seen how much she cost from opening Thomas's mail, so there was no excuse for wearing tatty shoes. Her anger went as quickly as it came. She'd just hit a wall, and was frustrated with herself more than anything. She'd be fine in a minute. Then she could think calmly again.

She actually didn't give tuppence for how the woman dressed. She could have turned up in flowery wellingtons for all Ruth cared as long as she did her job well. Which she hadn't for Thomas. Ruth had no idea if this solicitor would help her. She had no idea what she should expect, or what rights she even had. What she wanted was quite simple – to have Christine Pelham explain why Thomas pleaded guilty. She wanted to know in detail about the evidence. Had the police got hold of this record? If so, who directed them to it? Who led the way to Thomas being charged? Until she knew all of this she only had scraps. If there'd been a trial it all would have been explained. Instead, she was left in limbo, scrabbling for answers to clear his name. Left with hearing accounts from people like Jed and Chloe.

He was guilty. And that's a fact.

I'd rather forget about that day. Forget about him.

CHAPTER SIXTEEN

Rosie stood in one spot, leaning against her cooker, and gazed at the police officer's bright yellow jacket. On the back in big silver letters the word POLICE. The brightness of it reflected extra light as he moved through the gloom. He'd barely walked through the front door when he saw her handiwork on the back door. Rosie trailed after him as he went to examine it, explaining her dilemma. The crudely cut lengths of batten nailed across it looked worse than they did last night.

He tutted mildly. 'Dear, oh dear, that's not going to hold. One kick and those battens will give. You'd be better off putting a bolt on the door.' He moved closer to inspect something, which he then pointed out to her on the left side of the doorframe. 'You've splintered it here. Let the nail go in sideways.'

Rosie held back a sigh and switched on the kettle. Her hard labour, her blistered hand and aching shoulders, all for nothing. He still had his back to her so she used the moment to comb her fingers through her hair and pick sleep from her eyes. She would have liked to put on a clean top as the one she was wearing smelled of stale sweat from all the sawing. She'd flopped into bed still wearing it, and tossed and turned until dawn. She was asleep when he knocked on her door. Her sour smell bothered her, so she excused herself, saying she was popping to the loo. In the bathroom she used the toilet, then ran a cold flannel under her armpits, then sprayed some Impulse on her skin and clothes.

When she returned the policeman was sitting at her tiny table, making a small hill of sawdust with his hand to clear a space for his notebook. Rosie pulled her two best mugs off the mug tree, and put a spoon of coffee in them, then fetched milk from the fridge, which she hoped was in date. She placed a coffee in front of him and he murmured a thank you, and she sat in the other chair by the side of the back door. There was a metre of space between them, which she hoped was far enough for him not to smell her.

After introducing himself and establishing she was who he wished to see, he informed her he was making enquiries about Anabel Whiting.

'Anabel's mum said you would call,' she said.

'Yes, well, as you can imagine, Anabel's parents are growing more concerned. Can I start by asking when you last saw Anabel?'

'Christmas Eve,' she promptly replied.

His eyebrows rose. 'Not since then?'

'No.'

'Any reason why?'

Rosie shrugged. 'No reason. Just Christmas, I suppose. People are busy.'

'Were you busy?'

She blinked, surprised at the question. 'Me? Not really. Just the usual Christmas shopping marathon everyone does. Buying too much food and whatnot.'

He glanced at her spartan supplies on the kitchen counter: a small jar of Nescafé, a scraped jar of peanut butter, a few slices left of a loaf of white bread, and by the sink an almost empty bottle of Robinsons squash next to a thimbleful of washing-up liquid. Most embarrassing for Rosie was the empty litre bottle of Metaxa on the draining board. Rosie nibbled the loose skin on the side of her thumb. He could look all he wanted. This was her home. She could live how she liked.

'So you saw her Christmas Eve?'

Rosie nodded and put her hand in her lap. She condemned Anabel for sucking her thumb. She was as bad biting her nails. 'We bumped into each other in town. Had a quick hello and that was it.'

'Anabel's mum said that over the last few months she's sensed something amiss between you. She thinks you've had a falling out, because normally Anabel mentions things you've been doing together in most of their chats. She also said that since you were eighteen you two always do something together on New Year's Eve. After their family party?'

Rosie bristled. Meg should keep her barbed comments to herself, and her nose out of Rosie and Anabel's business. 'Well, this time we didn't,' she said flatly. 'I went to a party across the road.'

His gaze rested on her for an uncomfortable length of time, though it was probably only seconds. 'Miss Carlyle, I'd like to cut to the chase. Your friend has not been in touch with her family since before New Year's Eve and she has not been in touch with her employer to explain her absence. If you have had a falling out, which might be the cause of her taking off, now would be a good time to say. It will lessen her parents' alarm at thinking there's a more sinister reason. We know she packed a suitcase, which is reassuring, but for her not to be in contact is apparently completely out of character.'

Rosie gritted her teeth to stop herself from telling him to back off. She couldn't tell him why Anabel had gone. She stared at him anxiously, and wasn't worried if it showed on her face. It would be strange if she wasn't worried about her missing friend. She was, of course, worried. Every day she was waiting for something to happen, for everything to come out, for the police to be banging at her door for a very different reason.

'Look,' she said. 'Anabel has been working through some things, so we've given each other some space. There's been no falling out. She's my best friend and if you want to know the truth I could do with her right now!' She pointed at the back door with a shaky hand. 'I'm living here scared out of my mind. I had to do that to the door yesterday because someone got in, because it doesn't lock!'

His expression showed only mild interest, which riled Rosie instantly. She'd hoped to receive some sympathy, not a lukewarm stare. She shook her head in disbelief. 'Someone came into my home while I wasn't here and touched my things,' she said in a tight voice. 'So right now I'd very much like it if Anabel came back and put us all out of our worry, but also to keep me company. Because until the letting agency gets the lock fixed, I'm here completely alone and vulnerable.'

'Have you reported the break-in to the police?' he asked.

She opened her eyes in disdain. 'And what good will that do? I'll get a crime reference number, and be directed to victim support. A fat lot of good that will do. It won't mend the door.'

He closed his notebook and tucked it in his jacket. 'The letting agency might take quicker action if they know you've reported it to the police.' He rose from the chair and picked up his police cap.

Something in the way he moved resonated with Rosie as he stretched his neck side to side, as if it had a kink, and she found herself studying him. Something was familiar about him, but she couldn't place where she might have seen him before. Maybe it was outside a nightclub. Coppers were always there waiting at the end of the night in case of trouble. She followed him as he made his way to the front door. He opened it and stepped out in the hall, but instead of leaving, turned and faced her.

'Anabel's mother hoped you might be able to help us with her daughter's whereabouts or give us names of people she might have gone to. Do you know where she is, Miss Carlyle?'

Rosie shook her head. 'If I knew I'd say.'

He placed his cap on his head and gave her a hard stare. 'I had a feeling you would say that. If you change your mind and can think of anything that might help, do the right thing and let her mother know.'

When the sound of his footsteps disappeared from the hall, Rosie closed her door, leaned back against it and let herself slide to the floor. His visit had shaken her. He had questioned her more like a suspect than Anabel's friend. He'd barely been interested in her telling him she'd had an intruder. His interest was all on Anabel.

A draught coming under the door chilled her lower back, the circulating air smelling fresher. Air from the hallway. She sat forward, away from the door, and picked up the trapped malodorous aroma inside her flat. On the table the coffee she made him was untouched. He probably thought the mug unwashed, her hands unhygienic when she touched it. Rosie stared at the stains on her leggings, and felt hot embarrassment wash over her. Anabel's antics had reduced her to this level. The weeks of worry had taken her energy to the point where she no longer cared about her home or her appearance.

She had to find Anabel. Not knowing where Anabel was, or what she might be saying, was scaring Rosie. She had Rosie's life in her hands. If Anabel shared their secret, it didn't just affect her. It affected Rosie. The fallout was far-reaching. Why couldn't she just come home right now and put an end to this threat? Rosie had always been there for Anabel. Why couldn't Anabel be there for Rosie? They were best friends forever, that's what they always said. Till the day they died.

Anabel needed reminding of that. As to where was she now? She had run away. Just like she did before.

CHAPTER SEVENTEEN

Ruth parked across the road from the Victorian house, and sighed in frustration at the sight of the two people in the front garden. After everything she had learned from her day at the hospital, and from meeting Catherine last night, her brain felt overloaded. She just wanted to go into her flat and close the door, and sieve through this information.

The man and woman in the front garden turned and stared at the sound of the engine. Two things surprised her. Kim was dressed in a healthcare assistant uniform, bluey-grey, and Tim Wiley was in his police uniform. Kim looked uncomfortable. Although Ruth didn't know her well, she saw from her stance the tightly folded arms across her chest, the shoulders hunched forwards and legs stiffly drawn together. She did not want to be there.

Ruth wondered if it was to do with what she saw last night when she looked out of her window, while standing there thinking about Catherine. She wondered how much trouble Kim was in if the police were here again. Perhaps more than a slap on the wrist. Something had been exchanged between Kim and the man in the beanie hat, of that Ruth was sure, as she saw him put something Kim gave him in his pocket. Whether it was anything illegal, she couldn't tell. But it had disturbed her, seeing him loping off down the street, the thought of drugs being passed right outside Thomas's flat.

She wanted to stay in the car. She could pull out her phone and pretend to make a call, if she knew how long Tim Wiley was going to be there. He might only just have arrived. She wondered if she should just slip past them. What she didn't want was to engage in a conversation where he might reveal who she was to Kim. He gave a nod, having seen her, and reluctantly she got out of the car and locked it.

'Afternoon, Dr Bennett,' he called, as Ruth crossed the road and pushed open the garden gate.

She responded cordially. 'Good afternoon.'

He looked powerful. The wide utility belt around his hips carried protection equipment. His black multi-pocket vest was packed solid. On his right shoulder he wore a personal radio, and a bodycam on his left breast. His heavy-duty boots, his vest, helmet, plus all the equipment, must weigh two stone or more. It was a wonder he didn't have more than just a foot problem. It must be feeling better if he was back at work.

Ruth acknowledged her neighbour. 'Hello, Kim. Nice to see you. Less cold today, isn't it?'

Kim was staring at her with puzzled eyes. Maybe at hearing the police officer address her by name? Or as a doctor? She could be wondering why Ruth hadn't mentioned it after being told a doctor lived in the flat before.

'I didn't realise you were a nurse.'

Kim gave a derisive look at her tunic. 'I'm a healthcare assistant.' An abrasive tone in her voice, Ruth suspected she'd just said goodbye to her friendliness. 'I do bank shifts. Gynae one day, chest unit the next, day after somewhere else again. You go where needed. But you already know how it works, with *you* being a doctor.'

Ruth heard the dig. She was meant to. She gave them both a polite nod. 'Well, I'll let you get on. I don't want to interrupt.' As quickly as she could without running she made for the front door. She had her key out ready, but his next remark stopped her.

'I'm surprised you live here, Dr Bennett.'

Ruth turned and made eye contact, keeping her resentment hidden. 'Are you?' Then rushed to say, 'I'm glad I bumped into you, actually. I wouldn't mind a word, if you have the time.'

A grin spread across his face. 'I have time right now. Miss Levey and I were just finishing.'

Ruth saw the relief in Kim as she closed her eyes and let out a sigh. Tim Wiley heard and gave Kim a hard stare, which she saw when her eyes were back open. She responded nervously, 'It won't happen again. I can promise you that.'

'It better not,' he returned in a stern tone. When nothing further was said from him, Kim shuffled awkwardly away, reaching Ruth and then quickly using her own key to open the door.

As it shut behind her, Tim Wiley smiled ruefully. 'Sorry about that,' he said, as if Kim had been interrupting them but was now dealt with. 'She's lucky you came along, otherwise I'd have taken her to the station.'

Ruth wasn't about to ask why and was thankful he didn't enlighten her. She wanted this conversation to end as quickly as possible. 'I'm sorry, but I told a white lie. I said I wanted a word because I didn't want anyone here knowing who I am. I hope you can understand that?'

He came towards her. 'Why don't we take this inside? I'm busting for a jimmy riddle and could do with a cuppa if there's one going.'

Ruth felt her stomach dip. She didn't want him in her home.

'I had something I wanted to discuss with you anyway. About your son,' he added.

*

In the galley kitchen Ruth took her time making the tea to get used to the idea of this unexpected visitor in her home. When he came out of the bathroom she'd expected him to follow her into the galley space, but instead he sat down at the desk, removing his helmet. She had no idea what he was about to tell her and just hoped it wasn't a ploy to get invited in. She didn't know if it was his over-confidence or his lack of awareness of what she was feeling that made her wary of him, or whether there was just something off about his character that made her uneasy. His behaviour at the surgery as a patient hadn't been *that* bad. He'd asked her out, but so what? He hadn't been especially flirtatious or pushy. Just… over-familiar.

Tim Wiley smiled appreciatively as she set down a mug of tea for him. 'Just what the doctor ordered,' he quipped.

Ruth sat in the armchair, then wished she hadn't when he stood up. He walked the length of the bookcase, running his hand along an empty shelf. 'So,' he said, in a whimsical voice, 'none of your neighbours know it was your son living here?'

'That's right. I'd prefer it to stay that way.'

His eyebrows lifted at her sharp tone, but it didn't dent his confidence. 'I'm not judging,' he said. 'I don't blame you. It must be difficult to live with.'

She could feel the heat rising in her face. She resented him knowing where she lived. Commenting on it like he did in front of Kim. Knowing it was Thomas's home and knowing she was Thomas's mother. Having knowledge of who she is.

'Well, a change of scenery is always good. Probably what you needed.'

'Yes,' she said quietly. 'I do.' A thought crossed her mind. 'Were you working on the case?' she asked hopefully.

'No.'

She glanced away, then remembered why she'd let him in. 'Outside you said you had something you wanted to discuss. That it was about my son.'

He walked back to the desk and picked up the mug of tea. He took a sip. 'I was going to suggest something. That if you want any help, I can assist.'

She stared at him. 'What are you talking about?'

He responded with a shrug of the shoulders.

Her disappointment was sharp. He'd tricked his way in by letting her think he knew something. When all he really wanted was to… She sprang from the armchair and angrily faced him. 'What is it you want from me? Because if it's my interest, let me tell you unless it's about Thomas, I have none.'

He reared back, pretending to show alarm, putting his hands over his ears. 'Whoa, Dr Bennett, you need to chill.'

Ruth marched past him, incensed. 'I want you to leave now. I don't know what your game is, but I don't want or need your help. I just want you to go.' She walked quickly to the front door and held it wide open by pressing back against it.

A moment later he sauntered to the door. In the tiny hallway, there was hardly room for them both. He tapped his finger on the closed bathroom door. 'It can't be easy going in there.'

He peered at her closely, then in slow movements he stretched his arms out and placed his hands on the front door on either side of her head.

'Can you please just go?' she asked tremulously.

'I am. I will,' he answered in a quiet voice. 'I just wanted to share something with you. A mate of mine was in on the interviews with your son. Your son denied all knowledge of it. Couldn't account for the drugs in his flat or in his locker. Couldn't explain what was found on his phone or why he was off his face when arrested. Then he gets to the magistrates' court and pleads guilty.'

'I don't understand why you're telling me this,' she whispered.

'What I'm saying is when someone enters a guilty plea it means they admit to committing the offence. The thing is, I heard he pleaded guilty on the basis that he didn't really do it. He was going for the middle ground. So it would have been interesting to see how that was dealt with if your son had gone before a crown court. That's all I wanted to say. If I upset you, that wasn't my intention.'

'Go now, please,' she said in tearful voice.

He dropped his arms and backed away. Ruth was then startled to see Henry standing in the doorway.

'Are you okay?' he asked her calmly.

Tim Wiley seemed not the least concerned at being found in this questionable manner. He stepped up to Henry in the doorway. 'Nothing for you to be concerned about, sir. She got a little upset.'

'I was addressing Miss Bennett,' Henry retorted. 'From what I saw I'd say she had good reason to feel upset.'

'I'm okay, Henry,' Ruth called out quickly. 'The officer was just leaving.'

Henry didn't move from his position, forcing Tim Wiley to shoulder his way past. Henry watched him go all the way down the stairs. When the front door shut loudly, Ruth slumped with relief. She had a vision of Henry pouncing on the policeman and rugby tackling him to the floor. Which wouldn't have helped at all. What she wanted was to quickly get over this drama so she could concentrate on what he said.

Thomas taking the middle ground. Not admitting to committing a crime.

Tim Wiley's behaviour confused her. Was it him who sent her the anonymous letter? Was he trying to tell her there was something wrong with allowing Thomas to do that? Christine Pelham would know the answer, but would she tell it to her late client's mother? Ruth wanted to know the implications, if any, this might have had for Thomas. She wanted to understand Thomas's reasoning and know if he fully understood his situation. How would he have fared if he'd gone before a judge that day? Might he have gone to prison? On Monday she would ring Christine Pelham again. She wanted answers now, more urgently than yesterday, because the events of today made not knowing all the facts even harder to bear. It had returned her thoughts to Thomas's suffering – alone, afraid, while she wasn't even aware or able to help him.

Henry put a glass into her hand and she gratefully sipped the whisky. He had closed her front door and ushered her into the armchair with her barely realising he was there. He had moved around her invisibly to hand her this drink. In the darkening room he stood by the window, quietly watching the daylight leaving the sky, his presence calming.

'You don't have to stay,' she said. 'I'm fine here, I promise.'

'I'm not the polite type, I assure you,' he replied. Then a beat later: 'I'm fine here, I promise.'

Ruth smiled, enjoying the gentle humour, his calming presence. She would like to know more about him. Her knowledge of him was new. He was her son's friend. She heard him draw breath and looked at him expectantly. Maybe he was thinking to leave. It had to be after five. Time for most people to be thinking of going home. He turned from the window and clasped his hands as if he had made a decision.

'Are you hungry?' he asked.

Ruth blinked at him in surprise. Food was the last thing on her mind. She should be hungry. She had missed lunch. 'I think I am,' she answered finally.

'There's a really good Indian restaurant within walking distance. They open at six but we could have a drink in the pub opposite first. How does that sound?'

'It sounds perfect,' she replied. It was exactly what she needed right now. A drink, some nice food and calm company. A chance to unwind. To think nothing at all.

CHAPTER EIGHTEEN

Henry was at the bar ordering her a glass of wine. She observed him from where she sat in a comfortable chair by an open fire. The pub was nice, and fairly traditional with wood panelling and beams, brass plates on the walls and copper jugs on the windowsills. Wonderfully quiet as well. Henry suited the place, she felt, he seemed kind of traditional himself. His dark suede jacket and shoes were well made, in a classic style that would never look dated. He had strong features – she couldn't say if they made him handsome or not, as all she could see was his intelligent face. Without his glasses it might appear less so.

He walked to their table with a pint glass in one hand and a wine glass in the other. He placed her drink on a coaster and sat in the adjacent chair, putting his pint down temporarily so he could adjust his position and move the chair to a better angle.

'That's better,' he said. Then he raised his glass at her. 'Cheers.'

Ruth did the same to him, glad they were not following through with the whole practice of touching glasses to clink, as it would feel too celebratory and not very grown up. Which they both were.

'Do you mind if I clarify something?' he asked.

Ruth shook her head.

'Is it Miss or Ms? It felt awkward calling you Miss the first time, as I wasn't sure.'

Ruth wondered if this was his way of asking why she had a different name to Thomas. 'Well, Bennett is my birth name.

Thomas's father and I never married, but I'm not often referred to as Miss Bennett. It's usually Ruth or Dr Bennett.'

'Ah,' he said. 'That makes sense.'

'What does?' she asked, intrigued.

'Why it didn't sound quite right or feel right somehow.'

Ruth laughed. 'What on earth are you saying? How can saying someone's name not feel or sound right if you don't know anything about them but their name?'

'You'd be surprised. My intuition tells me things.' He drank some of his beer, and then carried on talking. 'So in what area of the medical world will one find you? Or are you a doctor of an entirely different kind?'

'I'm a GP,' she said.

'So you have to know something about every illness then?'

Ruth glanced at him appreciatively. 'It's nice that you think that.'

He shrugged. 'Well, I can't imagine ever going to see my doctor and thinking maybe I better not go about that. He won't know what it is.'

She laughed again. 'You've just made me realise something that's made me feel a whole lot better. Because you're right. Who goes to the doctor thinking that?'

He looked at her quizzically. 'Why did you need to feel a whole lot better?'

Ruth lowered her gaze. He was good at listening, she realised, quick at picking up on things. 'Just something today,' she said. 'A nurse I met on a ward I was visiting viewed me as inadequate, I think.' She glanced at him now. 'Silly, I suppose, to let it affect me.'

'Are you working at the hospital?'

'No, just visiting. I'm working as a GP in Bournemouth. I just wanted to see the hospital.'

He nodded. 'I confess, my experiences of visiting hospitals, or doctors for that matter, is limited, but I'm sure they must be stressful places to work at. I suspect this nurse was stressed because she was unable to see what was right in front of her nose – a very knowledgeable doctor.'

'Well, that's kind of you to say,' Ruth commented, all of a sudden feeling self-conscious the conversation was still about her. 'And I'm glad to hear you have little reason to see a doctor. Your health must be robust.'

A frown appeared on his brow. He stared hard at the fire grate. 'I'm trying to think when I last saw a doctor,' he said, in a pondering tone. 'Have I seen one since the snake bite?'

'Snake bite?' Ruth exclaimed. 'What, in England?'

'No.' He shook his head. 'Nangetty, Australia. Three years ago. It was lucky a doctor was on site. Even luckier, it was only a baby. Fangs are tiny.'

Ruth looked at him in horror. Her voice rose a little. 'You got bitten by a snake in Australia?'

'I did,' he said, focusing back on his surroundings. 'A dugite, no less. Pretty lethal things really,' he said in a matter-of-fact way. He smiled at her. 'Still, I live to tell the tale. Fight another day.'

Ruth was curious. He'd said little about himself. Revealing something like this happening for some people would have been a big moment. He'd toned his reveal down to make it sound like a wasp sting. 'Were you on holiday?'

'No. Work. My other work that is, when I'm not acting landlord. Though, my sister pretty much takes care of all that. The house was left to us jointly by our parents. I just keep the bills down by keeping up the maintenance. Marlene doesn't want to give up the family home, so I support where I can.'

Ruth's wine was nearly finished, but she didn't want to draw attention to the nearly empty glass. She was enjoying hearing about him. 'So your other work. What does that entail?'

He gave a small laugh. 'Apart from snake bites, you mean? Well, it takes me to places both far and near and lets me do what I love best. Dig about for old things.'

Ruth felt her breath catch. In an instant she was back in Pompeii and nineteen years old again. Feeling the hot sun on her skin and the bone-dry earth under her feet.

Henry must have noticed her manner change, as he was looking at her concerned. Then he mildly tutted. 'Tom told me his father died before he was born. That he was training to be an archaeologist. I wish I recalled him telling me that sooner.'

Ruth had believed Pietro was already an archaeologist when she met him. It was only afterwards she understood he was still studying and that it would take him a few more years until he qualified. Not that it mattered. They were young. She summoned a smile for Henry. 'Honestly, I'm fine. It was a long time ago. Please, carry on. You can't leave me in suspense. Is that what you do?'

'Well, I suppose the two fields are closely related in that they piece together the past. But I don't just study dinosaurs. I study a vast amount of other things.'

Ruth scrutinised him. 'Is that a grin you're suppressing?'

He stared at her deadpan. 'No.'

Ruth drained her glass, watching for a sign of any glee. 'Shall we make a move?' she suggested. 'I'm starving now.'

He drank the last half-inch of his beer and stood up. 'Good, because I could eat a Tyrannosaurus.'

Ruth waited until she had put on her coat and was ready to depart before giving him a small smile and a pointed stare. 'I bet you couldn't wait to say that.'

Henry looked amused. It had been a pleasant half hour. Probably the nicest half hour she'd had in a long while. And that was all thanks to Henry Thorpe. Despite him denying it earlier, he was a very polite man.

CHAPTER NINETEEN

Rosie peered bleary-eyed in the direction of the bathroom. She left the door open at night as it was the only room in the flat with a window. It was still dark. She turned the lamp on, then pulled her phone out from under her pillow and squinted at the time. She groaned. Not even six o'clock. And awake to another day of nothingness.

She hadn't spoken to another soul since Saturday. Not since the police officer. She hadn't stepped outside these four walls. Since then, and all through Sunday until now, she had been entirely alone. She closed her eyes. *What to do?* Would she feel better if she went back to work? She would have to get up now to get ready, to shower and put on some make-up, to throw something in a lunchbox to take with her. Then decide whether to take the short or the longer route past Costa Coffee where she would hand over her reusable cup and order the same as always. A skinny latte made with coconut milk and flavoured with sugar-free cinnamon. She'd then walk with her earbuds in and listen to her playlist, unless talking with Anabel, and by the time she arrived at work she'd be up to facing the day.

She would have to decide at some point. Her sick note ran out in a week. She would need another one, an appointment with her usual doctor, not the one seeing her today, so she didn't have to explain anything and would be able to just say nothing had changed. She was still the same. Poor sleep, low mood, anxious most of the time. Which was why the thought she would be better back at work was daft. She wasn't thinking. She'd not worked for over three months. If she had broken a leg, she'd expect to be off work for that long, but what she had wasn't mending.

Panic attacks. Warnings that something wasn't right.

She knew what caused it, of course – days on end of quietly worrying if Anabel was going to carry out her threat. She had said it so boldly. 'I need to tell someone what we did, Rosie.'

The insomnia and anxiety started right then. Night after night she couldn't sleep and while awake she couldn't not think, the internal voice in her head on a loop. *Will she? Won't she? Will she? Won't she*? Like pulling a million petals from the same daisy. Never getting to the end. To the part that mattered. To only what mattered. *Will she tell our secret?*

Anabel didn't care if this upset Rosie, didn't care that Rosie would be worried sick with not knowing what Anabel was thinking or planning or doing about their secret. She just distanced herself from the situation and ran away, like she had nothing to do with it. *She* had everything to do with it.

She breathed in deeply and tried to release the tension from her face. Her mobile was still in her hand. She checked her emails. Nothing from Anabel. Maybe Rosie should send a second email and tell her not to bother coming back, that no one cared. She might come running then, desperate to be wanted and needed and cosseted like a big baby.

Rosie puffed out her cheeks with pockets of air, holding it until she felt pressure in her teeth. Today she was not going to spend every thought on Anabel. She was going to fill her mind with calm. Let positive images soothe her. She was going to rise from this bed soon, shower and wash her hair, and for once blow dry it. Then dig out what cleaning products she had under the sink and clean the flat. If she was clean and her home clean she might feel more normal.

Taking a moment to imagine it all looking clean she stretched her limbs out like a starfish, getting her energy ready. Her right hand brushed the far pillow and something light fell into her palm. Rosie turned her head to see. In an instant she was bolt upright on the bed with the object flung to the end of the room. Her shocked eyes saw it skid as it hit the small area of lino and stop by the table and chairs.

'Fuck. Fuck. Fuck,' she cried, between snatches of breath. Someone had left this here during the night. Someone had stood by her bed, *looking at her asleep.*

Her eyes flew to the back door, her brain clocked immediately it was shut. It was exactly as yesterday with the battens still in place. Making herself move from the bed she stepped cautiously to the bathroom. Through the open doorway she saw the handle of the latch on the window fully down, tightly closed. The window was big enough to climb through, but it wasn't open, which left only one other way in.

Rosie whimpered. *A stranger had opened her front door.* It had a Yale lock that opened the door from the outside with a key, but only if the night latch wasn't pushed across. Rosie had never been able to use that small metal button. The entire lock was painted over. The button showed as just a bump in the thick layers of paint. She would have to scrape it all away to free it to see if it even worked. When she moved in six years ago she was handed two keys. One she gave to Anabel so she could let herself in and not have to hang about waiting for Rosie to open the door. Anabel was like her sister. Rosie's bedsit was her second home.

On a night out a year ago Rosie took a different handbag out with her, leaving her key behind. She'd had to climb on Anabel's back and get in through the bathroom window, because Anabel confessed to losing hers. She'd used it recently, so it had not been lost long, but she had no idea where it might be. They never got around to getting a new key, so Anabel then had to wait to be let in.

Rosie wanted to believe more than anything that Anabel had found the lost key, that it was her who came into her home last night. If Anabel phoned right now and said it was her, Rosie wouldn't even be cross. She'd actually want to hug her instead. Wanting that to be the way it happened wasn't enough for her to believe it, though. Not while a memory of Anabel soaked to the skin kept pushing hope away. She'd got drenched walking to Rosie's in a downpour of icy rain, then sat shivering by the front door for nearly three hours. Rosie stripped her and put her in a hot bath. Her skin was so white it was see-through, showing lots of little blue veins. She was shaking so hard when suddenly she flopped, terrifying Rosie like nothing ever before. She'd thought she was going to lose her. The paramedic said half a degree colder and they'd have taken Anabel to A&E. They advised against hot baths and to let her warm gradually. That was at the beginning of September, four months ago, the last time Anabel stayed at Rosie's. Anabel definitely didn't have the lost key then.

Stubbornly she had waited, had sat cold and wet, because she wanted to talk. She was so desperate to blame Rosie for what happened in the summer that she was prepared to lie about their secret for what happened when they were children. 'I'll tell them it was you, Rosie. No one knew I was even there, remember.'

Had Anabel found her key after searching hard for it? Had she let herself quietly in in the middle of the night, or been persuaded to hand it over to a blackmailer? It was a sickening thought either way. If it wasn't Anabel, whoever it was, wasn't likely to be going to the police. They'd blackmailed Anabel and trespassed inside Rosie's home.

Rosie had to sit down before she could look at the object on the floor. It had to be a message from Anabel, whether it was delivered by her or brought there by someone else. She was trying to get Rosie into trouble. Her insides knotted with fear, bringing pain to her belly. She breathed in through her nose and out through her mouth, slowly. She tried to calm her mind down and try and think.

Rosie drew her legs up and rested her feet on the edge of the chair so she could put her chin on her knees. The fear swamping her flinched her muscles and nerves, causing reactions in all sorts of ways. Stomach aches that made her have to run to the loo often, or bend over it to be sick. Dull headaches most of the time she had to ignore, as paracetamol didn't work on them. Since this feud began she had been plagued by some sort of physical upset almost every day.

Bumping into Anabel on Christmas Eve Rosie had prayed it would turn around their relationship, that it might be a pivotal moment. Hearing Anabel laugh had filled her with hope of them getting back to normal. Until she looked into her eyes and saw a lost soul. From then on, Rosie had been waiting for Anabel to make her next move.

She was only helpless if she did nothing. She put her feet to the floor and picked up the object. She got up from the chair and went to a kitchen cabinet. Inside was a choice of jars. Rosie picked a family size jar of Branston pickle that had been there for years. Twisting the tight lid off she saw the brown pickle looked surprisingly fresh. She pushed it down into the wet pickle, imagining it like quicksand, disappearing the object away. Satisfied, she screwed the lid back on and put the jar back in the cupboard.

Thinking calmly now, she planned her day. She would clean her home. Shower. Wash hair. Start to peel paint off the button on the front door. Then go see this doctor. Rosie would keep it low-key and just say she was feeling a little better, and leave it at that. So the doctor could delay her idea of sending Rosie to a counsellor. Right now Rosie had bigger things to sort out than her mental health, which would all go away in an instant, anyway, when she found Anabel.

She pulled open a drawer beneath the counter for her sharp knife. Like the breadknife, it had never been used. She'd bought it thinking she would need it for cooking, but as she didn't cook more than beans on toast or fried egg, it was still brand new, the point very sharp. She might start cooking one day. Get a slow cooker and make stews and bring some in a food flask to work. She could freeze it in batches. Start eating healthy and making... She went suddenly still. A memory of a conversation about cooking was trying to come through. Rosie's instinct was to concentrate. *A woman. Snooty tone. Hair perfect, like it'd been glued to her head. Talking about soup. Blending soup. Chilli in soup.* Rosie's eyes suddenly gleamed in satisfaction. 'Gotcha,' she quietly said.

The woman had talked about every home-made soup she'd ever prepared, like she was the second Mary Berry. She kept pushing plastic containers at Anabel, saying how brilliant they were. *Tupperware.* A party Anabel had talked her into going to with the enticement that there'd be free food and wine. They were offered only one glass of wine each and a bowl of Pringles to share the entire evening. But it wasn't this memory that made Rosie think of this boring woman, it was what she overheard her saying to Anabel in the kitchen. *An offer to move in and house share.* On their walk home Anabel said the woman was probably asking everyone, that they weren't even friends, but that wasn't the impression Rosie got, as in the kitchen they appeared to like each other.

Rosie had a sudden urge to see inside this woman's house again, as a possibility occurred to her that she felt strongly might well be true – Anabel was hiding there, and had been since she ran away. Letting her little Tupperware friend make her home-made soup, while she cried on her shoulder and told her all about what horrible Rosie had done.

CHAPTER TWENTY

Ruth met the whole team at the seven thirty Monday morning meeting. Six doctors, two nurse practitioners, two practice nurses, three healthcare assistants, plus the practice management and administration team and receptionists were all there. The only absent staff were the cleaners. Ruth found herself saying hello and thank you for the welcome a fair few times. Dr Raj sat beside her and took it upon herself to introduce Ruth. She had a big smile she used often and seemed to be the regular spokesperson, as she was asked a number of things by the others – the same thing more than once from a few. But 'Are there no biscuits today?' was the question asked most often. Joan answered that one a few moments later by bringing in a box of Border biscuits.

Ruth sat silently throughout the meeting, enjoying her tea, listening to the topics discussed: previous minutes and updates, complaints received and handled, office needs, improvement ideas to the car park and pavement at the front. General business – new staff – Dr Bennett. On leave – Dr Michaels – baby due February.

It was nice sitting there feeling like she was part of the team, not just there short term, like it was her normal life. It made her aware of the future, that one day she could live again and not be suspended in time, and that evenings out like Saturday night would happen again, with other nice people. Eventually, she would be able to feel happy for more than an hour or two. But it made her feel wretched for even having such thoughts. *He's barely cold.* Ruth wanted to suppress the voice in her head. *She's leaving her boy already. Snatching at anything to be happy, to quick fix pain.* The taunts were unbearable and she was grateful to hear a chair sharply push back on the floor so she could focus on something else.

Carol Campbell and several other doctors stayed seated at the table, waiting for the rest to leave and the noise to die down.

Dr Campbell smiled at Ruth. 'Anything that delays facing the storm is always good.'

Ruth smiled in return, thinking Dr Campbell had a thing for saying the dramatic and that she wouldn't be surprised if she was in an amateur dramatics group.

She then said, 'We just thought we'd take the opportunity to welcome you and give you the chance to put names to faces.'

The man opposite Ruth held up a finger. 'Jim Miller, in case you missed my name first time round.' He smiled with strong white teeth. Too white for his age, so perhaps veneers. 'I'm the old fart who is retiring shortly.' He winked. 'You might want to keep that in mind for the future.'

Ruth would be going home when Thomas's name was cleared. She would not be staying for Jim's job, though flattering of the senior partner to suggest it.

A few groans went round the room and Dr Raj pretended to play a violin. 'Poor old Jim. All that free time to have fun. Our hearts bleat for you.'

'Don't you mean bleed?' the slightly chubby man beside Jim said.

'No, Colin, I don't,' Dr Raj replied precisely. 'Jim is going to live on a sheep farm, surrounding himself with little bleats, so we will join in their song.'

Ruth's lips parted in a silent laugh. Dr Raj's quirky humour appealed to her.

Jim Miller held up his hand to quieten everyone. 'Enough levity. Dr Bennett will think we're all a bunch of clowns and won't want to come to any of our fun evenings.' He looked across at

Ruth. 'Dr Raj gives us cooking lessons once a month, letting us crowd into her home and her kitchen. Dr Hurst, to your right, hosts a book club in her home, also once a month. You are very welcome to join us.'

Ruth gazed at the people around her, all unaware of her deception, of the real reason she was there – to get to know one of their patients. It now made sense why she hadn't managed to contact the nurse. She was off sick from work and was perhaps staying with family. Ruth was eager to meet her after what Jed Nolan revealed. 'Well, thank you,' she replied. 'I'm sure I'd love to.'

Carol Campbell said, 'So, Ruth, while you have us all here, is there anything you'd like to ask?'

Ruth would like to have asked about Tim Wiley, but thought better of it as she would have to disclose concerns, which involved more than just being asked out by the man. She did have a query about one other patient, though. 'This won't take long,' she said. 'The patient I'm seeing at ten o'clock is Rosie Carlyle. I saw her on Friday as well. Today is a follow-up to see how she fared over the weekend. I don't know if any of you are familiar with her? Dr Michaels has been treating her.' No one said anything so Ruth carried on. 'Rosie Carlyle, twenty-seven, is being treated for depression, anxiety and insomnia, but I haven't found anything in her notes to suggest a trigger. She's on repeat medication, including zopiclone. But I think she warrants counselling.'

Jim Miller sat forward and drummed his fingers on the table slowly for a second. 'Before this lovely holy building stood here, the Carlyle family were patients at my old practice. I haven't seen the mother in years, but I remember the woman, sadly. I haven't met her daughter as a patient here, but I have an image of her in my mind from years ago when I went to the family home to sedate the mother. Her daughter was at the table with a bowl of tomato soup, dipping bread into it. I felt bad because I startled her, and the soup splashed down her top.

'That image has stayed with me because her father's body was still out on the driveway. The daughter, I believe, was thirteen. She'd been in her dad's car while he was washing it. The car was parked on a sloped driveway, which I believe is now gone after what happened, as his two sons took a jackhammer to it and levelled it. Anyway, the daughter was sitting in the front of the car playing the radio, I believe, when somehow the brake was let off and the car rolled back killing Mr Carlyle. It was a tragic accident, but I'm not sure if Mrs Carlyle handled it well with her daughter. Her husband was only forty-seven at the time. Fit and well. A paramedic.' He paused for a moment. 'Bereavement counselling was offered to the whole family, plus further counselling for the daughter to help her cope with what she may have caused.' He sighed. 'The mother didn't want to know. Her sons were grown men, so may have gone to their own GPs nearer to their homes. I don't know. With what happened, though, it would not be surprising if Rosie Carlyle was having symptoms years after that traumatic event. Especially if not dealt with at the time.'

Jim Miller's account had been well worth hearing and Ruth was glad she'd referred her patient for a mental health assessment. It may help her to talk to the experts about things she may have blocked from her mind, or may be always thinking about. Ruth would be alert for any openings in the conversation that would allow her to ask about it, so long as Rosie seemed comfortable with that. Ruth wasn't about to probe carelessly, she had more sense than that. The same as she wouldn't poke at a wasp nest.

Ruth thanked everyone and said she had no more questions.

The meeting ended, the doctors rose from their chairs and headed out of the door. Ruth made to stand, but Dr Raj placed a hand on her forearm. 'Dr Campbell said you worked in Bath?'

Ruth nodded. 'Yes. For a long time.'

Dr Raj's amber-brown eyes opened wide. 'And you came here instead? Bath is such a fine place with all its historical buildings and history. I could live there tomorrow. Do you have family here?'

Ruth swallowed the tiny ball forming in her throat and shook her head. 'No. It's just me.'

Dr Raj looked surprised. 'You're a beautiful woman. I was not expecting that. I imagined you with some handsome husband and a brood of small children.'

Ruth must have shown something on her face, because Dr Raj lightly patted Ruth's arm. 'Pay no heed to my nosiness, my dear. My family tell me I'm terribly nosy. And when not nosy, matchmaking. When you come to my home for a cooking lesson, I'll be sure to invite only the good stock from my family.' She smiled impishly. 'One or two of them might be worth you viewing, Dr Bennett, even if I say so myself. They are both very handsome.'

Ruth laughed. She couldn't help it. The woman, whether intentionally or not, invented amusing situations like a born comedian. Ruth liked her. She brought a nice aura to the day.

'Listen,' she said. 'I have something less pleasant I wanted to share. It didn't feel right saying it straight after what Jim said. Rosie Carlyle. Her friend has been a patient of mine for a few years, and she's mentioned a couple of times some worrying things about their friendship. Joan's had dealings with her too. Said she's a crafty one with finding excuses for extra meds.'

Ruth slowly nodded. 'Thanks, I will bear that in mind.' She thought that perhaps Rosie had been judged a little unfairly about her need for more medication. Ruth would reserve judgement. Rosie lost her father in a traumatic way. Lord knows how she might have been affected by that.

CHAPTER TWENTY-ONE

Rosie Carlyle had made more effort with her appearance, which was a good sign in Ruth's book. Her hair was tied back and shiny, her jumper and jeans clean. Daily habits like washing and dressing could lead an anxious person to have positive thoughts by creating a positive self-image. Ruth clocked the puffy eyes and pallor and thinness of Rosie, but stayed with the positives for now. She said good morning, warmly, but didn't overdo it by being too smiley. 'How was your weekend?'

'So-so,' Rosie replied, in a so-so tone. Then with a little energy to her voice, like she wanted to emphasise the next point, added, 'Absolutely nothing happened at all.'

Which made Ruth instantly think something absolutely had happened. 'It's okay if you don't want to talk, Rosie.'

Rosie's cheek bulged where her tongue pushed against it, while her derisory gaze swept over Ruth. She then inspected the back of her right hand, which showed knuckles freshly grazed and looking sore.

'That looks painful,' Ruth remarked when Rosie looked up. 'And recent.'

Rosie nodded. 'Happened an hour ago while I was scraping paint off a door. Scraped my knuckles as well.'

Ruth made a wincing sound. 'So you're decorating, are you?'

'No. Fixing the front door. The latch has been painted over so I'm freeing it so it can work.'

Ruth kept her voice light. 'Does this have anything to do with your things being touched?'

Rosie gave a sharp laugh. 'You could say that.'

Ruth wanted to keep her talking. 'What's happened?'

'Like I said. Absolutely nothing happened at all. Unless you count being questioned like a suspect because my friend disappeared. We've been friends since we were ten. Like sisters. And I'm getting it in the neck because she's run away.'

'Do you know why she's run away?'

'I certainly do,' Rosie answered in a hard voice. 'It's a habit of hers. She runs away when she's scared.'

'Of what?'

Rosie shrugged. 'Just things she's done.'

Ruth was thinking about how old Rosie was when her dad was killed. Only just a teenager. She wondered if this friend helped comfort her. 'Do you think she'll let you know where she is?'

She shook her head. 'No. She doesn't want to see me.'

'Why not?'

'Something happened. She doesn't like me anymore.'

'She blames you?'

'Yes. I think it's a cop-out, to be honest, so she can feel better about herself. It's easier to blame me than to look at herself and see her own behaviour. I've supported her all our lives, and this is the thanks I get. I get grilled by the police because they think I know where she is. But I don't.'

Ruth thought of something. 'Did you tell them about the things happening in your home?'

Rosie gave a snort of disgust. 'I told the copper who interviewed me. He saw the door the person got in through. Wasn't interested in taking details. Said I should report it to the police, so the letting agency takes getting the door fixed more seriously. Can you believe that? You tell a policeman about a crime and he tells you to report it to the police like he isn't one himself.'

Ruth sympathised. Systems sometimes didn't make sense. She was thinking if what Rosie said was actually true, the police should be concerned. Having someone unknown come into your home was a serious matter. It was not just a broken door Rosie was dealing with. 'So not a very pleasant weekend, then?'

'This morning when I woke I thought it might be better to be back at work, and then something happened that made me realise I wasn't ready.'

'I notice you've been off sick for a while. Dr Michaels is on maternity leave—'

'Damn, I didn't know that,' Rosie interrupted. 'I was going to ask her for a new sick note next week.'

'Well, I'm happy to write you one. It would be a chance to see how you're getting on. I think you're right. It sounds like you're not ready. So counselling might be a good option, but don't expect an appointment next week. It can take a few weeks before you get one. What happened this morning to make you think you weren't ready?'

Rosie shook her head. 'Nothing. I just all of sudden had a panic attack. Couldn't breathe. Felt sick. Had to sit down.'

'Do you think this has anything to do with how you're feeling about your friend?'

She shrugged. 'Maybe.'

'Has there been a problem for a while between you?'

'Yup. It was building all last summer. During September we barely spoke. I tried. We then had three months of silence. Christmas Eve we said hello, but nothing more since.'

'So about the same time you started to feel anxious and not sleep well?'

She gave a big nod.

'Rosie, before we finish, can I ask if there's any history of depression on your mother's side?'

'No.'

'And she's fit and well?'

'Yes. Hardly ever goes to the doctor.'

'Same question about your father. Any depression on his side?'

'No.'

'And he's fit and well?'

Ruth watched as Rosie stared down at the floor and felt bad about asking when she knew full well the father was dead. Rosie lifted her head and quietly said, 'My father died.'

'I'm sorry to hear that,' Ruth said, intending to leave things there.

'It was an accident. He was cleaning his car. Me and my friend were playing out in the front garden. I went in to get us a drink of squash. When I came out the car had rolled back over my dad. Killing him.'

Ruth kept her eyes on her patient. She told the story with apparent honesty and without contrivance. But it was not the same story Jim Miller told. *The daughter was sitting in the front of the car playing the radio, I believe.* 'That must have been a terrible shock, Rosie. For both you and your friend.'

Rosie nodded. 'It was. My friend ran away.'

A few minutes later Rosie left and Ruth was alone. She didn't know what to think. She was seeing Rosie's sore knuckles. Caused from trying to fix a door. So she could feel safe. *She's a crafty one*, was Joan's opinion. It had certainly been interesting to hear her put her friend in the picture and herself away from the scene, leaving it to the listener to draw conclusions. Did the friend have something to do with what happened? Is that why she ran away?

Ruth suspected there were many interesting details stored away that her patient might never tell. It could be it was easier to quash the image of herself if she could picture her friend instead. She didn't say her friend was in the car, just that she was there. Pinpointing any further detail might flip that image, leaving Rosie there alone. In the car. Aged thirteen. When her dad is accidently killed.

A difficult memory for anyone to bear. Especially for the child who caused it. The question was, if Rosie was to be believed, which child caused it? Rosie? Or was it her friend? It would be a terrible secret to keep if that was the case. It struck Ruth that Rosie might be right. Her friend didn't want to be friends any longer. It might in fact be the best thing to happen. That they went their separate ways. If staying together meant creating unpleasant memories of that day.

CHAPTER TWENTY-TWO

Ruth drove almost to the end of the road before she found a place to park. She stepped out of the car into a gust of wind, instantly wishing her hair was tied back. She shut the car door and pointed the fob to lock it. Then, picking up her briefcase and bag, she felt the wind push her along the street, only to have to stop a few seconds later as her hair whipped across her face, covering her eyes. She put her briefcase and bag at her feet, then gathering her blowing hair she pushed it down the back of her collar.

Ready to carry on, something made her pause. She sensed a figure behind her, who really should have passed her by now. She looked over her shoulder and thought she saw a shape move quickly behind a tree. She wasn't too concerned as it was far enough away for her to have time to run to safety, if need be. It was a creepy thought, however. She stared hard in the direction of the tree, in case someone was there, to let them know she was aware. Then, determinedly, she carried on.

A minute later she let herself in the front door and was relieved to close it behind her. She heard voices as she made her way up the stairs. A young man was standing at the top. Ruth came to eye level with him, then stepped up the last tread. A young woman behind him had styled intricate braids into her very pale pink hair, which looked extraordinarily pretty. They each carried a badminton racquet and gym bag. They both smiled.

'Hi,' they said in unison. The man's greeting came with a small bow.

Ruth caught only first names, as they introduced themselves speaking quickly. Akito and Tilly. They lived in the two flats upstairs. Ruth introduced herself.

'You're the doctor,' Tilly said. Then she scrunched her nose. 'Sorry, that came out bold. Kim told us yesterday.'

Ruth wondered what else Kim shared.

Akito put one finger to his lips as he glanced down the stairs. 'Shush,' he quietly said. 'Kim is always there.' He hadn't said it impolitely, more conveying a fact.

Ruth caught him studying her, unobtrusively. She realised why, when he asked, 'Why don't you join us for a game of badminton? We'll happily wait for you if you'd like to come.' He had probably been assessing if she looked fit enough. She'd used her car to get to work that morning, as the rain threatened to turn heavy. She declined his offer with a smile and said maybe next time. She waited until they were at the bottom of the stairs before putting her key in the door.

Inside the flat she kicked off her shoes and stepped into Thomas's slippers. Then, her coat still on, she went into the galley kitchen and took a frozen ready meal out of the tiny freezer. Grilled chicken and broccoli. She pierced the film and set the microwave for three and a half minutes.

The humming of the microwave started and followed her to the bedroom, where she pulled on soft grey comfy joggers and a thin woollen top. The room was looking cluttered – the floor had disappeared – from living out of the suitcase plonked in front of the bedroom door. She couldn't even close it to hide the untidiness.

When the food was ready, she picked up a knife and fork from the draining board and carried her plate and glass over to the desk so she could sit and eat. Thomas must have done the same, or else sat with the plate on his knees in the armchair. Ruth tucked into her meal, enjoying the silence after a rather noisy and very busy day. She hadn't had a minute to spare all day. Not even time to contact Christine Pelham again. The woman hadn't called yet. Maybe she was concerned at hearing from her deceased client's mother?

She cleared her plate and was pleasantly full. She would get up shortly and wash it, then take Thomas's diary and curl up in the armchair. The two books on the desk in front of her were the ones Thomas lent to Henry. In the restaurant Henry told her he'd brought them back. That he'd left them on the desk, but forgot to say before they went out. That was the reason he came to the flat on Saturday. She'd half-expected to hear from him yesterday. Maybe a text or a call? She might have suggested treating him to Sunday lunch at a nice pub somewhere. But she was not going to dwell on it. They barely knew one another. He was not obliged to contact her. An impromptu decision to eat together hardly made them friends. It was a tricky one. She would have had less expectation if they'd split the bill. If he hadn't treated her. If he hadn't said it was his pleasure after such a lovely evening.

Her mobile rang, and she thought it might be him. She glanced at the screen and felt immediately guilty. She answered the WhatsApp video chat and said hello to her sister.

Pauline's face filled the screen. 'What the fuck, Ruth, are you doing in Bournemouth?'

Ruth bit her lip, not knowing how to begin this. She was about to break her sister's heart.

'I had to find out from your ex-colleague you're there. What is this? You've given up your job, I hear. A job you bloody love. What's going on, Ruth? I haven't heard from you since Boxing Day. Where are you even staying? A hotel?'

Ruth had no way of preparing Pauline. She had told no one about her visit to Bournemouth last August. She had told no one she was in Bournemouth on that terrible day. She could have told Pauline. She trusted her. Pauline had been her big sister and confidante her whole life. They were close. And since their parents passed they were even closer. Her one comfort in all of this was that she never had to tell their gentle, sweet parents. They were gone, a year apart, before Ruth reached forty. So there was only Pauline to tell.

Ruth took a shaky breath. Then had to wipe away her sudden tears.

Pauline's eyes were glued on her. Her voice rose by another decibel. 'Ruth, for fuck sake, talk to me.'

Pauline had always had a loud potty-mouth for as long as Ruth could remember. How she managed to control it in her job as a head teacher was a mystery, as outside of it she swore like a trooper. Every other sentence had a swear word.

Ruth held her phone to show Pauline around the living room, then put the camera back on her. 'I'm at Thomas's flat. I've been here since New Year's Eve. I've got a job as a locum GP, and I'll be staying in Bournemouth until the GP I'm covering is back from her maternity leave.'

Pauline began to talk, but she put her hand over her mouth. Ruth could see she was flummoxed and none of this was making sense. Ruth had to tell her.

'I have something to tell you, Pauline, which I never wanted you or anybody to know about. In August last year I had a voicemail from Thomas asking me to go to Bournemouth Crown Court. He didn't want to talk about it over the phone, said we would discuss it when I arrived. He was expecting me to turn up the next day, but I drove down that evening and booked into a hotel for the night, hoping to see him. He didn't reply to my text so I went to the court the next morning. Thomas hadn't arrived when I got there. I met with his solicitor and then his barrister and I was told Thomas was appearing in court to be sentenced. His barrister told me Thomas had pleaded guilty to stealing drugs from the hospital. There was no trial. Thomas was late, and I worried he'd be given a tougher sentence. I tried phoning him, but there was no answer. Then his barrister told me why. The police got in to his flat and found him.

'And that's why Thomas took his life, Pauline. When you asked me what caused it, I couldn't bring myself to tell you all this. I'm here in Bournemouth because my darling boy was accused of a terrible crime, which I know he could never have done.'

Pauline's shoulders were shaking with short jerky movements, her face buried in her hands. Her whole body now heaved a sob, which echoed in her cupped hands. Ruth watched silently, wishing she was there to comfort her. Instead, she had to watch her cry. A minute passed before Pauline wiped her face with her sleeve. Her face was ravaged, her eyes wet with tears.

She sniffed and wiped her nose, using her sleeve again. She breathed slow jerky breaths. She sniffed again, then stretched her eyes and mouth wide to gain control.

Then she gave Ruth a teary smile. 'You beautiful, stupid girl. Don't you know you never had to keep that from me? I loved him, you silly woman. I would never need convincing he was innocent. He was made from the same cloth as you. You only know how to do what is right. So did he.'

The two sisters kept company, mostly staying quiet with soft glances at one another, until they were ready to say goodnight. Ruth had so much to tell her still. About Catherine. About Thomas. About the baby that was due. But that was okay. She'd tell her when they spoke again, which knowing Pauline, would be soon.

CHAPTER TWENTY-THREE

By Wednesday afternoon Ruth felt like she was wading through mud. In a moment of quiet between patients, there was a light knock on the door, interrupting her thoughts, and she was glad when Joan came into the room. 'Well, of all the strangest things,' she said, in a stage whisper, while staring at a white envelope in her hand. 'I've just had a woman come in and hand me this, said she'd been asked to bring it here to give to Thomas's mother. Well, who might that be? I asked.' Her eyes turned to Ruth to convey the punchline of this strangest thing. 'The new doctor, she says.'

Joan was clearly waiting for Ruth to join in the wonder of this strangeness. Ruth couldn't say a thing. Her eyes were fixed on the white envelope. She ignored her brief anxiety from keeping this connection with Thomas a secret. Her entire being filled with an unthinking elation at hearing herself called *Thomas's mother.*

Joan came up to the desk, waving the envelope lightly in front of Ruth's eyes, still waiting for Ruth to respond. 'So what do I do with it? Open it, bin it or stick it in a letterbox? Though it won't go far, being blank.'

Ruth raised her eyes from the envelope to look at Joan. 'I guess you could put it on the desk,' she said quietly. 'Or you could hand it to me.'

Joan gasped, her expression surprised. 'So, it is for you? You didn't mention you have children.'

Ruth noticed the small change in her voice, in her body language, reinforcing her awareness that Joan cared and was now a little hurt. She gave her a sad smile. 'I don't, Joan. Not anymore. Thomas was my son.'

Joan raised a hand to her bosom, and her eyes turned suspiciously bright. She made a little noise in her throat, gave a small cough. Then said, calmly, 'Do you want me to shuffle the rest of your patients to the other doctors? Let you get on home?'

Joan was reacting as if Thomas had just this moment died. 'Joan,' Ruth said in a tone to get her attention. 'There's no need for any of that. I'm fine. I promise you I don't need to go home. I'm actually curious about the person who gave it to you.'

Poor Joan's eyes were flitting around at hearing a normal question. She responded fast. 'Shoulder-length brown hair, about thirty, about five foot five. Pink rain jacket.' She placed the envelope on the desk, looking a little flustered.

Ruth wondered for a moment. 'I don't suppose she was pregnant?'

Joan shook her head, and gave a weighty sigh like she was blowing up a balloon, perhaps thinking her answer was not what Ruth wanted to hear.

'Thanks, Joan,' Ruth replied, at the same time slipping the envelope in a drawer.

'Do you want a cup of tea?' Joan asked.

Ruth nodded. 'Please. Normal tea, if you have it.'

Ruth took a deep steadying breath as Joan went out the door. She was curious to know how this person knew she was Thomas's mother *and* the new doctor there. The only people who would know that, as far as she was aware, were Jed Nolan, because she'd said she was a new GP to the area, maybe some of the ward staff if he then told them, Henry, and Tim Wiley. Unable to wait, she slipped the envelope out of the drawer and opened it, wanting to read it before Joan returned.

She recognised the paper and writing straight away. It was from whoever sent the first letter. The front of this envelope was blank, but it had been hand delivered this time. By a female. So not the doctor, the landlord or the policeman. Unless they'd used their wife or girlfriend or sister. She unfolded the small sheet of paper with the same scraggly edge at the top, torn from a spiral notebook, the same paper as sent before when asking her to come to Bournemouth. It wasn't signed. Like its predecessor, it was a short message.

Dear Thomas's mother,

I'm so glad you decided to come. I had started to give up hope. It has been very difficult imagining you thinking your son was bad. The fact that you're here now reassures me you are here for him. I think the most horrible thing for anyone is not knowing what happened. Please stay.

Ruth was moved by the simple composition. It felt sensitive. The first letter had started with a blunt greeting. *To the mother of Thomas De Luca.* She felt a rise of frustration, wishing she had more to go on than just encouragement to stay. If this person would just talk to her, it would be so much simpler to get to the bottom of it all. They had to know something.

She put the letter away as the door opened – Joan returning with the tea, which she placed down carefully and not too near Ruth's keyboard. She held her hands together lightly across her stomach. 'I'm not going to intrude,' she said, a little primly. 'I know I can look gruff, but I'm a very good listener and I'm very unshockable. That's all I wanted to say.' Then she was gone.

Ruth had a tear in her eye as she picked up the special-looking cup by its delicate handle and took a sip of the tea, before placing it back onto its matching saucer. Some gestures made you cry.

CHAPTER TWENTY-FOUR

Ruth was surprised to find Henry in the house after she closed the front door. He was standing at Kim's open doorway, talking quietly to her, wearing his corduroy jacket. He briefly acknowledged her, turning his head at the sound of her footsteps, then continued his conversation. Ruth carried on quietly up the stairs and was at the top when she heard Kim's door shut. She thought she heard Henry say something. She turned and saw he had his phone in his hand and was looking at the screen. He hadn't been speaking to her. He raised his head unexpectedly, and caught her looking down at him. She felt awkward. As if she'd been spying.

'Sorry, I thought you called something,' she quickly said.

He flicked the back of his hand up at her, in what she supposed was a gesture of denial, though it looked more like *a shooing away.* 'No. You're all right. I was just here for a quick word with one of the tenants.'

'Okay,' she replied, in a breezy tone, when he said nothing more. She turned her back, then went into her flat and quietly shut the door. 'Well, fuck you, Henry Thorpe. You rude man.'

She spent an unsettled evening after that, the flat seeming empty and silent. She heard sounds from above. A TV on – either Akito or Tilly liked it loud. She wasn't sure which one lived in the flat immediately above. She hadn't managed to get a television yet, and wasn't keen to listen to music on her phone. She scrambled eggs in the microwave for supper, which she ate with bread and butter, in favour of the fish pie in the freezer. She then wandered from lounge to bedroom, back to lounge and to the window where she sat and stared out at the rain, until nearly nine when she went for a bath.

Her fingertips were like prunes from lying there too long, thinking about everything and nothing. The purple sea and red-brown sand she saw the first day. Her journey to Bournemouth, the radio on, mind occupied with worry. Faces of old colleagues. Her neighbours. A drawing, made when Thomas was five – her and him, standing on lime-green grass, with a blue cloud and a yellow sun in the sky.

For the first time, she was missing home, missing the familiarity of sounds and smells and views from her window. She was missing her modern two-bed with a not-too-big back garden. Bought while keeping in mind that a small house would be easier to manage when working full time, and bringing up a child alone. It was a house she had grown to like, with lovely dove-grey-painted walls. It had plenty of light, and faced a meadow.

Nothing like Thomas's flat. Lying in the bath, looking up at a stipple ceiling, at a dull light in an opaque encasement, at small turquoise tiles on walls in need of grouting, was depressing. She sat forward and pulled the plug, looping the chain around the tap. She pulled a stripy towel off the back of the door, and hurriedly dried. She was going to make some hot milk and add some whisky, and then climb into bed.

*

Ruth didn't know if it was the dream that woke her, the tot of whisky, or a noise outside the front door. She thought it might have been the dream, and wished it hadn't woken her. It had been so vivid. Thomas sat in the passenger seat of her car and talked the whole journey home to Bath, telling her what happened – how glad he was not to be blamed, how well he would sleep after this, how excited he was for tomorrow to get out and walk and stretch his legs. He would walk for miles, he said.

She stared at the faint light in the hall. She should have closed the bedroom door now that her suitcase was no longer in the way; it was under the bed, her clothes on the shelves of the bookcase in the sitting room. She turned the bedside lamp on and, sleepy-eyed, stumbled to the end of the bed and pulled the door away from the wall, careful not to catch her toes in the process, feeling the resistance as it scraped the carpet. Her hand suddenly dropped, as if she had a stroke, mesmerised by what was on the back of it. A dark blue suit, a pale blue shirt, a tie hanging over them, a pair of black socks bulging from the right jacket pocket. In the left pocket, a brown folded envelope.

She inhaled three shuddering breaths, before she cried out in despair. She gazed at the clothing longingly, knowing without a doubt that he'd put them there ready to wear to court. She lifted one of the sleeves of the jacket and held it to the side of her face, rubbing her cheek against the fabric, then placed it back down, neatly. She reached for the envelope and saw it was for her. *Mum.* In a daze she found her way to his armchair, and sat with the envelope pressed to her breast.

Her boy was going to tell her why he left.

For a long time she sat in the dark watching the rain dribble down the windowpane, too scared to read his last letter to her. She would be with him, feeling what he shared. All his last thoughts. He would be here right beside her. As this was his home, he would have written it here. She turned in the chair and switched on the lamp, then carefully unsealed the envelope. She pulled out a sheaf of papers. Documents, as well as handwritten sheets. Her eyes focused on the handwriting, which was so familiar. She began reading.

Mum,

First, thanks for coming. I'm writing this letter as if tomorrow is already here, when in fact it is still the evening before, but everything I need to say can be said now. I wish I was there right beside you as I know this has come as a horrible shock. I'm so sorry, as you're probably sitting alone in your car, still in the car park, and you have to face a long drive home. I'm so sorry that I didn't talk to you yesterday, instead leaving you a voicemail, but I just wanted you here. I thought it best to write this in case we didn't get a chance to talk. I imagine Mr Cadell has handed it you. Mum, you're probably in shock so why don't you put this letter down and go get a coffee first? You'll see from the car park a hotel almost facing. They have a nice coffee bar there. Go get some and uncramp all that tension you must be feeling right now. A quick walk will do you good. I would love to go with you, but clearly, things have not gone well and I've been taken into custody. I'm hoping it's because they think I'm a flight risk or something like that, and that there will still be a trial.

Ruth raised her shocked face, unable to absorb what she had just read. She could hear her son's voice plainly as she read his words. Her thoughts scattered as she tried to readjust shattered emotions. She had expected it to be a suicide note – his parting words. She rose out of the chair, and moved in a way that was not careful, banging into the wall as she entered the galley kitchen. She clumsily poured whisky in a glass, sloshing some on the counter. Her hand shook as she raised the glass, bumping her lips against her teeth hard before she got a chance to open her mouth. She felt the liquid run down her chin as she swallowed, leaving a slight burn.

Breathing shallowly, she returned to the chair.

I hope you've done that, Mum, but if not, make sure you do before driving home. I need you to look after yourself. This is going to come as a series of shocks. Please forgive me if it sounds like bullet points, but there's a lot of information I need to send your way. Fingers crossed, you won't have to do anything at all. But I have to prepare for either outcome. So here goes.

I was carried off a ward by police officers. I had been on duty. Mercifully, I have no memory of what was, apparently, my very disruptive behaviour. I woke in A&E in the presence of two police officers. When deemed fit, I was arrested for assaulting a security guard. I was taken to a police station. I was offered legal advice, which I declined, as frankly I didn't believe what I was meant to have done. I was put in a cell and given something to eat, then taken to an interview room where I was questioned about any medical conditions, any prescribed medication. Had I taken any medication that day? What food and drink had I consumed? Was it possible I'd taken drugs by accident? Eyewitnesses described my behaviour as verbally and physically aggressive, which resulted in me throwing a security guard to the ground. I couldn't explain my behaviour. I couldn't recall the morning at all. I was taken back to a cell, but a short time later was brought back to the interview room and was informed that a serious concern had come to light. Police officers were speaking with the hospital. Was there anything I might like to tell them? There wasn't. I was then informed my locker had been opened by hospital security and a quantity of hospital medications were found. Could I explain that? I couldn't. After which I was returned to the cell.

I was advised I would be staying, while enquiries continued. I then asked for legal advice. A duty solicitor spoke to me over the phone, advised me not to talk to the police without her present. When she arrived, I'm not sure what I expected. Perhaps someone who would take one look at me and say, 'Don't worry.' She didn't say that. She was direct. I was still being held and the police were still investigating.

During the next interview I asked on what grounds my locker was opened. I was informed a member of staff reported being able to see drugs in my locker. My locker was locked. That might sound strange, but it isn't when I explain. At some point in the past, someone had prised a vent slat wider in order to post something or get something out. It bent the slat upwards. It wasn't wide enough to worry about, you couldn't get fingers through, but it gave a view of the top shelf. Anything of value, I kept at the bottom of the locker, out of sight. The discovery was made by my consultant. Concerned for my welfare after my behaviour, he checked the area where I change, even the rubbish in a bin. He told the police he saw the whole shelf full of drugs. On the basis of that discovery, my flat was searched. The police found an even larger quantity of hospital drugs under my bed. In my locker, a number of syringes were also found.

It was confirmed my locker key and house key were presently with my possessions at the police station, being held by the police, and that I had not lost them. I was informed that certain items of mine, including my phone, were being examined. I told them I didn't take the drugs and couldn't understand how they had been found. Shortly after, I was charged, my fingerprints, photograph, DNA taken, then released on bail and given a date to appear before a magistrates' court.

A week before I was due in court, I met with the solicitor so she could take me through the initial details of the prosecution case. The charges were laid out. It was frightening. 'Contrary to section…' this and that – so many numbers and letters referring to so many different Acts – is a phrase that will stay with me a long time. She didn't sugar-coat the seriousness of the offences, the possible outcomes. I was in a position of trust, in a job where risks to others were high if I failed in my duties. I was on duty when I assaulted a person trying to carry out their duty of protecting others. She showed me the report of a blood specimen taken at the hospital the day I was arrested. Midazolam. Though she read it as A1-hydroxymidazolam. The witness statements from staff on duty were damning, because they all said the same – concern for their personal safety and their patients, fear that I carried a weapon. Pretty heavy, hey, Mum?

Theft of hospital medications, procured so as to go undetected, as the quantity and batch numbers and dates showed they had been taken over a period of time. Data from my phone uncovered three deleted texts from three different contacts. All untraceable. Everyone knows, I'm told, that drug dealers only use burner phones. The conclusion being, dealers must have known my number to do business with me, and that I must have a burner phone somewhere. I admitted to deleting the texts – I thought they were a scam and didn't reply. The police were sceptical, pointing out that as a doctor was I not concerned at being approached three times about drugs. I was concerned, and at some point would have checked it out, but I had other things on my mind then. They expressed no surprise – I was busy building a side business.

The solicitor explained that an early plea might reduce a custodial sentence by a third, as it saves the courts the time and expense of a trial. If the case went to trial and I was found guilty, I would not be open to any reduction of a sentence that an early plea offers, and may well face a maximum sentence for this offence, as this offence hit numerous aggravating factors which could impact on the sentence issued by the judge. She asked if there was anything that might assist my case, suggested I might like to get some character witness statements, preferably from someone like my employer. Not helpful, I have to say. My consultant is already a witness for discovering the drugs.

So, this is what happened. I pleaded guilty at the magistrates' court, was convicted, and due to the seriousness of the offences, was referred to the crown court for sentencing. That is when the clock started ticking. Truly, a miserable time. I needed a barrister that would help get me the shortest sentence, and hired someone good to speak on my behalf. So, I was all set to go along today and expected to be going to prison. Except I discovered something yesterday, and will be changing my plea to not guilty.(By that I mean I discovered something today. Not to confuse you. Just wanted to remind you I'm writing this as if tomorrow is already here.)

So, there you have it. You know as much as I do now, and will know what's happened in court. If you're reading this, I'm still convicted, and can't be with you right now. Perhaps the judge didn't like that I pleaded guilty at the magistrates' court but wouldn't admit to committing any offence.

So, last few things for worst-case scenario. I won't be coming home any time soon.

My bank details and debit card are enclosed, to pay legal costs or whatever.

My flat rent is paid up to the end of September. I should get back the deposit. Henry Thorpe is my landlord. Big ask, if you could pack all my things and take them to Bath with you for safe keeping. Ask Henry if he can mind the bike as it's too big for you to get in your car.

Details of my mobile provider, PIN, etc, are enclosed. Please cancel them. Again, use my account to settle any bills. Also, Netflix, gym membership to cancel.

The man on the top floor, where I live, is called Akito. Please can you give him twenty pounds? I owe it to him from July for a food delivery, and clean forgot. Last thing, which you probably won't want to do, but if you need to stay overnight while sorting out my stuff, stay at the flat. Henry won't mind.

This one – don't overthink it. I want you to visit Catherine Dell. Details are with the other paperwork. Say hello, but then can you look at her with your doctor hat on? It could be the stress of all this, but she passed out the other day. This… her… is the hardest part of all of this. I'm in love, Mum.

Okay, that's about it. You're probably sitting there exhausted. I love you, Mum. Please don't let whatever happens take over your life. Whatever happens will not be forever. This will pass. Love you.

Ruth took in the sound of the rain, her senses working together again as Thomas's voice quietened. She rose from the armchair and went to the window and placed her hand against the cold glass. She listened to the gentle pitter-patter. Everything he had faced. Everything explained. She understood, now, why he pleaded guilty. The evidence said he was guilty. Midazolam in his system supported that. Used for anaesthesia, sedation, trouble sleeping. Fast acting. An extremely small amount could help you chill. A side effect – amnesia. In susceptible individuals, a paradoxical reaction – involuntary movements, verbalisation, uncontrollable crying, disinhibition. Everything explained.

Except for two things. What he had discovered. And what she was stuck on – his end behaviour. Staying positive. His suit hung ready. His letter to her. His intentions. Nothing to suggest he had given up hope.

So why did he kill himself?

CHAPTER TWENTY-FIVE

Rosie stared with a hopeful look in her eyes at her image in the mirror. She was conscious of the effort it took to not lose that look. She felt peculiar, as if something had taken place inside of her at some time during the night. She had dreamed of when she was at her happiest – falling into bed tipsy and giggly with Anabel telling her to shut up and go to sleep, while snuggling into her back, sharing her bed like best friends did. She had woken and felt like she was someone different, and felt a flutter of nerves as a thought popped into her head – *Anabel would like this Rosie.*

She turned away and continued getting ready. She pulled on a pair of black fleecy leggings and a warm black hoody over the thermal vest. On her feet she put on warm socks, and then her Uggs, the only footwear that ever kept her feet truly warm. She then picked up the rucksack she'd tossed on the bed earlier, dug out from the wardrobe. It wasn't her usual brightly coloured one, but charcoal-grey.

Taking it to the small kitchen table, she put in the items she got ready before getting dressed. A flask of coffee, some bags of crisps, a bagel, gone slightly hard, and a couple of triangular cheeses. In a side pocket she put a can of lemon Fanta. In the front pocket, her purse, phone, earbuds, keys, gloves, thermal hat. She then put on her padded jacket. It covered her thighs and would keep out the cold as it was filled with feathers. She was ready. She turned the light off and opened her front door, closing it quietly behind her.

She walked purposely to the end of her road and turned right. It would be a pleasant walk with roads still quiet and houses still asleep. A normal Thursday morning. By the time she reached her destination she expected she would see the odd light on in a window. While she walked she tried to recall whether there were trees or bushes in the garden that might obscure windows. She seemed to remember steps going up to the house, and a side entrance with a glass back door. There was definitely a bus shelter opposite, which couldn't be a more perfect a place to sit. Even better if the windows had plenty of coverage from posters and timetables. She would then have somewhere she could legitimately sit all day without being seen. The road, as she recalled, had houses only along one side. It really couldn't be better. A bus shelter placed in a perfect spot, with only the sea to watch her.

She was enjoying this walk. The anticipation of finding Anabel was making her nerves giddy. 'Ready or not, here I come,' she sang softly, as she passed parked cars, turning her head fast to look in the space between them, as if ready to frighten a child playing hide and seek. She was being silly. Probably from the thought of seeing how shocked Anabel would be. Rosie hoped it would be a nice shock.

The cold air on her face was refreshing. She should walk more often in the cold and dark. It was the best time to think. She suspected Anabel's mum spent every night in the dark wondering where her daughter was, and if she was coming home. It was cruel of Anabel, really, to put her mother through that. *Please find her, Rosie*, the poor woman had asked.

Rosie would tell Anabel off for that. She had a mum who cared deeply and she was sending her to an early grave, shaving years off the woman's life, by letting her worry like this. *Not on, Anabel. You're not meant to be heartless.* Rosie was going to tell Anabel that.

She was going to tell Anabel to her face that what she did last New Year's Eve was wrong. The problem was, Rosie had not addressed Anabel's behaviour in the past. She had let her get away with it. Pretended not to notice when Anabel tried to outshine her, to oust her from happiness, even from her own home. Anabel had loved the fact that Rosie's parents loved having her visit them, and she would visit even when Rosie wasn't there. If Rosie had been of a weaker mind, she would have ended up as a depressed child. Then after what happened, Rosie had to rise above the pettiness, she'd had to be the stronger person. Because Anabel could not come to terms with what she had done, instead she ran away. Just like she was doing now.

Rosie sometimes wondered if Anabel would have been better if she had become a nun. She could exist in a world where every day she could go to confession and cleanse herself of sin. Rosie wished she'd suggested this when they were only thirteen. It would have made Anabel's life so much easier, and hers in the end. Their next birthdays they would be twenty-eight. They were unmarried, single, without children, without ever being engaged, or living with anyone in a meaningful relationship. Rosie didn't need to question why.

Their secret stopped them from living their lives.

Anabel was right, and it wasn't really a threat, it was a fact. *It's not going to go away.* Unless one of them told it. It was with them forever.

It had taken till now for Rosie to realise it. They should have let what happened end their friendship when they were thirteen.

Rosie arrived at her destination clear-headed, the sea behind her still dark, the waves glowing as they rolled over. Her soul had not been quiet and peaceful for so long. An empty space inside was soothed. She enjoyed feeling her body relax, turn languid. She gave no apology for what she was about to do. It was with calmness she was going to help them and not with anger anymore. Whatever happened would be done out of love, for a friendship that was forced to survive because it had to carry a secret. A secret that broke Anabel. Rosie had to take responsibility for that. It was her father who had died. She should have owned up to what happened. She was doing something she should have done a long time ago – setting Anabel free.

CHAPTER TWENTY-SIX

The last two days Ruth had kept herself stupidly busy and was exhausted. She winced as if in pain, and had to breathe hard and not move for a second.

Pauline grumbled behind her. 'Don't stop walking, or I'll drop the fucking lot.'

Ruth felt her mouth grin. She could be dying right now, yet all it would take is for Pauline to say, *I'll drop the fucking lot,* and she would feel so much better. She *made* Ruth grin. That was about the fifth swear word out of her mouth in the last minute. Determined to stay a little happy, she tried to shove the disagreeable thoughts of Thomas to the back of her mind and carried Pauline's suitcase up the stairs.

She should have waited until she had more facts. In a matter of days she would have a more complete picture than the one given by Thomas. Yesterday, the replies to emails she sent poured in. Apple agreed to assistance that she no longer required – Thomas had beaten them to it, providing her with his PIN and password, but it had been kind of them to respond. The bank sent a respectful reply and would close Dr De Luca's account upon receiving evidence of her identity and relationship to Thomas, and the death certificate. The hospital sent condolences and invited her to go and see them. Christine Pelham had a window in her diary for three o'clock Monday, if Ruth would like to see her then.

She should have waited and not looked. Left well alone, and waited patiently instead. She would then have not seen what was on his phone. Being hasty, she went through his texts and found the one he should never have sent – the phrasing of which sounded an extra alarm bell for Ruth.

It sounded cold and dismissive. And while it wasn't exactly saying she was 'asking for it', there was a slight echo of that in this phrase.

You wanted it, we had sex. Nothing more.

No wonder he'd been cautious of the police seeing it. There was no other interpretation. He was justifying having sex like he was doing the nurse a favour. But to then cast her as wanton? Couldn't he have lent some dignity to the situation, used the 'it's not you, it's me' excuse, to let her down gently? Instead, he had sent a blunt message.

Ruth recognised the number. She had phoned it enough times. She was not surprised, of course, after what Jed Nolan revealed. It was the nurse's phone number. The number for the woman Ruth had been trying to contact since coming here.

Had *she* phoned the police about Thomas because he hurt her feelings? Ruth wasn't trying to come up with a reason the police shouldn't have been called – if they were needed it was the right thing to do. But she couldn't help thinking there was a motive other than the safety of staff and patients behind it. Thomas sent that message to the nurse, and in the contacts on his mobile he put her name down as *Don't Answer*. Ruth would rather not have known. She didn't want to ever feel anything but love for her son, didn't want her memories of him changed. She couldn't undo what she'd seen, or stop this slow crawl of shame.

In the flat, Pauline plonked her bags down and took a quiet wander around the rooms. She returned briefly to fetch one of the bags and quickly disappeared again. Ruth stayed in the sitting room and waited to be called, as knowing her sister she was preparing a surprise.

On a corner of the bath was a lit tealight in a glass holder, its scent already sweetening the air. It had black calligraphy on the glass that she would look at later. Her sister pointed to it. 'Well,' she said in her head teacher's voice. 'That's to let him know it's not just any naked woman in his bath. It's his aunt, so he'd better keep his eyes shut.'

Ruth was touched. Pauline had come to terms with where her nephew had died with gentle humour.

'Do you fancy a cuppa?' she now asked.

Pauline looked askance at the offer. 'Fuck, no, I haven't broken my back carrying bottles up here to drink tea. We'll save that for the morning. You grab the pillows from your bed while I pour us some wine, because I'm not sitting on a hard chair all evening and I'm not sitting on the floor without something to cushion this bony arse. Why the fuck hasn't Thomas got more than one armchair?'

Ruth laughed, already loving having her sister there. She had turned up with only a half hour warning after texting for the postcode. She hugged the thought that Pauline would be there all weekend and didn't want to rush one minute of it away. She was enjoying every second, listening to her now talking to herself in the kitchen.

'What the fuck are you meant to do in here? Apart from barely breathe it's so small. Ruth, where's your glasses, before I empty out the fucking coffee jar to use?'

Ruth went to the kitchen and rescued her, letting the loveliness of her soak in. Together they set out all the delicious goodies she'd brought with her. Crusty white bread and soft cheeses, smoked salmon and fat black olives, and a vine of sweet tomatoes. For afters, dark chocolate to sup with their wine. It was a feast, a celebration of their love for each other and for the boy they had loved with all their heart.

Seemingly in a blink, their first evening passed and was nearly over. Ruth, first to admit a need for sleep, kissed her sister's cheek and told her she'd be sharing her bed. She left Pauline sitting up in the armchair with Thomas's diary in her lap. She deserved to have this close time with him. She'd been part of the boy's life since he was a baby. She deserved to feel the same comfort Ruth gained from reading his words.

*

Saturday was a perfect day for walking. White clouds covered the sky and kept the air warm. They started at Bournemouth Pier and walked along the beach to Sandbanks, one of the most expensive places to live in England. Millionaires Row in Dorset was made up of just thirteen houses. The waterfront mansions in the peninsular left no room for more to be built. The houses went for millions, and one property there was once owned by John Lennon. It was a stunning place to live with uninterrupted views of the south coast and Poole Harbour.

Ruth glanced at her sister and saw her face concentrated in thought. She'd been quiet for most of the walk, but that was her normal pattern in the morning, more so after drinking. She would rally somewhere around teatime and want to party all over again. Their plan was to have lunch in Sandbanks, at a pub preferably, where they could sit awhile before taking the four-mile walk back.

Pauline glanced at her. 'When was the last time you had your hair cut?'

Ruth grimaced. 'Probably last March or thereabouts. Why? Is it awful?'

Pauline shook her head. 'No, but there's no point having it long if you're only going to wear it up.'

Pauline was right, she did mostly have her hair tied back. It kept it off her face, especially in the wind. Otherwise it could blow in her eyes like it had when she'd got out of the car on Monday.

She'd forgotten about that, how she'd become aware of somebody possibly following her. She inspected her sister's hair – a lighter shade of blonde than hers, and layered to shoulder length. It suited Pauline, so it would probably suit her too as they had similar shaped faces. At fifty-two Pauline was aging well. She had a face that could look plain at times and then suddenly quite stunning. But today her skin looked tired, a little grey.

'You're right. I should do something with it.'

'You should,' she replied, sounding unexpectedly firm. 'You're still in your forties, and you don't need telling you're a catch. You're like what's her fucking face in that film we like. Adaline. You never age. You've got bosoms and curves, while I got the angles of a fucking ironing board.'

Ruth felt slightly worried. There was an undercurrent of anger in Pauline's voice. 'What's up? You sound strange. Is everything all right with you and Nigel?'

Pauline sniffed as if her nose was wet, and shook her head. 'Nigel is a wonderful man, as ever. I've been so lucky. When we couldn't have kids I wondered what the future held. Twenty-five years on and I'm still happy.' She smiled a little then. 'It helps that the fucker has a brain of his own and stays out of my way when I need me time.'

Ruth grinned, relieved nothing was wrong. She shoulder bumped her sister, sending her nearly into the path of a man running by. 'You're such a bitch,' she called lightly. 'Now, to get back to the subject of getting my hair cut, it might have to be on the agenda soon anyway.' She gave Pauline a sly smile. 'If I don't want it pulled, or getting sticky fingers stuck in it.'

Pauline came to a stop as if poleaxed, her mouth hanging open. She gazed at Ruth's waistline. Ruth felt a momentary sadness that she was quick to hide. This joyful moment was not about her being a mother, but it was the next best thing. She stepped in front of her sister and took her face in her hands. 'Thomas's baby. You're going to have a great-nephew soon.'

'Oh my God,' she exclaimed, her eyes like saucers in her shocked face. And then louder, in a shout that carried across to the people standing at the fringe of the sea. 'Oh my God! I'm going to be a great-aunt!'

Lunch became a celebration and they shared a bottle of champagne. Pauline wanted to know everything. Who she was, what she was like, the whole story. Ruth told her everything she had learned so far about Thomas, and only finished talking as they came to the end of their walk back. It had done Ruth the power of good. Spending a day outside walking this stunning coastline, breathing in the sea air, and having Pauline to confide in.

*

Ruth scrutinised herself in the mirror and was glad she'd had a nap after the celebratory lunch. The sleep had sobered her. Otherwise they would not be going out again. She was taking Pauline to the same Indian restaurant she went to with Henry. It was an easy decision, and would round off the day nicely. Almost ready, Ruth's lipstick ended up on her cheek. She turned shocked eyes at her sister standing in the bathroom doorway. Hardly believing what she'd just heard.

'What did you say?'

'I said, would you like a cup of tea?'

Ruth waited for the punchline, but Pauline's eyes were serious. So was her voice. She wasn't joking. Her blouse only half buttoned was hanging out of her jeans. She looked tired.

Ruth stared at her concerned. 'Don't you want to go out?'

Pauline shook her head. 'I want to talk to you instead. I *need* to talk you. I can't…'

Her eyes squeezed shut. Her hand was hard against her mouth. Ruth let the lipstick roll out of her hand into the sink, immediately worried. Her instincts all day had been telling her something was wrong. Pauline drank more than she usually did. Her mood had been off, her earlier quietness and the anger in her voice. Something was wrong. She gazed at her sister. 'Hey, what's going on? You can talk to me about anything. What do you need to tell me?'

Pauline shook her head. 'We're not having this chat in the bathroom. I'm going to make some tea, and then we'll sit down.'

Ruth had been sat on the bed, waiting quietly while Pauline made the tea. It was now poured and waiting for her. She had butterflies in her stomach as she joined Pauline in the sitting room. Pauline was sat cross-legged beneath the windowsill. Ruth sat in Thomas's armchair, and saw her tea beside her on the small table. She would leave it to cool awhile.

Pauline raised her head. She looked exhausted. Not just tired. She looked in pain.

Ruth's stomach churned. She didn't know if she was strong enough to hear more bad news. She was terribly afraid Pauline was going to say she was ill.

Pauline shifted on the floor, and breathed in harshly. 'This isn't fucking fair,' she said quietly. Her gaze was intense. She badly wanted to tell Ruth something.

Ruth quietly observed, then it hit her. Pauline needed permission, because this was going to hurt Ruth. 'Pauline, just tell me. Because this isn't fair either. Just say whatever it is.' Her voice was deliberately firm, what Pauline needed. Ruth saw her calming already.

She had pulled herself together. Ruth now just had to listen.

Her voice was quietly composed. No longer laden with heavy emotion. 'I want you to know, I love you, and I would do anything to not have to say this. Give an opinion on something so private. You must have known, I would have thought something when you gave it to me. I can't leave without telling you my thoughts, after reading Thomas's diary.'

Ruth took slow breaths, her chest barely moving. Pauline glanced at her. Ruth forced herself to nod for Pauline to continue.

'I think something perhaps got out of hand with the woman Thomas slept with. The subtext… The way he says things. I'm picking up on something dark. It sounds like it wasn't normal sex. It sounds like he…' She broke off, and shook her head. 'Christ, this is so hard. Look, let's leave it there. I'm so sorry I had to say any of this.'

'Finish what you couldn't say,' Ruth said quietly.

'I can't,' she protested.

'Well, let me say it for you then. Like he went too far.' The eyes staring out of her face had dulled. She stood up and moved past Pauline as if unseeing. 'I'm going for a walk.'

Pauline jumped up to stop her leaving. 'Don't leave like this. *Please.* You need to talk.'

'There is nothing to say,' Ruth replied in a hollow voice. 'You said it all.'

Pauline's eyes suddenly flared. 'For Christ's sake, Ruth. Don't leave me feeling the bad guy. You fucking gave me the diary to read. You must have known I would have thought that.' She stared at her sister beseechingly, until something she suddenly realised made her gasp. 'Oh for fuck sake,' she cried in despair. 'You haven't read it the way I did.'

'I'm going for a walk,' Ruth said again. 'I'll see you later.'

'Let me come with you, Ruth,' Pauline pleaded.

'No,' she replied. Her voice was distant, tired. 'I need to think about my son. I need to be on my own to do that.'

*

Ruth returned to the flat at midnight and Pauline was sitting up waiting, still in the same state of dress she'd been in hours before when standing in the bathroom doorway. Her blouse not fully buttoned. Ruth went into the bedroom and came back to her with Thomas's letter. She handed it to her wordlessly and went to bed.

She wanted to tell Pauline everything would be all right, but she couldn't. How could she when everything kept getting worse?

Her beliefs about her son were being sorely tested. Her beautiful memories of him being rocked. She wanted to turn back time and she couldn't. She couldn't undo what she now knew. She was in too deep and could only go forward and discover more things.

Crowding her mind was the overwhelming fear that Pauline might be right. And that Ruth might need to prepare herself for a darker truth about her son.

CHAPTER TWENTY-SEVEN

The sisters were preparing to say goodbye. Pauline's car was already packed, but she'd come back upstairs for a final check for anything missed. She was leaving more behind than she was taking. A fridge full of food, a half dozen bottles of wine, a bottle of Jack Daniel's, some nice smellies in the bathroom and some paperbacks left by the bed for Ruth to read.

She grabbed Ruth in a fierce hug and pressed her face into her neck. 'Let me say this quickly, and please don't think I'm only saying it to make you feel better. I sat up all night and read every page of his diary again. I then read his letter. I was wrong, Ruth. No matter what I thought initially I know I was wrong. Thomas would never have done harm to anybody, let alone a woman.'

Ruth tried to pull away. 'It's all right, Pauline. I understand.'

Pauline gently shook her. 'No, listen to me. I was wrong, I'm telling you. I'm a teacher, Ruth, and I read every page again. The nuances of his internal monologue showed something different, or rather it highlighted something. There was no anger or hatred of this woman coming off those pages. There was only despair. Anxiety. Fear.'

Ruth wasn't convinced. She hadn't told Pauline about the text message. The bluntly worded message Thomas sent. She hadn't told her what she had felt from reading those words. The slow crawl of shame that was blunting her love for him. 'Maybe,' she said in half-hearted way, in an attempt to stop Pauline talking.

'No! Not maybe!' Pauline's voice rose with urgency. 'Ruth, when he says how bad he feels, it's a passage four lines long, that's poorly punctuated, without capital letters in some place. I think he was drunk while writing it. Put in full stops and commas, it says something completely different. I think his thoughts were just streaming out without pause. He was just fast-talking to himself. Read it again.'

'When did he say he felt bad?' Ruth asked, in a dispirited voice.

Pauline eased back and gazed at her. 'You need to read all of it.'

Ruth gave a slow shake of her head. 'I keep putting things in the way,' she quietly answered. When really she hadn't been able pick it up again. Not while her heart was at war with her mind.

'When I'm gone, read it. Read the entries in April. You'll see what I mean.'

'So you think he didn't do anything wrong?'

Pauline shook her head. 'I think he pissed someone off. What happened to him was an annihilation. The way I see it, he either stumbled across someone committing a crime and they knew, or a psycho targeted him. And I mean that, Ruth, so be careful. You're a doctor, you know the most dangerous thing about this individual is that you can't spot them.'

The sisters hugged warmly to say goodbye, and Pauline gave her last parting advice. 'Stay alert. Question everything twice. Someone knows you're looking into this. That copper for a start. And Thomas's landlord. Plus that wanker of a doctor. And then you have the mysterious letter writer. And the nurse you can't track down. One of these people will know something. For all you know the consultant could be the guilty fucker. He found the drugs. Your woman downstairs. You say she's a nurse, and likely to be dabbling in drugs. Is she selling or receiving? If selling, where's she getting her stash from? She lives below you. Do you know if she has a spare key to this flat? She might have come up here and put the drugs under Thomas's bed. Interesting that her main observation of the police was them taking away the sports bag. I'm leaving you a lot to think about. But that's what you've got to do, Ruth. Think all of it through.'

The two sisters moved out to the tiny hall. Pauline gave a sad smile. 'Right, I'm off. Just one last thing to do.' She opened the bathroom door. Then, as if Thomas was standing there, she said to him, 'Look after her till I get back and don't be sulking about what I said. I love you, you big lump, so see you soon.'

Moments later she was gone and the flat was quiet again. It was still morning. Ruth knew she would go stir-crazy if she stayed there all day alone. She fetched a warm jacket and put on her trainers. She was going for another walk, but this time she would pay attention to where she walked. If asked where she went last night for the best part of five hours, she could only say the sea. The only images she could recollect was the expanse of the beach and sea and the long path she took, and a carrier bag being swept along by the wind. She kept track of it the whole way, occasionally thinking its journey ended as snagged on a bramble, then it would take off again, ahead of her all the way until she reached the point where she had to turn back. Today, she would have a wander around the shops and streets and see a bit of life going on. She hadn't dismissed what Pauline asked her to do. She was taking the diary with her to read when she stopped for a coffee.

Kim was sitting on the wall when Ruth came out the front door. She hadn't spoken to her for a week, and hadn't seen her apart from a glimpse when she was talking to Henry at her door. Kim looked like she was going to ignore her, so Ruth decided to talk first.

'Kim, can I talk to you?'

Kim looked surprised, and gave a noncommittal shrug.

Ruth took that for a yes. 'I could see last time we spoke that I'd upset you, by not telling you what I did. You probably thought it was arrogant of me. I just want to say sorry. I didn't set out to deceive you, it would just have sounded strange me saying it then. Like I was being flippant, I suppose.'

Kim gave her an appraising look, then raised her eyebrows and let out a deep sigh. 'The trouble with you doctors is you forget you're allowed to be ordinary. You don't have to be on your guard twenty-four/seven. I get that when you mention it, people probably start telling you their problems. You won't get it from me.' She pulled a funny face, distorting her features in a mimicry of death, tongue poking out the side of her mouth, eyes fixed open. Then smiled normally. 'Unless I'm croaking it, of course. Then yours is the first door I'm banging.'

Ruth smiled in return. 'I will remember that. I'm off to the shops. Do you want anything while I'm out?'

'No. I'm good, thanks. I'm going out myself soon.' She hopped down off the wall. 'I'm glad you told me, because I've wanted to say to be careful of that copper that was here.'

Ruth scrutinised her, wondering what she was getting at. 'Why?'

She pulled a different face this time, her mouth twisted. 'Odd, that's why. Something odd. I can feel it.'

It was Ruth's turn to sigh. 'I'll bear it in mind. Thanks, Kim.'

*

Mid-afternoon, Ruth exited a small tourist shop, pleased with her purchases of teas and biscuits. She'd had free tea given to her every day at work and wondered if everyone put money in a pot. She'd be happy to do that, but in the meantime would bring in her contribution and hand it to Joan to add to the supplies. She settled her shopping into one bag and was about to walk on when a fat raindrop landed on her nose. She looked up and saw that the heavens were about to open. She pulled her hood up and hurried in the direction of the pub. It made sense to go there as it was only a street away. The fact that it was Catherine's pub should make no difference. She wasn't there this time to watch for her, but to shelter from the rain.

Ruth ordered a falafel wrap and a glass of white wine at the bar, then made herself comfortable at a table in a corner, sitting facing the wall so it felt more private. She started to read the entries from the beginning of April, and was pleasantly surprised by his opening sentence.

1 April

Today is why I became a doctor. For patients like Molly. She puts everything into perspective. She's a professor of English and is 39 and is dying. She told me, you don't need a long life to have lived. You just need to have lived all your yesterdays. She inspires me and makes me grateful. This page is for you, Molly, so when I look back I'll remember today.

Ruth was glad she was facing the wall. She forgot how hard this would be. What rubbish it was to say words can never hurt you. Words could tear your heart apart. People used them every day to destroy one another. Someone in the world right now saying *I don't love you anymore*. Words had always had power. Otherwise, every time someone told someone their loved one was dead, it wouldn't hurt. They were just words. She took a sip of wine and calmed herself.

2 April

Smashed it in theatre today. Mr Mason actually congratulated me. Well executed, he said. Now feel a bit punch-drunk so falling into bed right now.

3 April

My phone went missing today. Jed said I didn't put it where I said I did, which was on the shelf by the scrub sink. I know I did, because I always put it in the same place. Only it wasn't there. It was on top of my locker. I hope he's not playing silly buggers with me. I'm too tired at the moment for games. Woke up feeling like I hadn't slept in a month. Went for a run after work to get some energy. Need to be fresher by tomorrow. Mr Mason's first patient is going to take up half the day. At least I've got tomorrow evening to look forward to.

4 April

What the fuck is going on? My phone went missing again. It's got to be her! I thought she'd gone quiet and all was forgiven. Now she's playing with my head. Jed suggested I'm burning the candle at both ends. Then Mason suggested the same. I've had enough of being patronised. She was off duty when I found it in a drawer! But tomorrow I'm having it out with her. Patients' notes and now my phone. She's trying to get me to react. I know she is.

Ruth stopped reading as a plate of food was placed down in front of her. She moved her wine glass out of the way as the man put down cutlery. She thanked him, relieved it was not the woman serving her, as she'd rather not have to get into a conversation if recognised. She just wanted to sit quietly and read.

5 April

Jesus H Christ. She cried. I mean, really cried. I asked her outright if she took it, and she didn't deny it, she just cried. To make matters worse she then starts telling people trying to comfort her that she doesn't think he meant to. Things just got out of hand. He's nice really! What the fuck! Is she telling them about our night in bed or what I just said to her in private? I'm so tired I can't even think straight and now I'm picking up shitty vibes from work colleagues. Thank God Mason wasn't there.

6 April

Don't have energy to write. drunk Mason suggested went home after morning list looked heavy eyed at table. euphemism I think he wanted say looked hungover. Well wrong not drank since January… feel bad what I done to her – am horrible man didn't mean anything just frustration things out of hand. fuck sake nicking now please get over it!!!

Ruth sat back in the chair, putting distance between her and the book on the table. Her pulse started to pound in her temple, her heart rate keeping pace with it. This was the passage Pauline was talking about. It was worse than Ruth imagined. She shuddered. She didn't know how Pauline could be so sure. Punctuate it, she said. Ruth wasn't ready to even try. Maybe in an hour or two or in a month's time she'd write it out on a clean piece of paper. Pretend like she was in a classroom doing an exercise in grammar. Then it might not seem so stark. She breathed fast, too much air, and couldn't slow it down. The wall in front of her and the noise behind made her feel she was back on that corridor with nowhere to run. No way to avoid not knowing. She gasped and air whistled into her lungs. Quickly, before she lost more control, she reached for her glass and gulped the wine. She gasped again, this time able to take a fuller breath. She concentrated on that. She had to sort herself out before she could leave. She breathed again.

How could Pauline change her mind? Ruth wanted to be that sure. But at the moment she was having trouble seeing him as the person she knew. And that was killing her. If in the process of clearing his name something more fundamental was destroyed, then for her the word Pauline used was the right one – annihilation.

Her joy at being his mother for twenty-five years would no longer exist. She would lose her son for the second time. There would be no coming back from that. Not for her. There were mothers and fathers who had lost far more, suffered far more and stood back up again. She knew that to be true. She knew also that it could never be like that for her. He'd been the centre of her world from the moment he was born. The only light she still had was the brightness of knowing such love. If something took that away, she would lose every part of him forever. He would be lost in the moment that light was snuffed out. Leaving a place of dark where she would never know it or feel it again.

CHAPTER TWENTY-EIGHT

For four days, Rosie had been watching. Seeing the same things. Bedroom curtains drawing back in the mornings, lights out. Then the reverse in the evenings, lights on, curtains drawn across. Miss Tupperware was as predictable as night follows day. Everything she did was precise. Rosie witnessed the same behaviours at the same times every day. At the kitchen window at six o'clock washing up. Outside the back door ten minutes later to place her bag of rubbish in the bin. Not throwing her rubbish in either, but placing it, tucking it down nicely to make it look neat. Back in the kitchen at seven thirty, her hair slicked down, wearing a fluffy dressing gown with wide lapels. Reaching in to the same wall cupboard to take something out, then putting it back, and a moment later exiting the kitchen with a mug in her hand. No doubt her nightly routine – bath and Ovaltine or whatever she drank. The dullness of her would kill Rosie if she was subjected to it day after day.

Each morning she had come out of the back door at exactly the same time. At six fifty she locked it, then drove off in her clean little car, her hair up in a bun, her clothes like an M&S advert. Only in a bad way. Like she picked all old age clothes. Blouses that weren't meant to be worn by someone her age, done up to the top, and skirts worn down past her knees. She wasn't much older than her and Anabel, yet she dressed like a prissy spinster, easily shockable by anything in the slightest bit revealing.

She'd then return at the same time each day, clearly from her job. The first day Rosie had been surprised, as her character suggested she'd be far too finicky to carry germs into her home. But she wore her nurse's uniform in the house after finishing work. Rosie was betting she was a terrible nurse, the patients probably too afraid to leave anything in a bedpan in case she wrinkled her nose. The minutes she spent tidying her car each day, after getting out of it, was insane. The sleek little car had to be left perfect. Wiping the driver's seat, then little marks off the windscreen and then around the mudguards. The woman should have chosen a better colour if she wanted it to stay this clean. If Anabel was in that home and wasn't dead, it wouldn't be long before she was. No one could survive someone this boring.

Rosie reached into her bag of sweets and pulled out another jelly. A collection of sweet wrappers littered the ground at her feet in the bus shelter, deliberately left so she could see the pile growing each day from the effort of her vigil. She sucked hard, rinsing her teeth with the sweetness, tempted to give up, to persuade herself Anabel wasn't there. After all, she had no proof. Her watching hadn't shown a single movement at the windows during the day. It was possible Anabel was in a room at the back of the house, watching telly or reading a book, but surely she would go into the kitchen sometimes?

She popped another sweet in her mouth and picked up her rucksack, preparing for a wet walk home, when something crossed her vision fast. A bright pink shape dashing to get to the small car, then disappearing inside it, as the car door opened and shut. This was the first evening the woman had gone out. Perhaps for church, it being a Sunday. Worn for the rain, the pink jacket was waterproof to the max. It couldn't have been Anabel wearing the rain jacket, because she didn't drive. But it was Anabel's jacket. Rosie was one hundred per cent sure. Anabel had bought it at a shop in Ringwood and wore it every day, loving its raspberry pinkness. Rosie watched the car tail lights disappear and then she crossed the road.

A light left on in the hall shone through the glass pane of the front door on to stone steps leading up to the house. Rosie bypassed the front door and then the bins by the side door until a gate stopped her going further. It blocked her view of the back garden. It was tall and locked, but not so high she couldn't climb over, she just needed to be quiet about it. This is where Rosie liked being thin, and agile as well. She grabbed the top of the gate and put her left foot on the metal latch, and then in one fluid movement she was up, over and dropping to the ground on the other side. She made hardly a sound, just a small creak from the gate.

The back garden was dark, with no light shining out on it. She edged her way around the house and came to the first window – a small square of frosted glass, which Rosie recalled being the downstairs loo. She could remember a white toilet roll on a shelf, one half of a sheet folded back and tucked into the hollow centre, like it was done in a hotel. The weirdest thing was, Rosie had gone to the loo as they were leaving, so did Miss Tupperware go in after every person to redo it?

Rosie stepped back and looked up at the windows. The two rooms were in total darkness. She could see an outline of roller blinds partially pulled down. She moved to the last window – the patio doors – and looked inside. The curtains were pulled back, and light leaked into the room from the hall allowing her to see the furniture. This was the room where they'd had the Tupperware party. She tried the door first, but no luck. She pulled her mobile out of her pocket, swiped down the screen, and tapped on the flashlight icon. She wanted to see the room in more detail, just in case Anabel was lying still on a couch. Or hiding in a corner. She relaxed and let the full beam shine into the room. Nobody was in there. It was tidy, but not in perfect order as expected. There were things on the coffee table and on the small dining table against the wall. The cushions needed straightening and magazines left on the sofa needed to be tidied away.

Rosie shone the light on the coffee table. Nail polish bottles and cotton pads and nail polish remover. On the dining table there was a mug, a woollen garment and some loose pens on paper. She aimed the beam around the floor and could see nothing belonging to Anabel. No kicked-off footwear or identifiable bag. She turned away, walking back to the gate, preparing for the climb back over. There, she stopped. Instinct turned her around and she returned to look in at the coffee table again.

Nail polish remover and nail polishes, and standing alone an even smaller bottle, something Rosie recognised. Dark glass and white chunky childproof cap. She couldn't make out the colour of the label or writing, but had an idea it would say something along the lines of how it stopped nail biting. It could be that Miss Tupperware had the same habit as Rosie. Or it could be it was being used to break another bad habit. It had a vile taste. Like earwax, but more bitter. Rosie should know. She had tried it. And now, she suspected, it was being used to stop Anabel sucking her thumb.

Her initial excitement at seeing it suddenly dwindled. It felt like nothing important anymore. She felt sad at the thought of this being done to Anabel. But more so, anxious. She didn't think it a good idea her being made to lose her comfort by someone who didn't know her, who wouldn't understand how sensitive she was right now. Anabel had a lot on her mind. The woman should make an allowance for the habit, and put off any changes for now.

Rosie leaned her forehead against the glass and looked in at the comfortable home. She was almost convinced Anabel was somewhere in this house. But why? Was it because Anabel was scared after receiving that note? Was it to have somewhere neutral where she could decide on Rosie's future? Was it because she had a new best friend?

If this was why she was there, then this nurse would know why Anabel had run away. She would know the police were looking for Anabel. So would she hide her?

Rosie had a bad feeling about this. She felt it in the pit of her stomach. Her first thought when she saw her washing hanging out on New Year's Eve was that it was Anabel. Rosie's bad feelings increased. Her mind crowding with dark thoughts of darker possibilities that might well be true. Anabel might not be acting alone. She might have found a friend to help. Was it remotely possible all of it was staged to frighten Rosie? Even down to Anabel sending herself that note? Anabel knew Rosie's home better than anyone else. She might have known the back door didn't lock. She came in that way sometimes.

Rosie wished she could be sure Anabel was safe, that something would give her that reassurance. That would take away the horrible thoughts of Anabel. Because if Anabel was innocent in this, it left another possibility – this nurse, for some reason, wanted Anabel in her home. She was giving Anabel safe refuge, but maybe she was just keeping her close.

Rosie acted without thinking. She tapped the glass door three times. The sound, loud outside, would be loud enough to be heard inside. Anabel would be like a scared cat right now.

Rosie waited and listened. Then gave a defeated sigh. 'I know you're in there,' she whispered.

The house remained quiet. Rosie's shoulders slumped as she walked away.

CHAPTER TWENTY-NINE

Christine Pelham had changed a bit since August last year. Her hair was nicely styled and had been treated to a good colour rinse, bringing in some warm caramel tones. She was wearing stylish footwear – block heel lace-up black shoes that Ruth would happily wear herself. Her manner had also improved. She placed down a cafetière of coffee that Ruth was looking forward to tasting, inviting her to help herself to the brown sugar lumps and the small jug of milk. She then sat at her desk, where a space had been cleared to give them an uninterrupted view. Otherwise, they would have been trying to see each other over a small mountain of files.

Ruth sat in a comfortable tub chair, thinking about the solicitor. There was something different about her, other than her appearance, more to do with the aura around her that showed in her eyes. A calmness.

'You seem changed,' Ruth said, deciding she would be frank.

Christine Pelham gave a small nod. 'You can see that with your doctor's eyes?'

Ruth shrugged. 'I don't know. Perhaps. There seems something settled about you.'

The solicitor gave her an appreciative smile. 'Well, your observations are correct, and also quite remarkable given we only met briefly and under tremendously stressful circumstances.' She paused. Then, making a decision, she reached for a silver photograph frame from among the things on her desk. She turned it round to show Ruth a fair-haired boy. His top two baby teeth were missing in his wide smile. 'My son, Toby. He's just turned five. Last summer he had an accident. He was hit by a car. He'd been playing outside, going up and down the pavement on his scooter while my husband was packing the car. He wasn't aware Toby had gone on the road. It was early evening and it was quiet, cars parked all the way along it with people home from work. Toby had gone in between two parked cars. Then a car drove along and the driver didn't see him come out from between them. Toby was incredibly lucky to get away with a broken arm and leg, as the bumper of the vehicle was at his head height. He could have suffered a head injury. Or worse. One of the doctors discussed the statistics for children of Toby's age getting hit by a vehicle.' She blew a short breath out of her mouth and appeared slightly flushed as she looked at Ruth. 'I hope me telling you this is okay. We've been truly fortunate and I was acutely aware of your loss that day in court.'

Ruth was thinking it would have been a very frightening experience. Her four-year-old had been injured quite badly. The shock of knowing how much more serious it could have been would have left his parents shaken. 'Has Toby made a full recovery?' she asked.

'Yes.' She nodded firmly. 'Thank God. My husband is a primary school head teacher. He spends all day with little people and is brilliant with them. He spent every day that summer with Toby getting him well again.'

Ruth picked up the cup of coffee in front of her, drinking it black as it smelt so good. She took a sip and it tasted good too.

'When did it happen?'

'Thirty-first of July. He was meant to be going camping next day, just him and his dad, which was why my husband was packing the car.'

Thomas died exactly three weeks later. The twenty-first of August. The week before he'd been with his solicitor, possibly in this room, going over his case for court. Did his solicitor have her mind fully on her job then? Her little boy had been injured. Was she fully concentrating at the time? Ruth was aware her thoughts right now were unkind. She glanced across the desk and unexpectedly felt sure that Christine Pelham wouldn't have shared this if her ability to do her job had in any way been affected. Which left perhaps the only reason for it. She was a mother. She'd experienced a near loss, and three weeks later was with a mother who wasn't as fortunate as her.

'So a very worrying time. I'm glad it turned out well, that he's made a good recovery.'

'Me too,' she replied. Then settled back in her chair. 'So, now on to you. What's brought you here?'

Ruth took only a second to consider what she wanted – the answer to her burning question. 'Did you think Thomas was guilty?'

Her eyes showed her surprise. She clasped her hands together. 'My honest answer? I don't know. But when I think about just him – his charming manners, open character, the kindness in his eyes – it's not difficult to imagine him not guilty.'

Ruth waited for her to say more.

She gave a small, resigned sigh. 'The evidence said he was guilty.'

'I spoke to one of Thomas's colleagues last week. He told me a record was kept of when Thomas stole drugs.'

Christine Pelham frowned. 'I don't recall seeing that. I'd have to look back at the case notes. Have you looked through Thomas's copy?'

Ruth frowned. 'Thomas's copy?'

'Yes. He would have been provided initial details of the prosecution case, a summary of the charges, his account, written witness statements, police statements, recorded evidence.'

Ruth was stunned. She had put all his stuff in a cupboard. Everything she had wanted to know had been available to her the whole time. 'I'll look for it,' she replied, in a bit of daze. She took another sip of the coffee to give her a moment to steady her nerves, then placed the cup down carefully. 'Do you think he did the right thing, opting to plead guilty?'

'Yes, I do. Even a barrister as fine as Mr Cadell would have to have the evidence to prove him not guilty. Thomas, I don't have to tell you, was a highly intelligent man. He made an informed decision.'

Ruth picked up her handbag and took out a brown envelope. 'Last week I found a letter from Thomas. It was in his suit jacket, hanging on the back of his bedroom door, gone unnoticed until I cleared some things out of the way. He wrote it the day before he was due to appear in court. It's a letter to me, telling me everything that happened. At the end he writes his intentions. He was going to change his plea to not guilty.' Ruth held out the envelope. 'I'd be grateful, Ms Pelham, and of course expect to pay for this service, if you could read it and give your opinion.'

For a second she appeared hesitant, like she wasn't going to take it. Then her hand slowly reached out. 'I'll read it.'

'Thank you,' Ruth replied, keeping her bag in her hand and standing, preparing to leave.

Christine Pelham also stood. 'I'll read it now, so please stay. I'll go to another office, though, as I'd rather read it in private.'

Ruth sat back down. She'd not expected it to happen straight away. 'Okay. Thank you. I'll wait here.'

Forty-three minutes later, Christine Pelham returned. Ruth had looked at her phone when the door shut, and again when it opened. The brown envelope was in her hand, presumably with the letter inside as it wasn't in her other hand. She went to her side of the desk and sat down. Then she passed the envelope to Ruth. 'Thank you for letting me read something so personal, so moving. I read it very carefully. Before I tell you my thoughts, what are you hoping for?'

Ruth was hoping for a magic wand to be waved, and her son not to be guilty anymore. She breathed. Paused. Then said what was in her mind: 'Thomas's letter says he's innocent. He doesn't understand how it all happened. He made a decision to plead guilty because of the evidence, but the day before court he learned something that was going to allow him to change his plea. What I'm finding hard to understand is why he was found dead in his bath the next day. But also – what did he find out?'

The solicitor slowly nodded as if agreeing. 'I don't have the answer to that question. I'm not going to be able to tell you why he died. I'm going to be very truthful with you. The letter doesn't prove Thomas was innocent, nor does it present any evidence to support that claim. Thomas pleaded guilty.'

Ruth gazed at her in dismay. 'So that's it. He'll be thought guilty forever? What happens in cases like this if someone dies before they are sentenced?'

Christine Pelham sighed. 'The death of the defendant brings the proceedings to an end. He will not be sentenced and so his conviction is not complete. He is on record as guilty. The record will show the facts of his conviction and his death and that no sentence was passed.'

She turned her palms facing up, as if to show it was out of her hands. 'There can be a number of reasons why this letter was written. First, to give his side of the story to you. You hadn't been made aware of what had happened. He has told you of his experience after being arrested, and that is all true. His decision not to follow through with what he intended could again be for a number of reasons.'

She sighed. 'This is incredibly difficult for you. As you're having to take leaps in the dark to understand his actions. What he writes contradicts what he intended, and now you have questions. What was it he found that decided him to change his plea? Why did he not come to court? Why, instead, take a different tragic direction entirely? As a solicitor, I would want to challenge those questions with more difficult ones. Did he find something? Was he intending to change his plea? Was he intending to come to court? Did he write this letter because this is what he wanted his mother to believe?'

Ruth felt a heaviness sink through her. Her first thought: she wished she'd never come and never shared his last letter with someone who didn't know him. It felt like she'd put a further black mark against his name. She didn't blame this woman. Not at all. She was doing her job, and today it seemed like she was doing it well.

She rose from her chair. 'Thank you for your honesty.'

Christine Pelham stood and held her gaze. 'I am so very sorry for what you're going through.' She walked her to the door and then shook her hand. 'This appointment has no fee. I wish I could have done more. I wish you all the best, Dr Bennett.'

Ruth swallowed hard. Unable to respond. Those difficult questions the solicitor asked – she was taking them with her. It was like slow torture to hear an alternative truth that others believed.

*

Ruth found Henry casually leaning against her front door, with his arms folded across his chest, in a relaxed manner. Ruth glanced at him in surprise, self-conscious and aware the strain from hearing difficult things in Christine Pelham's office was probably showing in her eyes and on her face. While he… looked absolutely bloody dandy. Not a ruffled feather in sight, as if without a care in the world.

'Hi,' he said.

'Hi,' she responded, politely. 'Did you want something?'

'A moment of your time, if now is all right? I'd like your opinion on something.'

Ruth opened the front door, curious. 'You know the way through. I'll just be a moment while I take off my shoes.'

His eyes went to the high-heeled shoes she was wearing. Chocolate-brown patent leather, with a tiny gold detail on the sides. Then to the pinstripe black trousers, tapering at the end and showing her slender, bare ankles. He withdrew his gaze, and murmured a sound not entirely understood, as it sounded like approval. Ruth inwardly sighed, and followed him to the sitting room, deciding she would keep on her shoes until he was gone. It annoyed her that he'd let her see a side to his character that was warm and amusing and interesting. It had left her curious to know him, until he waved her off like a nosy neighbour to Kim. Thinking of him and his attractive smile and low deep voice, and the warm dryness of his palm as he'd taken her hand to cross the busy road after leaving the restaurant. And now standing here stirring her attraction again, bloody man.

'So,' he said. 'The kitchen. I'm thinking to knock down the partition wall and put one along the length of this room instead. It would make this room a little shorter, but not by much, and it might even improve on how it looks now. A door could close off the kitchen, a sliding one to maximise space. It would still be a small kitchen, but the new wall could be lined with more cupboards, and more importantly, an oven could be installed. I suggested it to Tom, but he wasn't bothered about using the hob or having a cooker.' He turned to her. 'So what do you think? It would mean a bit of upheaval for a short while.'

Ruth knew exactly what she thought. He could have told her this over the phone. She shrugged. 'It's entirely up to you. If you want to make improvements, please go ahead. I'm sure I'll manage. I'm out at work all week. You can have the run of the place. So please feel free to do whatever you want. It's your property.'

He studied her for a moment, and made another murmuring sound. 'I thought it might be something you would wish to have done, but as I'm not sensing any interest, perhaps I'm wrong. Which is entirely your decision. I'll just leave it for now. Rethink doing it at some other time.'

Ruth shook her head in exasperation. 'You know, I didn't ask for us to go out for a meal, or have a drink together. As it turned out it was a pleasant evening, I thought we had a friendship perhaps beginning. Then you turn back into a landlord, and a rather aloof one at that. So I hope you'll forgive my not jumping up and down in a show of enthusiasm, as I think I'd rather stick to the microwave, to be honest.'

His head lifted in surprise, and Ruth was further maddened to see him looking slightly awkward. 'I see. I'm sorry, I shouldn't have come,' he expressed in a quiet, reserved tone. 'I'll leave you alone. I think that's probably what I should do.' He glanced at her. 'I think I've made things rather awkward.' His self-deprecating smile clearly showed that he thought he'd done something unwise. 'I'll see myself out,' he said.

'Henry, would you like a drink?' Ruth asked in an exasperated tone.

He hesitated at the sitting-room door. His eyes found hers. Ruth felt butterflies in her stomach. He gave a short sigh. And looked at the floor. 'I think perhaps not. But thank you all the same. I'll say goodnight and… I'll see you around,' he added, in a noncommittal tone. Then he went out of the room and Ruth heard the front door quietly shut.

And all of sudden, inexplicably, she felt tearful.

CHAPTER THIRTY

Ruth was struggling. Since her appointment with Christine Pelham she felt overwhelmed. She'd not been able to find the case notes in the storage cupboard. She lost two nights of sleep and knew if she didn't change direction soon she was going to hit a wall of deeper depression than she could handle. She needed to come to a decision. Should she stop searching for answers? Should she go home? Or should she stay? She was drowning in misery and with nothing to pull her out of it. She wanted *her* Thomas, her memories of him to remain absolute. She wanted to feel what he had always given her, what only he could give – a completeness. Her job as a mother had been cut short, and all she had to hold onto was that she had done it well. She hadn't missed out any important parts or left gaps in his soul. Everything she was hearing was pushing that from her, and without it she had failed.

It might have been better to have stayed ignorant and not questioned the truth. Having her belief in his innocence questioned was bringing the worst type of pain. A different reality. The fighting spirit coming through in his letter may have only been intended to make her believe he was strong, that it was only in the last moment something took that strength away, but he'd been all right up till then. Not suffering. And not afraid. Did he write the letter because it was what he wanted his mother to believe?

She pushed back her chair and stood up, the Post-it on her desk the last straw. These kind people she worked with didn't know why she was there. Joan knew about Thomas, that he had died, that the new doctor had lost her son, but she didn't know the rest of it. Ruth felt like a traitor every time one of them showed her a kindness. Especially when it came on top of her telling a lie. On Monday Carol Campbell had ushered her out of the building with a hopeful look in her eye, perhaps wondering if Ruth might stick around and apply for Jim Miller's job. Ruth had told her she had an appointment with a solicitor about a property she was looking at, so that she didn't miss her appointment with Christine Pelham.

At the Monday morning meeting everyone had enthused over the biscuits she'd bought. On Tuesday she found a flowering plant on her office windowsill and knew it to be from Joan, who'd waved it off as something she'd just had lying around. The white ceramic pot looked new, the campanula, with pretty, violet bell-shaped flowers, fresh. And today the Post-it from Dr Raj with her address neatly written so Ruth knew where to go for the cooking lesson she was hosting that evening. Ruth couldn't go. It would be wrong to accept an invitation when she was there under false pretences. She would rather not have to add to her discomfort.

She wound her scarf around her neck and gathered her things. The offices were quiet, and she was now going home. As she exited the car park she turned right onto the road, the opposite direction to her flat, but carried on and let her subconscious guide her.

*

Ruth parked on a side road, then headed towards the town. She would have to give some reason to Catherine Dell for why she was visiting. She could say a woman who worked in the pub down the road pointed out where Catherine lived, so she thought she'd call in and see how she was, as it was her who helped Catherine after she fainted.

The man who opened the purple door looked distracted, with a mobile pressed to his ear. He briefly spoke to her. 'Go right to the top, up both flights of stairs.'

Ruth did as she was told and climbed two flights. Catherine Dell was waiting at the top, leaning over the bannister. She hollered down the stairs. 'Thanks, Pete. I owe you.' Then to her visitor. 'He answers the door if it's for me, to save me going up and down.'

She looked properly at her visitor, and her expression changed. Her voice hushed with surprise. 'I didn't dream you. It *was* you helping me.' Her beautiful brown eyes filled with tears. 'You're Thomas's mother.'

'Yes, I am,' Ruth managed to say, an ache in her throat at being with this young woman. She didn't need an excuse for why she was visiting after all. Catherine recognised her. Thomas must have shown her a photograph. Her chocolate brown hair fell in soft waves down her back. Over her neat bump she wore a man's white shirt, teamed with a pair of black leggings, her ankles exposed. Her slightly puffy feet showed pearly pink toenails.

Catherine stood still and stared at her, her eyes showing how emotional this was for her. Ruth stepped closer. 'Would it be all right if I come in to say hello?'

Catherine led the way into a cosy sitting room. A two-seater sofa was angled to face a faux wood burner, with glowing fake coals behind black lattice doors, with a small matching armchair on the other side of the fire. In front of a tall window was an old pine desk piled with exercise books that Ruth eyed curiously.

'Am I interrupting?'

'No, not at all. I'd just finished marking the last one,' she replied.

'So you're a teacher.'

'Yes.' She nodded. 'I teach Spanish in a school, and then twice a week in the evenings I run courses in Italian and French.' She smiled. 'It's how I met Thomas.' She laughed softly. 'He joined my Italian group and tried very hard not to speak it for at least two lessons.'

'You're kidding,' Ruth softly exclaimed, with a lightness in her voice that had been absent for a while.

'No, I'm not. He said it was the only way he could think of to ask me out. I asked him why he didn't join my French group, so at least he'd learn a new language. He said he picked Italian so he wouldn't have to concentrate.' She became aware her guest was still standing and invited Ruth to sit down. 'Would you like some tea or coffee, or something else to drink?'

Ruth sat down in the armchair. 'I'm fine thank you, Catherine. I'd rather you just sat down and we talked. I'd really love to hear more about you and Thomas. And how you are, with everything that's happened, and now close to having your baby.'

She sat down on the sofa holding her bump with one hand and brought her legs up as well. 'My ankles are getting swollen so I need to keep them up.' She sank against a cushion, looking comfortable. Then, quite matter-of-factly said, 'I fell in love with Thomas in an instant. It probably took less than five minutes for me to be aware. It was both the scariest and most exciting moment of my life. I don't regret a minute of it.'

'This must have been so hard for you,' Ruth replied.

She smiled sadly. 'Yes. One minute we're thinking about our future and the next moment it's snatched away. The last time he was here, which was two days before he was due to go to court, he said he wished he'd never met me to save me from the experience. I told him he could not dictate my fate.' She paused while she looked down at her bump. 'I'm only sorry I wasn't with him the night before, but I didn't want him worried or guessing why I was getting sick. But it might have saved him if I had.'

Ruth leaned forward in the chair. 'Don't think that way. Don't change what was a kind act into a reason to blame yourself, Catherine.'

She gave a half smile. 'That's what Thomas would have said.'

Ruth gave a confirming nod, and saw she was eased. 'Can I ask you something? Did you write me a letter asking me to come to Bournemouth?'

'No.' She shook her head. 'I was going to contact you, but then I thought I didn't want you to feel the burden of me being pregnant. I was going to wait until after the baby was born before coming to see you and introducing us. Why are you asking?'

Ruth sighed. 'Someone sent me a letter, which they didn't sign.' She pulled a sad face. 'Basically asking for me to come and do what I already intended to do. Clear Thomas's name.'

Catherine let out a shaky breath, her hand rising to her chest. 'Oh, I'm so very glad. I hadn't wanted to ask what you thought. Thomas had no doubt you would know he was innocent, not for a second did he worry about it, but I was afraid you might not think that. Everything was so clear cut, and unless you knew him like we do, you could be easily persuaded to think him guilty.'

Ruth was silent, needing a moment to herself. This young woman had just explained something so simple – you didn't need proof of something if you had no doubts in your heart. Nothing had given her a reason to doubt him – she had kept faith while Ruth had floundered.

'Did Thomas tell you about the difficulties he was having at work?'

She nodded. 'You mean with the poor nurse? He felt so bad for shouting at her after believing she'd taken his phone. He just wanted her to admit it. What he couldn't understand was why she was behaving the way she was. He knew he'd been drunk when they slept together, but in the morning she seemed all right about it. He said she was nice. He didn't get the feeling she was expecting anything more, but he felt bad about the casualness of sleeping with her. When she began texting he realised he'd misread her feelings for him.'

'Do you think Thomas might have misread her from the beginning?'

Catherine shook her head. 'No. She was exactly as he described.'

Ruth stared at her confused. 'You've met this nurse?'

'Yes. Thomas introduced me when I went to meet him from work one day. She seemed kind. Not awkward or anything. But then I read a text she'd sent him, and it was like she had forgotten he was with someone else, as she asked if she could visit. I was going to talk to her, but then it didn't happen because after Thomas was arrested he was no longer working at the hospital, so he wasn't having to see her anymore. But he thought of her. He worried that he'd caused her to unhinge, perhaps.'

'Do you think this woman could have had anything to do with the drugs found in Thomas's flat and in his locker?'

Her expression was uncertain. 'I didn't think so. I know Thomas wondered that, but she doesn't seem like that type of person. If anything, I'd say she was too uncomplicated to think of something so devious.'

'Did Thomas think of anyone else it could have been?'

She sighed deeply. 'I'm not sure Thomas would even have noticed. He was running on empty his last few weeks at work. He wasn't sleeping. He was worrying how he was being regarded.'

'So no clue as to who might have done this? No one you've since thought of as suspicious? Did he have enemies?'

Catherine considered the questions quietly for a few seconds. She shook her head sadly. 'When it happened I thought of nothing but who could it be. I came to the conclusion that it had to be someone very jealous. Thomas had something that not everyone has – a passion to learn. It was like watching someone receive a special gift when he raised his head from a book. He'd talk about something he learned like it was magic. If someone envied that trait, it could make them want to take it away from him.' She stared at her bump reflectively, then placed her hand there. 'When I think of what happened, I see it like a domino effect. Every piece set perfectly, waiting for the first one to fall over.'

Ruth felt comfortable with Catherine and they chatted about a few things, getting to know each other. Catherine's mother died when she was fifteen. Her father remarried and was living in Brighton. Her one sibling, her sister Helena, lived in Belgium.

She was visiting in a month's time to stay until after the baby was born. Ruth asked if there was enough room for them all to be there and Catherine showed her around. A small kitchen with a washing machine and a cooker. A bathroom with a bath where she could bathe the baby. Her sister would sleep in the sitting room, she said, as the two-seater was a sofa bed. At each stop Ruth noticed things that told her more about Catherine's character. The rows of books on shelves in the sitting room, colour-coordinated. The well-kept kitchen and bathroom, with uncluttered surfaces. The small candle on the kitchen windowsill in front of a framed photograph of Thomas. Then, in the bedroom, alongside a neatly made bed, a neatly made cot with baby blue blankets and sheets, facing a rooftop window where mother and baby could look at the sky. They would have plenty of room, she said, for her and her baby.

Ruth hugged her goodbye. They swapped phone numbers, Ruth giving Catherine her work number as well. 'Look, I'm going to be in Bournemouth for a little while. I honestly don't know if I'll ever be able to clear Thomas's name, but I want you to know that talking to you has made me want to carry on trying. When I call a halt for whatever reason, I'd very much like for us to get to know each other well. I'd like you to feel you can have a friend in me. A support. A babysitter. Or really whatever suits.'

She had tears in her eyes again, and Ruth couldn't help smiling. Pregnancy hormones were such an on-and-off tap of tears that you never knew when they were going to come.

'I hoped you'd want that. Not only will you be this baby's only grandmother, you're the person his father loved most in the world.'

Ruth was fortunate not to trip going down the stairs, as her own tears fairly blinded her. It had been a visit she had desperately needed. Feeling all the love in that home made her heart ache, but in a good way. There was some happiness to be found ahead. There was something to look forward to that was not sad.

CHAPTER THIRTY-ONE

Rosie waited for the front door to open again.

If she hadn't caught the bus this morning, and the wrong bus at that, and been taken on a detour to the bus station she wouldn't have seen the missing person posters taped to the windows. Seeing Anabel's face staring at her from the posters decided her. She would make this call. Hopping on the wrong bus because it was on the right side of the road was meant to have happened. Every other day she walked. If this nurse was hiding Anabel, she was now going to be in trouble. Rosie's senses must have guided her to take a bus so she would see Anabel in a poster. Like a good omen.

Rosie called from a payphone before boarding the correct bus. She made sure to sound emphatic and positive. The photograph of the missing woman in a poster at the bus station was definitely the woman she saw on the steps of a house opposite a bus shelter, opposite the beach. She then used reverse psychology on the call handler by suggesting her call might not now be needed. Perhaps the woman was no longer missing, and it was her home where she was standing when spotted. But being a concerned citizen, she thought it best to report it just in case.

On her journey on the correct bus, she fretted she would not make it in time to see the police arrive. But she had to wait another forty minutes after getting off the bus before they turned up. Clearly they weren't in a rush, perhaps thinking a missing woman reported being found alive wasn't a great emergency. If she was reported dead, Rosie thought, it would be urgent. Rosie had hoped to see them arrive at speed with blue lights flashing and sirens going, but of course they wouldn't arrive like that. Anabel wasn't a criminal, not as far as they were concerned. She was someone reported as missing, possibly vulnerable, who needed a gentler approach. Rosie wished she was able to see what was going on inside the house to make sure that they looked for her properly and searched under beds and in cupboards and even in the attic. She would like to be inside the house to be sure it wasn't a cursory search, and to be there when Anabel was found.

She dug out her emergency cigarettes and lit one. Knowing the police were inside the house right now was jangling her nerves, but she mustn't show that or slow down. At this time of the morning walking along the beach was fine so long as you had a stick in your hand and there was a dog in the distance. She couldn't wait in the bus shelter, not with a police car parked across the road, but that was okay. She was still close enough to see that the female officer was not young and the male officer had black-rimmed glasses on.

The front door remained closed for a long time, and that reassured her. It hadn't been an in-and-out visit. In all probability Anabel had shown herself, and they were now talking to her, reassuring her she was not in trouble. They might even have her talking on the phone to Meg, while Miss Tupperware made them all tea. She was there, in her home. She had opened the front door. When Rosie made the call she hadn't thought about the woman not being there, so it was lucky really, her own routine today not being the same. If they hadn't got an answer, as would have happened yesterday, the police might have gone away.

Rosie slowed down. The front door was opening. The female officer came out first, then the other officer followed. Rosie watched for Anabel to appear and was tempted to get ready to wave. Seconds ticked by. What was keeping her? A quick visit to the loo? A long goodbye to her new friend? Rosie watched the doorway intensely. Perhaps Anabel was getting her things, or getting dressed or... The nurse had come to the doorway, standing with arms folded close to her chest as if feeling the chilly air. Rosie was astounded as she gave a little wave to the officers. Her gaze darted to the police car. The officers had the doors open and were getting ready to get in. And now the nurse smiled and gave a second wave.

'Oh, you twats,' Rosie cried, as the car began to move. In a second they were gone and the front door was closed. Rosie was left staring at it in a daze.

She was shocked. She had expected to see Anabel. Had they searched the house or just sat and drank tea? Had they been fooled? Anabel was probably hiding behind the bath panel. No, that didn't make sense – she wouldn't fit there. But somewhere like that. Somewhere not obvious. They'd taken an hour to get here. Had they called ahead to make sure someone was home first, giving Anabel time to escape? If she was on foot she couldn't have gone far, but if she'd jumped on a bus or taken a taxi she could be miles away by now.

Rosie slumped down on the sand, the rush of adrenaline gone. Her mind was exhausted. She was beginning to think she was never going to see Anabel again. This was not an adventure anymore – it had passed that stage a while ago. It was no longer fun. She was worried. This wasn't like Anabel. To keep something like this going for this long would show she had no feelings for her family. But she loved her mum and dad. She'd been missing three weeks. Long enough to have sorted her head out, if that's what she was doing. She was incapable of withstanding the pressure of knowing she was causing her parents to suffer. Anabel was a marshmallow – soft all the way through. Her heart wasn't made of iron. She would never be able to do this for this long, unless she was forced to and had no choice.

Rosie gazed at the house with a sense of foreboding. Maybe she was still inside, and maybe she *was* behind the bath panel. But not in one piece. Perhaps Miss Tupperware had chopped her up or even made her into soup. Rosie felt her stomach churn and bent over quickly to bring up what little she'd eaten that morning. A packet of crisps. She spat bits of sick from her mouth and then rinsed it out with some water. She was thinking up the craziest things. Crazy imaginings she needed to control. Her vigil was not over yet.

All she needed to do was knock on the door and ask if Anabel was there. A few hours from now it would be the accepted thing to do, because by then she would have heard the rumour of Anabel being there. The police would have told Meg they'd checked it out, and Meg would have told Rosie. It would then be only normal to call at the house and check again. And as Rosie had been to it before, invited there for a Tupperware party, it was natural it would be her who would come calling. She knew the woman. The woman knew her. She was Anabel's friend.

Perhaps if Anabel heard her voice, she'd come out from where she was hiding. That's all Rosie wanted now – for Anabel to show herself so she could stop imagining her behind a bath panel in a space where she wouldn't fit. Rosie was sorry she'd thought such awful things, but that's what best friends did when they fell out. They thought up horrible things about each other. It didn't mean they weren't still friends. Anabel wouldn't want that and neither would Rosie. Deep down they loved each other. Anabel needed her. Rosie had to keep remembering that. She mustn't give up on her. Right now her friend was probably very afraid, thinking Rosie didn't care. Rosie would show her she did. She would find her and she would tell her she would always be there for her. Nothing would change that.

CHAPTER THIRTY-TWO

Ruth lied about why she didn't go to Dr Raj's house, citing an unexpected visit from her sister as the reason. Dr Raj was gracious and said she should have brought her sister along, but no matter, she could come next time. In the meantime, a sample of their cooking was in the fridge in the kitchen for her to take home with her after work. It just needed heating. 'Just a teaspoon of water over the naan bread before you warm it will make it more moist.'

Ruth thanked her, and felt horrible for deceiving the woman. 'Well, I'll do that,' she said, nodding. 'I'll look forward to my supper this evening.'

'It was nice for you to have a surprise visit. More important to be with family and miss something you can come to anytime. My nephews are going nowhere, so we have plenty of time for any matchmaking.' She smiled, seeming satisfied about that, then glanced at her watch. 'Okay. Well, now let's hope we have a good day.'

Ruth closed her office door. She had five minutes of silence to enjoy before patients arrived. Then she would work hard all day, to make up for her deceit. And she would spend this evening quietly and let her mind rest. She had an appointment tomorrow at the hospital with someone called Janice May, where she would hear another side of Thomas's story. But for now, she was going to enjoy feeling close to him again.

Just after midday, Mary and Sally, the receptionists, entered her office full of excitement. Mary was holding a large bouquet of brightly coloured flowers, while Sally held the door for her. They both were beaming. Then Sally spoke, 'He asked us to deliver them. He's waiting out in reception.'

'Ever so handsome,' Mary exclaimed.

Ruth immediately thought of Henry. She came out of her chair and around her desk to inspect them. A small white envelope was tucked in the flowers. Ruth retrieved it and read the card. He'd written, *Sorry*. 'Give me a minute,' she said to them. 'I'll be out in a moment.'

When the door shut, she breathed in shakily, realising how much Henry had affected her. Then, calming her expression, she went out to meet him. Ruth felt instant disappointment and then an anger as Tim Wiley rose from a chair, smiling at her like they had a connection. She flew past him and straight out of the entrance door to breathe in air.

'Hold up,' he called after her, making her walk faster and then further around the building so that when he caught up they were somewhere private.

He wore faded jeans and a black leather jacket, and he was handsome, but Ruth didn't find him attractive. She found him disturbing after that episode in her flat.

'What do you want?' she asked bluntly.

He spread his hands. 'To say sorry, of course. I was bang out of order. Scared you, instead of reassuring you I was on your side.'

'There are no sides, Mr Wiley,' she retorted sharply. 'My son is dead. There are no sides to that.'

'Come on,' he cajoled. 'You know what I mean. I want to help. You can only be staying where you are for one reason. So you can question neighbours without them knowing who you really are. You want to prove he was innocent. You haven't come here just for a change of scenery. I can help with that.'

'Really?' she answered curtly. 'How do you propose to do that?'

'By bringing to justice the guilty party,' he answered in a tone equally sharp, surprising her. He was serious. He wanted to do this, but why? What was his motivation to help? Ruth couldn't trust him. Shouldn't trust him, according to Kim. What did he really want?

'If you come near me again, I'm going to report you to the police.'

He laughed harshly. 'You do that and you'll never get answers.'

'Please leave, Mr Wiley, or I'll call them now.'

He let out a heavy sigh, then started shaking his head at her, like she was disappointing him. 'Good job I don't take offence and I know you've been under enormous strain.' Then he gave a casual salute, tapping two fingers lightly to his temple. 'I'll be seeing you, Doc. Stay safe now.'

*

Ruth brought home the food from Dr Raj, carefully wrapped in containers and tinfoil, but not the flowers from Tim Wiley. She gave them to Mary and Sally. They had a choice either to take them home or put them in a bin. She instructed all three receptionists, including Joan, not to book Tim Wiley as a patient with her again. If he required a doctor, he was to see someone else. The mood she was in, they didn't question her reasons, nor mention the flowers again.

Kim was just coming out of the front door as Ruth was about to let herself in. Ruth stepped in her way to stop her leaving as she wanted to talk to her.

'Kim, that police officer. Has he come here before?'

Kim's manner was immediately cagey, and Ruth lost patience. 'I'm not concerned about the reasons he was here to see you. I just want to know if he's been here before?'

Kim eyed her warily, clearly startled by her new neighbour's sharpness. 'I think this must be his patch. I've seen him a few times on the street. Seems to always turn up at the right place, wrong time.'

'Right. Thank you for telling me,' Ruth replied, heading for the stairs without further comment.

'Is everything all right?' Kim called after her.

Ruth gave no answer, just continued on up to her flat. She was thinking about the time she thought someone was behind her, darting close to the tree, thinking it might have been Tim Wiley.

Once safely in the flat, she put the food in the freezer compartment for another evening. She had no appetite to enjoy it now. She was going to open one of the bottles of wine Pauline kindly left behind, and have more than one glass to unwind.

Tim Wiley's visit to the surgery had greatly unsettled her. She couldn't work out what his interest was. One part of her was telling her he was not attracted to her in the normal sense, as she wasn't picking up quite that vibe, but that it was something else, a connection he felt he had with her that she most definitely didn't feel. Was it because he'd been with her at the most intimate time of seeing her son dead? Did he feel that moment connected them? He was older than Thomas, probably mid-thirties, so in between hers and Thomas's ages. Was he trying to replace him as a son? Or act like a father figure for Thomas, be someone who had lost a son? Whatever his feelings or thoughts she never wanted anything to do with them.

An hour on and she was bathed and nicely relaxed, and drinking a second glass of wine. She heard a light tap at the door. She hoped it wasn't an invitation to play badminton or Kim curious to know more. Not bothering to cover her vest top or tie back her tangle of damp hair, she opened the door. Henry, the one person she hadn't expected to see, stood there looking strangely awkward. Adjusting the glasses on his face, then turning his attention to a whisky bottle in his hand, his gaze eventually found hers.

'Is this a convenient time?' he asked, in a tone that gave nothing away, his voice that of someone she knew but didn't know well.

Ruth left the door open for him to come in. She walked ahead, leaving it up to him whether he chose to follow. In the living room she picked up her glass of wine and went to stand by the window. Henry stood in the centre of the room with an air of uncertainty about him. She heard him sigh, but her attention stayed on the wine glass in her hand. If he had something to say, he could say it. She wasn't in the mood to make things easy for anyone today.

She heard him put the bottle down on the desk. Then he spoke. 'You're here to feel close to your son and I would have taken advantage of your loss by putting my attraction for you before that. So I come bearing a gift as just a friend, if you'll allow that?'

Ruth lifted her gaze and saw him fiddling with a button on his jacket. He was behaving like a nervous teenager on a first date. It was this that provoked her to tease him. 'So this attraction for me has now gone,' she said softly.

'Well, yes, of course,' he instantly replied.

'So it was fleeting, then? Nothing to really worry about?'

'Yes,' he agreed.

'Barely even a crush?' she commented.

He murmured something quietly, still fiddling with the button on his jacket. Ruth hid her amusement. The threads would snap if he twisted the damn thing any tighter. She took a sip of her wine while watching him, then said in a low playful voice, 'That's a shame.'

It would be hard to miss the flush that came to his cheeks or hear his intake of breath. Finally, he looked at her. After that they didn't need words. Their eyes told each other what they thought.

Before dawn he left her bed, and she knew it was to protect her reputation, to prevent anyone noticing him leaving her place. It didn't feel like a bad thing that he was leaving in the middle of the night, but like he cared. He dressed in the dark and left as quietly as possible so she wouldn't wake.

CHAPTER THIRTY-THREE

Her limbs next day felt wonderfully heavy, and if she could have curled up somewhere soft she would have slept all the hours, showing no inclination for physical exertion. Fortunately, her workload was keeping her busy, but not so busy she couldn't concentrate and do her job.

Ruth shivered, wishing she'd put on her jacket. It had seemed like a good idea at the time to drink her tea outside in the cold, to help blow away the cobwebs. Joan seemed unaffected. Hardy. Capable of enduring swimming in the sea in winter, no doubt. 'Do we have time for a second cup of tea?' Ruth asked. 'Only this time inside in the warm.'

'I'm sure we can find time,' she answered in an offhand manner, her attention on the car park. She pointed to the grey Volvo over in the corner. 'You might want to park closer to the building. Use the bays by reception.'

Ruth frowned. 'Why? It's fine there.'

'Our CCTV doesn't capture over there.' Joan's expression was serious. 'It's dark over in that corner by the time we leave.'

Ruth was curious. 'Have you had cars broken into?'

Joan shook her head. 'No. Not yet, we haven't. It's not that which concerns me. It's yesterday I saw a car on the road outside. Saw it there again the evening of Dr Raj's do. I got ready here and saw it when I came out of the building.'

'Maybe it was a lift for one of the doctors. For Sally or Mary maybe?' Ruth suggested.

'No.' Joan shook her head again. 'Sally only lives around the corner, and Mary drives herself.'

Ruth was confused, wondering where this was going. 'So what's the problem with a car being there twice? It could have been there to pick someone else up. Someone working in a shop, or maybe waiting for someone who was with them, who nipped into the chip shop?'

Joan stared at her. 'I'll tell you what the problem is. I saw it a third time a week or so ago when you were riding your bike. Which is why I'm glad you're using your car now, and why I want you to park it closer to the building.'

Ruth was more confused. 'I still don't get the point of what that has to do with me moving my car.'

'The point is,' Joan said in a firm voice. 'You were lucky you weren't hit by it. Any closer, you'd have been under the wheels.'

Ruth was bewildered. She had no recollection of this happening. Which in itself was not good, that she wasn't even aware. Her voice was mildly sceptical. 'Are you sure?'

Joan pointed straight at the road. 'I'm as sure as I'm standing here, that car was deliberately too close. I was in shock watching it, waiting to see you flying off the bike.'

Ruth felt a different shiver. How could she not have known a car was that close behind her? When only last week she'd been conscious of a car for another reason. She kept the worry out of her voice. 'What make of car was it?'

Joan turned a glum face. 'A fast car.'

Ruth raised her eyebrows.

Making Joan wave her hand in agitation. 'Maybe maroon or black. I don't know what else. My eyes were on you and the bumper. Not the make of the car. So, do me a favour, park by the entrance so we know you're safe.'

*

Her three o'clock patient was on time. Ruth was glad she suggested a further follow-up. Rosie's skin and eyes looked brighter. There was more energy about her. Then a moment later, Ruth revised her opinion. It was nervous energy. Rosie had a taut expression, her small frame tense in the chair, becoming visibly obvious the longer she sat there. She was unable to relax.

'How have you been?' Ruth asked, to kick things off.

'Fine.' Her voice sounded equally tense. Clipped. Sharp. One-word answer.

'You look well, if perhaps a little tense.'

'Walking. Fresh air.'

'Well, that's good to hear. Good for your physical wellbeing.' Ruth gave a small encouraging smile. 'And how are you *feeling*?'

Her response was fast, showing she was irritable. 'Absolutely brilliant. Hunky-dory. What else do you want to know?'

Ruth glanced at her speculatively. Rosie was more than irritable. She was upset. Which was probably increasing with being questioned. Ruth wouldn't press her to talk. She fully realised Rosie was only there for a new doctor's note, which Ruth had prepared already. She passed it across the desk to her.

She rose from the chair and stared at Ruth. 'It's not you,' she said, in a calmer voice. 'I just haven't got time to sit here. I like coming here to see you, actually.'

Ruth was touched. Feeling a tiny breakthrough. 'Well, I hope you keep coming, then.'

Rosie sighed. It sounded like relief. 'Yeah. I will. I've got to find my friend, though, now.'

'Has she been in touch?'

Rosie shook her head. 'No, but I'm getting closer to finding her.'

Then she smiled, and Ruth was stunned. It looked like a genuine happiness. It transformed her face, softening her features.

'Well, good luck,' Ruth replied. 'Perhaps on your way out, you could make another appointment?'

Rosie nodded. Then out the door she went. On a mission to find her friend.

*

In half an hour she would be finished for the day as leaving work at four o'clock – for a second non-existent appointment about a property – at the hospital this time. She was feeling guilty for lying. Every new day she worked here, she liked her colleagues more and more.

Joan entered the room after a light tap at the door. 'You have a visitor,' she said. Then seeing Ruth's eyes, she raised a hand to calm her. 'I think you'll like this one.' She grinned. 'I like her, and I've only spoken to her for a second.'

Ruth curiously followed Joan out to reception. Then stopped still, not wanting to interrupt what she was seeing. A small girl, perhaps six or seven was having a conversation with Catherine. Using her hands to speak very competently, judging by Catherine's slower responses. Saying something very funny as well, judging by Catherine's fit of giggles.

'I'm going to pee myself, if you keep making me laugh,' Catherine said involuntarily, before quickly signing what she said out loud.

The girl laughed, and clutched her belly. Then pointed to the toilet. The mother then tapped her shoulder to draw her attention. They had been called to see the doctor.

Catherine waved goodbye. She then glanced around and saw Ruth.

In an instant in her heart, Ruth knew. Catherine was completely innocent. It would be unacceptable in any way, shape or form for her ever to be involved in what happened to Thomas. She was a beautiful human being. As Catherine drew near, Ruth greeted her. 'What a lovely surprise.'

Catherine touched her bump and stayed still for a moment. 'Think this baby's wearing boots.' Then she smiled. 'It's literally a hello and goodbye. And I hope we're not interrupting.'

Ruth shook her head. 'Of course not.'

'Only, we're off for a check-up.'

Ruth liked the way she used plural to denote she was more than one. 'Perhaps if you're free over the weekend, we could meet up?'

'There's a good pub on my road. We could have a drink there.'

'I know.' Ruth nodded. 'I saw it the evening you fainted.'

'Okay, well, text me, just let me know when you'll be there.' She smiled. Gave a little wave. Then she was gone.

When Ruth turned, Joan was standing mesmerised. 'What a lovely young woman.' She sighed.

Ruth went back to her office thinking Joan was a romantic at heart, but also completely correct in her assessment.

CHAPTER THIRTY-FOUR

Ruth knocked on the door for her appointment with Janice May at exactly four thirty. A woman with grey curly hair invited Ruth into a small room, which Ruth immediately recognised as The Quiet Room – a term used by hospital staff for the place where relatives could take time out to gather strength or reflect, or for them to hear bad news or sad news. The armchairs and low table and box of tissues were all that was really required, as the tea or coffee or water could be fetched once any news had been imparted. On the low table already were a white jug flask, some mugs, a bowl of sugar sachets, tea and coffee bags and pods of UHT milk.

The woman held out her hand. 'I'm Janice May. Please accept my sincere condolences for your loss, Dr Bennett. Your son was a lovely man.'

Ruth took her hand and stared at her in surprise. 'You knew Thomas?'

Janice May smiled warmly. 'I asked to be the one to speak to you, to tell you everything we know, because I liked him. I didn't want you to hear about him from someone who didn't really know him. I hope that's okay?'

Ruth sat down, already relieved. She would rather hear the facts from someone who knew and liked Thomas. The woman offered her a drink, but Ruth declined politely. 'I've had a lot of caffeine today, but thank you.'

Janice May sat down and sighed heartily. 'I can't imagine how difficult this has been, and how hard it is for you to be here. I'm going to say everything in simple terms and hope none of it is too painful to hear. I work in human resources and was involved in the disciplinary procedures against Thomas. On the day Thomas was arrested, he was informed by letter that suspension on full pay was necessary while a formal investigation into his conduct was carried out by the investigating manager. This involved gathering information and witness statements. We learned very soon, of course, that Thomas had been charged. While we had enough reasonable belief that misconduct had occurred and were at liberty to take formal action of dismissal, we nonetheless continued the investigation.'

Ruth had held her breath while hearing all this and breathed a little shakily. Janice noticed. 'Do you want me to stop for a moment, or ask me any questions?'

Ruth nodded. 'May I ask about locker keys?'

'Of course. When issued with a locker, you're provided a key. The master key is held in a secure place by security services. Thomas's main locker was in the changing room in the theatre department, as while working on the Surgical Unit, which covers the wards, Outpatients and the A&E department, he of course also worked in theatre. My understanding is he had possession of his key that day and hadn't lost it. In the morning, in fact, he was working in theatre.'

'Yes, that's what I heard,' Ruth replied. 'May I also ask about a record that was kept from February of last year of the drugs that went missing and when Thomas was on duty?'

Her brow furrowed with deep wrinkles. Her voice lowered with surprise and confusion. 'I beg your pardon? What record?'

Ruth could tell by her reaction she had no knowledge of this record. 'I was told about it from someone who saw it the day after Thomas was arrested. It was taken from him and shredded. But he had a good look at it and was able to see dates when drugs were taken were all on the days Thomas worked, except for one date, which he said was incorrect as he worked Thomas's shift that day.'

Janice's eyes had opened wide. 'Oh my word. This is the first I've heard of it.' She breathed harshly. 'I'm really shocked. There was no record kept. It took days to work it all out, going through batch numbers and dates and the drug ordering books. It was slow work as medicines had been taken from different departments, but pharmacy was not able to pin down dates of when the drugs were taken because they had not been noticed as missing. The check was only carried out after a list of all the drugs was given to us by the police. I would really like to know who told you this.' She looked at Ruth candidly. 'Do you think this person was telling the truth? That he did actually see a record?'

Ruth found herself nodding. Jed Nolan told her reluctantly, and would rather not have told her anything. 'Yes. I do,' she answered. 'He told me about the box of diamorphine recorded missing.'

Janice's mouth dropped open. It took a moment for her to speak. 'No. Not a chance of that happening without it being noticed. Are you sure he wasn't winding you up?'

Ruth could see Janice was rattled. She had picked up a clean empty mug and seemed surprised it didn't contain a drink. 'This is so strange. That someone could have been doing this. You must have been appalled. Lord knows what the investigating manager will make of it. And Mr Mason will want to know.' She shut her eyes briefly. 'He hated it was him who found the drugs in Thomas's locker and wished he'd never gone looking. But I think he felt it was his duty. Staff were verbalising concerns. There were suggestions his water bottle be checked, but that was impossible without knowing which bottle he'd been drinking from. Most of them drink out of tin bottles now or mark their plastic bottle with their name. Anyway, a few of them set off, checking the theatre where he worked and various places where he'd been standing. You see, despite Thomas's conduct, he was liked. Mr Mason could see something special in him. He said this in his statement and intended to say it in court. He called him a true doctor. He felt he let Thomas down.'

Ruth reached for some tissues to hand her. Her eyes were welling.

'Sorry,' she said. 'I'm behaving unprofessionally.' She gave a watery smile. 'What I liked about your son was his graciousness. When he came in for a hearing, held in May, he made it easy on everyone by saying how sorry he was for them having to do this unpleasant job, and that it wasn't easy having to tell someone they had done something wrong.'

Ruth felt her heart catch. She gave a soft laugh. 'That sounds like Thomas. When he was small I told him off about something that I can't remember. Maybe for leaving clothes on the floor or something. But what I do remember is him solemnly saying this must have been hard on me, having to tell him off.'

Janice sniffed then wiped her nose. 'I don't know if anything will come of what you've told me, but I will let you know any outcome. Though it could take a while.'

'The doctor who told me is Jed Nolan,' Ruth said. 'He worked with Thomas.'

Janice gave her a small hug goodbye. It had been an emotional meeting for both of them.

The sky was dark when she came out of the hospital. She breathed in the refreshingly cold air. The meeting had helped and she was glad she had gone. It hadn't been all doom and gloom as she had feared. Thomas didn't leave under quite as black a cloud as she thought. He was liked. Before pulling out of the car park she checked her phone. She had no text messages or missed calls. She hadn't heard from Henry all day, and hoped this wasn't a step back again.

*

She spotted the police vehicle as she turned into her road. Immediately her guard was up, thinking of ways to avoid seeing Tim Wiley. She could carry on driving and come back after he'd gone, or try sneaking in through the door from the back garden and take refuge in Kim's flat. Kim was outside smoking so she could ask her quickly.

Through the windscreen she saw two police officers and stopped panicking. They were not him. As she parked and got out of the car, she saw them talking to Kim, who pointed in Ruth's direction. The officers turned to look at Ruth as she came through the front garden gate.

'Ah,' Kim said. 'You're home. They've been looking for you, Ruth.'

The shorter officer stepped forward. 'Dr Bennett, if we might have a word,' he said in a tone that sounded official.

Ruth's mouth went dry. What did they want? A dozen thoughts flashed through her head. Had something happened to Pauline? Was it something to do with work? Had Carol Campbell discovered why she was working there? The little boy she examined this morning… Had she missed something? Her meeting half an hour ago… Had Janice May decided to tell the police about this record? What did they want with her?

'It would be better to have this talk inside, Dr Bennett.'

'Sure,' she replied calmly, trying to keep a lid on her fears. 'If you follow me, we can talk in my flat.'

She was aware of him all the way up the stairs, and wanted to slow down the short journey. She was in no hurry to hear what he had to say, all too aware that some things could not be taken back once spoken out loud. They were life changing. She turned on the light in the small hall and then in the living room. She didn't bother to sit or take off her coat, in case she needed to flee.

'How can I help?' she asked.

From his breast pocket he took out a notebook and opened it at a page. 'I believe you know a Mr Henry Thorpe.'

She felt her heart thump. 'Yes. I do.'

'Can you confirm what time he left your flat this morning?'

Ruth felt her throat close. 'I'm not completely sure. Perhaps four o'clock.'

'Did you see him leave? Walk down the street?'

She shook her head. 'No. I was in bed. I just heard him leave.'

'Okay. Thank you for that. Prior to his being here, did you notice anyone on the street or a car parked out there, perhaps?'

'No, I didn't.'

He closed his notebook, without writing anything. Was it just a prop to help him talk? She wondered if he would try to stop her if she walked out the door. It was the only way she was not going to hear anything. And now he was preparing to tell her. He had done the big build-up. Now for the news.

'Henry Thorpe was found at approximately 0600 this morning, on this street, just yards from the front door. I'm surprised you weren't disturbed by police sirens or ambulance.'

'My bedroom doesn't have windows or external walls. I hear only noise from the stairs,' Ruth replied, her brain working on autopilot to give these facts. While waiting for him still to say the worst…

'Doctors say he has a severe concussion following a head injury. We were unable to talk to him until the doctors gave the go ahead at just after four. He'd been unconscious until then. He remembers only leaving your flat. Nothing about what happened to him after that.'

Ruth gazed at him blankly, and then her body remembered to breathe. She moved closer to study his face in case this was a lie. 'He's alive,' she uttered in a shocked voice. Then her thinking speeded up and her eyes flashed her anger. 'You should have said that straight away,' she said scathingly. 'Next time you impart bad news, try not to draw it out. The person you're telling might have a bad heart.'

Her criticism appeared to bounce off him. His manner remained impersonal. His tone strictly polite. 'We don't think this was an accident. Did Mr Thorpe voice any concerns while he was here with you? Any mentions of seeing something or someone that concerned him?'

She stared at him coolly, trying to calm her anger. 'No.'

'Do you know if he's had any problems with anyone recently or in the past?'

'No.'

'What about with family or with work?'

'No.'

He gazed at her with a wry smile. 'That's a lot of nos.' Then his eyes went to the bookcase, to the neatly folded female clothes. 'Your neighbour downstairs says you haven't been here long.'

'That's right,' Ruth replied, in a clipped tone.

'And that you're a doctor?'

'Yes.'

His expression showed he was curious. 'Your neighbour is surprised at you living here. She thinks you should be living somewhere more upmarket.'

'Does she?' Ruth's tone was getting sharper.

He nodded. 'Yes. She can't work out why you'd live here. Though she tells me the previous tenant was a doctor as well. Young, though, so perhaps not in the income bracket to afford more.'

Her stomach clenched. Did he know this address? Know about Thomas?

He looked around the spartan room, then at Ruth again, taking in the quality of her clothing, her shoes and briefcase, as if he was trying to work her out. 'I can see why she might think that.' He murmured as if in agreement. Then said, 'We may need to talk to you again.'

Riling Ruth some more. Was that a way of telling her she was considered a suspect? 'I don't think I have any further information I can give you.'

'Well, something might come to you later. Or to us, for that matter.'

Ruth held back from verbally sparring with him. She had to go. Henry could be dying. Until she spoke with a doctor she couldn't know. Her heart was racing with worry. '*Please.* Can you tell me the ward he's on?'

Her urgent plea seemed to throw him. It also seemed to bring a return to his manners. A seriousness appeared in his eyes. 'Yes, of course. I should have said sooner. He's in the ICU.'

Ruth gave a short nod. It was all she could manage. Henry must be in a bad way.

CHAPTER THIRTY-FIVE

Rosie saw the lights go on in the house. She would give the woman a chance to take off her coat. Yesterday after the police drove away, Rosie left and went home for a few hours. When she returned in the evening, the car had gone and Miss Tupperware wasn't home. She had the same result this morning, so was relieved this wasn't another wasted journey.

Confident she looked her best in smart black jeans and cream crew neck jumper, Rosie walked across the road. She was in a brighter mood after her visit to the doctor, and was glad she went. She was more relaxed and better able to knock on the door.

A moment later the woman presently stalking Rosie's dreams peered out at her curiously. Then recognition showed in her small brown eyes. She gave a half smile. 'Oh, hello.'

Rosie smiled back. 'I came with Anabel to your Tupperware party. I'm sorry I can't remember your name, though.'

'Chloe,' she said. 'And likewise, I've forgotten yours.'

'It's Rosie,' Rosie replied, thinking Chloe just told a pork pie. There was no way she didn't know Rosie's name. Anabel would have spoken about her. Lots of times, and probably not in a very nice way. But that was okay. She was here now and they were past the pleasantries. 'You can probably guess why I'm here. Anabel's mum said the police got a call saying she was here. Turned out wrong, obviously, but I wonder if I can come in and talk to you?'

Chloe held the door open wider. 'Sure. Come in. I'll put the kettle on.'

Rosie stepped into the hallway and wiped her feet on the mat. She remembered the white baluster and spindles on the stairs, and that behind the closed door at the end of the hall was the loo. The door to the right of it led into the lounge, the door to her immediate right into the kitchen.

She had her back to Chloe, which was as well given what Chloe said next. 'I'm surprised Meg hasn't phoned me. I didn't think the police were going to tell her. She must have been waiting all day yesterday, and now today wondering why I haven't called.'

Rosie had a job to mask her surprise. Though some, she supposed, would be acceptable. 'I didn't know you knew Anabel's mum.'

'Oh, yes,' Chloe said in a high voice. 'Meg works with my mum. They're both estate agents, which is how I have this house. My mum's got an eye for a bargain. She owns it, not me. I asked Anabel if she wanted to move in as it has three bedrooms. Meg is selling the house Anabel's flat is in. Her upstairs tenants have gone, so Anabel will be giving up her flat.'

Rosie did a better job hiding her second surprise. She'd always known Meg owned the property, and Anabel rented from her. She hadn't known Meg was selling, though, and Anabel leaving it. 'Is that how you know Anabel? Through your mum and her mum?'

Chloe took Rosie's jacket from her and hung it on a coat rack at the bottom of the stairs. She faced Rosie and her expression was puzzled. 'No. I work with Anabel on the ward. I thought you knew that. I moved from obstetrics to surgical last year and we hit it off.'

Rosie followed her into the kitchen and glanced appreciatively at the shiny black wall tiles, separating white gloss cabinets and white countertop. Two bar stools with black seats were lined up against a slim breakfast bar. 'This is lovely. You have so much room. It's a nice size space to cook in.'

'I know. I'm so lucky. Because cooking is my favourite thing,' she said, with a happy smile. She opened the cabinet above the kettle and Rosie saw the contents artfully arranged on the shelves. She'd guessed right about Ovaltine being her nightly drink, though there was also a jar of Bovril beside it. Chloe took out a tin of coffee. 'This okay? Or do you prefer tea?' she asked.

Rosie was leaning against the breakfast bar, between the stools, to keep out of the way. She nodded. 'Coffee's good.' She waited until the kettle silenced itself before she spoke again – Chloe must have boiled it just before Rosie arrived as it took only seconds. 'I'll be calling Meg later. I'll let her know you weren't aware the police told her, if you like?'

Chloe's expression was grateful. 'Can you? That would be great if you could. It's a bit awkward to talk to her in present circumstances. My mum said she's barely coping. The doctors have her on tablets to just get her through the day.'

'I can well imagine,' Rosie replied in a sombre tone. 'Yeah, I'll do it. She checks in with me every few days, asking if I've heard from Anabel. I have to give her the same answer each time. *Not yet, Meg.*' Rosie let out a weary sigh. 'To be honest, Chloe, I'm worried sick. I was praying all the way here that she would be with you secretly, and didn't want the police to know. I'm worried she's disappeared for good. It's not like her not to be in touch with her mum.'

Chloe stopped what she was doing and stared into Rosie's eyes. 'You mustn't think that,' she said in a motherly voice that sounded downright odd coming from someone her age. 'She probably just needs time to sort some things out.'

'Like what?' Rosie retorted more sharply than intended.

Chloe stepped back. 'I'm sure I don't know.' She sounded slightly offended.

'So she didn't say?' Rosie pressed.

'What do you mean?'

'When you saw her. She didn't say what things she needed to sort out?'

'I'm really not sure what you're trying to say,' she replied calmly. There was a short silence, while she studied Rosie as if trying to fathom her. Then she put her hand to her mouth and made a little sound. 'Oh, I'm sorry. Poor you. I've just realised you're not here just for Meg. Anabel's your friend.'

Rosie reined in her irritation. She would get nowhere if she lost her temper. If this woman was toying with her, and secretly knew all there was to know about her and Anabel, she was going to have to play along. If she was playing a cat-and-mouse game, Rosie would have to let her catch her. Right now, her best chance of finding anything out was to play dumb, make mistakes, not be clever. Earn her trust. Then Chloe might relax and let something slip. She might even shout up the stairs and call Anabel down.

'I was so sure she was here,' Rosie said, adding some disappointment into her voice. 'She likes you. I was hoping she'd talk to you. She's been in a bad way for a while. She won't talk to me. She was like this when we were kids. She'd bottle it up or run away to hide, like she has now.'

Chloe averted her gaze, giving nothing away.

Rosie took a gamble. She started towards the kitchen door. 'Look, I'm sorry. I shouldn't have come. Anabel wouldn't want me dragging you into this. Thanks for the offer of coffee, but I'm just going to go, if that's all right? It was selfish of me.'

'She told me a little…'

Rosie turned slowly and gazed at Chloe like she was some sort of miracle. 'That's amazing, Chloe,' she said in a hushed tone. 'You've managed to get her to talk. That's the best thing for her. She has someone she can talk to.'

Chloe raised her hand to reject that idea. Her reply was firm. 'I'm not who she wants to talk to. She wants to talk to a friend's family. Tell them what happened. That's what she says she wants to do.'

Rosie felt her heart stop. She managed to nod. Then she closed her eyes, needing a moment to work out if Chloe could be believed.

It seemed like she knew a lot. Was she being clever, by not saying the friend's name? Had Anabel really not told her it?

'Are you okay?' Chloe asked.

Rosie glanced at her, taking in the sleek bun and the diamond-patterned cardigan buttoned up to the neck. She gave a sad smile. 'Yes. Just relieved. After last year, it's all been a bit of a mess. Anabel will hardly talk to me. It's hard to get her to accept she had no choice. She was not to blame for what happened afterwards.'

Chloe's reaction showed she knew something. She became busy at the counter, spooning coffee into the mugs. She must have sensed Rosie watching because a moment later she laid the spoon down and hung her head. Rosie couldn't see her face, but she could hear the heaviness in her voice as she spoke. 'Anabel told me she did something bad. That her whole life has been on hold. She can never move on. I asked her if this was something she should tell the police. She said her friend needed her to be strong.' Chloe turned and gazed at Rosie. 'Last year upset her. It upset us all. I don't know any more than that. Do you?'

Rosie shook her head. 'I don't. That's why I'm here, Chloe. I want to find out how I can help her. I think she needs help.'

Chloe gripped her hands together, biting her bottom lip between her teeth. She sighed. 'I'm sure that's true, but I don't know where she is. Anabel was here, but not anymore. She's been gone over a week. I came home after work and Anabel and her suitcase were gone.'

Rosie breathed slightly easier. This was going well. She just needed to know one more thing. 'Chloe, when Meg and I searched Anabel's flat, I found what looked like a blackmail letter in her bin. Meg doesn't know. Did Anabel say anything about it?'

She nodded. 'Yes, she said someone posted it. She was actually happy about it. She said that someone knew, and soon she wouldn't have to hide anymore.'

'Shit,' Rosie whispered, and then seeing Chloe frown she spread her hands expansively. 'Anabel could be in danger. What sort of person sends a blackmail note? Do we have any idea who sent it?'

Chloe shook her head. 'She didn't say. She was behaving like she hoped to get another. Maybe she's gone back to her flat. When was the last time you checked there?'

Rosie stared at Chloe and then gave a low groan. 'Christ, how stupid am I? Not since I checked it with Meg.' She sighed. 'I wish I'd come to see you sooner. Thanks, Chloe. You've been a great help, but I'm going to shoot. I want to go check it now.'

As she stepped out of the front door, Chloe held out a carrier bag towards her. 'She left this behind.' Anabel's pink jacket was in it. 'Stay positive. She'll come back when she's ready. When you see her would you give it back to her, and send her my love?'

Rosie said she would.

'Thanks.'

Rosie wanted to leave, but something in Chloe's manner stalled her. 'What is it, Chloe? Has my coming here upset you?'

'No, not at all,' she replied. 'I just realised something. When you came here last year you didn't remember we'd met before. On the ward that day. You brought back a patient from theatre when it had all just kicked off.'

Rosie blinked in surprise. She should have twigged earlier that Chloe would have seen her. She had said it upset us all. She was including Rosie in that statement.

Rosie replied with the truth. 'It would have been hard to have noticed my own mother while all that was going on. And I so rarely go to the wards I don't get to see someone long enough to recognise them.' She smiled. 'I'll say hello next time.'

'When will that be?'

Rosie stilled. Chloe's phrasing caused a tingle in her spine. *When will that be? Say the bells of Stepney.* She shrugged the tune out of her head, and made for the steps, calling over her shoulder. 'As soon as Anabel's found.'

At the bottom of the steps she stood and waved, then set off for the walk home, feeling the light weight of the carrier bag in her hand, thinking… everything happening was because of what happened on the ward that day. Poor Anabel had been in a state. Rosie stayed and helped her calm down. People were searching for whatever the doctor had taken, thinking he put something in his water, picking up and putting down every other person's bottle of water, like it was a race to be the first one to find his. Afterwards, when it was discovered what he had done, what he had stolen, Rosie returned the empty patient trolley back to theatre and called it a day. Anabel had needed her. Though, it wasn't long after that, she rejected the comfort Rosie tried to give. She didn't want to be consoled.

Rosie had taken note of Chloe's advice. She would check Anabel's flat one more time, but she was going to stop looking if she didn't find her there. Everything had shifted. She couldn't ignore what Chloe said, that Anabel wanted to talk to this friend's family. To tell them what happened. Rosie would need to act fast. There was no way she was letting Anabel tell her mum. Rosie was her daughter, not Anabel. She would hear it from Rosie. Not anyone else.

Anabel wanted to share their secret. Which was a shame. They had kept it so safe while they were friends. It would be nice if Anabel wanted to become friends again, but that probably wouldn't happen now.

CHAPTER THIRTY-SIX

Ruth entered the hospital through the main doors and headed straight for the stairs. She went up one flight to the first floor, turned left and walked along the corridor, passing a prayer room, getting a glimpse of a golden glow stained-glass window, until she came to the Critical Care Unit. The two whiteboards on the wall listed the departments beyond the double doors: Coronary Care. Cardiac. High Dependency. Intensive Care Unit. Where Henry was now a patient.

She had been in no fit state to drive, and had called for a taxi. She had waited on the pavement for it to arrive. While the two police officers climbed in their vehicle. Then the officer, who had spoken to her in the flat about Henry, unexpectedly surprised her. He wound down the window and gave her an unopened bottle of water, which she drank with a thirst. He then gave her exact directions to the Critical Care Unit so that when she got to the hospital she didn't have to stop and ask someone or look for floor maps.

At the entrance to the unit she paused and attempted to prepare herself for what she might face. Too much knowledge and experience at a time like this was making her visualise the worst outcomes.

The doors were closed. Ruth pressed the intercom button, and a few moments later a nurse came to the door. Ruth used the only reason she might be let in, as she was not next of kin or a relative: 'Hi, I'm here to see Henry Thorpe. The two police officers who were here earlier to talk to him informed me of his admission as soon as they were able to contact me.'

The nurse held the door wider and let Ruth in. 'I'll take you through. He's in bed three, but we'll be moving him shortly.'

Ruth was desperate to know his condition and again used what she had. 'I'm a doctor and I would be grateful if someone could tell me about Henry's condition. I understand he has concussion?'

'Yes,' she said. 'Why don't you come over to the desk and I'll get the consultant to talk to you? He's looking at Henry's notes now.'

The doctor sitting at the desk was dressed in light blue scrubs. From his face he looked to be around his late forties, but his body could have belonged to a much younger man with lean muscled forearms and slim strong neck. The nurse introduced her and he stood to say hello. 'Hi, I'm Douglas Freeman. Henry has given me permission to talk about him to you, otherwise we'd have to wake him. A very forthright man, Professor Thorpe. He made it clear you were not to be left in the dark should he become addled, or you have questions. He said you had enough nonsense to deal with already.'

Ruth felt her chest contract, and a tingling down the sides of her nose. *Damn you, Henry.* Bloody man had got under her skin. She was going to look all kinds of fool if she started to cry. 'Can I assume that him being as clear-minded as that is a good sign?' she asked.

He smiled with his eyes. 'You can. But cautiously. Henry received a blunt injury to the back of the head. I think this caused him to fall face forward and receive a second blow to the front of the head as he hit the pavement. When paramedics got to him his GCS was nine, so certainly concerning. His neurological findings steadily improved from about eleven o'clock this morning, his GCS then scored top marks of fifteen. So pretty good. His brain has no doubt been given a shake, and impact over a wide area of the skull has left him with a sickening headache. But CT is good. No bone displacement. No bleeding. No injury to his neck.

'He's out of the woods and doesn't need to be on ICU any longer. It was mainly precautionary, so we'll be moving him to a ward soon. We'll probably keep him in for a couple of days, then send him home with guidance on management of concussion and have him attend a follow-up appointment to see how things are.'

Ruth felt enormous relief. Concussion was no picnic and Henry might have symptoms for a while, but far better that than brain damage or death. She thanked the doctor and said she would have a peek at Henry, but not tire him.

His eyes were closed and she was able to examine the large bruise across his forehead. He had been lucky not to have fractured his skull or broken bones in his face. No grazes on his hands suggested he hadn't put them out to break his fall, that he had fallen without awareness. She shivered at the thought of that, how much more seriously injured he could have been if his head had hit the edge of the kerb. A hospital gown covered his chest, acting more as a sheet than a garment as his arms weren't in the sleeves. Ruth cast her eyes over the readings on the monitors. Apart from his blood pressure being a little low, it was all good. All reassuring.

'You know it's rude to just stand and stare, Dr Bennett,' Henry said quietly, making Ruth jump guiltily and give a little yelp. She'd been sure he was asleep. His eyes were still closed.

'How did you know it's me? Your eyes are closed.'

His lips curved in a small smile. 'And they'll be staying that way. The lights still hurt. I told you, my intuition tells me things.'

'Really?' She laughed softly. She then poked her tongue out at him. 'And what does your intuition tell you now, oh, Mr Clever Clogs.'

'That you're probably taking advantage of a man unable to defend himself.'

Ruth sat down gingerly on the side of his bed, careful not to cause any movement. 'How are you?'

His hand reached out and touched her lap. She held it there, resting her hand over his.

'Don't be worried, Ruth,' he said, speaking low, and slowly, probably so as not to jar his hurting head. 'It's all fixable. I asked Marlene to check on you all and make sure you're all feeling safe. Especially Kim, as she's on the ground floor.'

Ruth shushed him as she saw him give a little wince. 'Don't worry about anything. We're all fine. They've got a doctor living with them if they need medical help,' she said in a jokey way.

He waited a moment before speaking again, till the frown eased between his eyes. 'Be careful. Make sure the front door is never left on the latch. Akito is an electronics engineer. Talk to him about installing a security entry system. Tell him I'll cover whatever it costs, whether he does it or gets someone in.'

He took slow breaths then and rested. His features became relaxed. Without the distraction of his glasses she admired the planes of his face – eyeline meeting side of socket, following on down to his cheekbone. In her bed last night she had looked into his eyes, and seen even more intelligence lurking in their depths. It would have been cruel beyond measure to have rendered them blank.

Ruth felt the presence of someone behind her and turned her head. The nurse who let her in was standing there with a porter. The nurse smiled. 'We're going to move him to a ward now.'

Ruth rose from the bed and leaned over Henry to place a light kiss on his cheek. He didn't stir and she wished they would let him sleep and move him later. Then she glanced around at the other beds, at the equipment monitoring the patients, keeping some of them alive, and knew Henry was lucky not to have to be staying.

Very quietly she thanked the nurse for looking after him.

*

Downstairs in the atrium she followed a sign to the public toilets. The full bottle of water she drank had filled her bladder. She hadn't been to the loo since leaving work, and since then she'd had a meeting with Janice May and then a meeting with the police. It was now eight fifteen. At the sink she washed her hands and checked her face in the mirror. Her grey eyes looked darker, her skin paler, and she felt cold. She was trying to keep disturbing thoughts at bay. Picking up her handbag she went back out to the corridor. She would phone for a taxi to take her home and then have a hot bath, a hot drink, and get into bed where she would be comforted by Henry's scent still on her pillows.

She pulled out her phone, raising it to look at the screen and then stilled. She saw Kim walking through the main doors, her puffer jacket over her uniform. Ruth watched her disappear into the lift. She must be working a night shift on one of the wards. She liked Kim, but she wasn't fooled. She had fed information about Ruth to the police officer, perhaps deliberately. There was something untrustworthy about her. Ruth couldn't take what she said at face value. She'd been questioned by Tim Wiley. But about what?

Focusing on the job in hand, Ruth dialled the same taxi firm she used earlier to now take her home. Five minutes she was told, and to wait by the entrance. Holding her phone she went outside and a couple of minutes later it pinged with a message informing her of the vehicle model and car registration just as the taxi pulled into the kerb. Ruth gave her name and gratefully climbed in and shut the door. As the driver pulled out, Ruth watched the back of his head. His beanie hat was covering his ears and she appreciated he must be cold too. There was a clear starry sky. It was going to be a cold night – colder than last night, which had been relatively mild. Another thing to be grateful for – Henry mightn't have fared so well if he'd ended up with hypothermia or pneumonia.

The beanie hat on the driver reminded her that Kim's visitor had been wearing one the night he entered the front garden. Was it possible he was there again when Henry was leaving? Perhaps Kim had a middle-of-the-night meeting with the man so that no one saw them? Ruth had other thoughts as well, even darker than this one, that she could no longer keep at bay. The thought had been there from the beginning, from the very second she heard Henry had been found outside on the pavement. Tim Wiley had done it. It was him behind her the night she got out of her car into gusty wind. Him hiding by the tree. Him in the car on the red-brick road. Him behind her getting too close to her bike. Had his interest turned to fixation?

She entered the house and considered Kim's closed front door. She would like to have a very frank conversation with her neighbour, one that involved Kim telling the truth, but Kim was currently at work in the hospital. Kim might know far more about Tim Wiley than she was letting on. She might know more about Thomas. It might be worth revealing to Kim that Thomas was her son. Tomorrow was Saturday and Kim would probably sleep through some of it. Before Ruth made any decisions, she would talk to the other tenants and see what they knew. Akito had pointed out Kim was always there. He was an observant man. He may have noticed more than just his neighbour downstairs.

Henry had asked her to speak to Akito. Thomas had asked her to settle a debt. In the morning she would carry out both requests. If she gained nothing after talking to Akito and Tilly, and then to Kim, she would take her concerns to the police.

CHAPTER THIRTY-SEVEN

Rosie was trying one more possibility before she gave up for good. Anabel's flat had shown no sign that she had been back. Through the letterbox Rosie saw brown envelopes and flyers dropped where they'd landed. No one had walked over them or through the front door. She now wanted to find Jed Nolan. Anabel spoke about him a lot, like he was a friend more than a colleague. Rosie had worked with him, too, but there had never been any familiarity between them. He only ever talked to her as a doctor when he needed assistance from a nurse. But he liked Anabel. He'd loaned her a self-help book last summer on how to be free of anxiety. Rosie learned long ago that Anabel attracted people who wanted to help her. Take Chloe – she'd invited Anabel to live with her. They must have formed more than a work colleague relationship for that to have happened. Yet Anabel denied it, making out like they weren't even friends after the Tupperware party. She hadn't even mentioned Chloe being a nurse.

Rosie held the new sick note in her hand. It was her excuse to be visiting her workplace. She was handing it in. She made her way towards the Surgical Unit, keeping a look out for anyone who might know the answer to her question. She was in luck. Liam, a porter, was up ahead, and someone she knew well. She'd slept with him once a few years ago and he still had a thing for her, despite being married with two kids. She caught up with him and was less than flattered by his shocked stare and opening comments.

'Blimey, they said you were off sick. I didn't realise you'd been that unwell. There's nothing of you. What've you been off with?'

Rosie gave a wan smile. She might as well milk it. It might get her more help. 'Oh, just some bug I picked up. How are you, Liam?'

'Good,' he said. 'Working all hours. Me and the missus are expecting another one.' He grinned. 'Falls pregnant at the drop of a hat.'

Rosie saw he was delighted at his prowess as a lover. She beamed at him. 'That's brilliant news, Liam. Congratulations.'

His chest puffed out with genuine pride and Rosie felt a pang of jealousy. She could have been his wife, and the mother of his two children. She could have been settled and content with a man who would never be unhappy, but for Anabel standing in the way of her happiness.

'Liam, I don't suppose you've seen Dr Nolan on your rounds? I need to give him something.'

His thick eyebrows moved up to his hairline. 'Rosie, you do know it's only six o'clock in the morning?'

She stared at him, trying to hide her surprise. She actually hadn't known it was so early. When she'd climbed out of bed she hadn't checked the time. She'd just got dressed and gone to the hospital. Maybe having no structure to her day had something to do with it. She had no landmarks to pass the time. When she was awake she was alone and when she was asleep she was drugged. The only times in the last few months she'd been conscious of night and day were when she'd begun watching Chloe's home.

She batted away his comment. 'This is normal for me, Liam. I'm always up early. But I thought it best to catch him before he started work. I'll just hang around.'

He didn't look fully convinced, pulling a face as though he thought she was a bit mad, but then said, 'Well, you're in luck. You won't have to. I just stocked the changing rooms in theatre and he was changing back into his clothes. He's been assisting with an operation half the night, he said, and was going home. If you hurry you might catch him.'

Rosie was already walking away, and called out her thanks. She wouldn't bother with going to the department, she'd head for the car park instead. She knew his car and would wait for him there.

If she'd been a minute longer she would have missed him. She'd barely caught her breath when he showed up. He hadn't noticed her and was yawning with his mouth wide open. He was good-looking, but not Rosie's cup of tea. He was too boyish, and his put-on public schoolboy voice irritated her. Surely he realised people who spoke that way naturally would notice? To her it showed a sign of insecurity, that he felt lacking in some way and had to do it to fit in. If he was from a working-class background he should stand up and be proud. The car she was leaning on was a Porsche, but it was so old that if it went too fast or over a bump the suspension would probably bottom out.

He startled as he saw her. If there were other people around or cars passing he might not have, but the stillness of her standing there in the pale morning light must have jolted him.

She smiled. 'Hi, Jed.'

'What are you doing here?' he asked, without returning a smile. 'And would you mind not leaning against my car?'

Rosie stood straight and made a show of examining the roof. 'Sorry, didn't realise it would hurt it.' She waved her hand in the direction of the building. 'Just dropping off a sick note.'

He eyed her for a moment before putting a key in the car door to unlock it. 'I thought you'd left.'

'No.' She shook her head. 'Just been unwell.'

He opened his car door without further comment, obviously not interested in why she was waiting there. Rosie decided to blurt it out. 'Have you seen Anabel?'

He bent and put his bag across onto the passenger seat, then straightened and turned to look at her. 'Why would I have seen your friend?'

Rosie smirked. 'Because you fancy her.'

He stared out into the car park, then seemed to reluctantly drag his gaze back to her. Rosie felt a heat come into her chest and rise up to her cheeks as she watched his eyes appraise her. His lip curled. 'If you can't find your friend, then I suggest you stop looking. She's clearly come to her senses and has made herself unavailable.'

Rosie gasped, and saw this bring a satisfied smile to his face. Her back teeth began to grind. Who the fuck does he think he is? He was younger than her and felt he could talk to her like that? So what if he was a doctor? He was hardly even qualified.

'Wanker,' she snarled. 'What the fuck gives you the right to say that?'

He tutted. 'Such language.' Then he climbed into his car.

Rosie stepped forward before he could close the door. 'I'm worried about her,' she said in a hard voice. 'Don't you get it? No one knows where she is.'

He looked up at her as she stood by the door. 'I've worked with you on and off for a couple of years now, Nurse Carlyle. I don't imagine for a moment you're worried about your friend. I don't see you putting up posters of her, though others have and the police have. I haven't noticed any postings from you on the Facebook page dedicated to finding her. You say no one knows where she is. How come you don't, if you're her friend?'

'Why don't you like me?' Rosie asked in a challenging tone.

He sat for a second and then eyed her with open disdain. 'You're not that good at hiding your feelings. I have a good memory of you at a New Year's Eve party. Your friend was having a good time. I was sitting close enough to you to see your stony eyes fixed on her face, and to hear what you had to say under your breath.' He reached out and pulled the car door closed, then he wound down the window. 'I hope I've answered your question,' he said, turning on the engine and pulling his seat belt across him. 'You're not a nice person. It's as simple as that.'

Then he drove away. Leaving Rosie with legs like rubber.

*

Rosie ignored the woman sitting across from her on the bus and exhaled into her cupped hands again. The nosy cow could look the other way if she didn't like what Rosie was doing. Rosie didn't care. She was more concerned that her mother would smell alcohol on her breath. She drank a glass of vodka when she got back home and then had to quickly sit down. It was the first drink she'd had in more than a week, and without food in her stomach it had gone straight to her blood stream. All the good progress she'd made in the last week – she'd not taken any extra medication either – undone in that few minutes of talking in the car park.

Jed Nolan had been a complete shit. Like he was so perfect. He wasn't even popular. He might be more educated, and she might only be a couple of years older, but she knew people better than him and knew most people would find him dull. He was like a second cup of tea after the first one satisfied your thirst. It didn't make an impact. You didn't really need it. You wouldn't bother if it wasn't poured. He was like that. So she could kick herself for letting him upset her.

It was the way he looked at her. The way he put Anabel out of reach as if she were too good for Rosie. It made her remember her parents' comments. *You're lucky to have her, Rosie. Make sure you're nice to her.* Anabel fooled them with her doe eyes and soggy thumb. It was probably her thumb sucking that Jed liked. He probably got off on it and had wet dreams. If Rosie was in that car park another time and his car was there, she'd pick at all the bubbling in the brown paintwork and see how he liked that. She bet his language would turn blue then. Seeing it was really a rust bucket.

The stop she wanted was coming up. The six-mile journey to Poole had taken only half an hour. As a child when she went to Bournemouth for the day it had seemed so much further. She grabbed onto the pole as the bus came to a standstill, to steady her balance while carrying a heavy holdall. She'd packed as if going away. She wasn't even intending to stay, she just needed to get away for a few hours to clear her head. This visit, though, would be good for another reason. It would give her a chance to tell her mum about the day Dad died. It would be her last visit for a while. How long depended on her mum. Once Rosie said goodbye she was going back to her bedsit to pack properly, then taking a different bus on a far longer journey. It might be years before she saw her mum again.

Off the bus, she managed her bags better. She was wiry and strong and kept up a good pace. At the Co-op, around the corner from her mum's, she stopped to buy a bunch of yellow chrysanthemums and a Toblerone. Likely leftover Christmas stock, it was a bonus to be able to buy her a big bar. It was her favourite chocolate, what she always brought back from a holiday. Rosie now felt more optimistic. Happier that she'd got something to give her.

A few minutes later she was touched by a wistful desire to return to the past, to relive her childhood again. She had played on this safe street every day after school, marking the pavement with chalk for hopscotch, or playing French skipping with Anabel. They'd take it in turns to stand with the elastic band around the back of their legs and loop the other end around a heavy kitchen chair. At the weekends they'd ride off on their bikes and spend the day on the beach, hanging out at the arcades looking for forgotten coins in slot machines. Those easy days had been full of fun.

She came to the two houses, side by side. Anabel's on the left with a sloped drive down to a black metal garage door, Rosie's on the right with the slope now gone, the garage bricked up, the space now a level slab of concrete to park one car. There were new people living in Anabel's house. Well, they were new as far as Rosie was concerned – she'd never met them, even though they'd been there years. Anabel's mum and dad moved house right after she and Rosie moved to Bournemouth to train as nurses. Today, knowing they were gone from the street and that she too might never come back, it felt like the end of an era.

Rosie walked past the grey concrete and up to the front door. She rang the bell, swallowing the sliver of mint she'd been sucking. A moment later her mum's face stared out at her from the front-room window. Was she frowning because she wasn't wearing her glasses or because she was in a gloomy mood? Rosie smiled, and waited for the door to open.

Jo Carlyle let her daughter in and left Rosie to shut the front door, walking from the hall and back to the front room without a word. Rosie quietly put down her bags, thinking she should have called. She pulled the flowers and chocolate out of the carrier bag, deciding the best thing to do was to ignore the stilted atmosphere. She'd make herself useful, offer to do chores, then treat them to a takeaway for tea. Over the meal she would explain what really happened. It was going to break her mum's heart.

When she joined her mum she found her in an armchair with a magazine in her lap, her gaze focused on the pages. Rosie glanced around the room and noticed it was nice and clean, the pile in the beige carpet showing slim runways left from an upright Hoover. There were new photos on the mantel, and she saw with some surprise her brothers looking older. Max was losing his hair and Ron had a paunch. Rosie could see only one photo of her when she was two, her mum was holding her dressed in a pale blue jumper and jeans.

Rosie chanced a look at her now. Her head was still in the magazine. At fifty-nine, she was trim and stylish and kept her grey-blonde hair short. She was wearing her work clothes, a blue-and-red silk scarf poking out of the neck of her blouse, and a navy skirt. She'd worked in the same job as a cashier at the same building society for the last forty years. Being a Saturday, she would have finished at twelve. Rosie should have delayed her visit an hour or two, given her a chance to unwind first. She knew her mother's routine by heart. She liked to sit for a bit after getting home, usually with a magazine, before changing out of her clothes. Her life was structured. She had Sundays and Mondays off, then Tuesday to Friday worked nine till five. Tomorrow she would change bed linen, do washing, then a trip to Aldi. Mondays she went for a swim or a walk after ironing. She liked the telly on in the evenings so she could watch her soaps, and unless it was her birthday or the birthday of a friend, this was the life she enjoyed. Rosie wouldn't mind it at all, peace and quiet and no one to answer to.

'I'm just going to pop these flowers in water, then make some tea,' Rosie said. 'Do you want one?'

Jo Carlyle rose from the chair and set down the magazine. Rosie sighed inwardly, relieved to see her responding.

'Ignore my bags in the hall,' she lightly laughed. 'I'm not staying.'

Her mum finally looked at her and then at the flowers. Rosie saw no humour in her face, no lightening of her mood. 'Have yourself a drink, Rosie, then go.' Her voice was stark.

Rosie felt the ground shift beneath her feet, feeling the weight of her insides plummet forcefully. Her mum was deadly serious. She was asking her to leave. Rosie stared at her in shock. She couldn't get her head around it. The last visit had been strained, but not so much as to warrant this. They'd eaten together. Rosie washed up, while her mum dried. They'd watched *EastEnders* together before Rosie caught the bus home. It hadn't been that bad. *This* felt final, like her mum wanted her to go forever. Had Anabel already told her?

Rosie gazed at her confused. 'What's wrong? Are you ill?'

Her mum had an emptiness in her eyes. Her voice was weary. 'You know, all your life I was waiting for it to show itself. I convinced myself I was wrong about you, that I was bad-minded. And some of the time I was able to sweep the thoughts away. Your brothers thought it. They used to say it plenty of times. They don't say it anymore. They don't talk about you.' She inhaled slowly, then as if with something more than the need to breathe out, she released the air like pushing something from her body. 'Your father, poor man, never saw anything wrong. He saw only good in people. You know what I can't get over. Is seeing you sat at that table, *eating*, while your father was lying dead outside on the ground. While that poor girl next door ran away. Meg should have run with her the moment you set your sights on her.' She gazed at Rosie dispassionately, her voice at one level as if anchored down so she could say nothing loud or fast.

Rosie gaped at her. She had always known her mother blamed her. It sat quietly in her eyes year in and year out. She had never voiced it, though. Never. Not once. Not even on the day of his funeral when she stared into Rosie's eyes and suggested Rosie didn't go.

'You think I don't know what's going on? That I don't pick up a newspaper? That I walk blindly past shop windows? I rang Meg as soon as I saw Anabel's face. I couldn't tell her I found out her daughter was missing from seeing it on a poster. You disgust me, Rosie. You hadn't even the decency to let me know Anabel was missing.'

'I didn't want you upset,' Rosie protested. 'I knew you would worry.'

'Cut the bullshit, Rosie,' her mother quietly said. 'You didn't want me to know or to ask questions.' She gave a low bitter laugh. 'I wouldn't have asked you anything. I already know it all. Your sweet friend came to see me last September. She sat in that chair by the window and cried over what happened to that doctor. She told me what you did on the ward that day. The trick you pulled to gee up his plight. When she finished I told her to get as far away from you as possible. To cut all ties and not look back. If I thought that's what she was doing right now, I'd be happy, but I have a terrible feeling something bad has happened to her. She'd never leave Meg to worry like this.' She stared at Rosie with desolate eyes. 'You broke her doing that, because everything inside of you is broken and you cannot stand the thought of her being happy. I've been waiting all these years for it to show itself and eventually it has. The vileness that runs through your veins finally burst out. So go, Rosie, and don't come back. You're not welcome in this home anymore.'

*

Rosie made it as far as Anabel's old house before the contents of her stomach landed on a patch of grass, leaving the green blades in a pool of yellow. Wiping her mouth with her sleeve she walked blindly on. Pain drilled a hole in her stomach and clawed her mind. Words tripped over themselves as she tried to come to terms with what happened. A word was beating in her heart like a small wild animal, trapped there. *Traitor.* All this time she hadn't known that her friend had gone behind her back and betrayed her to the one person that mattered. *How could she?* 'How fucking dare she?' Rosie roared up at the sky, scaring the old man she was passing.

She spat on the ground to clear the vile taste from her mouth. Anabel hadn't told everything. She was a coward. According to Chloe, Anabel wanted to tell the friend's family about it. Well, she had the chance to do that and hadn't so far. Rosie would know if her mum knew that. Rosie couldn't wait to tell her a great big fat lie. That she got in first and told their secret. Rosie would make sure to let Anabel know she included every last detail.

She went into the Co-op for the second time that day. She made straight for the counter, placing down a twenty-pound note, and walked out with a bottle of vodka without waiting for change. From her rucksack she retrieved the plastic bottle and emptied out the water, replacing it with the vodka. She had a bus journey to survive and this shock to cope with, and she was going to need to drink plenty to manage that. She took her first drink and looked up at the sky again. Not to roar at it this time, but to promise it something that could not be said out loud.

Anabel Whiting, you will be fucking dead as soon as I find you.

CHAPTER THIRTY-EIGHT

Don't have energy to write. Drunk. Mason suggested went home after morning list, looked heavy-eyed at table. Euphemism, I think he wanted say looked hungover. Well, wrong. Not drank since January… Feel bad what I done. To her, am horrible man. Didn't mean anything, just frustration. Things out of hand, fuck sake, nicking now. Please get over it!!!

Ruth had spent the time waiting for Akito and Tilly to get back from the shops by adding punctuation to the words Thomas wrote on 6 April. This last attempt read marginally better if its meaning was referring to the three days before, and his emotional outburst of words a result of all the things that happened in that short period.

Third of April his phone went missing. He thought Jed might have moved it and was playing games. Fourth of April it went missing again and he suspected the nurse as having taken it and put it in a drawer. His consultant and Jed suggest he is tired. Fifth of April, after he confronts her, she cries and tells colleagues he's really nice. *I don't think he meant to. Things just got out of hand.* She was talking to colleagues after Thomas confronted her. She was referring to what just happened between them. He'd accused her of taking his phone. She was crying…

Ruth felt her chest tingle. She recalled what Catherine said. *He felt so bad for shouting at her after believing she'd taken his phone. He just wanted her to admit it.* Had Thomas written *nicking* as a harsher way to say *taken*? Jed also mentioned that Thomas… *Shouted at the poor girl.* Ruth wondered at the possibility that this is what the nurse meant. Things just got out of hand because he shouted at her. Whereas normally, he's really nice. Had she been defending him because of his colleagues witnessing his behaviour? It was a different image of her, if so, than the one Ruth had started to imagine. This nurse sounded more like the one Catherine described. Ruth would like to meet her so she could judge for herself what she was like. It would be good to think she was nice, and to know Thomas never hurt her. That her call to the police wasn't done out of spite, but out of necessity. These troublesome thoughts, she so wanted to not have, taking little bites at her mind. She phoned Catherine earlier, apologising for not being able to meet her this weekend, due to unforeseen circumstances, and felt guilty when she came off the phone. Catherine didn't have a single troublesome thought about Thomas, while his mother did.

Her thoughts were interrupted by a sharp tap at the door. She opened it to a smiling Akito and Tilly. The lovely twosome had gone out shopping as soon as they heard Henry's request. Their immediate response was to help. Practical help as well, listing what Henry might need when he got home: a bed brought downstairs or someone to stay with him? Ruth couldn't say as she didn't know Henry's home situation. She glanced at them fondly, enjoying their enthusiasm and energy. She could imagine them working well together in a crisis in countries where earthquakes and tsunamis happened and volcanoes erupted. She grabbed her keys and followed them up to Tilly's flat, which she now knew was the one above her.

Ruth was handed a mug of tea, which she hadn't noticed Tilly making. Both she and Akito seemed to make things happen effortlessly, and to do lots of things together. She wondered if they were more than friends and if they shared their flats. On a small table by the window a game of chess was in progress, and placed tidily on the floor under one of the chairs was a man's pair of Crocs.

Ruth glanced at Akito and saw him busy with his laptop, searching for information about the job he was tasked with. He had an idea to install security cameras at the back and front of the house as a start. Ruth knew she needed to interrupt him. She pulled a twenty-pound note out of her jeans pocket and placed it next to his laptop.

He gazed at it. 'What's that for?'

Tilly was looking on curiously, and Ruth stared from her back to Akito. 'Thomas asked me to give it to you. He forgot to pay you back for a food delivery you paid for in July.'

Akito placed the note between his palms in front of his chest, his chin lowered to rest on the tips of his fingers. He sat in silence, for possibly a minute, then carefully removed his heavy-rimmed glasses so he could wipe his eyes. In his emotional state, his English became broken. 'How are you knowing Thomas?'

'He was my son,' she replied softly.

Ruth watched the changing expressions on their faces. It was something she would remember for a long time. The quick glances at her, and then the more comfortable longer looks as it sank in who she was. Akito sat up straight, then he bowed his head at her. 'It is an honour to meet you, Dr Bennett. We liked your son very much.'

'Please, call me Ruth,' she said, feeling overwhelmed. 'And please forgive me for not telling you both sooner.'

Tilly smiled kindly. 'How could you tell us, after what happened? We may have been people who didn't like him. Have you come here so you can feel close to him?'

'In a way, Tilly,' she replied.

'Dr Bennett has come to make sense of it all, I imagine,' Akito said in a grave tone. 'Like we have been trying to do.'

Ruth gazed at him earnestly. 'You're right, Akito. I'm trying to make sense of it. Can I ask you both if there's anything you remember worrying you?' She saw Akito exchange a look with Tilly.

Tilly tugged at her fingers for a moment, then stopped and kept her hands still. 'A couple of times Akito had to bang for ages at Thomas's door before he'd open it. He looked spaced out. We thought he might have taken something. He said he'd fallen asleep in the chair and was bone tired and hadn't heard the door.'

Ruth could see her concern and knew this was what they had thought at the time. She cleared her throat with a small cough. 'Thank you, Tilly, for your honesty. Obviously hearing that is a bit of a blow as I'm here trying to clear Thomas's name, but anything you remember, good or bad, any visitors or situations you thought strange, it might help.'

They looked at one another again. Akito gave a small nod. Then Tilly spoke for both of them. 'Akito and I have talked about this a few times. We told the police about the sports bag right from the start, but they said it didn't make a difference that it wasn't Thomas's bag because the drugs were found under his bed in it.'

Ruth was confused. 'Are you saying it was someone else's property?'

Tilly nodded. 'Yes, but only the bag, Ruth. That was the police's argument. You see, the bag belonged to Akito. He'd given it to Thomas when Thomas was taking stuff to the charity shops. It was something he did every now and again, mainly taking books. He always asked if we had anything we wanted taking and mostly we didn't, but on this occasion Akito had some dumbbell weights he never used. He put them in a sports bag for Thomas to carry, because a carrier bag was too flimsy. He reminded Thomas the bag was not for charity and to bring it back. The next time we saw it was when the police took it from Thomas's flat.'

'How does this help Thomas? It's not like the bag materialised out of nowhere. A stranger hadn't put it there.'

'You asked about strange,' Tilly replied. 'Well, this felt strange. If Thomas had the bag for a while, say a few weeks, it wouldn't be strange, but Thomas went to the charity shop the day before he was arrested. So it doesn't make sense he'd come back with it and use it to store drugs in.'

'So what's your theory?' Ruth asked.

'Our theory?' Tilly sighed. 'We've gone back and forth over the same ground. On that Friday we know Thomas was at work. Akito asked him if he was up for a game of squash in the evening. Thomas said he couldn't, as after he got back from the charity shop he'd be getting ready for work and didn't finish until nine. So Thomas, me and Akito were out of the house at the same time for most of the evening. We think someone must have got in during that time, saw the bag and filled it with drugs, then hid it under Thomas's bed. Then when Thomas got home, he didn't see the bag so wasn't reminded to give it back to Akito.'

Ruth didn't want to get hopeful at this stage; she'd rather play devil's advocate and test their theory. 'So how did this person or persons get in? Is Thomas's flat easy to break in to, and not leave a sign?'

Akito shook his head. 'I tried. I couldn't. The only way in is with keys. Through the front door and Thomas's door. Henry has keys to all the flats. His were accounted for because he left them with his sister as he was away for four months last year. In Thomas's job he has to change in and out of his clothes, and use a locker. It would not be impossible for someone to have taken a copy of his keys.'

Ruth hesitated. She did not want to raise suspicion on someone they knew. 'Do you know if Kim was home?'

'Kim,' Akito said, 'was working a twilight shift. We all walked out of the house at near enough the same time.' He shared a look with Tilly, then said, 'If she'd not been working… I…'

Ruth helped him out – she could see he didn't want to say what he was thinking. 'You would have suspected her? Why?'

He shrugged. 'We're not judging her on smoking weed. It's the occasional visits from the police and the occasional visitors we get in the front garden, so she can pass something, that lead us to think she's occasionally breaking the law.'

Ruth instantly thought of Tim Wiley. He'd been there to question Kim. Was it possible he thought Kim had something to do with the drugs found under Thomas's bed? Was that the reason he wanted to help prove her son innocent?

'There was a police officer here last Saturday talking to Kim. I suspect it was to question her about something I saw the night before. She was acting suspiciously. A man came into the front garden and I think she gave him something. The police officer who came to see her is PC Tim Wiley. Have either of you met him? Kim thought this was his patch.'

'No,' Tilly replied. 'The same one came each time, though, so it might have been him. He's tall and has dark hair.'

Ruth was grateful that they were trying to help and had been Thomas's friends. She would see them later, she said, after she visited Henry and let them know how he was. They in turn said they would try and remember anything else that might be useful.

Tim Wiley was tall and had dark hair, so it probably was him. It was probably him she glimpsed at the garden gate the night she looked out the window at Kim. Which meant he came then and the next day. Maybe he felt responsible for what happened. It didn't help that she thought it might have been him who assaulted Henry. How did that place him in all of this? He was either overly familiar because he wanted to help her or, more worryingly, he was a bad cop. Ruth was in a quandary. Did she put these concerns aside and still approach Kim? Suppose they were working together? Henry said to be careful. Where Tim Wiley was concerned, she would be *very* careful. She was a little afraid, which was a good thing. She would keep reminding herself of that. Why should she be afraid? She didn't know enough to know who she could trust.

CHAPTER THIRTY-NINE

The bruise on Henry's forehead looked worse, blackish, caused by the haemoglobin in the blood losing oxygen. It would look worse before it looked better. Ruth would expect to see changes of colour and shape and size and it could take weeks to fade. She was concerned, though, about him being sick, and hoped the nurse was right and he'd pushed himself too hard, first going for a walk, then trying to read a newspaper. He was presently lying on his side as it was more comfortable for him with the back of his head off the pillow, because he could now feel where he'd been hit. Ruth pulled the curtains around the bed as he groaned.

'Damn noise in this place, could it get any louder?'

Ruth sympathised. Henry had been moved to a general ward. So many patients said they came out of hospital more tired than they went in, because of the noise. There was a Boots and a WHSmith in the main entrance. Boots was bound to sell earplugs. That's what he could do with, though the nurses would have to know as they might think Henry wasn't responding when they asked him to open his eyes. He was holding her hand as if it was the most natural thing to do. It felt strange to think that two days ago they slept with one another and Henry had done more than hold her hand. She felt heat in the region of her navel, then blushed when she saw Henry squinting at her.

'Something bothering you, Dr Bennett?' Ruth stared at him half amused, half perturbed, he was so quick to detect change. He closed his eyes and his tone became serious. 'The police were here, Ruth. They're going to be talking to you. They know who you are.'

Ruth lightly squeezed his hand. 'Thanks for the warning. I'll be sure to hide the bat when I get home.'

'Be careful,' he said. 'They're looking to charge someone with attempted murder.'

'And what, they'll think it was me?' she lightly mocked.

'They might,' he replied. 'They might think about who you are, and wonder why you're staying where you are. Wondering if you're wanting to blame someone for what happened. They may think you suspect me as I'm the landlord with keys to where Tom lived.'

His words instantly sobered her. It would be ironic if while trying to clear her son's name, she was charged with a crime she hadn't committed. 'I'll be careful, Henry,' she said. Wishing she had come clean from the beginning and confirmed what he had hoped was the reason for her being there. She would hate for Henry to think for a second she ever suspected him.

She could see he was trying to sleep. She would leave now and catch the hospital shop before it closed, if it wasn't already. It was Saturday and ten after five. Failing that, she'd find a shop on the way home. On the bedside locker was a bottle of freshly squeezed orange juice and a toiletry bag, so someone had been to visit. Ruth hoped it was his sister, Marlene, and that she wasn't going to find out that Henry was married and lived with a wife.

She knew so little about him. She didn't know where he lived and whether he lived alone, or lived with his sister when he was not off exploring with his other job. The consultant on ICU addressed him as Professor Thorpe, so she imagined he gave lectures as well. Her dossier on him wouldn't even fill a page. She rose from her chair and leaned over to kiss him like she had the night before. She knew *some* things. She knew she liked being near him and knew she liked kissing him.

'See you tomorrow,' she whispered.

*

Arriving home she was greeted by a light coming on as she walked up the path. Akito worked fast, she'd not expected anything operational in this short a time. Kim sat on the front doorstep and grumbled. 'Can't sit on the wall. That thing comes on every time I move my arm.'

Ruth eased back as the smoke from the cigarette blew in her face. Kim waved her arm at it. 'Sorry. I'll smoke by the gate from now on, otherwise the whole front garden will light up.'

She stubbed out the cigarette and sent the dog-end flying over the wall. Ruth sat down beside her, before the woman had time to get up. She wasn't sure how to start this conversation or even how much she should say.

Kim glanced at her speculatively. 'How's Henry? Akito said you were visiting him.'

'Yes. He was very lucky, Kim. Bad concussion, but it could have been worse.'

'You're not kidding. He could have been killed,' she replied heatedly.

'Shame PC Wiley wasn't on our road then,' Ruth slipped in. 'It would have been helpful to have caught the person who did this.'

Kim shook her head. 'Nah, you don't want him around. Told you, he's odd.'

Ruth turned to look at her. 'You say that, but you don't say why. Why was he here talking to you? Was it to do with the man who came here to see you?'

Kim gaped at her. 'Blimey, you don't hold your punches.' Her eyes flashed. 'That was my brother, all right?'

Ruth kept her gaze calm. 'Is he not allowed in your flat, then? Or is it always a quick visit, for you to give him something?'

She laughed harshly, eyes almost popping out of her head. 'Blimey, Doc, keep them punches coming, why don't you?' She stood up and fished her cigarettes out to light up another. She took a pull of nicotine and blew the smoke out the side of her mouth. 'He has trouble sleeping and don't like seeing doctors. Had enough of them when he came back from Iraq. Combat-related PTSD. It don't help him them knowing it. It don't make it go away. He gets scared at night. So I give him the odd zopiclone or a Mogadon.'

'From your own prescription or from where you work?' Ruth quietly asked.

Kim stared at her mutinously, then a moment later changed the direction of the conversation. 'You have secrets and all. What's someone like you doing living in a crummy flat? You never did say. And Henry seems very accommodating loaning you a dead tenant's bike. What gives, Ruth?'

Ruth gauged her manner. She was annoyed, but not angry. It seemed like she was telling the truth about her brother. 'If I promise to tell you the answer, will you answer some of my questions first?'

She nodded. 'Go on then. What do you want to ask?'

'Do you have a key to my flat?'

She reared back as her reply shot out. 'No, I fucking don't.' She was angry now. No two ways about it. Her eyes were shooting daggers.

Ruth tried to calm her. 'Hey, don't get het up. I'm only asking.'

'Well, fucking don't. That copper asked me the same.'

'When did he ask you that?'

She shrugged. 'A day or two after that poor bloke died.'

'So was he part of the police investigation?'

She shook her head. 'No, he weren't. He was just a bloody nuisance, hanging around the street, which is how he caught me giving Fred a few pills.' She looked at Ruth straight. 'I'll tell you why he's odd. He knows I've nicked them, and yet he's done nothing about it. It's like he's using it as an excuse to be here. He caught me red-handed the day he was here and he made a big show of it in front of you, but I knew he wasn't going to do anything.'

Ruth was intrigued. She had a creeping feeling she was on to something. 'Why do you think that is?' Kim took a drag of her cigarette and averted her gaze. 'Come on, Kim, you must have some idea. Why's he not doing anything about it?'

Kim turned her attention to the house. Ruth saw her looking up. She pointed her cigarette at Ruth's window. 'Because he was here the night that bloke died. It was about ten o'clock at night, and Fred, my brother, had just called. We were standing just over there,' she said, pointing at a bush. 'I could see PC Wiley up at that window. A minute later he comes waltzing out. He clocked me, and his face was dead serious. He said he knew what I was doing. That was it. Then he was gone.' She sighed, then sounded relieved. 'First person I told that to. So your turn now. Why are you here?'

Ruth was sitting in stunned silence. She had learned something she had never expected to hear. PC Tim Wiley had been involved with Thomas while he was alive. He had involved himself in her life too. He knew about her. Her first day at the surgery, he was there. Why was that? Was it pure coincidence that they met again? For a second time she wondered if it was him who'd written to her. Had he been waiting for her to come, perhaps tracking her movements? Ruth shivered. What did he want from her? She raised her head and saw Kim hunched down in front her. Her eyes concerned.

Kim stared at her worriedly. 'You look like you've seen a ghost.' Then her manner lightened, trying to get a response. 'You don't have to tell me, I'm not going to twist your arm. Come on, you need to go inside.'

Ruth reached out and touched her forearm. 'I'm okay, and you deserve to know the truth. He was my son, Kim. Thomas. That's why I'm here.'

Kim stared into Ruth's eyes. Whatever she saw had her enfolding Ruth into her arms. 'Come here, you silly woman.' She patted Ruth's shoulder and quietly said, 'What did I tell you about not being a doctor twenty-four/seven? You're allowed to be normal. You're allowed your own life. You're not just a doctor. You're a woman and a mother as well.'

'Not anymore, Kim,' Ruth cried.

Kim eased back so she could look at Ruth's face. ''Course you are, you silly thing. You think of him, don't you?'

Ruth nodded.

'Well, then. You remember that. You're Thomas's mother. I want to hear you say that.'

Ruth gave a teary smile, and inhaled a shaky breath. 'I'm Thomas's mother, Kim,' she said.

CHAPTER FORTY

Rosie couldn't remember getting into bed, but that didn't matter. What mattered was, for the first time in a long time, she slept all night long. She had expected to toss and turn after yesterday but, surprisingly, she felt strangely free, her mood calm. Everything was going to be all right. No more worrying or hiding from the past. It was a terrible thing her mum said, and the poor thing would suffer, but Rosie absolved her of blame. It wasn't her fault. It was Anabel's. Happy-clappy Anabel, who always managed to get in first and cast doubts about Rosie's character.

The pressure in her bladder made her draw up her knees. She didn't want to get up out of bed yet. She wanted to stay there a little longer. But the need to urinate wouldn't let her settle. She pushed back the covers and put her feet on the floor, and made her way to the bathroom. It took a second for her to register that she wasn't pulling down pyjamas, but having to unzip jeans. Hardly surprising when she couldn't recall getting into bed. She focused on her arms – this was a surprise, she was wearing Anabel's jacket.

While still on the loo, she tugged her arm out of the sleeve and wondered what the heck she'd been doing. She liked it, but not enough to start trying it on in the night. Surely she would remember putting it on? As the jacket came off, small stones fell from a pocket. Rosie dropped the jacket on the floor while she sorted herself out and pulled up her pants. She then stepped out of the jeans and picked up the stones, and saw they were small pebbles. They must have been in a pocket since Anabel last went to a beach. Rosie took them over to the small bin by the sink and threw them away.

She padded barefoot from the bathroom to the kitchen and flicked on the kettle. Another surprise – her Ugg boots on the floor. She had worn trainers to her mum's, so she had no idea why they were in the middle of the kitchen. She needed a hit of caffeine to wake up her brain, so put a large spoon of coffee in a mug, and got milk out ready from the fridge. She picked up the boots and felt grains of sand against her fingers and then between her toes from where they'd been on the floor. She put them by the back door and got on with making her drink, adding lots of milk so she could drink it fast.

With half of it swallowed down, her brain was working no better, she was unable to remember anything from last night. Why she was wearing Anabel's jacket was a mystery. Maybe she subconsciously put it on, to have something of Anabel's next to her, while she mentally said goodbye.

On the table, her rucksack was open at the neck and she gazed curiously at the blue Smirnoff bottle next to the empty plastic water bottle. She definitely didn't remember buying that. The half-bottle from her mum's Co-op, yes, but not this second one. Rosie got out her purse and checked it for a receipt. Then checked the bag as well. Not finding one she went back to the bathroom and searched the pockets in her jeans, then the pockets of Anabel's jacket. Leaving only her coat to check. Five minutes later she was flummoxed. She had searched everywhere, her coat was nowhere to be found. She had everything else. Her keys, her phone, but not her black coat.

Rosie tried to think what she might have done with it. Was it possible she'd left it on the bus? Or in the shop where she bought the second bottle of vodka? Had she taken it off while walking and dropped it on the street? She grabbed her hair on the top of her head tying to think, but nothing was coming to her. She was an irresponsible idiot. To have got that drunk while out alone. To have drunk herself into a state of oblivion and unable to remember. Anything could have happened to her. She needed to think about that, and sort herself out. She could have got picked up by the police and thrown in a cell overnight. She was lucky it was only a coat she lost.

She grabbed the empty bottles out of her bag and shoved them in the bin, not wanting to see the evidence of her stupidity. When washed and dressed she'd walk along the street and see if it was lying anywhere. With that in mind, she walked over to the front door – she might have dropped it in the hallway getting out her keys. On the floor outside the door she saw a white envelope, the M&S carrier bag Anabel's jacket was in, and her own coat. *What the hell had she been doing?* Rosie picked up the envelope and knew straight away who it was from. She gave a short bitter laugh. Anabel had finally got in touch. Had she given it to Chloe to give to her and the woman put it in the bag? Or had Anabel delivered it herself, but ever the coward she hadn't posted it through the letterbox in case Rosie heard? She would have seen Rosie's coat and gathered she was in but probably drunk. Rosie fetched the bag and coat and shut the front door.

She set the envelope on the kitchen table, not in any hurry to read it. Rosie wasn't interested in anything Anabel had to say after learning of her betrayal.

She got washed and dressed, putting on clean jeans, taking her time, and then made herself a second drink before opening the envelope. Two sheets of white paper were filled with Anabel's writing. Her first word was a lie. If Rosie was dear to her she would never have done what she did. Rosie sat down on the bed to read the letter.

Dear Rosie,

I should have written this letter to you when we were thirteen, and not let fourteen years go by. I should have said then what

I need to say now. The first time I saw you out of my bedroom window, I knew you were going to be my friend. Riding a bike in the middle of the street with your arms open wide. You had your eyes closed! You were so brave. I remember thinking you would crash into a parked car or go over an uneven surface and get really hurt. Watching you, I knew even then my life was about to change. I'd never had a friend like you, but you knew that didn't you, Rosie? You sensed I never had any friends. I should never have looked out that window again, but I couldn't stop myself. I was drawn to you. You made me come alive, Rosie, like my very own sun, making me grow and flower. I felt invincible with you. Everything we did, you made so exciting. You were afraid of nothing. Climbing the tallest tree, walking the highest wall, standing on a railway track. Every day was an adventure. You made bad things fun. Running from a shop with a stolen item. You always got the good things, like chocolate and biscuits. Do you remember when I came out with a box of soap powder? You laughed so hard. You thought it was brilliant. We couldn't eat it, so we trailed it all the way along the road like Hansel and Gretel. You were magic, Rosie.

It was the following year when I realised you were hiding who you really are. You know you're different, don't you, Rosie? I sensed it the first time when I came to your bedroom and saw you on the floor with that huge jigsaw puzzle, made with hundreds of tiny pieces. It was a picture of a woman riding side-saddle, wearing a billowing blue dress. I was scared to move in case I stepped on it. I held my breath watching you place the last four pieces. It was in the middle of the picture and I wanted you to hurry and fill in that small gap, so I could see the last tiny part of her face and hat. Then you did that startling thing. When you broke the picture apart instead of placing those pieces, I think you were saying that nothing and no one had control over you.

When I look back I now see what you did with us. You made a nearly perfect picture where you could fit in, and for a while were able to do that, until that day tore it apart. Have you ever wondered what we might be like if we had never met? If what happened hadn't?

I think I knew on that day something big was going to happen. I've asked myself if the reason was to bind me with you forever? Your father just a means to an end in achieving that? If I told what happened that day straight away, it might not have made a difference to how I feel now, but it would have been known what we did.

Rosie stopped reading. She didn't want reminding of the moment her life changed. She remembered being starving afterwards, and hiding a T-shirt stained with soup. She had not been able to satisfy her hunger for weeks. Her stomach felt cavernous and no amount of food was able to fill it. After it happened she had to shake Anabel to get her to listen. They couldn't tell anyone, otherwise they would both get taken away. Anabel had it easy. She ran away and hid in a cove up the coast. She was gone for a whole day. Meg thought it was from shock at seeing the dead body on the drive, but Rosie knew the truth. She ran away because she played a dangerous game that went wrong. Rosie had it worse. In trying to protect them she anchored herself to Anabel for life. She was reminded every day of this by the absence of her father. How Anabel wormed her way into Rosie's father's heart. Rosie could see it in his eyes – his eyes didn't brighten in the same way when he looked at Rosie. He never gave Rosie a pet name.

Anabel stole him from her. But it didn't satisfy her or stop her from stealing again. She stole Rosie's happiness every chance she got. Then try and look innocent of any blame. *She knew* she hurt Rosie. She just didn't care. Rosie now had to consider her next move. She couldn't keep letting Anabel go first.

CHAPTER FORTY-ONE

Ruth could think of better things to do on a Sunday afternoon, but none as pressing as this. After what Kim said to her last night, she had no choice. She parked in the thirty-minute zone, right outside the entrance to Bournemouth Police Station. If she had to, she would come back and move her car somewhere else. For now, though, she would leave it there and hope this didn't take long. She could feel her legs trembling as the automatic doors opened for her to enter. At the front desk she waited for one of the officers behind the glass to notice her, wishing she were not quite so tall to give her time to be unnoticed and collect her thoughts. A policewoman with short dark hair and wearing spectacles with large round lenses looked up at her expectantly.

'Hi,' Ruth said. 'I wonder if might I have a word with someone in private about a delicate matter concerning a police officer.'

The woman's face subtly changed. Her owl-like gaze became solemn. 'If you give me a second, I'll take you through to a room where we can talk.'

Ruth was surprised it was that simple. She just wished her nerves would catch up and relax. A moment later the woman opened a side door and led Ruth to an office with a desk and chairs and plain walls. The policewoman gestured to a chair on the far side of the desk, before she sat down herself.

'I'm PC Mandy Dawson. How can I assist you?'

'My name is Ruth Bennett, and I have some concerns about an officer's behaviour, I'm afraid.'

PC Dawson inclined her head. 'So, there are a number of ways we can do this. You have a choice to fill in a complaint on the website, or you can contact a solicitor and have them make a complaint for you, or you can fill in an IOPC online. That's the Independent Office for Police Conduct. Or we can do this here. I'll just need to find the inspector.'

Ruth was startled. She just wanted a chat. Nothing formal. 'Can't I just have an informal chat with you, and perhaps someone have a quiet word with him?'

The woman frowned. 'I'm afraid it has to be an inspector.'

Ruth gave a hesitant nod. 'Okay.'

'Right, I'll try not to be long. Would you mind waiting?'

In truth, Ruth wasn't sure she had a choice. She had done nothing wrong, but she had said a worrying thing. It made sense that a senior ranking officer was required, except it also made it feel more alarming.

'Would you like some tea or coffee?'

'Coffee, please. Oh, and my car. I've left it in the thirty-minute zone.'

'Okay, I'll let the front desk know.'

Ruth shivered as the door closed, wondering if it was a mistake to have come. Was she reaching the wrong conclusions about him and overreacting? He'd bought her flowers and asked her out. Offered to help. Was she making herself look an idiot? On the other hand, there was Henry to consider and what Kim said yesterday, that she'd seen Tim Wiley in Thomas's flat the night he died.

A few minutes later another officer brought her some coffee in a mug. He said hello, but nothing more. Close to thirty minutes passed before the door opened again. It wasn't PC Mandy Dawson returning, but a tall grey-haired man wearing stripes on his shoulders.

He sat down in the chair vacated by PC Dawson. 'My name is Sergeant Phillips. Thank you for waiting. I know PC Dawson explained it would be an inspector, but unfortunately the inspector is dealing with a serious incident.'

Ruth nodded, relieved to be dealing with a less senior officer. The less senior, the less serious it felt. 'Well, that's fine with me.'

He held her gaze, and gave a quick nod of acknowledgement. 'Well, let's begin then.'

They went through the formalities: full name, age, address, occupation. The sergeant raised his head when he heard Ruth's address, but then lowered it again and carried on writing. He now looked across the desk at Ruth. 'How long would you say this situation has been going on?'

Ruth was unsure how to answer. It was going to sound trivial. 'I wouldn't call it a situation. Just one or two encounters.'

'And when did these happen?'

'Well, the first week of January, I met him as my patient. I'm a GP and it was my first day there. He informed me we'd met before, that he'd been my driver to take me to the morgue to see my dead son. He asked me out for a drink after telling me that. The second time was at my home. He was on duty and had come to see one of my neighbours about a police matter, I presume. Then he came up to my flat and suggested he could assist me in some way. It was an uncomfortable moment.'

'Was he there by invitation?'

Ruth gave a vague nod. 'Well, kind of. I didn't want him to reveal my real identity to the tenant he was talking to, so I said I wanted to have a word with him.'

'So what is it that made you uncomfortable?'

Ruth stared at him frankly. 'I felt he got in my home under false pretences. He more or less invited himself in. He implied he had some information to tell me about my son.'

'Okay. Is that the sum of it?'

'No, not quite. I asked him to leave and in my hall he kind of cornered me?'

His eyes were a dark blue with a level gaze directed at Ruth. 'Did he touch you?'

Ruth shook her head. 'No. He blocked me. Putting his arms either side of me as I was stood against my door. He spoke about my son's case. Said his mate was in on the interviews and my son didn't admit to the crime, but then at court pleaded guilty.'

'And is this true? I mean about your son.'

'Yes, as far as I'm aware, that is what happened.'

'Any other encounters?'

'He turned up at my surgery last Thursday with flowers and a card that said, *Sorry*. He said he didn't intend to scare me at my flat, but to tell me he was on my side.'

Sergeant Phillips now sat back. 'I recognise your address. You mentioned you didn't want your real identity known.'

'Yes,' Ruth answered. 'My son died there last August. I'm in Bournemouth to try and uncover what happened.'

The sergeant gave a small sigh. 'Right.' He nodded. 'I'm going to stop here and speak to one of the officers. Would you mind waiting?'

Ruth said the same thing herself hundreds of times to patients. Of course she wouldn't mind. What else would she do? The door opened much sooner than she expected. It was Sergeant Phillips returning, accompanied by the officer she saw at her flat Friday evening, whose name she couldn't remember.

'Hello again, Dr Bennett. You may recall my name from Friday, but just to remind you, I'm PC Jason Kirby, and here to help matters along.'

Ruth was nonplussed by the policeman's presence. She didn't recall him saying his name. The sergeant was now looking at her with an expression hard to determine. 'I'd like to offer my condolences, Dr Bennett. I met with your son, Dr De Luca.'

His words took the wind out of her. She was shocked at hearing him say her son's name. She hadn't mentioned Thomas's name to him. This whole moment felt strange. The man had only been gone out of the room ten minutes, and yet it seemed like a change in the situation.

He remarked on her startled face. 'I do apologise. I think I shocked you a little. I should have explained first my reason for stepping out of the room was to verify a few things with PC Kirby, as your address hit a chord with me, and then, of course, the mention of your son put all the pieces together for me.'

His explanation gave Ruth time to gather her wits. 'Thank you for your condolences, Sergeant. I appreciate it.'

His expression was curious. 'So… you're here hoping to uncover what happened with your son, which I entirely understand. Your son had no previous record and a sterling future ahead of him, and in a puff of smoke it's gone. A sudden death in the aftermath is always a shock in these situations.'

'Yes, it is,' Ruth agreed.

He smiled at her kindly. 'It's fortunate you being here as PC Kirby was going to ask you to come to the station and give a statement in regards to what happened to Mr Thorpe. He can do that with you now if that's all right.'

Ruth knew she shouldn't be shocked. Henry had warned her, but right now she was feeling at a disadvantage. It felt like a blunt pause. 'Yes, of course,' she replied. 'Henry told me yesterday that the police might talk to me.'

PC Kirby sat down in the chair vacated by Sergeant Phillips. It must be an important chair to sit in as they were all taking turns. Then again, it did face the hot seat. *Her seat.* The sergeant sat in the chair next to Kirby. Ruth felt a shiver of unease. She stared at the officers before her and tried to remember why she was there. That had been only half addressed, as Sergeant Phillips had not brought it to a natural end. As how could he, when she hadn't given him the officer's name.

PC Kirby began the conversation. 'Before I take your statement I'd like to go over a few things if I may. I understand you started a new job as a GP the first week of January. May I ask where you were working prior to that?'

Ruth answered confidently, 'I worked as a GP in Bath, which is where I normally reside.'

'And when did you come to live in Bournemouth?'

'New Year's Eve, two days before starting my new job. Last year I took over the payments on my son's flat, but was unable to move here sooner due to giving notice on my old job. I came to Bournemouth to find out what I could about my son's case. There being no trial, I knew very little of what happened.'

The sergeant glanced at her curiously. 'Have you been here to ask us about it or contacted the CPS?'

'No,' Ruth quietly admitted. 'I'm not yet ready to do that.'

He nodded thoughtfully. 'So you've been trying to gather information on your own, I take it?'

'Yes,' she replied, and noticed him give a nod to PC Kirby to continue, which he was quick to do.

'You told Sergeant Phillips that you didn't want your real identity revealed. Would I be right in thinking you didn't wish for the other tenants to know you were related to Dr De Luca?'

'Yes, that's correct,' she answered in a steady voice.

'And why is that? Did you have reason to think they might have been involved or be in possession of information the police didn't have?'

Ruth gazed at him coolly, thinking to ask for a solicitor. His questions didn't seem like they were leading towards him taking a statement. 'I would have thought that was perfectly obvious. I had no idea of the reaction I would get if it became known I was the mother of the previous tenant, who had been convicted of stealing hospital drugs.'

He nodded. 'I understand that. But it would also allow you the anonymity to ask them questions.'

'Yes, that too,' she said, agreeing with him. 'Again, obvious, I would have thought.'

He shrugged. 'I'd like to ask you about your relationship to Mr Thorpe. Did you know Mr Thorpe prior to coming to Bournemouth?'

'No. We had two conversations on the phone. Both concerning the flat. The first one was to discuss the lease. The flat still had Thomas's things. At that point I paid a further month's rent. The second was where it was agreed I could take over the renting of the flat for the foreseeable future. The keys were posted to me, and I met with my new landlord a few nights after moving in.'

'And did a relationship begin between you then?'

Ruth debated how to answer this. She was damned if she was going to come out of this looking shamed. 'No, but let me be clear. I warmed to Henry Thorpe that evening. He was kind about my son. The second time I saw him we went to a pub and an Indian restaurant together. The third time I saw him I thought him rude, as he barely acknowledged my existence. The time after that – a discussion in my flat about a kitchen. The last time was Thursday, not including my visits to the hospital to see him. He let me know he was attracted to me, but felt it would be wrong to pursue his feelings because of my reason for being there.' She paused to make sure she had his full attention so she could look him defiantly in the eye. 'I made love with Henry Thorpe for most of that night before he left my bed, and it is probably the best sex I've ever had.'

Ruth noticed the sergeant put his hand across his mouth, and suspected she'd amused him. PC Kirby, however, was unfazed by her candour and continued. 'Did you have any reason to think he might have been involved?'

Ruth lifted her head sharply. 'What are you implying?'

'I'm not implying anything, Dr Bennett.' His gaze was steady. 'I merely wonder how you viewed Henry Thorpe. He was your son's landlord. A stranger to you until recently. You've met a handful of times, during which time Mr Thorpe suffered a serious assault. I would have thought you might be curious to know if we had any leads?'

Ruth felt cornered. If she said she was curious, it might come across as a delayed response. She breathed in and counted to ten. She was going to knock this line of questioning on the head. She gazed at both men. 'I came here with concerns about an officer, which I don't feel have been paid proper attention. You have not cautioned me or read me my rights, and yet you, PC Kirby, are questioning me like a suspect. Now do I need to call a solicitor or what? Because right now, I'm very close to doing exactly that.' She stood up. 'So, gentlemen, while I excuse myself to use a bathroom, make up your minds and let me know on my return.'

CHAPTER FORTY-TWO

A fresh mug of coffee was waiting on her return. The officers had switched seats and Ruth was now facing Sergeant Phillips. He regarded her with calm eyes. 'We were going to get to the subject of this officer,' he said. 'I have concerns. You have my full attention.'

'Good,' she replied, in a matter-of-fact manner. 'Then I can go straight to the part I didn't tell you. When I heard what happened to Henry my first thought was this officer had done it. I have nothing to support that, apart from a feeling this man is trying to get close to me for some reason. Then yesterday evening I learned something, which is why I am here today. This officer was seen leaving my son's flat the night he died.'

The silence that followed allowed Ruth to hear the small groan of PC Kirby's stomach. Sergeant Phillips glanced at him, then his whole attention focused on her. 'You have come in contact with him by chance, it would seem, when he had previous dealings with you during the time of your son's death. It is the same officer who drove you to view your son at the mortuary. One of the reasons I stopped earlier was to check which officer was given that duty. I would like you to tell me this officer's name, Dr Bennett.'

Ruth felt her stomach dip. Her being there was feeling more serious. She just needed to say it, and the sooner the better. He had fooled her into letting him into her home. 'His name is Tim Wiley,' she said.

PC Kirby was plainly surprised. But not the sergeant. He slowly nodded at her. 'First, I'm very sorry this has happened. You saw this officer in his uniform, I believe? Talking with another tenant?'

'Yes. That's right,' Ruth replied.

'Acting in his duties as an officer?'

'Well, yes. He said he was going to take her to the station.'

'He's also your patient, I hear?'

'Yes. That's how I met him. He had a problem with his foot. I offered to write him a doctor's note, but he said he was on leave that week and didn't need one. Which is why it didn't seem strange to see him in uniform when talking to my neighbour. I assumed he was back at work.'

His eyebrows rose at this. 'I see,' he said in a quiet tone, clearly thinking more than his voice was letting on. He looked thoughtfully at the table, then seemed to come to some decision. 'Well,' he said, sitting up straight, his eyes making contact with hers. 'There's no easy way say this, Dr Bennett, but Tim Wiley was not on leave. He left last September. He's no longer on the force.'

Ruth gaped, shocked. Confused. What he said didn't make sense. 'But he was in uniform. He had a radio. He was wearing exactly what you all wear.'

'He's acquired it somehow,' he answered in a pondering tone.

'How can that be?' she asked. 'Why isn't he on the force anymore?'

Sergeant Phillips paused a few seconds before he spoke again, perhaps giving her time to adjust to this news. Then, calmly, he answered. 'His wife died last year. After that he struggled, which is understandable. Then, in August, he had what I would call a breakdown. We offered him every support, to take as much time as needed, to see a counsellor. We wanted him to go to Occupational Health, but instead he resigned. So you see, Dr Bennett, what we've learned from you is worrying. Tim Wiley is no longer a police officer, but sadly he's impersonating one.'

Ruth was utterly bemused. 'Why would he pretend, though, with my neighbour? What would he have done with her if she'd kicked off or something? Leave her on your doorstep?'

The sergeant placed his hands on the table, readying himself to stand. 'Well, that's what we're going to find out, Dr Bennett. In the meantime, if he tries to contact you, contact the police straight away.' He stood. 'Thank you for bringing this to our attention. Once again, I'm sorry this has happened. I'll leave you in the hands of PC Kirby while I get on with reporting this. But if you have any concerns or want to add any more, please get in touch.'

When Ruth walked out of the station an hour later, because she had to stay to give a statement for Thursday evening, she felt disjointed. Unsettled. Mostly, plain disturbed. Tim Wiley was out there and was perhaps a dangerous man. She kept asking herself what he was doing in Thomas's flat? What was Thomas to him? Why was he there so late at night? She couldn't see an answer. Couldn't see one good reason for his being there. Her son had spent his last day on earth in the company of this man. Knowing that made her more wary than anything else she had learned so far. Had he said something to Thomas that might have turned his mind? Had he taken away Thomas's last hope somehow? Ruth screwed her eyes shut. She didn't want to imagine any of that happening, but without knowing his reason for being there she could only see Tim Wiley in a bad light. She realised something. She hadn't asked Kim if she saw Thomas up at the window. Or if it was only PC Wiley she saw? The shock of finding out what Tim Wiley was doing was finally coming home to her. How much more in danger she was feeling now.

*

It was gone seven by the time Ruth managed to visit Henry. He was sitting up in bed, more comfortable and in better spirits. Ruth expected he'd be discharged in the morning. If it wasn't Sunday, he would probably be home already. She felt strangely shy with him more awake and able to focus on her, especially as he seemed able to read her mind. Why else would he be regarding her with amused eyes?

'Oh, shut up,' she quietly said.

'You know, there's a name for that,' he replied. 'When you start talking to yourself.' He chuckled as he took in her exasperated face.

'Really? I didn't know that,' she answered in a wry tone. 'But I do know there's a name for men like you. Maddening.'

She sighed and lowered her gaze and he caught hold of her hand, his eyes concerned. 'What's happened?'

She glanced at him, thinking she would never be able to hide anything from this man. She didn't want him to worry, but if he could remember anything it would help. 'I just came from the police station and told them that after you left my bed I decided to follow you and hit you over the head.' She gave him an amused stare, before adding, 'Because you were a lousy lover.'

'Ha,' he responded. 'So that was why. I did wonder.' A serious look entered his eyes. 'Has Akito managed to start anything yet?'

She nodded. 'Yes. A motion sensor light is up already. He did that yesterday. Today he was looking at door entry systems. He mentioned video doorbell intercom, using our phones, but I don't think he's staying with that idea, probably because not everyone wants to keep checking their phones.'

He agreed. 'Yes, and not everyone has a smartphone. I'm not sure if Kim has one.'

'I also told them that I thought of the police officer you met in my flat when I heard what happened to you.'

His eyes narrowed. His tone of voice showed concern. 'Really? Was that wise?'

She gazed at him. 'Well, that depends on how you look at this situation. The man who came to my home is not a policeman, and hasn't been since last year.'

'Wow,' he quietly commented. 'That's concerning.'

'It is,' she agreed. 'But not nearly as concerning as finding out he visited Thomas the night he died.'

Henry sat forward, away from the pillow. 'He was with Tom?' His voice was quietly shocked. 'What was *that man* doing with Tom?'

Ruth shook her head. 'I don't know, and I can only think it was for something bad.'

Tears welled up in her eyes. Henry pulled her closer and then against his chest, where she quietly cried for a few moments. When the tears stopped, she used the corner of his sheet to dry her face. Then she told him about all the things she now knew, starting from the beginning with her search for the nurse, the anonymous letters, the reason she was working where she was, her chat with Kim, her visit to Jed Nolan, her visit to the solicitor, then with the hospital, who Tim Wiley was, and what he said, what the coroner said, what the post-mortem found, what Akito and Tilly said, what Catherine said, who Catherine was, and about her baby, and about what Pauline said, and about Thomas's letter in his suit hanging ready for court.

When she finished talking she rested back against Henry's chest, exhausted. She had been speaking for almost an hour. Henry smoothed her hair, then gently tugged it to raise her head so he could kiss her. 'So here on a mission then, Dr Bennett.' Then softly said, 'Bravo.'

'I haven't done anything to save him yet,' she replied, wearily.

'Go home and sleep. Don't think any more tonight. Rest your mind if you can.'

Ruth nodded, wondering if she had energy to even stand. 'Can't I just sleep here?' she whispered.

He smiled at her. 'As tempting as that is, you won't get any rest here.'

She sighed and made an effort to sit up. 'Fine, I'll be good and go home. Tomorrow, I have to work,' she said. 'Will I see you afterwards?'

'Well, I hope so,' he replied. 'As a landlord it's my duty to check up on my tenants after an incident. I dare say I'll knock on your door, Dr Bennett.'

Ruth had a grin on her face as she left the ward. She loved his humour, and that he didn't take himself too seriously but knew how to be serious. He was quite a special man and part of her recognised that what they had between them could lead to her ending up hurt. She was only temporarily in Bournemouth, and his life was spent travelling from one destination to the next.

She climbed into her car and considered the matter some more. She shouldn't look too far ahead, or look for sadness before it arrived. Otherwise, what was the point of living? Of experiencing anything? In any case, you couldn't stop hurt. If it was meant to happen, it would happen. No point waiting for it to arrive. She should have learned that by now from loving Pietro and Thomas.

There was no warning, which was just as well, otherwise you wouldn't love with all your heart.

CHAPTER FORTY-THREE

The Monday morning meeting came to an end. There was little change from last week, with just two new items: a pharmaceutical rep would be calling on Wednesday to introduce a new medication, and the patients' toilet was being fitted with a new hand dryer as the old one had broken again. Joan was clearing the table of mugs and small plates, empty except for a few crumbs left of the caraway seed cake Dr Raj brought in, which had looked delicious, but which Ruth couldn't eat because she was churned up with what she was about to do.

In another minute Dr Miller, Dr Campbell and Dr Raj would leave and she would lose the moment. It was really just these three she needed to tell, but she was most fond of Dr Raj and would have liked to have told her when they were alone. She raised her hand to gain their attention. She was nervous. This might go very badly. They might not like her very much after they heard what she said, but that couldn't be helped. She had decided to do this when she woke up this morning, even if it meant losing her job.

'Thank you,' she said. 'I just need a moment of your time. I need to bring to your attention one of our patients. His name is Tim Wiley, and some of you may have heard he brought flowers to me at the surgery last week.'

Ruth saw Joan silently nodding like she was the confirmer of some terrible deed, and was grateful she was there too.

'Yesterday, I was at Bournemouth Police Station and discovered this man is impersonating a police officer. He was a police officer last year, but he is not anymore. Mr Wiley is now being looked for by the police. If he should turn up, may I suggest we call them? I encountered a problem with Mr Wiley on my first day here, when I saw him as a patient. Afterwards, he asked me out, which I declined.'

'Oh my dear,' Carol Campbell uttered, unable to hide her dismay. 'How awful for you.' She glanced around the table. 'Have either of you had dealings with him?' Dr Miller and Dr Raj shook their heads. Carol looked back to Ruth. 'Thank goodness you went and spoke about him.'

Ruth held her gaze. 'I don't think it's a coincidence my meeting Mr Wiley that first day. This morning I checked his record. He signed on here as a patient the day I started. I think he knew I was coming.' Ruth could see the intrigue in their faces. 'He informed me we had met before, when he was the officer who drove me to view my son's body at the mortuary last year.'

'I'm so very sorry to hear that,' Jim Miller instantly said. He gazed at her sadly.

Ruth wanted to look away. 'Please don't be kind. I really don't deserve it. I came here with a purpose. To get information about my son. My son lived here. Last year he was convicted of stealing hospital medicines and was due to be sentenced. Instead, he ended his life. From his barrister I learned the name of the person who called the police. I wanted to get to know her, to find out what she knew. I didn't believe my son was guilty. I still don't believe it. This person is also a patient here, but I haven't spoken to her. Not because I haven't wanted to, but because I've been unable to get hold of her. I will entirely understand if you wish to report me, and of course I expect to have to leave here straight away.'

'Why was your son living in Bournemouth?' Jim asked. His expression was guarded, which given what he had just heard was generous of him. He could have shown anger or disappointment or even open distrust.

'He was a first-year doctor,' Ruth replied.

He sat quietly for several seconds, then said, 'Why don't you grab some fresh air? Let's say we meet back here in ten minutes?'

'Of course,' Ruth replied. His request reminded her that while he may well be retiring soon, he was still the senior partner in the practice.

Dr Raj, who had been unusually quiet, spoke out. 'Is that really necessary, Jim? I would like to say something in response to Dr Bennett.'

Jim held up his hand. 'Sunita, this is not the time.'

'Well, it is for me, Jim.'

Ruth wanted a hole in the floor to open up and swallow her. The last thing she wanted was to cause a disagreement. They had all been so kind. She gazed at each of them. 'Look, you all have every right to be disappointed. And Dr Raj, please say whatever you want. You should air your grievance.'

'Trust me, Dr Bennett, I am disappointed. In my hero, sat over there with his restricted brain strangling him. Whatever is the matter with you, Jim Miller?' she said to him. 'Dr Bennett has just bared her soul. So what if she has come here for her own personal reasons. Don't we all do that? Wouldn't you take every opportunity to find out something about *your* son, or your daughter, Lucy? And you, Carol – why are you hanging your head? It isn't the worst thing for someone to do. I would go to the ends of the earth for my children.'

Dr Raj was right, Carol Campbell's head was very nearly touching the table. Ruth should just leave and end all this embarrassment. A hiccup came from Carol and Ruth was astonished to see her eyes were damp when she raised her head.

'For pity's sake, Carol,' Dr Raj crooned. 'Don't get so upset. Dr Bennett has proved how strong she is.'

'Halle-bloody-lujah,' Joan said loudly into the room, making everyone realise she was still there.

'Joan, please wait your turn,' Dr Raj said in a clipped voice. Then she turned to Ruth, her gaze stern. 'Yes, I am angry. Right now probably not with you, but with life. You have faced great hardship, Dr Bennett. You have then crusaded alone. I have always believed a mother knows her child. I am less believing when a mother says she is surprised by her child's failings. Perhaps in some cases it is true. A child can hide from their mother. But it is also true that for some it is easier to feign ignorance than to admit knowledge of a child's behaviour. I think you would find it very hard to fool yourself. Please don't fall on your sword now, because of this slight embarrassment you find yourself in. There isn't one of us who wants you to leave. I know Jim is already rehearsing a speech to that effect.'

He nodded at Ruth. 'Well, something along those lines.' He raised an eyebrow at her. 'Along with a reminder of the Data Protection Act and patient confidentiality.'

She nodded back. 'Honestly, Jim, I'm happy to go. I've really caused an upset. I had no right.'

Carol Campbell stood up, only slightly taller than Ruth sitting down. 'You're going nowhere,' she said. 'Apart from down the corridor to your office. And then later to the pub with us. Is that clear?'

'Crystal,' Ruth replied, feeling she needed a good cry herself. She didn't deserve such an easy time. They were all far too kind. Then Ruth registered what Carol had said. They were not going to believe what she had to say next. 'This evening might not be possible. A friend of mine is coming out of hospital. Someone tried to murder him last Thursday after he left my flat.'

Carol threw her hands up in the air, looking and sounding wonderfully dramatic. 'Someone *please* get this woman a bodyguard, before we get any more shocks.'

*

Ruth was determined to see each of them individually during the course of the day. She didn't want anyone to feel railroaded into agreeing for her to stay. She felt it was only right that they had time to consider their decision. Carol's response was to tell her to shut up, in the nicest possible way. Dr Raj wanted to see a photograph of Thomas.

She left Jim until last, entering his office after his quiet response to her knock at the door.

Jim stood and gestured for her to sit down in a patient chair by his desk. 'How are you?'

She smiled at the question as it felt so familiar in this setting. 'I'm fine thanks, Jim. How are you?'

He sat down and gave a nonchalant shrug. 'Been thinking about you on and off all day, to be honest.'

She stared at him seriously. 'Jim, I meant what I said this morning. I'm still willing to leave without any hard feelings if you've changed your mind. To be honest, you weren't given much of a choice by Dr Raj.'

'Perhaps not,' he agreed. 'But I would have arrived at the same decision eventually.' He looked at her openly. 'You fit in so well. There isn't anything you need our help with; it's like you've been here for a very long time. That, of course, is down to your experience. It was a brave decision to give up your partnership. I wondered why you did. And now I know.'

'It was an easy decision, but I should have come much sooner. I let four months go by.'

'You must have found it all very hard to deal with. Both before and after.'

'There wasn't much of a before, Jim. I found out what he'd been accused of the same day I found out he was dead. I walked into the court knowing nothing, other than that my son would be there. It was his barrister who told me everything.'

He shook his head slowly, his eyes expressing his feelings for her situation. 'God,' he said quietly. Then after a moment he sighed. 'Let's hope you get a resolution. I'd like you to stay. I too meant what I said. Come April, this chair will be empty and will need someone in it. Maybe when you get a day off you might consider this town as somewhere you might like to stay.'

'Maybe,' she said, humbled that he would still consider her fit for his job. She realised something. She didn't miss her old job. Maybe her future could be somewhere else. It was something to think about. Thomas liked it here. She might like it too, one day.

CHAPTER FORTY-FOUR

Her mood sank at seeing the police car parked on the road. It was not a sight she wanted to be greeted with after coming home. She parked further away and spotted a female officer walking slowly along the pavement, head down, looking at the ground. Ruth got out of her car. The officer didn't look up, leaving Ruth to carry on to her flat. Outside the front door Kim and Tilly were talking via intercom into a metal panel fixed to the wall. Ruth joined them and saw four buttons with nameplates next to them. Her name was printed neatly in one of them. Above Kim's name, and below Tilly's and Akito's.

'Hi, Ruth,' Akito's cheery voice called from the speaker. 'It's working. I can see you. When it's convenient I'll fit a video control panel in your flat. Ours are all done.'

'Thank you, Akito,' she replied, not really wanting it done at this moment because she wanted to get ready for Henry's visit. 'Does it take long to do?'

'Half an hour, tops. It's set up. I just need to fix it to a wall.'

'Okay. Come down when you want.'

Ruth smiled at Kim and Tilly. 'He's brilliant, isn't he?' she remarked, stepping through the open front door intending to go straight upstairs. She'd leave her door open for Akito and have a bath while he was there. She wanted to wash and blow dry her hair. Give a flick around the flat, make sure the bathroom was clean and…

'Ruth!'

Ruth turned. Kim was standing there watching her. 'That's the second time I called,' she said. 'Everything all right?'

Ruth nodded. 'Yes. Why? Sorry, I was lost in thought.'

Kim continued looking at her and Ruth twigged – she was referring to their conversation. 'I'm fine, Kim. Honest. And thank you for being lovely.'

Kim produced a white envelope from her pocket. 'This was in the letter basket for you. Tilly and I saw it when we came out to check the intercom.'

Ruth took it from her, then guiltily noticed her drawn face. 'Are *you* all right?'

She shrugged. 'Bit tired is all. Night shifts bugger up your sleep pattern.'

Ruth was concerned. Kim looked washed-out, her form a little shrunk. 'Could you stick to days?'

She pulled a face. 'Could, but nights pay more.' She rocked back on her heels and put her hands in her pockets, looking self-conscious.

Ruth was going to say she should see a doctor, but Kim was putting up her guard, deflecting Ruth's concern, pulling herself up straight. 'A few early nights is all I need. I said the same thing to Henry earlier – it's what he needs too.'

'Henry?' Ruth said, surprised.

'Yes, he called earlier. His sister drove him. He didn't look like he should have been out of bed, but he wanted to say a quick hello and check on us all.'

'Poor thing,' Ruth said, thinking maybe she might not see him now. 'Well, I'm going to kick off my shoes and flop in a chair. I think we're all pooped.' She gave a small laugh.

'Yeah,' Kim said quietly. She turned as Tilly came in smiling and bounded up the stairs with her pretty pink hair swinging in a ponytail. 'God, I envy her energy.'

*

In the flat Ruth pulled out her phone and saw she had a text from Henry.

Studies show that those who receive a house call from their doctor have a 100% faster recovery rate.

She chuckled and thought up a reply. She was about to write it, then changed her mind. Henry was probably wiped out after getting out of hospital. He might think he wanted a visit from her, but what he needed was a quiet first night home.

Mr Thorpe, you're out of touch. I see a lot of my patients now by video call. May I suggest we schedule you one for tomorrow? In the meanwhile, your doctor's orders are to rest.

A few moments later a sad face emoji and a kiss pinged back.

Ruth put her phone away just as Akito arrived. She'd still have a bath and then spend the evening reading all of Thomas's diary, from beginning to end. She felt ready to read the pages she'd been avoiding. People had been there for her all day, making her feel strong again. She hadn't been there for Thomas at his time of need, but now she could be there for him in spirit.

*

By the time she reached the end of July and midway into August, Ruth's emotions were as ragged as the torn tissues in her lap. A separate pile lay sodden on the arm of the chair. She wept from reading of his days without hope, as he mentally and physically spiralled. Tilly might well have been right – Thomas might have been taking something, as he mentioned colleagues' concerns about his tiredness and forgetfulness in the days leading up to his arrest and, on one day, his admission of irritableness. Ruth flicked back to that date. She wanted to read it again, hoping she was imagining too much about his behaviour.

15 April

Well, what a fuck-up of a day. Mason had me in the office wanting to know what was going on and all I could do was stare at him blankly. He jabbed his finger at the patient's notes wanting to know where the results of the blood test were. I flippantly suggested he search the computer. He already had. Then he realised I didn't even know what blood test he was on about. He asked me to take it yesterday, apparently. Christ, what was I meant to say? I couldn't fucking remember. So I denied it. Great decision that was. He called in Elliot, and the senior reg confirmed he heard Mason ask me, but best of all, he watched me write it down. In your notebook, Dr De Luca. So I pulled it out, and there it was. Blood amylase test for Albert Morgan. That's where I should have apologised. But no, I felt so fucking irritable, I walked out. Jesus wept. Talk about ironic. Only the night before or Monday I'd been wondering if I'd unhinged her! But it's me acting like a nutjob. I need to get a grip. This is not me! A scary thought keeps coming to my head that I've got fucking schizophrenia!

Ruth turned to the page in the diary where she left off, determined to finish reading the last few entries. She was not surprised Thomas thought he might have schizophrenia. It was not rare. He would have been worried about his behaviour. His forgetfulness, in particular. Thomas always had an excellent memory. She found it curious that once he left the hospital, in the months he was waiting to go to court, his thinking became crystal clear. She would have expected him to become increasingly more anxious and unable to think straight. Yet every page thereafter was a thoughtful account of something notable or pleasant. He'd surfed several times, taking pleasure in being out on the waves, describing a deep blue sky or the warmth of the sun, and a bird soaring high. He'd described moments with Catherine, the scent and softness of her skin, the freckles on her arms, her schoolteacher's voice when he wouldn't let her concentrate on preparing next term's schoolwork. He was clear minded every day.

She read some more. Sixteenth of August, they had a picnic in her car because it started to rain. Seventeenth of August, he hooked up the television in the bedroom. Catherine had fainted. They stayed in and watched *The Age of Innocence* and *The Remains of the Day*. Eighteenth of August, he had a haircut and polished his shoes. Nineteenth of August… Ruth felt her breath catch. He had taken his patient's advice. His words cut right through her heart.

19 August

Today will be one of my yesterdays, and I spent all of it with Catherine. It doesn't get better than that.

Ruth felt her eyes burn from the salt of fresh tears. She wished there was a way to let Molly know that her words had helped her son live his days. There were no more entries after that. The following pages were blank. There was no way of knowing what he did in the last two days, or what time he died. The date of his death was recorded as 21 August. The morning of that day he was due to appear in court. Time of death was estimated as occurring approximately ten hours before his body was found. So at or around midnight. But he could have died before then. He could have died on the twentieth and would have the wrong date on his headstone when the soil on his grave settled and it was able to have one. Ruth knew it was silly to let it matter. Whether it was an hour before midnight or an hour after didn't change anything. She would still imagine him in water going cold. The first officer on the scene said, 'The water in the bath was cold,' and those words would stay with her. But it was tormenting her knowing Tim Wiley was in Thomas's home on the night before, on the twentieth, at around 10 p.m. Ruth had not got around to asking Kim if she saw Thomas as well. Had an hour or so before midnight changed something in Thomas's mind? In his letter he said he had discovered something that made him decide to change his plea. What changed that decision? Was Christine Pelham's difficult question the reason why? Did Thomas say he found something because it's what he wanted Ruth to believe? To give her something to hold on to so that she could think he was innocent? Ruth wished she knew all the answers.

What had Tim Wiley wanted with her son at that time of night? Had he been posted there to guard Thomas's home? Did Sergeant Phillips know more than he was saying? Was he protecting one of his own? He said Tim Wiley had had a breakdown. Had it been triggered solely by his wife's death? Or had the man had something else on his mind? Something that would not let him be a policeman anymore?

He was breaking the law now. Had he broken the law before?

CHAPTER FORTY-FIVE

All the photographs were gone. It was the first thing she'd done this morning. The memory of their holidays was now in the rubbish, the only reminder the bits of Blu Tack left stuck on the walls. She was leaving this life and wanted no part of it anymore. Rosie was leaving today and not coming back. Everything she was taking was piled on the bed. The rest she was leaving behind or binning. The wardrobe still had clothes hanging in it, all cheap, impulsive buys, bought over the years which she would never wear. The drawers under the bed the same, still full of old jumpers and shoes. The small, flat screen TV on the kitchen counter was unearthed from the drawers, wrapped in a jumper. She'd forgotten she had it and thought it must have been put there because it was broken, but it worked fine. It was on now in the background and the picture and sound was good. If she had room in one of the cases, she'd pack it.

She tied another bin bag and added it to the pile by the back door. Old food from the fridge and cupboards, the rest was paperwork, accumulated over the years. Earlier, she'd checked pockets in clothes and compartments in handbags and in kitchen drawers and was fairly confident of leaving nothing with her identity.

She did a final check through the drawers and cupboards and was lucky and shocked to notice the jar of pickle. If she hadn't opened the cupboard door again… someone from the letting agency might have taken it home along with the other jars and tins left behind. She could imagine their surprise when they pulled out more than a spoonful of pickle to go with their cheese. She tied it in a thin carrier bag before hiding it among the rubbish in the black bin liner.

She took a minute to assess where she was with everything. It was really only the rubbish to put out and her packing to do. She hadn't made up her mind where she was going yet – she would do that when she got to the bus station. But it wouldn't be a bus she was taking, it would be a National Express coach to somewhere far away.

She picked up a few specs of dirt off the floor. The bedsit was still looking good from her day of thoroughly cleaning it, so the letting agency couldn't say she'd left it in a state. Turning her attention to the bed she started folding the clothes she was taking. When she had a neat pile ready she unzipped one of the cases and saw grains of sand left over from a holiday. She carried the case to the front door to shake it outside in the hallway. She couldn't take it out the back door because it was nailed shut with battens.

When she returned she found herself face to face with Anabel.

The case fell from her hand, onto the floor. Her ears were muffled, because she couldn't hear what was being said. Rosie walked over and turned up the volume on the television. Anabel's photo was in a corner of the screen. The reporter wore a bright red coat. Her voice was clear and pronounced. 'The body was found early this morning by a local fisherman. It is not known how long she might have been in the water.'

Rosie snatched at the remote and hit the off button fast, then unplugged the television from the socket. Her gaze went to the carrier bag, the one Chloe gave her with Anabel's jacket. She pressed her clammy palms together as bile rose into her throat. Sunday when she woke she was wearing Anabel's jacket and still couldn't remember why or when she put it on. Sunday she found a letter from Anabel outside her front door. She spent all day then, and all of Monday, thinking about the past. In her dream last night Anabel had been wearing her jacket. The amount of tears in it would let the rain in. It was definitely not waterproof anymore.

She pulled it out of the bag to check it, then shoved it back in. There was nothing wrong with it.

She cupped her hand under the cold kitchen tap and rinsed her mouth, then dried her hand with the end of her top. Anabel's jacket had pebbles in the pocket. She had been found in the sea. Had Rosie been with Anabel Saturday night? When Sunday morning her boots were on the kitchen floor, she wondered, had she gone out again after getting back from her mum's? She was so damn drunk, she couldn't remember. She hadn't found a receipt for the vodka. Maybe Anabel gave it to her as a present. Why was she wearing Anabel's jacket and why did she dream of Anabel wearing it? She leaned over the sink and tried to think. She was too scared to put the news back on in case she heard it was a suspicious death.

One thing was for sure. Her plans were going to have to be delayed by a day. If she went before offering her condolences it might increase Meg's suspicion there was something wrong between her daughter and best friend. The police might want to question her again. She didn't want anyone to come looking for her or create another missing persons poster. It was better to let Meg know her plans. She needed to show she had stood by Anabel. Even admit to spying on Chloe's house because she was so worried. The shock of now losing her friend was a shock too many. She couldn't stay after that. This town had too many sad memories.

Ten minutes later, hands deep in her pockets, head down to protect her face from the cold, she walked along her street with the carrier bag hanging from her wrist. She would start her new life tomorrow instead. It would give her time to think about where to go. She knew a nurse once who worked abroad out of season, cleaning caravans and putting up tents in holiday resorts. She got to see France and Spain that way and said it had been fun. Rosie wouldn't mind doing that, then in the summer she could apply for other jobs, be a children's entertainer or a holiday rep. She had a nursing qualification so she was bound to get something.

She noticed flowers in a bucket outside the petrol station shop and detoured across the tarmac to inspect them. There wasn't much of a choice and some were too colourful. She dithered, thinking not to bother, then spotted some white chrysanthemums. Pulling two bunches from the bucket she went inside the shop where she found a condolence card. After paying the assistant she borrowed the man's pen and wrote a few words to the family. She then continued her journey with carrier bags hanging from both wrists.

Meg's house was grander than the one she left behind next door to Rosie's mum. It had been a new build when she bought it, with five bedrooms and a garage. It didn't appeal to Rosie, as she wouldn't want to live on an estate where your make of car was judged as a sign of relative success. Meg's pink car was parked on the road, but there were no police vehicles. The poor woman would have had their visit first thing. Rosie knocked lightly, half hoping Meg wouldn't hear so she could leave the flowers and card in the porch.

Meg opened the door quickly and Rosie wasn't surprised to see her looking haunted. Her face was a sickly white but her eyes were dry, which Rosie was thankful for. She didn't fancy having to comfort her. She wanted this visit to be short.

'Hello, Meg,' she said softly. 'I'm so sorry for what's happened. I saw it on the news.'

'Come in,' she said.

Rosie closed the door quietly behind her, and slipped off her trainers. Meg didn't like shoes indoors. On the doormat Rosie saw today's mail, and noticed a hand-delivered white envelope partially hidden beneath a Domino's Pizza flyer. She picked the mail up and put it tidily on the shelf of the shoe cabinet, minus the white envelope, which went into Rosie's deep pocket.

She hadn't been to Meg's house in a while, maybe more than a year, so it felt strange. She followed Meg into the immaculate sitting room and saw that she'd been looking at photo albums.

Rosie wondered if she should offer to make her a cup of tea. The house was silent. Anabel's brother was in the navy and was probably flying home from somewhere, so Mr Whiting was probably at the airport waiting for his son.

Rosie relieved her wrists of the plastic bags and placed them down on the sofa. 'There's a card and some flowers in one, and Anabel's jacket in the other. I thought you might like to have it,' Rosie said.

Meg walked over to the sofa and picked up the bag with the jacket. She looked dazed. Leaving Rosie in the living room she went through the archway into the dining room to stand at the window, looking out at the back garden. The carrier bag was dropped to the floor as she hugged the jacket to her chest. Rosie could hear her sniffing it, then saw her bury her face in the material. She would leave her in peace, not bother offering tea.

She moved closer to the archway so as not to have to talk loudly and disturb the quiet atmosphere. 'I'm going away, Meg,' she said. 'I don't want to stay in this town without her. I'm letting you know so you don't wonder where I am. I might not be here for the funeral.'

Meg's shoulders stiffened. She turned slowly, then stared right through Rosie. 'I don't think Anabel would have wanted you there,' she replied, her eyes wide with unmistakable hatred. 'I certainly don't.' She then turned back to the window, saying not another word.

A few moments later, Rosie pulled the front door shut and walked down the path. She felt something hard settle in her chest that was singularly comforting. She imagined it like an internal armour, protecting her. She was on her own now. Meg was the last tie to cut. She was free to go wherever she wanted. She felt the smoothness of the envelope in her pocket. When had Anabel posted it? Rosie had not read all of her letter yet. She was burning to know what Anabel wrote to her mum. Had she told their secret? Had she written to Rosie's mum as well?

Rosie hoped not, because what good would that do? It would hurt the people who cared about her. She was dead now. Her voice should remain silent. Their secret taken with her to the grave. That's what Rosie would do. Leaving this town to help keep it safe. If one day a blackmail note drops though her letterbox, well, she would deal with it. Rosie was leaving so this blackmailer could never contact her again. She'll keep it safe then until the day she dies.

CHAPTER FORTY-SIX

Ruth swallowed the two paracetamol with the glass of water Joan handed her. She had the beginnings of a headache, and could do with getting some fresh air, but there were two police officers out in reception waiting to see her.

Joan took the glass from her and handed her a mug of tea. 'Do you want me to tell them you're not well?'

Ruth put the mug of tea on the desk. 'Did they say what they wanted?'

'No, but they said it wouldn't take long.'

'Fine,' she said. 'Give me a minute and then show them in.'

Joan closed the door quietly, leaving Ruth to wonder what the police wanted with her. Maybe they were there with an update on Tim Wiley. After yesterday's embarrassment, she would have preferred them to have come to her home and not her workplace. Her colleagues had been incredibly kind. She could do without them being reminded of why. She drank some of the tea and kept calm, then heard the knock on the door.

Joan showed the two officers into the room, then hovered by the wall until Ruth nodded at her to go. She had this. PC Kirby was familiar to her, and she vaguely recognised the female officer accompanying him. From where, she wasn't sure. Ruth invited them to sit down, and was grateful when PC Kirby declined.

'We shan't take up too much of your time, Dr Bennett, especially hearing you were unwell. We just called by as we wanted to show you something PC Nayland recovered from your street. We want to know if you recognise it. Mr Thorpe doesn't.'

Ruth remembered the woman. She'd been walking along the road with her head down as if searching the ground.

'What is it?' she asked.

PC Nayland unzipped a soft briefcase and pulled out a clear bag. She held it out close for Ruth to see what was inside. PC Kirby then spoke. 'Mr Thorpe doesn't think it's his, but we wondered if it might be yours or could have been your son's.'

PC Kirby was probably extremely efficient, but Ruth didn't care for his subtle dig. 'Which I may have worn that night, of course, I suspect you mean?' she retaliated in a cross voice.

He seemed genuinely surprised by her answer. 'No. We wondered if Mr Thorpe arrived at yours wearing a hat or you offered to lend him one when he left your home?'

Ruth felt her face warm. PC Kirby was a hard one to work out. How he was with her at the flat and at the station was different to how he was with her today. It was a useful behaviour for a policeman, she supposed. It had kept her on her toes. She examined the black beanie with its thin grey stripes. She shook her head. 'It's not mine, and Henry wasn't wearing one when I opened the door to him. He could have had it in his pocket, but that's something I wouldn't know.'

PC Kirby looked pleased at hearing this. 'Well, we managed to extract hairs and send them off to the lab. If it belongs to someone whose DNA is already in the system, then we'll know the owner.'

Ruth was a little startled. She thought that it was a lost cause and no suspect would be found, but now they were showing her what they thought of as evidence.

'Do you think the person who attacked Henry wore this?'

PC Nayland spoke up with a strong clear voice. 'From where I found it, I would say there was a strong chance it belonged to the perpetrator. There are a lot of hedges that stick out over the pavement along that street. The hat was found caught under a large bush. The space beneath it is big enough to crouch under. From its condition, it hasn't been there long.'

Ruth was amazed she could tell all that from a hat hanging off a bush. Her face must have shown her scepticism because the officer nodded understandingly. She gave Ruth a nice smile. 'I haven't got a crystal ball, but I am very good at looking for things. The hat might never have been found, unless it was washed to the ground by a heavy downpour. I had to get down on my hands and knees to peer under all the hedges before I found it.'

Ruth was impressed. PC Nayland hadn't just theorised, she had physically tested out her theory. Ruth, though, was wishing she had a crystal ball to put her troubled mind at rest. The man who came to see Kim in the front garden was wearing a beanie. Ruth hadn't known at the time that he was Kim's brother. If it was Fred's hat and he'd been in trouble with the law before, the police were going to go looking for him. After Kim's kindness, Ruth hoped it wasn't him who attacked Henry. She couldn't warn Kim either. If it was her brother who attacked Henry, then he was a danger to others. Ruth hoped it wouldn't be long before PC Kirby had the results of the DNA test. All the while Ruth was withholding information she was behaving irresponsibly.

PC Nayland put the bag away in the briefcase and the two officers headed to the door just as it opened. PC Kirby stepped back as Dr Raj stepped in. 'Sorry to interrupt you, Ruth, but I wanted to let the officers know that I'm free now.'

Ruth wasn't aware they were waiting to talk to Dr Raj too – it couldn't be about the same thing. It must be for something else. A missing person by the sounds of it, as she heard Dr Raj say she heard on the news that her missing patient had been found, and that it was a tragedy.

Ruth's door closed, and she drank in the silence and the last of her tea. It was lukewarm, but still drinkable. She looked out of the window at the view at the side of the car park. Tarmac, a fence, and then small red-brick houses. Not like the houses in Bath, built with large, honey-coloured stone cut with clean edges. She missed the colours of the city of Bath. There was something so tranquil about the light on the buildings, with the backdrop of dark green hills. It was a place that effortlessly rested the spirit and pulled at the imagination to take your mind off troubled thoughts. It was easy to imagine horses and carriages, and hearing sounds of hooves clip clop across cobbles.

She was aware of feeling out of sorts, aware she had a lot on her mind. Thomas, Tim Wiley, Kim, and her brother Fred. Her visit to the police station, their visit to her. She had been looking forward to seeing Henry after work, but now thought she wouldn't be very good company.

There was a knock on her door again and Joan entered wearing an apologetic face, her head at an angle, hands clasped together in front of her chest. 'You're in high demand today,' she said in an exasperated tone. 'I've had the police on the phone and they want to know if you can do a home visit. They're at the home of Rosie Carlyle as she's just had extremely bad news. Her best friend is dead.'

Ruth frowned. 'Is that why the police were here to talk to Dr Raj?'

Joan nodded. 'Yes. The missing woman was Dr Raj's patient. Poor thing drowned herself in the sea. They're probably wanting to know about her state of mind.'

Ruth put on her coat and picked up her briefcase and bag, thinking of Rosie's state of mind. Rosie hadn't mentioned her friend was officially missing. She would be devastated. She had lost her friend while they were still at loggerheads. Ruth wondered if it was reported on the local news. She hadn't read a newspaper or seen a television since coming to Bournemouth, and had given up thinking about what was going on in the world. She had enough to contend with in her own world. She glanced around the office, mentally checking she had everything. She had the necessary medications with her if required, but she would rather go down the route of listening and talking before resorting to other measures. Rosie Carlyle was already dependent on enough drugs without pushing more at her.

'Joan, do me a favour. While I run to the loo, pull up her postcode so I can put it in the satnav. Then let them know I'm coming, would you?'

Joan said she would, and a few minutes later handed Ruth a slip of paper. 'Make sure you go home when you're finished, and you give us a call so we know you're done. Then get some rest.'

Ruth smiled. 'Yes, Mum.'

'I'll give you "Mum",' Joan replied. 'If I was your mum, you'd have gone home and not be rushing about even more. I'm surprised you have only a headache after yesterday.'

Ruth walked away feeling realigned. Joan was a good tonic for levelling things. Nothing was too serious that it couldn't be lightened in some way. She should be taking Joan with her to see this patient. Though, maybe not, she might be too scary. She smiled at the thought, then put Joan from her mind.

In the car she sorted out the satnav and selected some music to play while driving. She found it best to approach these situations with a soothed mind – it helped her to deal better with the expressions of grief. Bach's 'Air on the G String' always soothed her. It was her go-to music – a medicine, almost. She would recommend music to Rosie. She couldn't promise instant results or that it would make her cry less, but she had been in Rosie's shoes, and hearing beautiful music had helped. Maybe not today for Rosie, but when she was ready she might try it.

CHAPTER FORTY-SEVEN

The people whose New Year's Eve party she went to were standing on their side of the road when Rosie walked along it. She gave the couple a small wave. She hadn't seen them while sober and hadn't realised they were so young. Younger than her, perhaps even in their late teens. She'd had a vague image of them being middle-aged for some reason. They were looking towards the house where Rosie lived, probably thinking the 1950s building rundown with its motley collection of curtains hanging at windows.

'What's up?' she asked in a friendly manner.

'Just having a nose.' The girl grinned. 'A copper was here. Went about five minutes ago.'

Rosie felt her calmness waver. 'Did they say what they wanted?'

She shook her head. 'In and out, then drove off. Reckon they were here for that old bloke who lives there. He looks a right perv. Rob reckons he's hiding so we're watching out for him.'

Rob looked like he could do with putting on some warmer clothes, as from where Rosie stood she could see the nipples on his skinny chest push against the thin material of his T-shirt.

She knew who they were referring to – the man who lived above her, who she could sometimes hear singing when he was anxious. 'The Grand Old Duke of York' was a favourite, which he sang longest. To their eyes he was old perhaps, and his behaviour odd. He was skittish at times and occasionally shouted at people as they passed by, his size scaring them. Poor bugger was a mess after fighting in the wars. Guy Fawkes Night she'd found him outside with his hands over his ears cowering in the alley. If it didn't suit her purpose right now to have them think it was him the police were after, she would have given them a mouthful and told them to fuck right off. Poor sod had no one to look after him. The police were bound to call again. They were probably wanting to question her about Anabel.

A woman came out of the front door behind them, gave Rosie a tentative wave, and Rosie realised her mistake when she shooed the teenagers in. They were her kids and it wasn't them who invited Rosie to the party, it was their mum. How bad was she not being able to remember whose home she was in? She was going to quit drinking when she started her new life. It had done her no favours. She only had to look at the last few days. She gave the woman a warm smile and then went to her flat.

She closed the front door and stared at the mound of stuff on the bed. She would have it cleared in an hour tops, then be out of there. She was not going to wait until tomorrow. But first she needed to read Anabel's letter, to see what she had to say to her mum.

A minute later it was screwed up in a ball and back in her pocket. It wasn't even worth shredding the sentimental crap about how sorry Anabel was and what great parents and brother she had. Like that was going to help them. They were never going to get over this. Rosie had done them a favour not letting them read it.

She took off her coat and got the suitcase she'd dropped by the front door, carried it to the bed and put the pile of clothes in that she had folded earlier. In no time it was full, zipped closed, and standing on the floor. She fetched a second suitcase up on the bed, glad it didn't need emptying of sand. It was Anabel's, bought by Rosie from Primark for her and Anabel's last holiday. Anabel used it, then asked Rosie to store it as she didn't have room for it in her flat. Her with her separate bedroom, kitchen and living room! She had the room, she just didn't want it to spoil the look. It was too deep to go under her bed, where she'd kept her other one, so it would have to have gone on top of her wardrobe, or God forbid behind her couch.

She hadn't been able to abide clutter. The amount of times they'd gone to Bristol to the nearest Ikea so Anabel could sort her things into little boxes or separate underwear with little plastic dividers. She had shelves for shelves in her kitchen cupboards just so tins at the back stood taller than the tins in front of them. Rosie used to watch her fuss about a teabag left on the draining board or a cushion moved off the couch, endlessly fussing, though she'd been happy enough to send clutter to Rosie's home. That didn't matter.

Rosie needed to stop thinking negatively about Anabel. Being angry with her wasn't going to take away all the hurt. She put her medication in around the sides of the case. She was going to wean herself off them once she was away from here. From now on she planned to be well. She'd had enough mental stress. More than anyone could imagine. When her new sick note ran out she would hand in her resignation, explaining that due to grief she was unable to work out her notice. That way they might not stop any pay. Until she secured a job she would have to stay in the cheapest places. She was not exactly used to luxury so it hardly mattered as long as she had a bed.

She checked the time. A minute to eleven. Another ten minutes and she'd be done. She'd take the bin bags out, come back and put the telly in the case, grab toiletries from the bathroom. She'd drop in at the letting agency on the way to the bus station and hand back the bedsit keys. She was paid up with her rent, so no need to hang around while they inspected the place. They could keep her deposit. That was the only reason they would want to check the bedsit, to find reasons not to give it back. They could make what they like of the back door. They had not sent anyone around to fix the lock, so it was down to them she was leaving it nailed with battens.

The few minutes outside left her hands like ice. She hurried back indoors to the warmth, desperate now for the loo. The cold always did that to her, made her bladder sensitive, and right now if she didn't get her jeans undone she was going to wet herself. Eyes down, hands grappling with button and zip, she barely had her bottom on the seat when she jerked back up as if she'd sat on nails, screaming and running bare-bottomed out the door, urine trickling into her pants and jeans.

Her eyes darted to the front door. It was closed, but she left it open when she went out. She shoved her hand across her mouth, to stop another scream. She had to be quiet. Jesus, this had been done in the last few minutes! *All that blood!* She couldn't breathe. She could hardly believe it. Maybe it wasn't real. A trick of the light? Imagined? This could be a parallel universe, her existence being played differently elsewhere. Still in a bathroom washing her hands, everything normal. It could be delayed shock? Her brain reacting differently. Telling her she should feel something about Anabel being dead. Or worse, it was Anabel fucking haunting her, coming to punish her some more. Like a horror film, where words appear through steam on a mirror.

She took a ragged breath. The only way to be sure was to look again. Trembling to the point where her legs would collapse, she held onto the doorframe and turned to face the bathroom. She whimpered. *It wasn't true.* She was not guilty of *that*!

Her eyes couldn't look away. 'It's not true,' she cried.

Falling on her knees to hang over the bath, she desperately tried to rub it away. Her hands got wet as she frantically smudged the letters. The wet felt sticky, was spreading and smearing all over the bath. She needed the taps on. Water to wash it away. She let it gush in, using both hands to wash at the sides, wash at the base, washing red water down the drain. She was panting and panicking, and pleading in her mind. *Please make it go. Please make it go. Make it gone.*

Her eyes fixed on the bath, searching through the swirl of water. An uncontrollable sob came up her chest. It would not wash away. It was still there. The red words wouldn't disappear. Three words pounding at her head. YOU KILLED HER. *You killed her. You killed her.*

'Shut the fuck up,' she squealed.

She sat back on her calves and heaved a cry. She needed to get up off her knees and get out of there. Whoever did this was coming back. She got to her feet, did up her jeans and grabbed a towel, drying her hands roughly. She needed to get her coat and bags and go. A minute was all she needed to be ready to leave. Coat done up over her damp jeans, she opened the door and made a sound somewhere between a laugh and a cry. She had timed it wrong. Another second and she would have heard the knock at the door. She would have had warning.

Something in his eyes said he was not there to question her gently about Anabel. His knock on her door was for a different reason. She saw him glance at her hands. Then at the cases on the floor. And at *her.* She slowly backed away. Disbelieving. Reeling. Her mind shouting out. *It couldn't be true. The words were a lie! She wouldn't have.* The promise she made to the sky never happened. They were only her thoughts. What she wanted to do. Not what she did. They were just thoughts. Played out in her mind. They were not real.

The police officer stepped forward and gazed at the suitcases. He shook his head at her. 'You might want to put them back. You won't be going anywhere today.'

CHAPTER FORTY-EIGHT

Ruth parked on the road a few houses down from the address. She locked the car and scanned the street for a police vehicle. The absence of one made her wonder if she was still needed. Maybe Rosie had been taken to hospital. She would have expected them to phone if that was the case, though.

On the wall by the front door the names in the plastic windows next to the buttons were hard to read. The piece of paper Joan handed her said Rosie Carlyle lived in Flat 3. The front door was closed, but not shut completely. Ruth pushed it open and entered a brown-tiled hallway, which was long and narrow and quite dark due to the staircase beside it blocking the light. It was hard to make out if the swirls in the carpet on the stairs was a pattern or dirt. On her immediate left a brass door number was screwed to the brown-painted wood. She moved down the hallway, past the next door, and came to number three. Rosie's front door was slightly ajar. Ruth tapped it firmly, and called out, 'Helloooo! Dr Bennett here.'

She received no answer and pushed it open. 'Hi, Rosie. It's Dr Bennett.'

Still no response. She stayed at the door and looked around at her patient's home. Ruth's first thought was it was dismal. It would depress anyone living there. It was not a flat either, but a bedsit. She could see a kitchen area to the left, straight ahead a barricaded back door, and to the right a partial view of a double bed. A small table had been squeezed into the remaining space with a single chair plonked to face the foot of the bed for some reason. The closed door to her left had to be a bathroom.

She called out again, wondering if Rosie was in there, and stepped through the doorway, only to jump out of her skin when the front door shut sharply. She turned fast and knew straight away that something was wrong. She'd been expecting to see a police officer, but not him. *Definitely not him.* Why was he there?

She greeted him, hoping she didn't appear nervous and was only alarmed by the shutting of the door. 'You gave me a fright. I didn't see you there, I thought the place was empty.' She glanced around as if curious. 'Has she gone to hospital?'

Tim Wiley shook his head. 'No. She's on the far side of the bed.'

Ruth walked forward a step to see the whole bedroom area. Instant shock shunted her heart into her throat. *What had he done?* Rosie was on the bed, sitting against the black metal headboard. A rope around her waist tethered her to it. One wrist was handcuffed to a chair, the other secured with a cable tie to the metal bed frame. Across her mouth was wide silver tape. Her eyes, though, were not scared, which gave Ruth hope. For whatever reason Rosie was not frightened of him.

Ruth flicked her gaze to him. 'What's going on, Mr Wiley?' Then her heart skipped a beat at the sight of the gun in his hand. 'Is that loaded?' she asked quietly, keeping her voice exceptionally calm.

He looked down at it. Then said something strange. 'It is, but I try to think of it as empty.' He used it to point at the chair at the end of the bed, the twin of the one Rosie was handcuffed to. 'You can sit there,' he said. 'That's your seat.'

Ruth stayed where she was. If she sat down things could get worse. 'Why am I here?' she asked.

He gave a half smile. 'You're the audience.'

Ruth didn't like the sound of that at all. What was she going to have to watch? 'I don't understand. Can't you tell me what's wrong, so maybe I can help? Does she need to be like that? Handcuffed?'

He pointed at the chair with the gun again. 'Sit down. I know what you're trying to do. Buy time, talk me out of this. Well, *this* has been a long time coming.' His voice was as calm as hers. 'You need to do what I tell you. Leave your bags on the floor and take your seat.'

'And if I don't?' she asked.

'I'll shoot you. Nowhere serious, side of an arm probably.'

Ruth stared into his eyes. He meant it. He would do it if she didn't obey. She put her briefcase and bag down and sat in the chair facing Rosie Carlyle at the top of the bed.

Tim Wiley unzipped his black police vest and took the weight of it off his shoulders. He dropped it down on the floor and stretched his neck from side to side. Muscular strain or tension, Ruth suspected. From a blue canvas bag she hadn't noticed by his feet, he fetched out two plastic bottles of water. She was surprised when he handed her one.

'In case you get thirsty,' he said.

Ruth was parched, and if not for Rosie opposite her, with her mouth no doubt bone dry, she would have glugged it back right away. 'Thank you,' she replied.

She remembered the letter Kim gave her when she felt in her pockets for something to use as a weapon. She had forgotten all about it. She kept the water in her lap for something to hold on to, and tried to think about how to get them out of this situation. Her damn phone was in her bag. If she'd put it in her coat pocket she could have tried using it, even if it meant blindly pressing keys through the material. The only things she could use as a weapon were the bottle of water in her hand, her car keys in her pocket, a thick envelope, and the chair she was sitting on. As he had a gun, though, there was no contest even if she had a knife. She would risk both hers and Rosie's lives.

Tim Wiley climbed across the bed, as there wasn't room to get around Ruth, and straddled the chair Rosie was handcuffed to.

His weight would prevent Rosie from grabbing the chair to use against him. He rested his chest against the flat spindles, looking reasonably comfortable. He had clearly thought this through before Ruth arrived – where he would sit, and where Ruth would sit.

Keeping the gun in his right hand he used his left to rip the tape off Rosie's mouth. She yelped, then licked her lips as if sore. Around her mouth was red. Ruth wondered how long she had been there. The crotch of her jeans was a darker blue, so perhaps a long time. Ruth gazed at her reassuringly, trying to impress on her that it would be all right. She just needed to stay calm.

He tapped the top of the chair with the gun and looked at Rosie. 'So, have you worked out yet why we're all here?'

'Because you're a fucking lunatic,' she replied scathingly. She glanced at Ruth. 'Check out my bathroom. See what he did to it. He's a fucking loony.'

He laughed drily. 'Says the one popping pills every day. The one pissed out of her head most of the time. Lost any more clothes, have you?'

She spat at him and spittle landed on his cheek. 'You fucker,' she snarled. 'Get a kick out of following me, did you?' She flashed angry eyes to Ruth. 'I told you, didn't I, what happened in my home? It was him all along. Coming in here, touching my things, watching me asleep. He's one of those nutters that gets power out of wearing a uniform. Probably follows women so he can steal their underwear. *Makes me sick.*'

Ruth felt her alarm grow. Rosie showed no fear speaking like that. She thought Tim Wiley was a policeman. From Ruth's point of view this was turning more dangerous. He wanted Ruth there for a reason and Rosie was ignoring that. While she admired her fighting spirit, antagonising him wasn't going to help. From his attitude he was not concerned by the spit on his face, which he casually wiped off using the corner of the cover on Rosie's bed.

Ruth wanted to catch her eye to warn her, but she was looking only at him.

'So,' he said. 'You can't think of a reason you might be tied up in the same room as your doctor and me?'

She stared at him brazenly. 'Do I look like a clairvoyant?'

He ignored her answer and looked at Ruth instead. 'How are you doing, Dr Bennett?'

'I'm fine, thank you,' she said back. 'I wouldn't mind leaving, though. That would be nice.'

He winked at her, making her worry even more at how relaxed he was, like he had all the time in the world to play this game. He leaned slightly to his right and pulled something out of his left trouser pocket. Ruth jolted in fear as she heard a click and saw a blade spring out from the flick knife. He pointed it at Rosie. 'I'm going to use it on you, if you don't start talking.'

Rosie glared at him. 'Do that and you'll have every person in the building here, because I'll be screaming, you twat.'

He shook his head. 'No. No one will come. They're all out. This has been planned, you see. The sooner you realise that, the sooner you'll know I'm deadly serious. You're going to tell Dr Bennett what you did.'

Ruth saw Rosie's eyes change. He had unnerved her. She was gazing at him, searching his face. 'Have we met before?' she asked. 'I mean, before now and the time you came to question me?'

He lowered the gun and knife to his lap and clapped his hands slowly. 'We have, but have you remembered where yet?' He picked up the weapons again. 'Now stop fucking prevaricating and tell Dr Bennett what you did.'

Ruth was doing her best to stay calm. The last moment, though, had set off an undercurrent of fear in her belly. His voice revealed a deep anger. Rosie needed to be careful. She was not hearing his anger. Ruth had no idea why he had them there, but she wanted

Rosie to comply and tell him whatever he wanted. It didn't matter if it was a bunch of lies if it got them out of there.

Rosie curled her lip at him. 'I don't know what you're talking about. You can use that knife all you want. You should be ashamed of yourself wearing that uniform. Your family must be so proud of you. Or… is that it? They don't want you? Got to do something exciting to prove yourself? Girlfriend throw you out, did she? Or is the wife keeping the kids? She don't understand you?' Rosie taunted.

He banged the gun on the chair. '*Shut up!* Don't talk to me about this uniform. Just shut up and be quiet.'

Ruth watched him shake his head, close his eyes, and breathe hard. She tried to get Rosie's attention. Then he opened his eyes and the moment was lost.

The face he turned to Ruth was changed. Gone was his brashness. He was looking at her differently, his eyes solemn, his manner that of someone having to impart grave news. Even his voice sounded different. Matured. 'I'm sorry you're here, but I could think of no other way for you to hear this.' He inhaled deeply, and on the release of breath his gaze dropped away. 'My wife was dying. I could see it in her eyes. A simple stomach ache one minute, the next she's writhing, the pain unbearable. She's begging me to get help, and I'm trying. I'm running around trying to get someone to her, but nobody is willing to listen, no one cares about the state she's in. Everyone's too busy watching a ward that has turned into a circus. Noise. Chaos. And everyone saying the same thing. She'll have to wait. *She'll have to wait!* She did. And then she died.

'You told me the day I drove you that your son was innocent. Something clicked after that… something I remembered. A nurse standing alone, aside from all the chaos, ignoring the noise, ignoring *my wife*, while her colleagues looked distraught and her friend stood there crying. She had this smile on her face. A bloody smile! While my wife was dying!'

He pointed the knife at Rosie. 'Her friend told me everything. I felt at peace after talking to her, and so did she. I explained why I had to frighten her. Why I sent her a letter saying she should have been caught. I needed to get to the truth. And she wanted to tell it! Saturday night, she was going back to her home. She could have stayed longer at mine, she felt safe there, but she said it was time to go. This morning when I heard she'd drowned herself… I felt a rage.'

In a flash he demonstrated how much of a rage. He was leaning forward with the knife right at Rosie's face, his anger spoken through gritted teeth. 'She told me what you did.'

Ruth gasped. The tip of the blade pressed against Rosie's cheek. If the chair tipped over onto the bed and he slipped the knife would go in her face. 'Please don't,' she begged, in little more than a whisper.

He breathed in sharply and sat back, turning his eyes to Ruth. 'How can you be so kind after what she did? My wife died because of her. They tried to say it was the cancer. The reason her bowel obstructed. But if they got to her sooner, she might have had a chance to be saved.'

Ruth felt sorry for him. It sounded like a traumatic experience, and in his mind Rosie Carlyle was instrumental in it. But now was not the time to berate her. She had just lost her friend. Ruth needed to appeal to his compassion. She needed to make him see Rosie was already suffering. 'Tim, please, whatever you think she did, this won't make it better. Let her go. She's had a shock already today.'

He sat up straight and looked back at her as if *she'd* shocked him. Then it was him who gasped. 'You haven't connected the dots, have you? You haven't worked out who her friend is. Anabel told me she wrote to you, wanted you to come and undo what was done.'

Ruth gaped at him. 'Anabel?' she uttered in surprise.

'Yes,' he replied forcefully. 'Anabel Whiting.'

Ruth was more shocked. More confused. 'But I've been trying to contact her. I came to Bournemouth knowing Anabel Whiting was the person who phoned the police. Hers was the only name I had, and I was hoping she might know something.' She closed her eyes and felt pressure build around her head. 'She can't be dead,' she whispered. 'How am I going to find out what happened?'

Ruth sat in a daze. Her mind connected the things she hadn't known – Dr Raj's missing patient was Rosie's friend, the same friend who had just been found. All this time Ruth had been knocking on the door of this friend, and trying to contact her by phone, she had been missing. And now she was dead.

Why hadn't Rosie said that she and her friend were nurses? The person who could have helped her from the beginning had been right in front of her. *Rosie.* Rosie with all her troubles would have wanted to help. If Rosie had said her name or Ruth asked what she was called, they could have searched for Anabel together.

Her head was spinning. How did any of this connect with Tim Wiley? How did he know it was Anabel who had written to her? What was he saying? He had been talking about his wife. He mentioned chaos on a ward. Rosie watching a distraught friend. He mentioned noise. *Everyone watching a ward that had turned into a circus.* Her breath caught. She suddenly knew. O*h, God, no.* This was about Thomas! This is why he wanted her there. Why he wanted Rosie there.

Thomas caused chaos – while Rosie was smiling – while Tim Wiley's wife was dying.

He wanted to punish them for that.

CHAPTER FORTY-NINE

Rosie was trying to work out how to escape. The police officer was obviously deranged. The death of his wife had sent him over the edge, causing him to kidnap a nurse and target another because he blamed them. Rosie heard him on the phone thanking someone. He said he'd stay until the doctor came. Rosie was in a state, he'd keep her calm. She was in a state – tied to her bed – listening to him lie to the person on the other end of the phone. She was now in a different sort of state. *This* was about last summer! He was referring to what happened on the ward. That's where Rosie must have seen him before. He'd been visiting his wife. He was on the ward the day Dr De Luca was arrested.

This was nothing to do with her and Anabel's secret. He sent Anabel that cryptic letter. It wasn't to blackmail her, but to frighten her. He came to Rosie's home and did creepy things to frighten her. All the terrorising – the words in her bath – this was all him. All the time she had thought these things were happening because Anabel told someone their secret. When it was a husband gone mad from the death of his wife and wanting to blame someone.

But why drag Dr Bennett into it?

Rosie was in shock a little since hearing Anabel had written to her. Asking her to come and undo what was done! What on earth did she contact Dr Bennett for? The doctor couldn't bring the man's wife back to life. The man was badly overreacting. So she smiled. So what? He was a policeman. He surely witnessed people smiling during times of stress. Some people even laughed. It happened sometimes.

Rosie glanced at Dr Bennett. She'd sat in a daze since hearing Anabel was dead. But why? Why did the policeman want the doctor there? If he were going to harm Rosie, he wouldn't want a witness. It didn't make sense. Rosie thought back to a few minutes ago, hearing in her head the distressed whisper. *How am I going to find out what happened?*

A shiver suddenly ran down Rosie's spine. It now all made perfect sense. Anabel had felt guilty – her behaviour last New Year's Eve caused a lot of grief – which is why she contacted the woman.

Dr De Luca was Dr Bennett's son.

It explained now why Anabel killed herself. She felt guilty for what happened to the man. Rosie gazed at her GP and wondered if she realised how much danger she was in. Dr Bennett wasn't there by accident. The policeman tricked the doctor there for good reason. He blamed her son, maybe even more than he blamed Rosie.

*

Rosie was now in a daze.

She was upset. Learning her doctor was Dr De Luca's mum didn't feel right. She was the new doctor where coincidentally Rosie and Anabel were patients? Patients who had known and worked with her son? Her being in Bournemouth had to be about him. She might be a bit touched as well. Her son was convicted of a crime and maybe she couldn't accept that. Though, what mother wouldn't want their son to be innocent? She was the best doctor Rosie had ever had. And now it felt like she'd been tricked. Like it was happening all over again.

Anabel had been good at pulling the wool over people's eyes. Rosie had seen her beguiling ways. Could recall how her mum and dad used to look at Anabel. Faces lit up when she came and showed them something. Told them something. *Such a clever girl,* her dad would say. *A hard worker*, her mum would say. *You're lucky to have her as a friend*, they'd chorus. Anabel had tried to fool Rosie. Saying she was going to a *pottery class*? When really she was going to see him. Rosie followed her on both occasions when she went to try and see Dr De Luca. Rosie knew it was only a matter of time before Anabel caused him a problem.

Rosie felt the bed shift as the policeman crossed it for the third time. She watched in amazement as he made coffee in the kitchen, searching her cupboards, finding a drizzle of milk in the fridge. He handed Dr Bennett a mug of coffee. Rosie hadn't even been offered a drink of water. The two of them now sat there sipping their drinks as if she were invisible! Dr Bennett must be in shock to be letting this happen.

He began talking to Dr Bennett quietly as if Rosie were no longer there. He sat sideways on the chair, the gun and knife on the bed. 'I wanted you to hear the truth. I should have told you a while ago what actually clicked for me the day I drove you. I believed you when you said your son was innocent. You said it so quietly, from the back of the car, but I heard you. It was that which made me think about what I saw on the ward that day. Why would a nurse be smiling with all that going on? Why would she just stand there watching a friend cry? After seeing one of their own brought to the ground by a bunch of coppers? Everyone else was affected, so why not her? It struck me as so out of place. So I began watching them. I could tell right off something was wrong. I kept tabs on them to see what I might uncover.'

He jabbed his thumb over his shoulder without looking at Rosie, to make it clear to Dr Bennett who he was talking about. '*Her* and her friend both off sick not long after your son died. This one drinking like a fish, her mate looking haunted. They looked guilty of something, to me. But I didn't know what. I remembered hearing your son had a knife on him. Main reason why none of the staff would come over and see Evie. I asked about it. My colleagues said nothing was found on him. It was Anabel's behaviour that convinced me I was not wrong to be suspicious. If she wasn't walking into a church, she was standing outside the police station, looking in. When I spotted her on Christmas Eve, I decided to send her a letter. The letter was more of a taunt, but it did the trick. It unnerved her. She was in the middle of packing when I called on her. Said she was going to stay at a friend's, and gave me the address, then oddly, she hands me Dr De Luca's hospital identity badge. She wouldn't say how she had it or why she was giving it to me, and I didn't press her, because the state she was in I knew I was going to talk to her again soon.

'I let a week go by then went to see her at this friend's house. She was writing letters about what happened. She wouldn't tell me what they said. She was going to get her friend to deliver them. There was something so bloody sad about her I gave her my address. When she turned up and asked if she could stay, I couldn't turn her away. She was afraid Rosie Carlyle would find her and prevent her from telling the truth.' He rubbed his eyes, and when he spoke again his voice sounded choked. 'I shouldn't have let her leave. She had her whole life in front of her. She must have felt so alone to do that…' He turned and stared at Rosie. 'I hope you know her blood is on your hands.'

Rosie gazed at the dry red flakes around her fingernails. For him to say that reassured her he meant this only figuratively. The blood on her hands wasn't Anabel's. It was probably blood from an animal. Some liver from a butcher's he squeezed the blood out of to write with. Rosie let out a relieved sigh. The promise she made to the sky had been only a fantasy. The words he wrote were only feelings. She wondered how much longer he was going to jabber on. So far the only interesting part was his admission of a further crime – he had let the police waste time searching for a missing person he knew where to find. He had sat in Rosie's kitchen asking questions, probably only to taunt her. Or to snoop around. Rosie left him alone while she went to the bathroom. Had he snooped about for her front-door key, made an impression in a little tin of modelling clay? It was all so sick. And Anabel? Anabel must have taken Dr De Luca's ID badge after he was arrested. Perhaps she took it to keep as a memento under her pillow. If that was the reason she had it, she should have kept it secret.

'I was going to come and see you. I called your surgery in Bath. The receptionist said you no longer worked there, you'd gone to Bournemouth. New Year's Day I saw you come out of your son's place. I followed you the next day to your new job, signed on as a new patient and was able to see you the same day. But it didn't go well. You didn't like me.'

Rosie gazed at him sceptically. She'd have more respect for him if he just admitted he fancied Dr Bennett. Her doctor was a good-looking woman. Rosie had been studying her face and could see the resemblance to her son. His hair, though, had been a rich dark brown with a slight wave. Not blonde like his mother. She had noticed the way women looked at him. A bit like this pillock sat by the bed, droning on, looking at the mother. He wasn't thinking about his wife now. His attention was all on Dr Bennett.

'I wanted to tell you about Rosie Carlyle. She was jealous of her friend because your son took an interest. Anabel told me what they did when they were kids. Rosie Carlyle got her friend to kill her dad.'

Rosie's outrage was instant. Her shoulders strained forward as she tried to reach him, the veins in her neck standing out as she screeched at him, 'That's a filthy lie you just said!'

He ignored her, and so did her doctor. Rosie glared. 'You fucking saddo. Carrying on like this because your wife died. You're pathetic. You stupid man.'

Rosie was about to hurl further insults, but his crumpled face stopped her. Astonishingly, he had begun to cry. Tears were rolling down his cheeks. 'I'm sorry I blamed him. He would have helped

Evie if he could have. *He* was not to blame.' He dragged the back of his hand across his eyes, and gulped air, trying to compose himself. 'If I'd known I'd have never gone to see him. I would have left him alone. But my pain was unbearable. He killed my wife as far as I was concerned. I couldn't let that go. Now it's too late to say sorry. But I am. I'm so sorry, Dr Bennett.'

Rosie saw Dr Bennett's face change. She saw her eyes register what the policeman just said. She was looking at him in shock. Rosie gasped. *Oh my God*, she thought. Then covered her mouth as Dr Bennett stared at her. She sat quietly then and didn't say a word. She watched Dr Bennett get up from the chair, walk over to her bag and get out her phone. Her voice was leaden as she asked for the police.

The policeman didn't try to stop her. He sat there looking drained, as well he should. He had just admitted to killing Dr Bennett's son. Rosie couldn't believe how it had all turned out. The police were coming for *him*. And not *her*.

CHAPTER FIFTY

Ruth was beginning to think the law was an ass. Since mid-afternoon she had been talking to the police and it had been a waste of time. Tim Wiley had been arrested, Rosie Carlyle had been rescued, and Ruth had been offered coffee. It was now nearly six o'clock and she was sick of being offered coffee, sick of being offered platitudes, and sick of Sergeant Phillips's sympathetic eyes. He had been brought in to talk to her as she was not leaving until someone gave her answers that made sense. He had talked for the last twenty minutes, covering a number of things Ruth had asked other officers. He understood every one of her concerns, but there was no proof her son was innocent. In the eyes of the law he was guilty, and would remain so. In regards to the unlawful killing of Thomas, in the eyes of the law he left this world by his own hand.

Tim Wiley, he informed her, held his hands up to what he did today, but he emphatically denied killing Thomas De Luca. He declared that Dr Bennett completely misunderstood. What he was sorry for was for thinking her son was guilty, but when he left Dr De Luca's flat he was very much alive.

Ruth argued Thomas pleaded guilty to a crime he didn't commit on the basis of having no choice against a law that judged only on the evidence. Sergeant Phillips pointed out that this approach would not have been allowed at his sentencing hearing. A defendant can't seek to distance himself from the offence he has pleaded guilty to. A guilty plea by the defendant was acceptance of committing the offence. And while it was true criminal charges were sometimes dropped when a suspect is proven innocent or not enough evidence found, this was not the case with her son. Drugs weren't just found in Dr De Luca's locker and home, his fingerprints were all over them. Those drugs had been handled by her son. So overturning his conviction was highly unlikely.

Ruth wanted to bang the table in frustration, but she needed to sit there and listen. Something new might come out of this discussion and hit Sergeant Phillips smack in the eye. Then he would look at her amazed and see she was right. Thomas was innocent. Ruth told him about the letters Anabel Whiting sent her. Wanting her to come to Bournemouth to prove Thomas was innocent. Did he not think this dead woman deserved to be heard?

He was not surprised at her receiving letters. They had in their possession a letter sent by Anabel Whiting, only that morning, but a letter did not prove someone else was guilty of her son's crime. Sergeant Phillips was not hopeful it would lead anywhere. Dr De Luca pleaded guilty to the crime. Anabel Whiting wanting the police to believe someone else was guilty instead was simply not enough to change that. He said the young woman who delivered the letter to the police station said she'd been left a bag of them on her doorstep with a note from her friend asking her to deliver them. But no matter how many letters she wrote, Anabel Whiting's words could not be taken as facts, he said. Her beliefs, while strongly felt, was not evidence.

Ruth shook her head at him after he said that. Why couldn't he see what was as plain as day – Thomas was innocent. He was not guilty of committing any crime. And Tim Wiley was a liar. He blamed Thomas for his wife's death. He blamed Rosie Carlyle as well. He went to see Thomas and was the last person to see him alive. Rosie Carlyle would back her up. She was there and heard what was said. He went to see Thomas for one reason alone.

In Rosie's home, Ruth had been silent for most of the time Tim Wiley talked and intentionally looked unengaged, but she'd been aware the whole time and missed none of what was said. He revealed he had been on a mission since his wife's death.

'He has a darkness in his soul,' Ruth blurted out. 'Did you see what he wrote in the bathroom? He was accusing Rosie Carlyle of his wife's death.'

Sergeant Phillips's eyebrows rose. His expression turned concerned. 'Is that your professional opinion?'

Ruth stayed silent, wishing she'd been a little more circumspect and shown professionalism and self-restraint.

He tapped a finger on his chin and regarded her seriously. 'If it is not your professional opinion, it might be wise not to say it again. It might also be wise not to see Rosie Carlyle as a patient again. Miss Carlyle has voiced concern over finding out her doctor was Thomas De Luca's mother. She would not have seen you if she'd known that. She has assisted in every way she can, backed up everything you said about Tim Wiley. But today has left her disturbed and untrusting of her doctor. You need to tread cautiously as everything is open to interpretation, including your own behaviour.'

Ruth gaped at him. She had had enough. Now they were using Rosie to raise doubts about her character. Tim Wiley remaining innocent of murder might make it easier for them. She and Rosie had been held prisoner, Rosie tied to a bed by an officer who once upheld the law. No one liked that sort of news. It left a smear. Like the one left on Thomas. She leaned forward in her chair, while her hands on the desk curled into balls. 'Care to explain that comment?' she asked in a firm tone. 'I don't want to misinterpret your meaning.'

His sigh said he didn't want to tell her. He spread his hands as if he didn't have a choice. 'Rosie Carlyle said her doctor sat and drank coffee with the police officer, while she was tied to her bed, and that the weapons were put down beside her. And another thing. Tim Wiley didn't write those words about his wife. He wrote them for Anabel Whiting. Granted, it was a horrible thing to say. The young woman ended her own life. But I think Tim Wiley was striking out, after forming a friendship with her, and wanted to hurt Miss Carlyle. I think, you'd agree, Tim Wiley's behaviour shows an unwell man. An unwell man since his wife died.'

Ruth sat back astonished. She felt sick to her stomach. She guessed this was how Thomas must have felt. Only much worse. Trampled over and unheard. In the last few months it occasionally frustrated her that he hadn't protested his innocence strongly, more strenuously, that he hadn't put up enough of a fight. She felt he had given up his freedom too easily. Ruth was nearly defeated by the same hopelessness. She now wondered, guiltily, if his reaction was down to his upbringing? It was the only thing that made any sense. If she could turn back the clock would she make him different? What would she have changed? Nothing. She would not change a single thing about Thomas.

Sergeant Phillips gave her a searching look. Ruth was not going to tell him her thoughts. She held his gaze. 'How can you be so sure Tim Wiley didn't do something to my son?'

He broke eye contact and looked away, and in frustration she banged the table. 'Can you please just answer me that? Why are you so sure?'

He raised his head and she saw in his eyes something that made her sure he knew something. 'What did Anabel Whiting say in her letter? Did she tell you who was guilty? Did she say it was her?'

When he remained silent Ruth rose from her chair. She was so close to the truth and wasn't going to walk away while the law decided to let the guilty go free. She would be ruthless Ruth if she had to be. If that's what was required.

She demanded justice and she was not going to stop until she had it.

CHAPTER FIFTY-ONE

From the back seat of the taxi Ruth saw the blue flashing lights of an ambulance close to where she had parked. She had already been on the way to Purbeck Street to collect her car, when Henry phoned her asking for help at that address. After what happened at Rosie's home, Ruth was taken to the police station in a police car. She had been completely confused about Henry being there, thinking for a moment he must have heard what happened to her. Until he explained Kim's brother also lived there. The police had been called by neighbours, because Fred was in a bit of a state. So Henry had gone with Kim to help calm her brother down. The whole situation felt surreal to Ruth. Learning Kim's brother lived at the same address as Rosie. Today felt like she was going around in circles. She shrank back from the car window when normally her instinct would be to rush forward. Right now, though, she felt rudderless and wanted someone to help her for a change. She was so damned tired. She pondered whether to collect her car and drive herself home, to her real home in Bath, and forget about ever coming back.

A small crowd had gathered. She spotted two paramedics, two police officers, and Kim standing in front of one of them blocking his way. Ruth then saw the reason for them all being there. A man was banging his fists against his head. He was hurting himself. Henry was with him trying to keep his arms down at his sides. She quickly handed the driver a twenty-pound note, grabbed her bags and exited the car.

The noise of them all was quite deafening as she drew close. Many voices, all speaking at once. Kim was arguing fiercely with a police officer. A paramedic was talking loudly to the man, the man was manically singing, and rubbish was strewn all around him and even stuck to him. Henry seemed glad to see her. He gave a relieved smile. Then his face looked pained as 'The Grand Old Duke of York' got bellowed in his ears.

Ruth could see at a glance the man was frightened. His hands had found their way back to his head. Thankfully this time to pat it. As she watched him check each of his pockets, then pat his head again, Ruth wondered if he was feeling for his hat. She stepped closer, so he would hear her. 'Fred, your hat is safe. Is your head cold?'

His eyes swivelled to her face and he sang faster.

Kim turned at hearing Ruth's voice. 'Ruth, thank God. Fred needs to go to hospital. He's had a terrible shock. He thought Henry was a ghost. The police phoned me, found him wandering on the street looking for his hat. He's been going through the bins. They couldn't get him to go into his flat. Henry drove me over and when Fred saw him he went berserk. He's got a gash where he ran straight into a wall, trying to get away. I couldn't calm him down so they had to call an ambulance.' She nodded her head at the officers behind her. 'They wanted to arrest him, but are happier for him to go to hospital.' Kim called out to the paramedics. 'She's our doctor. Can you let her look at him, please?'

Ruth gave Kim a reassuring look. She was guessing that it was Fred who hit Henry. If he thought Henry was a ghost, he must have thought he had killed him. Kim must be feeling terribly scared for her brother. Her poor face was blotchy from crying. Ruth would hug her afterwards, but right now she needed to deal with Fred. She stood calmly in front of him, noticing the cut above his eye. Feeling the sheer size of him. He was a big chap, with a solid neck and his large head, more prominent with a crew-cut. She imagined when he was younger and in combats he would have looked twice as formidable. Ruth put him in his mid-forties. 'Would you like my scarf?' she offered. 'It will keep your head warm until we get your hat.'

His response was to sing louder. Ruth knew singing for some people helped relieve stress, but Fred didn't seem to benefitting. It seemed more like a form of pressurised speech. His thoughts were probably racing, while dealing with high energy. She held out the soft blue woollen scarf, and saw his eyes grow interested. She stepped closer and placed it around his neck, ignoring the stickiness on his clothes. She gave him a soft smile. 'How are you, Fred?' she asked.

He shook his head and waved his hand agitatedly in front of his eyes. Ruth turned to a paramedic. 'Could you turn off the flashing lights, please?' she asked. 'I think it upsets him.'

The sturdy woman nodded, and a moment later the street turned darker, and the noise level noticeably lower. Fred had stopped singing and was humming instead. He was now on the move, walking in fast circles through bags of rubbish.

'Do you want to sit down, Fred? Are your legs tired?'

His humming sounded like he was agreeing, but his walking picked up speed and carrier bags were splitting open with cans and bottles rattling across the pavement, rotting food releasing a stench into the air. The paramedics and police were discussing ways to calm him. Then, like a wound-down toy, his movements got slower and slower until he was at a complete stop, and he slumped. Ruth approached him. She would be truthful with him. 'Fred, the paramedics would like to take you to hospital so that a doctor can check to see if you're well. Would that be all right if they took you to the hospital?'

He looked undecided and searched the faces around him. Kim quickly came forward. 'I'm here, Fred. I've not gone anywhere. There's no need to be frightened. I think, Fred, you need some help with all this pain in your head, so it would be good to see a doctor.'

The poor man began to cry. He grabbed Kim's hand. Henry came over to reassure him. 'Fred, I'm honestly fine. It was only a bump to my head.'

Fred reached out his hand and touched Henry's chest. Words rushed out of his mouth in a mournful wail. 'Didn't mean to kill you. Was waiting for Kimmy. Got scared you'd make me go home. Sorry. Sorry. Sorry.'

Henry gently held Fred's hand against his chest. 'See. I'm not dead. Everything will be all right. You just need to get well now, Fred.'

A few minutes later Henry and Ruth stood and watched the ambulance drive away. Kim had gone with Fred. The two police officers were tidying the rubbish and clearing the pavement with a shovel and broom from their car.

Ruth turned to Henry. 'How's your head?'

'A lot better,' he replied. 'How's yours?'

Before his call for her help, she had texted him from the police station to say she wouldn't be able to see him tonight because she had been helping the police with their enquiries, and was only now leaving there to go and pick up her car from outside the patient's home. She would tell him another time how bad a day it was. She gave him a shaky smile. 'A bit woolly.'

He searched her face. 'I had a curious notion,' he said. 'When I saw you get out of the taxi, it occurred to me you might be finding all of this too much. What you're doing is so very hard when there aren't any assurances. I was unthinkingly eager for you to prove Tom innocent, without acknowledging the plausibility. Don't carry on, Ruth, if you can't prove it. Tom wouldn't want you to, and I say that because I genuinely believe Tom knew you would be faced with an uphill battle.'

She blinked back tears and put on a brave smile, then scanned the road. 'Where's your car?'

He pointed to a beaten-up dark green Land Rover.

'Do you want to come back to mine?' she asked.

He nodded, then stepped out of the way as a shard of broken glass skidded past his feet, and a voice behind her quietly said, 'Bloody dog shit!'

One of the police officers was shuffling backwards, dragging his left foot along a clean stretch of path, trying to wipe something off his shoe. He then stepped on some damp newspaper to wipe it some more. His colleague watched and chuckled.

Ruth had some wet wipes in her bag and fetched them out. She pulled a few sheets free ready to give to him. From a pocket in his jacket he took out a pair of blue rubber gloves and put them on. Then took off the shoe and sniffed at it gingerly. He threw back his head and laughed. 'It's pickle. Blimmin' pickle.'

His colleague switched on his torch and aimed it at the ground where the officer was standing. He advised him to mind out for the large curve of broken glass sticking out of the sludge right behind him.

The officer put his shoe back on and turned to look. A moment later he gave a low whistle.

'What have you got?' his colleague asked.

'A load of photos of pretty girls in swimsuits.'

The man might have gone and looked if Ruth and Henry weren't there. Instead, he carried on clearing up the rubbish only to be disturbed again by another find by his fellow officer.

'Need to bag this,' he said.

Ruth couldn't see what it was. She was standing too far away on a clean patch of pavement, but even close up it would be difficult to see in all the rubbish and the dim light from the street lamp.

The officer pointed it out to his colleague. 'Just to the right of that Sainsbury's bag, by the broken glass, there's a badge.' He aimed his torch. 'Look at the sludge, the curved glass is a broken jar of pickle, a full one by the look of it. Now, see what's sticking out of it?'

'Ah,' he exclaimed. 'I thought you were on about a birthday badge type of thing. Yes, definitely bag it.'

The officer got a bag ready to put it in, while his colleague picked it up with gloved fingertips. 'I think we should bag the broken glass and lid as well,' he said. 'This feels a bit weird. Who puts an ID badge in a jar of wet food?'

Ruth felt her heart pound. She stepped carefully around bags of rubbish to get closer. She couldn't take her eyes off the rectangular piece of plastic. Henry stepped beside her. He must have sensed her anxiety. He placed his hand on her forearm. With great effort she stayed calm and used a tone of voice to convey she was merely interested. 'Whose name is on it?' she asked.

The officer who found it glanced at her. Perhaps it was because she was a doctor he read it to her. 'Says, *NHS Foundation Trust. Valid until 18/03/2027. Dr Thomas De Luca.*'

He says some more, but she can't hear him. Her eyes have turned away from his moving lips to scan the rubbish. Thomas's ID had been found due to the actions of a disturbed man. The man he injured went to help him, and she was there because she had been asked to assist as a doctor. If the police officer had ignored his dirtied shoe, it might have remained hidden forever.

She realises the significance of this find. She has no doubt it being found at this address had something to do with Tim Wiley. This find might be the proof that was needed. But beating down her hope of proving Thomas innocent is the thought that even this find might not be enough. She knew only that Tim Wiley was given Thomas's ID by Anabel, and it had now been found in rubbish from the flats where Rosie lived. She didn't know any more than that.

He had tricked Ruth into coming to Rosie's home today to hear the truth. He wanted Rosie to say what she did. He had spoken about the dead nurse kindly. About Rosie, scathingly. She recalled something he said which now troubled her.

You haven't connected the dots, have you? You haven't worked out who her friend is.

Whose truth had he wanted her to hear? *His? Rosie's?*

Why did Anabel think Rosie would prevent her telling the truth?

Ruth shivered. She couldn't afford to lose this opportunity to prove something wasn't right about Thomas's case. But who did she accuse, and of what did she accuse them? She needed to light a fire for Sergeant Phillips to take action. She needed to accuse someone of something.

It took her a few moments to gather her courage and say, 'Can you call Sergeant Phillips, and let him know what you've found, please? And tell him where it was found – in rubbish belonging to the flats where Rosie Carlyle lives. The identity badge you're presently holding belonged to my son, Thomas De Luca. I believe this was stolen by Rosie Carlyle, who is presently answering questions at the police station. It's really quite important that you inform Sergeant Phillips that this NHS ID has been identified by Dr Ruth Bennett as being the property of her deceased son.'

His face showed shock as he stepped out of her hearing while he made a call lasting more than ten minutes. He didn't tell her what was said, but at one point he called to the other officer to stop tidying the rubbish. They were to wait by it instead.

Henry was staring at the officers, quietly dazed. He turned to Ruth in utter bemusement. 'How on earth did you know it would be his?'

Ruth swallowed past the ache in her throat. 'I didn't. But today I was inside the house and I heard an ex-police officer say that a young woman who was found dead today gave him Thomas's ID badge.'

She gulped for air and Henry stepped forward to hold her. She leaned against him, letting go her tears. Thinking about Thomas.

CHAPTER FIFTY-TWO

Ruth didn't protest when Henry helped her off with her trousers and blouse and pulled a T-shirt on over her head. She felt the coolness of the covers as she climbed into bed. She would have preferred to lie down on a sofa if Thomas had had one, as she wasn't intending to sleep, just rest. 'I just need an hour,' she said. 'If I nod off, you'll wake me if anyone calls, won't you?'

He had persuaded her to rest without her phone clutched in her hand, that he would keep an eye on it. 'I will, I promise. Now try and rest. You can't do any more now. Whatever the outcome.'

The pull of sleep after his reassurance was almost instant and she struggled not to give in to it. As she drifted off, she thought when she woke up she'd send a text to Carol, and a more personal one to Joan, and let them know she wouldn't be at work tomorrow. Or rather confirm she was taking their advice to take the day off. She wasn't traumatised, but she wouldn't be able to concentrate on her job. They were aware she'd been held captive as the police had gone to the surgery asking about the phone call requesting Dr Bennett visit Rosie Carlyle's home. When Ruth got around to checking her phone after Tim Wiley's arrest, she had six missed calls from the surgery. She called back and spoke to Joan, and then the strangest thing happened – one by one, Carol, Jim, and Dr Raj asked how she was. Joan had her on loudspeaker as they were all waiting anxiously to hear from her. Ruth had felt their genuine concern and warmth, and she really didn't know how she deserved it.

If she stayed, her colleagues could become friends. There was a future for her here, if that was what she wanted. Images came of her on a beach with a baby boy, letting his tiny feet feel the sea. Him as a toddler with a tiny bucket of water spilling out over the sand. Him running away laughing. Her licking sand off his ice cream. Him in her arms asleep. If she stayed, that baby boy would be her life.

Her last conscious thought before she sank into darkness, *Thomas would've loved being a father.*

*

She woke to silence and wondered about Henry. His face had been pale beneath the bruising earlier. Getting quietly out of bed she crept to the sitting room. The reading lamp on the table was on. Henry was fast asleep in the armchair, her phone resting on one of the arms, ready to answer if it rang. She debated whether to check it, but it was set to ring loud – Henry would have heard it if it rang.

She wanted to know what was happening. She and Henry left after more officers arrived to examine the rubbish. She had climbed into his Land Rover in a daze. He moved a pair of wellingtons from the footwell so she could put down her briefcase and bag. Out of the window she saw her car. Henry said he'd drive her to collect it tomorrow.

She wondered about Rosie. She had accused her of stealing Thomas's badge when she knew it was a lie. She was not taking heed of what she told herself in the beginning. She could hold onto the idea of Thomas being innocent only so long as she didn't try and pin the blame on another innocent person. What Ruth had just done was so wrong. Tim Wiley had obviously thrown Thomas's image away as a sign of his contempt. Rosie's garbage just happened to be close by.

Sickness returned in her stomach. It all seemed too easy finding Thomas's badge, the chain of events working out so well. It worried

Ruth, yet it also made sense that something like that could happen. When the police arrived at Rosie's home they found suitcases in her bathroom, put there by Tim Wiley. She had planned to leave Bournemouth today, she said. It stood to reason she would have rubbish to throw away before she left. If her rubbish bags were the last ones put in the communal bins, they would be the first ones Fred pulled out. But Ruth feared that this new evidence still wouldn't be enough. Nothing might happen. That was the reality she might have to face.

Henry turned in the armchair and Ruth saw her phone slide off the arm and disappear down the side of the cushion. She watched him sleeping, and felt guilty. He had only been out of hospital a couple of days and should be in a bed. When all this was over she didn't want to say goodbye to him. It was a crazy thought. The hours they'd actually spent together wouldn't even add up to a full day. She'd seen his car for the first time a couple of hours ago. She still didn't know where he lived. Yet she felt connected to him. She crept back out of the room and returned with her dressing gown to lay over him. Then, careful not to disturb him, she slid her hand down by the side of the cushion to feel for her phone. She touched the smooth hard plastic and pulled it out, and stared in surprise at what she found. Not a phone. But some sort of camera.

Ruth wondered why the little camera was in the armchair. If it had needed charging it would have been plugged in at a socket, and been taken away for examination by the police. Then she would have found it with his returned possessions in a bag like his laptop, phone and iPad. It had to mean something that it was found in Thomas's chair. Henry might know, but it would mean waking him.

She stared at it in the palm of her hand, dithering about what to do, when the solution suddenly came to her. Followed by an anxious thought. *Would he be home?*

Panic made her heart beat fast and hurried her out of the room, barely stopping to grab her coat, before winging her feet up the stairs. She would ask him if he would look at it straight away. She needed his urgent help. She would follow him inside his flat if need be, and give him no option.

Akito knew exactly what it was when he opened the door to his flat and it was held out to him. 'It's Thomas's cycling camera,' he said.

CHAPTER FIFTY-THREE

Rosie was getting impatient waiting for someone to take her home. She'd been told an officer would take her soon, but that was an hour ago. It had been a long day. First she was taken to the hospital to be checked out, and then to the police station. She had spent hours at the hospital, and after examining her the only thing the doctor was concerned about was that her weight was low. For a patient who'd been held at gunpoint, handcuffed to a bed and threatened with a knife, Rosie would have thought a doctor would have at least been concerned about her state of mind. Even the copper sitting with her had looked surprised, her eyebrows rising up her forehead.

She could have gone home then, admittedly. The female police officer had offered to take her. They had finished with their evidence gathering so she was allowed to enter the property. But Rosie suggested instead that she go with the officer to the station to give her statement there and then, as it might help her stop thinking about the red words on her bath. No one questioned her about Anabel's death. She had heard nothing suspicious about how it happened. So it must have happened like Officer Wiley said, Anabel drowned herself.

Rosie put her hand in her jeans' pocket and pulled out Anabel's letter. She had grabbed it from the side of the bed just before the knock on her door, nearly forgetting it. She might as well now read all of it. Wiley said when he went to see Anabel she was writing letters, and she was going to get her friend to deliver them. Anabel must have been referring to Chloe.

Rosie began reading the second page of the letter.

You dared me to do it, Rosie. You'd done it three times already. I was sure your dad would notice what we were doing, but he just carried on cleaning his car, walking back and forth to the garage to collect more cloths or change water. You said it was a game. It would be funny when your dad finally noticed his car had moved from where he'd originally parked, that we had to use each time he walked away to move it another inch. So I did it again and got it perfect. Do you remember that, Rosie? I do. I remember everything. You daring me one more time. Only this time I had to close my eyes. You would keep watch. I remember every single moment of it. Closing my eyes, releasing the handbrake, feeling the car move, getting ready to slam on the footbrake and pull the handbrake back up. Then I hear the sickening thud. The sound of his body. You knew he was there, Rosie, and not safely in the garage. Don't pretend you didn't. And you've known I've always known that all along.

You see, I worked it all out, Rosie. It was never about them. It was about me. You couldn't bear it, that there was something in me people liked. You couldn't bear seeing me after years of living with that secret, still able to be kind to you, to go on holiday with you, share everything I do with you. I had no choice, Rosie. I couldn't leave you to choose someone else to play with.

Last New Year's Eve, when I saw you watching me be happy, you couldn't hide what was in your eyes. You so desperately wanted me to think you were okay with it. And for all of five minutes I believed you. In that moment I felt guilty for all the love I'd denied you over the years. I was thinking it was a new start. I could be a real friend to you.

The night I got cold waiting for you. You put me in your bath. You hugged me in your bed to keep me warm. That was the last time I loved you, Rosie. Because I knew this friendship couldn't go on. I knew something big was going to happen again. And it did, didn't it, Rosie? Last summer happened. I blame you for that. If you had told someone what we did all those years ago, we would have gone our separate ways, and no else would ever have got hurt.

I'm telling everyone, Rosie. There'll be no need to hide anymore. I put flowers on your dad's grave today and told him again I was sorry. Maybe you should while you still can. This is fair warning I'm giving you, Rosie. The tide is coming for us. Make no mistake about that.

Anabel

Rosie put the letter away. She was not going to worry about it. She was going to concentrate instead on getting over this day, and leave the past behind. Right here and now in this place, while sat on this uncomfortable chair, is where it stopped. Anabel was not having any part of Rosie's future.

The padded seat was only comfortable for a short while. Her bum had gone numb from sitting there so long. Considering all the fuss made by the officer taking her statement that she rest when she got home, they were taking their sweet time. She wanted a drink, a large one. After what she'd been through, she deserved it. It crossed her mind she might get compensation. She heard some victims got money when a serious crime was committed against them. She'd settle for a stop at the shop on the way home to buy a decent bottle of vodka. She could pick up a scouring pad at the same time to get her bath clean. It was paint, one of the officers said, so it should come off with a bit of scrubbing.

She was unsure about tomorrow. She still wanted to leave, but didn't know if they'd want to ask her more questions. But what more was there to say? She had given chapter and verse, starting from last summer with the death of Dr De Luca, and how it had affected so many of them. Because he was so young, she said. How it made Anabel really low, which in turn caused Rosie to be depressed as they were best friends. She told them about the horrible note she found in Anabel's home, and then how she lived in terror after discovering someone had been in her flat. What Wiley had done had freaked her out. *Hanging out her clothes.* Rosie had seen the shock on their faces, which stayed after she added in the part about her being asleep when he came in her home the next time. She told them of her first meeting with the police officer, and how he questioned her about Anabel, when all the time he knew where she was. He wasn't interested in her broken back door.

She told them about opening the door today and thinking he was there on police business, only to discover he had a gun. She let them know that he thought it was her fault his wife died. She didn't even work on the ward, she worked in theatre, and was only there to bring back a patient. And while it was sad that his wife died, what happened to Rosie was unfair. Someone should have realised he was mentally unbalanced. She told them reluctantly about Dr Bennett. How she thought it was strange her doctor knew the policeman. She didn't want to think badly about the doctor, but she wished she'd known she was Dr De Luca's mum. It felt like Dr Bennett got a job where she was a patient because she knew her son, and that didn't feel right at all. She liked Dr Bennett, but now she felt awkward and wasn't sure she could trust her. She believed there was no misunderstanding of what Officer Wiley said to Dr Bennett – Rosie heard it too. He definitely killed her son. Which was truly awful to hear. Poor Dr Bennett had been completely shocked.

Rosie looked at her phone. Half past bloody nine. She wouldn't be getting home till gone ten and her nearest shop would be shut by then. She uncrossed her legs and shifted her bottom to get comfortable, then saw the door handle move. Finally, she thought, someone coming. She eagerly got up as the sergeant she saw earlier entered the room. She hoped he wasn't going to give a long-winded apology. They both stepped forward, her to leave and him to come further in. She laughed awkwardly, then noticed PC Nayland behind him, and gave her a smile, pleased it would be her driving Rosie home.

'Right then, are we off? I'm hoping to catch my shop before it shuts, so I can get something to clean my bath.' She looked at the sergeant. 'Thanks for the tea, sympathy and sandwiches.'

His gaze was stern, though perhaps that was just his face. His job. Or his age. He probably wanted to go home too.

'Apologies for the wait, Miss Carlyle, but officers have been busy after discovering certain items in household rubbish from the property where you live. One of the items is an NHS identity badge. An allegation of theft has been made against you after the property was identified as having belonged to Thomas De Luca.'

Rosie stepped back. 'What do you mean? I haven't stolen anything! Am I under arrest?' she asked in a tremulous voice.

'No,' he replied. 'We'd like to interview you on a voluntary basis. Before any questions are posed, you'll be cautioned.'

Rosie inhaled slowly. She needed to stay calm. She hadn't stolen it. She'd thrown it away. But she could hardly admit to that. The doctor was dead. She should have handed it in. Officer Wiley left it on her bed, but that still didn't excuse her actions. She quickly thought. They couldn't prove it was in her possession if it was found outside in a bin. No one saw her with it and Wiley told Dr Bennett it was given to him by Anabel. Therefore, it must be him who put it there.

She just had to stay alert and not let them rile her. She put on a suitably shocked face, and wondered if she could ask for a more comfortable chair. A cigarette as well. She needed to go outside and collect her thoughts and then come back in and tell them this wasn't right. She was the victim here. She would talk to them, and then they would see she was innocent.

CHAPTER FIFTY-FOUR

Tilly had offered her tea. She'd turned off the music Akito and she had been listening to, turned on another lamp, then went to get out of her pyjamas and into some clothes, probably feeling the tension in the room. She returned and helped Akito, giving Ruth space.

Ruth paced back and forth across the carpet, wearing only a coat over her T-shirt. Akito had been on his laptop too long. He sent Tilly to fetch things, different cables, stopped her when she started asking Ruth about an included transfer cable. He'd used his micro, he said, to connect to the USB cable. But that was over half an hour ago. Henry was still sleeping downstairs in the armchair, unaware she wasn't there.

Her heart was still pounding, more so, because in a moment Akito was going to squash her last hope and tell her it was roads and scenery and the cars in front of Thomas, filmed from his helmet while cycling.

She turned to look at him, but his eyes were still on the screen. 'How are we doing, Akito?'

He didn't look up.

'He's got earbuds in,' Tilly explained. 'He can't hear you.'

Ruth stood in front of him and now he looked up, startled. He gazed at her apprehensively. She noticed he'd backed his chair into the corner against the walls. She hadn't seen him moving it. No one could get behind it. She felt a shiver run down her chest. Tears were filling his eyes, his face turned terribly pale. One hand hovered over the laptop lid, the other removed his earphones.

'What have you found?' she asked.

His voice was distressed. 'You don't want to see it, Ruth.'

She placed her hand over her mouth, pressing hard, before slowly taking it away. 'Is he hurting himself?' she whispered.

Akito shook his head, shaking the tears out of his eyes onto his cheeks. 'No. Someone else is.'

*

Tilly sat up front beside Henry in his Land Rover. She'd pulled Henry from his sleep and gathered clothes for Ruth to wear. Ruth sat next to Akito in the back seat, needing to see what he had seen. In his flat before he let her watch, he told her about what she would see. The sound, he warned, was good, and a lot of the time she would hear only the voices. It was thirty-seven minutes long.

The first few minutes were of Thomas, his hands gripping the arms of the chair, dragging it forwards. Then his legs in jeans and feet in white trainers walking. The camera at that point was clipped to his clothing, before being unclipped and positioned in the armchair. It showed a view of his desk, the sitting-room door, and the wall.

Ruth had watched only these opening scenes, recognising Thomas's old trainers, when Tilly returned to the flat and said she should dress. She didn't bother with the socks and trousers, only the footwear. She buttoned up her coat instead.

And now the damn thing wouldn't work. She stared at Akito accusingly. 'Why won't it come on?'

'It needs charging, Ruth. That's all that is wrong. When we get to the police station I can plug it in.'

She stared at him tearfully. 'Is it bad, Akito?'

He gently held her hand and in a gentle voice, he said, 'Yes.'

Ruth kept her eyes closed for the rest of the journey and only opened them when the vehicle became stationary. Henry turned to her with concerned eyes. 'Are you okay?'

She shook her head. 'I'm afraid of what I'm going to see.'

He nodded like he understood. Then he turned to Tilly. 'Let's you and me go in and prepare the groundwork. Let's give Ruth a minute to herself. Akito will bring her in when she's ready.'

Ruth had to climb out of the vehicle, else she would scream. She needed to walk away for a minute before she lost control. She had let over four months go by before coming here. Her only thought was that she should have come immediately. Her son had been accused of a terrible crime and then he died and all that should have mattered was that she get to the bottom of it, not leave it until today to learn something like this… *Someone was hurting him.*

She had thought nothing would surpass that being the worst day of her life. Her heart beat violently as she prepared to get ready and go in and join Henry. She could not stand there forever. Henry had parked the Land Rover in a car park she was sure was only for police vehicles. As no other vehicle was without blue-and-yellow markings. Not that it mattered. Henry would move it if asked.

She gazed around her, and then gave a small gasp. *Rosie.*

Rosie was standing outside the entrance of the building with a phone pressed against her ear, perhaps calling for a taxi for a ride home – which the police should offer to do after what she had gone through. She was going back to an empty home to be reminded of what took place only hours ago. She would probably have to change her bed before she could climb in it. That's if she could bear even to get in it.

Ruth climbed back inside the Land Rover and saw Akito had the laptop working. The passenger door beside him was open. Tilly had come back, or else not gone with Henry straight away. Ruth watched curiously as Akito handed her a USB memory stick. She palmed it and wordlessly went back across the forecourt, back into the police station.

Ruth shivered. Her legs were cold, her coat over her thin T-shirt doing little to warm her. 'Sorry for disappearing, but I needed some air.' She sighed heavily. 'I just saw one of my patients, Akito. I told the police something about her that's not true.'

Akito didn't respond. She noticed his closed expression, and wondered if he and Tilly had had words. 'I see you managed to charge it. What was that you were giving Tilly?'

He briefly closed his eyes, before looking at her. 'It's not the battery, Ruth. I told you a lie because I thought the police should see it first, but now I'm thinking that once they see it you might not be allowed to. It will become evidence.'

Ruth was trying not to think what that meant. 'So what do you suggest? Henry is already in there, waiting for us.'

'You can watch it here. I made a copy of it. Tilly is now handing it in to the police.'

Her mouth went dry. The same dread she experienced just before she walked into the mortuary was descending on her. It was the pain she feared. The pain she would feel if she saw him suffer. When he was a child it would be a small pain in her stomach if he fell over and hurt himself. A momentary clenching of her insides. When she saw him lying so completely still, no matter how hard she watched for a flicker of life, the pain was like a knife inside her. She was filled with cuts.

Akito handed her some earphones, and asked if she was ready. She nodded. Whatever was in this film she was going to watch all of it. She was going to sit quietly and not say a word. She had not been there for her son when he most needed her. The least she could do was to witness what he had faced.

CHAPTER FIFTY-FIVE

Ruth watched as Thomas walked towards the sitting-room door. He looked taller from the back as she caught a brief glimpse of his neat hair above the collar of his blue shirt, before he disappeared out into the hall. His voice was shockingly clear, and terse.

'You took your time. I didn't think you were coming.'

A female voice answered, 'I had to work.'

'Come in. Close the door,' he replied curtly.

Thomas came through the sitting-room door, his expression remote. A young woman came in behind him. She was pretty, her hair in a ponytail. Her jacket matched the colour of her gloves. She placed her shoulder bag on the desk, before reaching inside it to pull out a bottle of red wine.

Thomas laughed. The sound was not pleasant. 'I'm not falling for that. You asked to see me, because I told you on the phone that I'm going to the police. So don't try and change my mind when I know it was you.'

She held the bottle out to him. 'The seal's not broken. Look. You'll hear it click.' She unscrewed the cap. 'See?'

Thomas stood with his arms folded. Not taking the bottle from her.

'Please! I brought some wine because tomorrow's going to be a hard day for both of us. Tonight, in fact, for me. After I leave here I'm going to the police station to tell them everything. Tell them you're innocent. So, please, I can't undo what I've done, but let me explain.'

Thomas turned his back on her. He shook his head slowly and sighed as he walked towards the far end of the room. His voice came from further away. 'I went to see your friend as my last hope. I thought it was her who set me up. I don't understand any of this. I don't even really know you. I can't even begin to understand your reasons. I'm not even interested in them. All I care about is that I now know it was you who planted those drugs on me.'

The woman was clearly watching him, though Thomas mustn't be aware as she put her hand in her coat pocket and pulled out a small dark glass bottle. She used both hands to untwist the lid. She dropped the cap straight in her bag and put the bottle back in her pocket, leaving her hand there.

Thomas came back to the desk with two glasses. Tumblers. 'These will have to do. I don't have wine glasses.'

'They're fine,' she replied. 'I'm just grateful you let me in.' She picked up the bottle of wine and poured some into a glass. Then paused when it was half full. 'I'm sorry for everything I did,' she said. 'Having the police watch you must be awful.'

Thomas frowned. What she said had taken him by surprise.

She pulled an awkward face. 'Sorry. I shouldn't have said. There was a policeman on the pavement outside your house.'

'Shit,' Thomas muttered. 'Not what I need right now.'

As he walked away her hand came out of her pocket holding the bottle and tipped liquid into the same glass she had poured wine in. She put the bottle back in her pocket then stirred the glass with her finger. She then poured wine in the second glass and was casually having her first sip when Thomas rejoined her.

'He's gone. He was here earlier. Wanting to see the criminal who killed his wife.'

The bitterness in his voice had her step back. She took a gulp of wine. Then in a tremulous voice. 'I will put everything right. I don't expect I'll be let out of the police station tonight, but I'll write to the hospital and let them know what I did.'

Thomas drank some of the wine. 'How did you get in here? I want to know everything. It's the least I deserve.'

'Your keys. I copied them. Same with your locker. You put them down in the changing room. Then while you were busy in theatre assisting with a three-hour operation, I pretended I had a toothache as an excuse to leave work. I pushed a wad of cotton wool under my gum when I returned. It looked good me coming back to work after seeing a dentist, and it allowed me to put back your keys.'

'And what? You just let yourself in here? I'm surprised the woman downstairs didn't clock you.'

'No one saw me. The house was empty. You were at the hospital. There are only four flats here. When I saw the Japanese guy, the girl with pink hair, and the blonde woman come out I knew the place was empty. I was in and out in ten minutes. There was a sports bag on the floor. I emptied my bag straight into it, then shoved it under your bed. Job done.'

He shook his head as if dazed. 'Fucking unbelievable.'

'You must have been shocked by what my friend told you. Does she know you've contacted me?'

'Shocked? It's hardly the word to describe how I feel. Like I told you on the phone, I didn't even really know you. And no, your friend doesn't know. She said you would deny it. Have you any idea what it's like not knowing how something like this could possibly have happened? I don't blame the police, and I don't blame colleagues for thinking me guilty. What else could they think? Drugs in my locker, I might have had a chance… But under my bed? Not a hope in hell.'

'Finding them in your home was important. It would ensure the police didn't look at anyone else in the hospital if the drugs were here as well.'

His mouth dropped open. He put his glass down hard on the desk and grabbed the bottle of wine to pour himself some more.

He drank it as if drinking water, then snarled. 'What I'd like to know is how my fingerprints were found all over them? We're talking hundreds of tablets here. Dozens of boxes.'

She gazed at the floor, then at the wall by the desk, until he wearily sighed. 'Just tell me. Think of it as a rehearsal for what you'll tell the police.'

'It took weeks,' she quietly admitted. 'Getting you to handle them, place your fingers on the boxes. A Herculean effort, to be honest. Can you read the label for me, Doctor? Is this the right drug, Doctor? Can you hand me that, can you pass me that? I never touched them, of course, unless wearing gloves and even then carefully. Weeks and weeks of slow collecting, which I then recorded as taken at the times you worked. One time I had to put drugs back, because the risk of them being noticed missing was too high. Taking a box of diamorphine was foolish. I got carried away, jotting the quantity down on a spreadsheet like it was a real audit.'

He laughed harshly and grabbed the back of his neck with his hand, the one that wasn't wrapped around his glass. 'Are you for real? Who the fuck were you recording it for? Or rather why? What did you hope to do with it? Show it to someone and say, *hey, I've been writing down all the drugs this doctor has taken*?'

Her face showed embarrassment. Or perhaps resentment. 'It was stupid. I know that. Tiny things are what trip you up. It was lucky only Jed Nolan saw it. If someone brighter than him had found it they'd have known it was iffy. It looked amateurish. When he had it snatched from his hand he thought the receptionist had grabbed it from him, but she was looking at the shredder by her desk, wondering what I put in. Stupid man believed it because he wanted you to be guilty. He was jealous.'

His voice was hard. 'The day on the ward. That was you, as well?'

She nodded. 'Yes. I swapped your water bottle.'

'And left me one with midazolam.'

'I thought it would send you to sleep. Mr Mason would then check on you and realise you'd taken something, then call the police.'

'Instead, I played right into your hands by knocking down the security guard. You've got no idea what you've done to me. Or perhaps you have,' he added scathingly. 'I thought I was an observant man, but I didn't see what you were doing right under my nose. All the coffees you gave me. Were they doctored as well?'

'Yes. A little. To make you not as sharp.'

'And my phone and my losing things?'

'It was just smoke and mirrors. Doing silly things like moving your phone out of sight for no reason other than to make you look unbalanced.'

'The texts? That was you too?'

'Yes. To make you look like a drug dealer. I paid cash for some phones, used each only once and not from the same area. That was stupid as well. It might have led the police to look at things too closely.'

'*And more.* Have you no shame?'

'I didn't, at the time.'

'You made it sound…' He snorted his disgust. 'Jesus, how can you be so brazen?'

He closed his eyes and sat on the edge of the desk. His shoulders slumped. 'Tomorrow I'm changing my plea. You know you're going to go to prison, don't you?'

'Yes, I know that. And you should definitely change your plea. You're not guilty.'

'Do you want me to come to the station with you?' he said in a tired voice. 'I will if you like. It can be quite daunting.'

She shook her head. 'I have to do this alone. But thank you.'

'Your friend said you had problems. You might suggest to your solicitor getting a psychiatric review. It may help your case. She said this is about her. Is that true?'

'Did she tell you about the man we killed?'

'Yes. She did. She told me how, as well.' His head flopped forward and jolted him. He raised his head and opened his eyes wide. 'Did something happen to you as a child? Were you abused?'

'No… Never.' She sounded surprised.

'What did she do, then? Do you blame her for his death?'

'Perhaps I blame her for making me feel,' she answered in a pondering voice.

'What's that supposed to mean?'

She shrugged. 'For making me notice how I was regarded. I had nothing to compare before.'

'So you need help,' he said in a sluggish voice.

She was gazing at him. He was unaware as his eyes had closed again. Her voice lowered. 'Yes. I think I do. The patient I was with earlier wouldn't shut up. I was looking at his tongue moving in his mouth and wondering how hard it would be to pull out. Some say it's the strongest muscle in the body, but I don't think it is. The jaw is stronger, surely…'

Thomas swayed. He looked nearly asleep, with only the desk behind him keeping him upright.

She pulled out a chair from beneath the desk, turning it towards him. She took the glass of wine out of his hand. 'Thomas, you should sit down!' she said in a loud voice.

He opened his eyes and made an effort to stand. He grabbed onto the desk as he swayed on his feet. 'Whoa! Shouldn't have done that. Haven't drank in ages… Need to sit… sorry…'

'Yes, you do,' she said, guiding him to the chair. She stayed close to him as he sat down hard. She pressed the glass back in his hand. 'Here, you may as well drink the last drop. It will help you sleep.'

Thomas raised the tumbler to his mouth. A dribble of red wine spilled down his chin onto his pale blue shirt. He then cupped the glass against his stomach, not noticing her leaving the room.

Minutes passed while he sat there quietly. Distant sounds were coming from outside the room. A toilet flushing. Then her humming.

Thomas roused a little, his voice slurred. 'Whatcha doin'? Hear water.'

Her tuneful humming woke him some more. He moved his hand through the air in a semicircle, back and forth, singing the words as if with a thick tongue.

'Alas my love, you do me wrong
To cast me off discourteously;
And I have loved you oh so long
Delighting in your company.'

She appeared through the door and came and stood beside him, and gave him a small clap.

He formed a grin, but could hold it barely a second. He hadn't the energy to control the muscle around his mouth. '"Greensleeves".' He clutched her arm. 'Pink sleeves.'

She put her hand on his shoulder and then down onto his back. 'Come on, up you get… That's it, push up. Put your hand on the desk to help. That's it…'

Thomas was on his feet. She had her arm around his waist. 'Now one foot in front of the other.'

'Bed,' he mumbled.

'Yes. A bath and bed.'

His head lolling to the side as they staggered sideways as they navigated their way out into the hall. Her voice was encouraging. 'Mind your head on the wall. Go forward. Keep going. Keep going. That's it.'

The timbre of her voice coming from another room was heard in the quietness of the sitting room. Minutes of hearing it followed by minutes of silence. Six minutes passed before she suddenly came back through the doorway and went straight to the desk. Her movements were quick. A little jerky. She picked up the glass she'd drank from and disappeared with it down the far end of the room. Thirty seconds later she was back at the desk. She placed his glass next to the wine bottle. From her pocket she took out the small dark glass bottle. She rummaged in her bag for the lid and left it on the desk beside the little bottle. The light from the ceiling showed her hands eerily pale. She had covered her pretty gloves with of a pair of latex gloves.

She took something from a side pocket in her bag and went back out of the room.

It was a further two minutes before she reappeared. She stood quietly by the door, breathing softly, her head angled as if listening out for him. A moment later in a solemn voice, she quietly said, 'There now. That didn't hurt at all.'

Then back to business she walked to the desk and reached for her bag. Her hand stilled midway. Her fingers opened. She had something in her palm.

She tutted. 'Be silly taking that.'

She picked up the bag with her left hand. Then went out the door.

It stayed quiet for several seconds, as if no one was there. Then she spoke: 'You shouldn't have warned me. You silly man.'

The front door was heard opening and then very quietly closing.

*

The image on the screen looked paused with no one in the room. Ruth kept her eyes glued to it, listening for signs of life. Her mind was tortured with imaginings of him slowly dying in that bath.

Akito closed down the lid of the laptop. Ruth was aghast and yanked it back up. He waited for her to take out the earbuds and hear him.

'It's finished, Ruth,' he quietly said. 'The last five minutes there's nothing to see or hear.'

Her breath hitched in her throat. Her voice quavered with disbelief. 'He's on his own, Akito. I can't leave him alone.'

He gently held her hand. He stared at her with gentle eyes, trying to calm her anguish. 'This isn't happening to him now, Ruth. Thomas has been gone a long time. He's not there now.'

Ruth put her finger on the screen. Willing it to make a sound. Then her face crumpled. 'He didn't want to die. He didn't choose to leave us. My boy. My sweet boy.'

Akito's voiced was choked with emotion. 'He's at peace now, Ruth. The police will now deal with this person.'

She gazed at him with stricken eyes, remembering what she learned today. 'It's too late, Akito. She's gone.'

CHAPTER FIFTY-SIX

Henry found Ruth outside an office building in a dark corner of the car park, standing in a daze. Her limbs couldn't move. She had no idea how long she had been there. Henry removed his jacket and wrapped it around her. She didn't feel cold.

He was staring at her worriedly. 'You need to come inside, Ruth. It's way too cold to be out here. You need to get warm. You're in shock.'

Which was undeniably true, which she couldn't care about.

Henry stepped closer and placed his arm around the small of her back, bringing her away from the brick wall, getting her to move her feet. She wanted to tell him not to worry. Her reactions were normal. Her body's response to fight, flight or freeze. It would eventually get back to its normal state. Her mind was another matter.

Ruth allowed herself to look in his eyes. She quickly shut her own. It was too soon to be comforted. If he was kind she would soften. Numbness was the only thing keeping her strong.

'What's happening inside? Have the police looked at the recording?'

'Yes. I believe so. Akito's been surprisingly forceful in trying to find out. He thinks the big bosses are coming to the station. Although he wasn't meant to overhear that.'

She gazed at him in surprise. 'It's a little too late for that.'

His expression saddened. 'I know. They want to talk to you, of course. But if you're not up to it now, I can take you home and bring you back in the morning.'

'No, I want to do this now. Thomas has already waited long enough. Tonight clears his name. Not another night will go by until that is done. I'm going to go inside, sit calmly, and wait to be called.'

Henry gave a short nod of encouragement. 'Akito told me what you found. You proved your boy was innocent. He would be proud of you.'

His word made her lips quiver. She pressed them hard and shook her head. 'No kindness please, Mr Thorpe. Not yet.'

He pulled her close for the briefest of hugs, then gave her space to walk on her own. Ruth looked up at the sky and breathed in the cold air, drawing it deep into her lungs. She wanted to be wide wake and do her best for Thomas. She glanced at Henry and became aware of him staring worriedly at something to the right of the building. Ruth turned her head, saw a police uniform, and vaguely stared. Out of the corner of her eye she saw a second uniform and then she saw pale hair and her entire being stiffened.

It was not too late. She had not run away. Her packed suitcases were still in her bathroom, put there by Tim Wiley, before Ruth was there. She had planned to leave Bournemouth today.

Henry tried to stop her, but she was already ahead, moving fast but carefully before the police spotted her. When two metres away, Ruth calmed her entire being. She would get only one chance before she was moved and the opportunity was taken away.

She called to her in a calm voice, 'Rosie.'

Nayland and Kirby turned in unison. Kirby shot out his hand, palm facing towards Ruth. 'This is not a good idea, Dr Bennett. I need you to turn around and walk to the entrance, please. Any untoward behaviour here could jeopardise an investigation.'

Ruth stared at him. He had yet to see the film. Otherwise, he would know there was nothing to investigate. Thomas had caught his own murderer on camera. The only thing left to do was to lock up the murderer.

'I assure you, I will not say or do anything to cause that. I merely wanted to ask Rosie why.'

'I really must insist you walk away now, Dr Bennett.'

Rosie turned and faced her. And right then, Ruth saw it. The calm face of a killer. Ruth was unable to detect any empathy in the pale blue eyes. Nor see in them any anxiety or fear or sadness. As if she had taken off her face and replaced it with one that was chilling. Where was the nail-biting, spiky, tense woman, whose face for one moment lit up when she smiled, who relied on medication for depression, insomnia and anxiety? Had any of Rosie Carlyle been real?

Rosie glanced at her. Ruth tried to hold her look. For a moment, she could swear she saw a reluctance come over Rosie's face. Ruth saw her stare at the handcuffs on her wrists. Then Rosie stared away, and calmly began talking.

'It was Anabel. She told me at her family party about the party we were going to afterwards, about who would be there. She must have seen something in my eyes when she said his name as she giggled like a teenager. Teasing me about him. I said nothing. I should have taken note of her relief. It meant something. When we got there Anabel straight away started to enjoy herself. I was at a table next to a doctor who couldn't sit still. His foot kept tapping on the floor and I realised he was staring at her. Her face was a little red from dancing. Then I realised he was staring because he liked her and was waiting to make his move. I was pleased for her. I saw his mouth drop with surprise and looked across the room to see what caused it. Dr De Luca with his jacket off, his bow tie loosened, unselfconscious, standing in the middle of the dance floor.' She gave a small laugh as she shared the memory. 'Drunk, of course. I would go rescue him, I decided, and stood up. It was the moment I had been waiting for. Then I saw Anabel move in front of him.' Rosie turned her gaze to Dr Bennett, and gave a small shrug. 'She always did things like that to make me feel unwanted.

She smiled across at me, and then she kissed him… She shouldn't have done that. It was cruel. So you see… It was her fault really.'

Ruth stayed perfectly still. Nothing Rosie had said surprised her. Nothing about her now could ever shock. The most shocking thing had already happened, already been seen, already been heard. On a laptop with its lid now closed down.

Ruth felt it only fair that she say something back. This would be the last time she would speak to her. Rosie should hear Ruth's side, so that she could properly understand.

Ruth stepped closer to Rosie, standing only feet away.

'I feel sorry for you, Rosie. You have an emptiness inside that can never be filled. You will never feel the joy of loving someone deeply. You will never feel your lips ache from smiling. Nor feel your eyes sting from crying, your bones ache from grieving. You will never feel closeness. You will never feel the lightness in your feet as you run to greet someone you love. What you feel is only the dregs. The worthless parts. You probably think all your vengeful actions, the harming and hating, is a great big feeling. But what you're feeling is a whole big nothingness. And you will feel it for the rest of your life.'

Ruth turned and walked slowly away. She did not care to look on Rosie's face again.

CHAPTER FIFTY-SEVEN

Rosie watched her walk away and wanted to call out that she was wrong. But not with Kirby and Nayland either side of her. She would write to Dr Bennett, instead, and tell her she was wrong. She felt Nayland's hand graze the top of her head as the policewoman guided her into the back of the car. Rosie was not going to talk to them again tonight. She wanted some hot food and something clean to wear, to be allowed to sleep. Then in the morning she would tell them everything. There was no point in denying the things she had done. Dr De Luca had captured her. *Thomas had captured her. Thomas,* who she might have loved, if Anabel had allowed it. The same as she would have with her father.

Anabel was wrong in what she wrote. Rosie hadn't known her father was there. She had closed her own eyes, after Anabel closed hers. She hadn't expected Anabel to keep them closed more than a second. She would open them and see Rosie's were shut, and know Rosie was betting that to happen. That Anabel wouldn't be brave enough to keep it up. The one time she judged Anabel wrong, she had to go and do it right. She couldn't punish Anabel for that. She hadn't deliberately killed him. Fate decided that would happen.

Same as it decided Tim Wiley to be the right person in the right place at the right time. She remembered tonight where she had seen him before. It wasn't on the ward. It was outside Dr De Luca's flat. He'd been standing on the pavement, stretching his neck as if it were tight, tilting his head from side to side. His being there gave her a perfect way to distract the doctor. Thomas had gone and looked out of the window to see if a policeman was there.

Rosie was glad to have this quiet moment to remember these things. It was all water under the bridge now. The three people she loved best were gone. Her father, Thomas, and Anabel. She had loved Anabel the most, which is why what she did hurt her the most.

Damn her for sharing the details of sleeping with him. For sharing how lovely he was, how his dark eyelashes were longer than both hers and Rosie's. *Damn her* for what she did. If she hadn't smiled right at Rosie, right before she kissed him…

That night could have been the beginning of something special for Rosie. De Luca had noticed her only that day. It had been a glorious day. He had been in an exuberant mood. The theatre list had gone well, the consultant was happy, everything on time with no mishaps. Everyone was in high spirits, a flow of pleasantries expansively being exchanged. An excitement was building for later for to bring in the new year.

Side by side, they washed their hands at the big sink, when all of a sudden he deliberately splashed water in her face. She turned to him and saw his eyes brimming with laughter. She looked around, sure his eyes were not smiling at just her. But they were. It was only her he was looking at.

'It's Nurse Carlyle, isn't it?' he said, in a cheerful voice.

Rosie had nodded like a fool, unable to speak. In the months he'd been working there, in all the times she'd seen him before, working in other specialities, doing rotations as part of his training, or passing him in a corridor, he'd not ever really spoken to her. Not like this.

He pulled her cap off her head and threw it in the sink. Making her mouth drop open. Then planted his hands on his hips. 'Well, Nurse Carlyle, I think we both deserve to go out and enjoy ourselves tonight. Don't you?'

She managed to mummer yes that time, which brought a firm nod of agreement from him.

'Then that makes two of us,' he stated. He then called out to a colleague for the name of the place where everyone was meeting. Then he smiled at her. 'So now you know. Hope to see you there.'

At the door, he turned and saw her watching him. He tapped a finger to the side of his head, as if he'd forgotten what it was he wanted to say. Then held up the same finger as the thought came back to him. 'Meant to say. Bring friends. Black tie, if they like. Or not if they prefer. Doesn't really matter. It's not strict. Tickets at the door will be same as club prices, but it'll be a good night.'

His words sent her into a spin. Her normal, rational thinking into overdrive. What dress should she wear? What shoes should she pick? Which lipstick, which earrings, which perfume? Should she wear her hair up or down, curling or straight? Things she never normally worried about – namely how she would look – sent her into a panic. So by the time she was ready, she clean forgot she had not yet told Anabel. So she could hardly believe her ears when Anabel said they were going to the Surgical Unit New Year's Eve party. Rosie hid her eyes when Anabel said his name, but not quick enough and was secretly pleased Anabel knew she was interested. It made it easier when your friend knew, so that they would know the right moment to disappear.

Rosie may have been able to forgive her, if she'd given Rosie time to hide her feelings. But to smile right at her like that. Just before she kissed him…

That smile, in that second, undid every bit of Rosie's love for her.

She tried to bring it back. When she was searching for her, when she thought she'd lost her, when she thought Anabel was in danger, or worse. She had tried to bring it back, and almost did when she thought she'd never see her again. She'd been almost there, almost back to loving her, until she went home and discovered Anabel betrayed her in the very worst way she could.

How did her mum put it? *The trick you pulled to gee up his plight.* The trick, she was referring to, was the call Rosie made on the ward to the police, when she told them her name was Anabel. Her mum was going to realise she had wasted energy on thinking about something so insignificant, in light of what she would soon hear. It would make it easier for her to disown Rosie. Easier to blame her for everything. Including Anabel's death.

Rosie stared down at the red stains still on her hands. She had not caused Anabel's death. She was sure of it. As sure as she was about her father's death. She hadn't been with Anabel when she died. She had only dreamed she was there. In the wind and in the dark, on the pier at the very end, wearing Anabel's jacket. She had only dreamed of hearing Anabel's short cry.

She glanced out the window at Dr Bennett. Her doctor was wrong. Rosie did feel a lightness in her feet. She had containment again. Anabel couldn't poke at it anymore. She didn't exist.

Rosie's eyes stayed on Dr Bennett, until she disappeared through the entrance of the police station. She had gazed at Rosie with a quiet, steely look in her eyes, her strength undiminished, which carried through to her voice. Rosie would miss having her as her doctor.

She was the best doctor anyone could have.

CHAPTER FIFTY-EIGHT

Ruth sat alone in the reception area, waiting for Sergeant Phillips to come. Henry was dropping Akito and Tilly home as it was nearly midnight. She felt a cold breeze on her legs from the automatic door opening. A smoker outside, standing too close to it. She shoved her hands into her pockets to warm them and felt the letter Kim gave her on Monday. She had been reminded it was there, when at Rosie's, when searching for a weapon. It seemed entirely absurd she had still not looked at it.

She pulled it out of her pocket and stared at the writing on the envelope. She barely shook her head. The urgency to know things had passed. What might be said that wasn't already known? Nothing more need be said. She had learned everything already from Thomas. She prepared to put it away when her eyes went to the poster she had noticed earlier. It had not been up on the wall the day she came here to collect Thomas's things. Somewhere, right now, there was a family at home grieving. With every minute passing made more unbearable, as time was reminding them, that yesterday the person they loved was alive.

The letter had been written on neatly folded sheets of white writing paper this time, rather than a spiral notepad. Anabel deserved to be heard.

Dear Thomas's mother,

I so wanted to tell you in person, I hope you believe that. Instead, I followed you. Watching you outside my home I came so close to getting out of the car. I was hoping somehow you would know I was there, and why I was there, and that I wouldn't have to say a word. I've never been brave. I watched you cycle away and felt so angry with myself. I came to the surgery to try again and almost caused you an accident. I'm sorry if I scared you. The car I borrowed I was still getting used to. Though, that isn't strictly true. I learned to drive when I was eighteen, a birthday present from my parents, but I've never driven. An experience when I was a child put me off ever wanting to be behind the wheel of a car.

I didn't have the courage to face you and tell you what happened. Which meant leaving you to find out on your own. Then I realised how impossible that task would be when there was nothing for you to find. If I could have proven what I believe to have happened to Thomas, I would have done it in a heartbeat. So in leaving all of this with you, I will share everything I do know.

It began with New Year's Eve last year when I danced with him.

I shan't embarrass you with details, but I thought he was wonderful. I one hundred per cent knew I was not his type. I am too quiet and probably not very exciting, but it was a lovely way to start the New Year. The mistake I made was in sleeping with him a few weeks later. It happened as these things do when alcohol is involved, but it wasn't unpleasant and I wasn't ashamed. When we said goodbye we knew we would never be intimate again, but that was fine with me. If anything, I had been given hope and a confidence boost that I might find someone to be with properly. The bigger mistake was in telling her. My best friend.

She wanted to have something to feel angry about. She didn't want the plain unexciting truth. That I had sex on the couch with a drunken man, and I was fine with that. She wanted to twist it in every possible way to make it become sordid. She wanted to create a storm. I knew it was just a front to disguise her resentment that it was ordinary me and not her he slept with. She so rarely set her sights on someone, and if I had known I would never have gone near him. I let her think he used me. It had happened to her, so I thought it might appease her if she thought the same happened to me. What I let myself forget was how dangerous she could be if denied attention.

Saying that lie was her opportunity to crush what she believed was hers before being taken away by me.

I became uneasy as she talked of payback. What could we do to him? In return for what he had done to me? I wouldn't listen to her, but that then left me in the dark about what she was planning. For a while it seemed as if nothing was happening. Then at work his behaviour towards me changed, as if I had done something wrong. Small things were happening. A patient's notes went missing. They had fallen down the gap at the back of the desk. It had happened before, things falling down the back because the desk never had a backboard put on. They were found the next day. Thomas thought I'd hidden them.

Then other things happened, his things went missing. I thought at first it was him being paranoid, but then I experienced the same. My phone went missing more than once, and I realised it was her. She laughed when she told me she'd been sending him texts from me. It was horrible, but I thought at least it was over.

I then started to hear worrying things about Thomas. He was arriving at work the worse for wear, a little unkempt and extremely tired. He was getting in trouble for forgetting things. I thought maybe he was ill. I truly didn't put it all together until the day he was arrested, and saw how out of it he was. She had to have given him something, in his water bottle, I suspect.

That day on the ward I wanted to get him into a cubicle so he could sleep it off, but she picked up the phone and called the police. She winked at me as she gave my name as the person reporting him. She asked everyone if they were all right, telling people to stay back, making things worse. Did anyone see a blade in his hand? Thomas was then taken away.

I thought then that she had done her worst. I should have known it would not be enough.

I have no proof it was her who put the drugs in Thomas's locker. She planted the seed, though, of where to look, of that I am sure. Mr Mason was mumbling to himself about leaking gases and Entonox, thinking along those lines for a reason for Thomas's behaviour, when next minute he's searching changing rooms.

I have no proof of anything I have told you. What makes it worse is she is a very accomplished liar. She would have made an incredible actress. She pretended to be shocked by what he had done. Isn't it terrible? she would say, sounding very sincere. It was a game to her, one she liked playing. If she said it enough times, I would believe he had done these things. The only thing she would admit to were the texts. The payback, as she called them. Everything else was him.

But none of it was about him. I'm so sorry to have to say that to you. He was just part of a vicious game so she could hurt me. I will never forgive myself for any of this. Thomas ended his life because I didn't stop her years ago and tell someone then what we did. Thomas came to see me the day before he was due to go to court. I told him as much as I could, about her using my phone to text him. But he probably thought it was too little too late to help. He left, and that was the last I saw of him.

I am telling everyone what happened, and I hope someone will take my words seriously and believe what was done to Thomas. He was innocent of everything.

The person the police need to be talking to is named Rosie Carlyle. She lives at Purbeck Street.

I wish I could have done more, and hope life brings you now only kindness.

Anabel Whiting

Ruth carefully folded Anabel's letter and placed it safely back in the envelope. Anabel had answered the question that Christine Pelham couldn't. Rosie had used Anabel's phone. That's what Thomas discovered. Which is why he invited Rosie into his home, why he set up his camera, hoping to get a confession. He had been right to be suspicious when she brought wine, but Rosie had still hoodwinked him, by getting him to look out of the window. She freely told him everything, because she knew Thomas wasn't going to be around to repeat it.

Ruth would keep the letter with Thomas's things and try not to think any unkind thoughts about a young woman who found it hard to be brave.

*

The sergeant's pallid face drew Ruth's concern. She could see the impact of today showing in his eyes. The awfulness of it all. 'Shall we go somewhere more private?' he said.

Ruth shook her head. Where they were was fine. There was no one else around them. No other customer at the reception desk or outside smoking waiting for it to be free.

He sat down beside her and nodded. 'Okay, let's just sit here instead. I'm sorry it's taken so long. Tim Wiley was helping fill in some of the blanks. He told us he left your son's ID in the home of Rosie Carlyle. For the same reason he sent a letter to Anabel. To unnerve her, see where it led. But that it wasn't him who threw it in the rubbish. You asked me earlier why I was so sure he didn't do something to your son. He revealed something during his statement. When he left your son he stayed out on the pavement for a while, and that's when he saw someone else going into the house. It was a woman wearing a pink jacket. He didn't see her face, though. After his wife died he started watching the two nurses, and one day he saw Anabel wearing it. Which is why he didn't tell someone. It confused him, he said, because he felt sure she wouldn't have hurt him.'

'Did he…?' Ruth had to swallow against the tightness in her throat before she could carry on talking. 'Did he say why he went to see Thomas?'

He nodded. 'Yes. He went there to tell Dr De Luca he blamed him for his wife's death.'

'Did he say how Thomas was?'

'Yes, he did. He said Dr De Luca was distressed. And said he would feel the same if he lost someone he loved in that way. That his behaviour had caused a great deal of sorrow. That he was more sorry than Tim Wiley could know.'

Ruth couldn't say anything to that. Thomas would have no doubt been kind. He would have let Tim Wiley say what he wanted, if it helped alleviate some of the man's pain. She didn't want to ask the sergeant anything more.

Sergeant Phillips glanced at her and saw tears on her face. 'We can sit here quietly, if you prefer? We don't have to talk about any of it tonight, if you don't want to?'

So that's what they did. They sat quietly until Henry's Land Rover arrived outside. They had not talked about any more of the awfulness. Their minds coming to the same conclusion. Tomorrow was time enough. Nothing was going to change from now until then. Everything would still be the same.

Except Ruth. For she is already changed. She is no longer a mother searching for the truth. She is no longer a mother of a son thought guilty of a terrible crime. She is no longer a mother who has lost sight of her son. She has been given back what was taken from her. She is a mother who is able to love once more with all of her heart and all of her mind. It is hers to hold for ever and never will it be in shadow again.

CHAPTER FIFTY-NINE

10 APRIL

The mouth-watering smells were making Ruth ravenous. She should have had something light to eat at lunchtime instead of waiting for the food at Jim Miller's retirement party. The buffet was a selection of cold and hot food. Unable to contain herself she swiped a sausage roll from a plate.

'Caught you,' Joan laughed, coming up behind her. 'I could eat everything, mind. I want to marry Dr Raj for her food. Don't know how she stays so slim.'

Ruth looked across the lawn to where Dr Raj was standing with some of her handsome family, giving them instructions. She was hosting the party at her home, and was probably thanking her lucky stars it was sunny and not April showers, so the gathering could be held outside. The food would be served after Jim's speech. Seventy guests had been catered for, all his family and friends, his work colleagues and their families. Yesterday was his last day. Ruth would miss him, as they all would. She had come to realise how calm a presence he was at the surgery. She wasn't stepping into his shoes. Carol, Dr Raj, and Ruth would be equal partners. They would work short-staffed until Dr Michaels returned after her maternity leave. A group was gathered around the doctor now, admiring her beautiful baby girl. Ruth had introduced herself earlier and had taken to her quiet manner.

Joan put a hand on Ruth's shoulder. 'Any more news?'

For a moment Ruth thought she was referring to Thomas. His conviction still remained because the appeal process was vastly complicated in a case where the defendant pleaded guilty. But she was less anxious about it now as in the eyes of the people he was innocent. In the days that followed Rosie Carlyle's arrest for murder, local newspapers and TV news reported the circumstances of Dr De Luca's death, which raised national interest and concern as Rosie Carlyle confessed to setting him up and committing every part of the crime. In her suitcase, some cheap mobile phones and some keys were found. The keys wouldn't unlock the front door when the police tried them. Henry told them the lock was changed, and fetched out the old key to show it matched the one they had.

Rosie Carlyle wrote to her from prison. Ruth didn't open the letter, nor reply. She has tried, without much success, to forget the pale blue eyes staring at her without empathy or remorse. In Ruth's mind, it was just the two of them standing there alone. The police officers, and Henry, were not there. In that moment, Ruth saw only Rosie. She couldn't be sure if it was an act of will, or her belief in the Hippocratic Oath, *First do no harm*, or if it was the spirit of Thomas that stayed her from extracting revenge. She had seen in her mind so clearly what she had wanted to do and how easy it would be to bring this woman to the ground and hold her there until she was dead.

Tim Wiley wrote to her as well. His letter she read, and it hadn't required a reply. It was to say sorry for the loss of her son. The ex-police officer was still waiting to go to court, but she didn't wish him a harsh punishment. Without Tim Wiley, she had come to realise, the truth might not have been found. His actions preceding the find of that camera was what led to it. If he had not left Thomas's ID in Rosie's home, she and Henry would not have come back to Ruth's flat where she then rested and Henry sat minding her phone.

Ruth wished Anabel Whiting had stayed with him. She had seen her in a photograph – smiling and with gentle eyes. She looked a sweet-natured young woman. Which was surprising. She would have lived tormented with the memory of that horrible game she was made to play. She had deserved a better friend than the one she had. If she hadn't kept it a secret she might have got free from her…

'Well?' Joan asked, right in her ear. Jolting Ruth out of these thoughts, back to realising what news she was actually being asked about.

Ruth reached across her chest and patted Joan's hand. 'No. Calm yourself, woman. She's only just gone into labour. Catherine's sister Helena will ring when it's getting close. And when I know, you'll know.'

Joan sighed. 'Good. I'll relax then.'

Akito came up to the buffet table. He had arranged the music. Ruth had enjoyed all of it so far. There'd been a lot of Frank Sinatra and Ella Fitzgerald. Louis Armstrong was now singing 'What a Wonderful World'.

'The microphone is set up, Joan. Just give me a thumbs-up when you want the music turned down.'

'Will do,' Joan replied.

Akito walked away and Joan sighed wistfully. 'I could marry him, too. Such a beautiful man.'

Ruth lightly dug her elbow in Joan's side. 'I think your Dom would have something to say about that, missus.'

Joan gave her husband a little wave. He was shy, she told everyone, but he seemed to be having a good chat with Akito and Tilly.

After that day, Akito, Tilly, and Kim had become more than just her neighbours. She counted them as friends, as she did Joan and her colleagues here today. Joan had been to her home in Bath to help with packing when Ruth went back and put her house up for sale. A lot of her furniture was in storage until she found a new home. For the present she was still living in Thomas's flat. Kim had voiced the possibility of Fred moving in when Ruth left. That, of course, would be up to Henry, but Ruth wouldn't be surprised if it happened. Henry had visited him and reported back that Fred was beginning to enjoy a better quality of life. The specialist mental health hospital had been a good choice for Fred's type of PTSD.

After that day is when many of her thoughts now began. After that day, Thomas's case notes were found on top of his wardrobe. Henry had spotted them when he was changing the light bulb above her bed. Ruth hadn't looked at them. She had the true account already, given to her by Rosie Carlyle.

She chewed the last mouthful of sausage roll and took a sip of her wine before smiling at the guest coming towards her. She looked really smart, her long legs in jeans, topped with a blazer and shirt, and her hair recently done. Ruth had warned Pauline not to swear today, not in front of her colleagues. She reached Ruth and Joan in a few easy strides. Ruth introduced her and Pauline managed more than a minute's conversation without a swear word. She then wandered off to find a loo and a drink.

Joan put a thumb up to Akito after getting a nod from Jim and he turned down the music. Jim picked up the microphone and thanked everyone for coming, and everyone went silent for his speech. Ruth's eyes were drawn to the man making his way down the stone steps that led to the back garden.

Joan plonked herself into a sturdy garden chair. She'd been knitting matinee jackets since February for this baby, broody for another grandchild. Ruth didn't like to stop her, but suspected three was more than enough. Catherine might be a mum that favoured modern baby clothes. It wasn't often Ruth saw a baby wearing a hand-knitted cardigan anymore. They wore JoJo Maman Bébé and babyGap more now.

Henry stood beside her and whispered, 'Have I missed much?'

Ruth glanced guiltily across at Jim. She hadn't been listening. The crowd laughed so he had just said something funny. Joan wasn't listening either. She was busy piling tissue-paper-wrapped packages into a gift bag to have ready to give to Catherine. 'No. Just started,' Ruth whispered back.

Another laugh came from the crowd and Henry used the opportunity to speak. 'I drove by a house up for sale on the way here. I stopped and had a quick peek. I think you'd like it. It's in a lovely spot with a view of the coastline.'

Ruth noticed Joan's eyes tear up at the pale blue cardigan with its tiny knitted collar. She felt her heart tug. She has learned to stay strong, learned that missing Thomas doesn't go away. His son will one day ask about him and she will tell lots of stories of what he was like as a little boy, and what he was like as a young man. She will make sure his son doesn't only know about how his life ended, but about how he lived all of it before that happened. She blinked to dry her eyes. She couldn't wait to meet his son, and hold him and give him a kiss from his father. She was not going to be overly sentimental or alarming when she did that. No, she'd quietly and composedly, deeply adore him, and always slip in an extra kiss.

'Might be too big for one person, though,' Henry added quietly.

After that day Ruth got to see where Henry lived. It wasn't with his sister Marlene, and it wasn't in a house, but on a barge. It suited him perfectly for the life he led. He could move it from place to place sometimes and use it while he worked. It was cosy, but Ruth preferred something more solid beneath her feet.

She glanced at him and noticed him twiddling a button on his jacket. 'No point in seeing somewhere too big. I hate decorating and gardening,' she replied.

'Yes, you're right. Be silly to see it, I suppose,' he agreed. Turning the button some more. 'You could always get a lodger,' he whispered.

Ruth gave a small shake of her head. 'No. I don't want to live with a stranger.'

She bit her lip to stop herself laughing. The button had just come off in his hand.

'It doesn't have to be a stranger,' he replied.

She gave him a casual glance. 'Well, if you get fed up on that boat, that might work. You like maintenance.'

'I don't mind it,' he agreed. His eyes found hers. 'Are you sure?'

Ruth took hold of his closed hand and uncurled his fingers. The button sat in his palm. 'Might stop you twiddling these off your jacket,' she said with a soft laugh.

When the clapping began and while people were still occupied, he kissed her. 'I'm very glad you came to Bournemouth, Dr Bennett.'

In the lull between the clapping and everyone getting back up to speed with their conversations, Pauline arrived back to the buffet table with eyes like saucers. Staring at Ruth she chose that moment to forget Ruth's warning and speak in a voice that everyone around heard. 'Fucking hell, Ruth. I nearly broke my arse coming down those steps.'

Ruth felt her eyes brim with happy tears. She loved her sister to pieces. She made everything normal, even after that day.

Last night after she turned the bathroom light off, Ruth heard her say, 'Love you, Thomas. Night night.'

*

Peter Thomas De Luca made his entrance into the world at twenty-seven minutes past midnight, weighing eight pounds seven ounces. Catherine had done brilliantly and smiled at Ruth sleepily. Helena had gone to Catherine's to rest. Henry had taken Joan for a short stroll along the quiet corridors of the hospital. To give Ruth a moment alone with her grandson.

She peeked beneath the hat keeping his head warm, and saw a shock of black hair. His skin was the red of a newborn, his hands and feet bluish, and perfectly normal.

Ruth lifted him out of the Perspex cot and took his weight into her arms. She bent her head to bring him closer so that she could breathe him in. She was in heaven. The most beautiful place on earth right now. Nothing could surpass the wonderfulness of this tiny little person.

She kissed him on his tiny soft cheeks, and one more kiss on his sweet little forehead. Making it three. One from her. One from Pietro. And one from Thomas.

Catherine smiled, with a gentle awareness in her eyes.

'*Il bellissimo bambino di Thomas*,' she said to Ruth. 'Thomas's beautiful baby.'

The words nearly burst Ruth's heart – the weight of emotions filling her was pressing it so tight, it could barely move to make its beats. Ruth held back the tears. She would stay strong for Catherine, just like Pietro's mother stayed strong for Ruth. The prize to love again and feel it with all your heart was something that helped you through the aching and the missing and the seeing and the hearing and the knowing of them. Because it is those you loved and lost that has helped you love again.

Ruth gazed at her son's baby and smiled. As far as she was concerned.

He was the most beautiful baby in the world.

He already had her heart. Wrapped all around him.

A LETTER FROM LIZ

Dear reader,

I want to say a huge thank you for choosing to read *The Silent Mother*. If you did enjoy it, and want to keep up to date with all my latest releases, just sign up at the following link. Your email address will never be shared and you can unsubscribe at any time.

www.bookouture.com/liz-lawler

I hope you loved *The Silent Mother* and if you did I would be very grateful if you could write a review. I'd love to hear what you think. I was inspired to write this story after staying overnight at a hotel. The road beside it led to Bournemouth Crown Court.

In the hotel was an attractive coffee bar, which was largely empty apart from a table in a corner where three people sat. They were an odd-looking trio. The older man dressed in a suit, the younger man in shorts and T-shirt, the woman in a jeans skirt and flip-flops. The man in the suit had a briefcase down by his side, and a folder placed on the table in front of him. From their dress code and close proximity I formed the opinion the woman and younger man were together, a mother and son, and having some sort of meeting with the other man.

While waiting for my drink to be made, I heard the woman's raised voice. 'Do you think he'll do prison time?'

The barista serving handed me my coffee, which I took to a table outside in the sunshine. I saw the younger man and woman later at a table together. I couldn't help noticing the anxiousness about them. Him tapping his foot and smoking fast, her with arms folded across her chest, and very slightly rocking.

I felt sure the man they'd been with must have been a solicitor or barrister. I didn't think about what the young man might have done. I thought about his mother, sat there silent, and wondered what answer she was given. Next day I found myself remembering her and wondering if she was driving home somewhere without her son. The sadness of that thought stayed with me.

I love hearing from my readers – you can get in touch on my Facebook page, through Twitter, Goodreads. If I'm late in responding please never think it's because I don't care or that I've ignored your name. It's only because I'm absent for a little while writing.

Thanks,
Liz Lawler

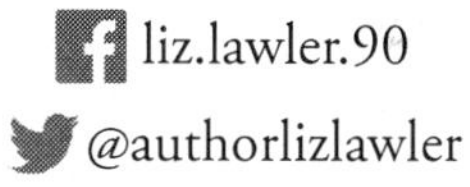

ACKNOWLEDGEMENTS

Thank you to Bournemouth for lending the most beautiful backdrop. It became the natural place to set this story, as the idea began there during one of my many visits. For the sake of the story, I've taken certain liberties by adding a place or street that exist only in fiction.

Amazing people have supported me along the way so there are many people I want to thank.

My agent, Rory Scarfe, and The Blair Partnership team, always there to root me on so that now I have some little green leaves. Only sixteen to go, Rory…

My editor, Cara Chimirri, for squeezing out every last drop of this story with your gentle hands.

Associate Publisher, Natasha Harding, for helping me get to the end. I look forward to beginning our journey.

The brilliant Bookouture team. Capability should be your byword. Thank you for everything you do, and for creating yet another amazing cover!

To Dr Peter Forster MBBS FRCA. Thank you so much for casting your expert eye over all of it. You have no idea how reassuring that is. You were there for me at the beginning with my first book, so I'm thrilled you were here for this one. You make it all better! All mistakes are of course mine.

To Dr Terren Tsunhei Ku – just an anaesthetist at Bath (is how he wished me to present him!). Thank you for the tutorial on toxicology and chemical analysis and about certain metabolites and diazepam patterns and about better drugs to use! Thank you for just a simple lesson!

To Detective Inspector Kurt Swallow. My sincere gratitude for reading this through with a policeman's eyes, and spotting my mistake! It would have been an offence to leave it there! Thank you so much, Kurt.

My thanks to Martyn Folkes for keeping me honest. My brother-in-law Kevin Stephenson and sister Bee Mundy for reading the first draft! Bradley Gould for my IT support. Harriet, my daughter-in-law, for being there for me on hard days! To my brothers and sisters for being there always. In age order from the top: Anthony, Robert, Marie, Patrick, Michael, Susan, Martin, Diane, Bernadette, Teresa, John. To our parents for bringing us our own football team.

To my husband Mike. Who keeps me completely sane. Which is all I need!

To the loves of my life, Lorcs, Katie, Alex.

To the lights of my life, Darcie, Dolly, Arthur, Nathaniel. It's about time we went out to play…

Finally, for Mum, my constant inspiration…

Printed in Great Britain
by Amazon

76890986R00218